To Car

Much love as
always

TAPING WHORES

BILL BAILEY

MINERVA PRESS
MONTREUX LONDON WASHINGTON

TAPING WHORES
Copyright © Bill Bailey 1996

ISBN 1 85863 850 X

First published 1996 by
MINERVA PRESS
195 Knightsbridge
London SW7 1RE

Printed in Great Britain by
Antony Rowe Ltd, Chippenham, Wiltshire

TAPING WHORES

ABOUT THE AUTHOR

Born in a small rural town in North Carolina, Bill Bailey began his itinerant life after graduating from university with a degree in philosophy. After three hilarious months' service, he talked his way out of the US Army and became a prison guard in Canada before prospecting unsuccessfully for gold in British Columbia. Having meanwhile accidentally married a Texan heiress, he proceeded to Houston, Texas where he managed a ranch, scrambled motorbikes, raced sports cars, worked as a bouncer, lectured, cut wheat, joined the struggle of the fruitpickers and organised the first white collar union in the US meat-packing industry. He competed in judo in Canada, the USA and Mexico. While participating in the civil rights struggle in Houston he discovered acting and subsequently moved to the UK. Within a year of his arrival he became the first full-frontal male nude on the British stage. In the course of his acting career he has worked extensively in film – in Hollywood and Europe – television and London's West End. Drawn into the Miners' Strike of 1984/5, he wrote and acted in a play which toured the coalfields in support of the strike. Now he lives with a foul-mouthed parrot.

Chapter One

Michael Regis sat at the table opposite Ian Castleberry, who was shorter and a little fatter than he appeared on TV. He was nearly fifty-one, and his double chin was prominent around his collar. Castleberry was toying with a napkin ring and looking a little distracted. Michael Regis was an arms dealer, though he would never have thought of himself as an arms dealer. His name appeared on numerous letterheads of firms as diverse as city banks and Belfast shipbuilders. But in fact the base of the pyramid formed by his wealth rested firmly on the ground of the arms trade. He visualised himself principally as a facilitator, and once even described himself as a mechanic when called on by a researcher from *Who's Who*. Both of them had a good laugh and the researcher was put at his ease, knowing that Michael Regis was a man who could laugh at himself. Regis was supremely and quietly confident, relaxed and charming. It was the kind of charm which could only come from old family and old money. The family was old, but the money was quite new. By the time that Michael was born, hundreds of years had whittled away at the historic family estates and all that was left was a mortgaged semi-detached house in Horsham. His family re-mortgaged it to send their promising son to Eton, Cambridge and Sandhurst. He rose quickly and effortlessly to lieutenant colonel and was assigned as liaison to General Buck Howard, the American NATO commander. It seemed that Michael Regis knew everyone, and everyone in their turn wanted to know the tall, handsome young colonel. Introductions were made. Links were formed. In time the tenuous strands of the web became channels for information, and Regis placed himself comfortably at the centre of the web collecting tolls for the passage of data.

Most people fail to realise that a large portion of industrialised economies are dedicated to the research, development and production of sophisticated arms. The money involved is so vast it would be hard to measure. There is such a torrent pouring into the industry that you can't count it fast enough. Straightforward documented trade lay above the surface. The bulk was below, passing furtively and without leaving a wake through foreign embassies, secret services, banking and the military. Michael Regis was virtually unknown outside the corridors of power, but, since he had tapped into this secret Gulf Stream, he was very well known inside. Very well known indeed.

They were having dinner at Le Bonheur, a discreet cellar restaurant near Victoria where Regis kept a table permanently booked in his name. It was a beautiful old converted wine cellar, and Regis's table was set into one of the arches at the rear of the room and could not be seen by the rest of the patrons. Anyone over six feet had to duck his head to enter, and it was lit by two period gas lamps set into the wall. The table was in use nearly every evening – if not by Regis, then by one of his friends like Ian Castleberry, who found it convenient for the Houses of Parliament. It was a table much in demand and was envied as much for its utter privacy as for the chef and wine list.

The wine waiter arrived and poured a drop in Michael Regis's glass, but Regis waved the waiter to continue. He knew the wine well. It was from his own reserve. He checked the clarity, though, as he raised his glass to Ian Castleberry.

"May as well have a splash while we're waiting, Ian," he said as he offered the glass for a toast. "And congratulations."

Castleberry looked up, a little surprised, but raised his glass. They clinked. "What's the occasion?"

Regis took a sip from his glass. "The Penhaligons have today withdrawn their objection."

The Minister very nearly dropped his glass of excellent wine. The blood drained from his face. "You're joking, of course." His voice was nearly a whisper.

"Oh, no, not at all." Regis smiled warmly.

For centuries the Penhaligons had owned the six hundred acres which adjoined the Castleberry Estate, a mere forty acres. The Penhaligon land was simply called The Monastery, after the ruins which could be still seen from the Chiltern Hills, but, for as long as anyone could remember, the site had lain undisturbed and was now well established as a wildlife sanctuary. It was wild and beautiful and it had blocked the Castleberrys for over one hundred and four years and the de Salles before them for longer than that. The Monastery was neither needed nor used much by the Penhaligons, except as a punishment for whoever owned those forty acres now occupied by

Castleberrys. Even the access road belonged to The Monastery, and, indeed, one shilling a year was paid to the Penhaligon estate for its use. Whatever had happened in the mists of time to cause such relentless hatred must have been powerful to have strained through the sieve of so many years. Generations of Penhaligons had been threatened and begged to sell the land and they had never been moved to part with so much as a square inch.

Ian Castleberry had come to view the ownership of The Monastery as immutable as the law of gravity and likely to outlast that law as well as most others. And what Michael Regis was telling him was that The Monastery was finally for sale. He would more easily have believed that the sun would rise in the west. The hand holding the wine glass was trembling. The wine spilled, and he found it necessary to grasp his right arm with his left to lower the glass to the table.

"How . . . on earth did you do it?" Castleberry finally asked in a weak voice. He knew Michael Regis well enough and could see that he was not joking.

Regis indulged in another sip of his wine.

"It's timing, isn't it? You know that. A man may be infernally jealous of his wife, but if there's something he really wants and the time is right, he'll prostitute her for it. Never seen a principle that wouldn't bend if you choose the right moment."

"And what was it with that swine Penhaligon? What on earth did you offer him?"

Regis smiled. "A horse."

Castleberry leaned back in his chair.

Old Sir Benjamin Penhaligon had an absolute passion for horses, for racing and training. Indeed, he had a good eye and a fine stable.

"Which horse?"

"Red Shadow."

"You're joking," Ian Castleberry said again.

Red Shadow was the most illustrious grandson of Red Sunset, a three-year-old, already a Grand National winner. He was owned by Harvey Gillmore, who had sworn publicly never to part with him.

"Harvey owed me a favour," said Regis. "He still has an interest in the horse but Red Shadow will be raced from the Penhaligon stable. The announcement should be made next week."

It was a little more than a favour. Harvey Gillmore was one of those Australian multi-millionaires who hit the shores of Britain from time to time like Pacific typhoons, flattening businesses, industries and newspapers, and reorganising them like their daddy's firms in Sydney or Perth. No unions, low wages, hard work. But because of the economy Gillmore was in a lot of trouble. Regis had organised a consortium of banks to refinance him in exchange for seats on the board of his holding company. For a price. The price was Red Shadow, or most of him.

Ian Castleberry laughed out loud – an explosion, a release from the emotion he felt. It was something he had dreamed of, a fantasy made reality by a few magic words at a moment when he was least expecting it. His mind had still been at Westminster and the interminable arguments with the Treasury when suddenly the heavens opened and a gift beyond his dreams had fallen from the skies. The Monastery was finally for sale. Original documents indicated that the properties had been joined together once and now, after hundreds of years, they were to be rejoined. It was too much to take in at one sweep.

Castleberry blinked. An angel was standing at the end of the table.

Michael Regis rose from his place.

"Ah, Jennifer. We've been waiting for you. This is Ian Castleberry. Jennifer Montgomery is a cousin of mine, one I acquired through marriage. I took the liberty of inviting her to dinner."

"I'm very glad you did, Michael," he said as the waiter seated her at the end of the table.

She had blonde shoulder-length hair and glittering blue eyes. Her dress was white, expensive satin, tight to the waist, then falling loosely to a hem just above her knees. The neckline plunged low but was discreet, and it suddenly reminded him of an arrow pointing the way downward. Indeed, he was immediately taken by Jennifer's sexuality and he felt his groin involuntarily tingle. He was a little embarrassed. She could not possibly be more than twenty-two years old.

"Thank you, Michael," she said as he poured her a glass of wine. She held the glass under her nose for a moment. "Hmmm. Brings back memories. A favourite of mine."

Jennifer smiled and looked towards Ian Castleberry, holding his eyes a moment before she spoke. "I was under the impression that ministers had little time for enjoying themselves."

Castleberry chuckled. "Just the propaganda we'd like people to believe. Everyone leaps at an invitation from Michael for an evening at his table. Which is conveniently close to the Commons."

He paused for a moment as the waiter served the soup.

"You, Miss Montgomery, are the second surprise I've had this evening. I'm not sure my heart can bear any more."

Jennifer Montgomery watched with a smile as Castleberry dabbed at the sweat on his forehead and receding hairline. It wasn't that warm at all. She turned to her cousin, who wasn't as tall as he looked, only a shade over six feet. But he seemed tall when he was standing. Even seated, he dominated the table. His brown, nearly black eyes were set widely apart in an olive skin which looked like a tan from a distance. A touch of the tar brush? she thought. His hair too was black and there was a lot of it. He must not have been less than forty but seemed fit, if not athletic. If it weren't for his large nose, he could have passed for a woman's dream. But it was not his looks which made Michael Regis attractive. It was his charm. He made everyone around him comfortable. He knew what to do, what to say and how to say it in the most pleasing way. He seldom drew attention to himself yet nevertheless others found themselves drawn to him.

Regis turned to Castleberry. "Jennifer is at RADA now, I believe—"

"Ah," she interrupted him. "No. Finished last spring. I've got my shingle out now, ready for offers leading to fame and fortune." She laughed. "Or at least to my Equity ticket."

Castleberry looked up from his excellent bouillon. "An actress. How interesting. I've heard that the profession is a little . . . uncertain."

"As is much of life, I've heard," she said, holding his eyes until he dropped them.

Regis had finished his soup and poured refills from the bottle. "Weren't you going to buy a flat in Hampstead?"

"Bought one. A house, actually. Lovely. Willoughby Road, a stone's throw from the Heath. Or rather, Father bought it." She smiled brightly. "A few things still need doing."

The entrée had arrived. As it was served, Jennifer observed that a question had been asked and answered in the English middle class style. The Minister had wanted to know how she could survive in such a difficult profession as acting and she answered that she already had a bundle, enough to afford a house near the Heath. Acting then became respectable, like gardening – a hobby, something to do with one's spare time.

She looked at Castleberry. He was sweating again, though he was clearly in good spirits. He was therefore drinking a little too much wine. A second bottle had arrived from the cellar. The hair he had left seemed to be ironed flat, and the slight curls round his temples looked rigid. There was something furtive about the man, despite his authoritative manner. He never held a frank look, always dropping his eyes to study a fork or the edge of the white tablecloth. When he looked at her, his eyes always first travelled down her cleavage before furtively crawling over to his fingernails.

The Minister held out his glass for a refill from the new bottle. Immediately he drank half of it. "I've got to say, Michael, that I've not felt happier in my life. A wonderful, wonderful piece of serendipity. I have no idea how to thank you."

"No need to thank me at all, Ian. I just happened to be in the right place at the right time. A word here, a word there and it was done. A mere bagatelle."

He popped a succulent carrot into his mouth. A bagatelle it was not. Much detailed planning and thought and civilised arm-twisting had gone into the operation. But he had enjoyed it. And they certainly had overlapping interests, particularly in the Middle East and Africa. Gillmore needed cash and, providing that the Minister for Trade and Industry could smooth the path a little, there would be plenty for the Australian with enough left over to satisfy his own immediate needs.

It was surprisingly quiet and intimate in their little cupboard. The bricks were painted white and reflected the illumination of the gas lamps, but the light was soft and faintly flickering. As they ate, the conversation drifted towards the islands of small talk. Ian Castleberry was glad in a way because his mind was in glorious confusion. The excitement of the news of The Monastery made his pulse race as ideas of what he was going to do and whom he was going to tell danced through his brain. And opposite him the lovely cousin kept catching his eye, he was sure of it. Between his new-found estates and Jennifer Montgomery he could hardly put a rational thought together at all. He was hardly aware of what he was eating, even whether or not it was good. Miss – he supposed it must be Miss – Montgomery had superb breasts. He would glance at that suggestive arrow of her cleavage and be torn as to which way to look. Either one side or the other, or let his eyes drift down to her small waist. When she was not looking, of course. He hadn't the courage to be direct and, besides, staring was rude. Yet he was more and more aware that she looked at him. Directly, frankly, with friendliness, sometimes with a smile. He wished that he had the courage of some of his colleagues to lock eyes and hold them. With males this was possible, but not with women. What was he putting in his mouth now? God knows. He just chewed it.

Castleberry was becoming a little giddy. Was it the wine? The wonderful news? Miss Beautiful Montgomery? It was hard to say. Could it be that good luck has a natural twin? She was definitely looking at him. Was she attracted? His heart beat a little faster still. Regis was talking, but he had no idea what he was saying. He simply answered with the right noises. Everything just felt so good for him. So right.

The remains of the meal were cleared and brandy served.

"I suppose I should have my solicitors press this thing straightaway, lest old Penhaligon changes his mind. Good Lord, after all these years. Hard to believe."

"There's no rush, Ian," Regis said. "He's not going to change his mind."

Castleberry had a sip of brandy.

"Can't wait to tell Catherine. And the boys will be delighted as well. Look forward to tomorrow, though. First time I can remember looking forward to tomorrow. Damned Treasury ministers. I think they are specially bred by Swiss gnomes and given clockwork hearts. Never mind." He tossed his napkin down. "There is a new dawn, Michael. Thanks to you."

"Would you mind, Ian, giving Jennifer a lift on your way to Highgate? Don't want to overload the taxi account for an aspiring young actress." Regis smiled warmly and squeezed Jennifer's hand.

"Of course, I'd be delighted."

The Minister looked at Jennifer and beamed. He was right. Nothing could go wrong on this night. His eyes followed their involuntary path along the downwards pointing arrow.

14

The Jaguar was parked in a dark shadow in the mews and Ian Castleberry almost imagined for a moment that it had been stolen. He held open the passenger door as Jennifer got in the car and he went round to the other side. As he slid into his own seat, he was aware that her dress had settled a little high on her crossed legs in the low seating position. He could just see a stocking top. And he was aware of her delicious perfume. What a beautiful girl, he sighed to himself as he put the keys in the ignition.

"Just a moment," said Jennifer as she looked intently at his face. The courtesy light was still on. "Something on your lip." She touched his lip softly with a long red nail. "There," she smiled. "Gone."

Ian Castleberry didn't know why he did it. He wasn't a bold man at all, but the wine and brandy and perfume were making him a bit giddy. His hand dropped to her thigh just as the courtesy light went out. She didn't move or shove his hand away, which surprised him. He felt the satiny silkiness of the stocking top and, above that, the warmth of her thigh. She still said nothing. He risked a look at her face, which he found close to his. And then he was kissing her, thirsty for the wetness as his mouth was completely dry. He was trembling and cursing himself for trembling, as his thoughts tumbled round like a tombola.

Luck was like that, wasn't it? It came in runs, just like bad luck. But she was so young! How could she be attracted to him? Well, he was a government minister, an important man. He appeared on television. A pity she had to be Regis's cousin, but what the devil?

His thoughts continued to tumble as he changed hands on her leg, fearful that she would now back away. But she didn't. As he put his left arm around her, he could hear her breathing deeply, a little hoarsely. He risked letting his right hand drift a little further up her thigh. He could feel the edge of her knickers, and she uncrossed her legs. Her arms went round his neck. Her legs were warm at the top, burning, and he put his hand softly on her mound as her pelvis began to move. Then he felt her arms disengage and she moved gently away.

"Better take me home now, Ian. This is no place for a fuck," she said, laughing gently as she took his right hand and put it on the steering wheel.

He was relieved in a way because he didn't know what to do next. Yet he was reluctant to let the moment go. She was so . . . hot. Where had that word come from, hot? A teenager's word.

"Yes," he said. "I suppose we'd better."

His voice sounded funny, and his hand trembled as he started the engine. They drove out of the mews, and he was reassured when she placed her hand on his leg. But he didn't know what to say, so he said nothing. It was too confusing.

Jennifer Montgomery looked at the portly middle-aged man driving the car, and thought for a moment about her cousin. Or her 'cousin', to be accurate. She and Michael Regis were related only by mutually rewarding business transactions. Not that she much looked forward to screwing the Minister for Trade and Industry who was clearing his throat on the other side of the Jaguar, but she did enjoy paying her 'cousin's' cheque for £1,500 into her account. She called herself a stratospheric whore because she cruised only at the highest atmosphere and served only the few men who could afford the private bedroom in the first-class cabin.

Jennifer Montgomery, whose real name was Sharon Stevens, was a Derbyshire girl, and her father still had a small electrical goods shop in Buxton. Her mother died before her tenth birthday and her father had almost immediately pressed her into service as proxy wife. Abuse was the word they used, but she didn't think it near strong enough or dirty enough to describe how it felt to her.

By her adolescence she had discovered several secrets. At the beginning she had withdrawn into herself, becoming secretive and full of remorse for what she was doing. For a couple of years she wet the bed, then had to endure her father's rage, and her sleep was interrupted by violent nightmares. She was powerless, and she felt the despair of powerlessness. But then, as her body had begun unfolding like a flower, when she was nearly fourteen, she gained a little confidence. She had always obsessively watched other people – how they walked, how they talked, the order of words, the effects of body language. So she learned to fight her father with the only weapons she had. She enticed him, teased him, promised him – and found that she could in fact manipulate *him*. Suddenly there were gifts, favours, even money.

When she left home just after her seventeenth birthday, she cleared out the shop till and the little safe sunk into the floor of his bedroom cupboard. By that time she knew that she wanted to be an actress. She moved to London but had to audition twice before getting into the Royal Academy of Dramatic Arts where she had done well.

When her savings and the money she had stolen from her father ran out, she decided very clinically what she was going to do and how she was going to do it. She answered the advertisement of a prostitute and asked her advice. Which led to the call girl circuit and then upwards to the very top drawer, to Veronica Hadley-White. Meanwhile she buried her Derbyshire accent under a very natural Home Counties inflection. The body language was harder, but she learned it.

When she finally visited Veronica Hadley-White, she was as convincing as the real article. Veronica asked that she remove her clothes and then proceeded to examine her as a buyer examines a horse. Every inch of her body was looked at in great detail and without comment. Her clothes, shoes and underwear underwent the same scrutiny.

Afterwards Veronica Hadley-White sat opposite her and said, "Very good body. Tacky clothes. I'll try you one time if you can manage to dress yourself properly. You only have one chance with me."

She must have been nearly sixty but looked and spoke like a duchess – or so Jennifer imagined. There were a number of rules, but the most important one was she must keep her mouth completely shut. She must not say anything about a client to *anyone*. *Ever*. At that level she could climb into bed with movie stars, kings and prime ministers. They paid well and for their money they wanted security. Absolute silence. They required the best, and so did Veronica Hadley-White.

And Jennifer Montgomery was one of the best in London. Not once in her life had she had a 'normal' relationship with a man, and she saw no reason why she should. She was now a freelance and had no more than two or three engagements a week, most of them regulars.

She leaned her head against Ian Castleberry's shoulder.

"I've never felt like this before," she said. "It's almost . . . electric. Isn't it?"

The Minister was startled. "You feel it too? Your hand is hot, like an iron."

Jennifer moved her hand, spreading her fingers, stroking.

"I hardly heard what you were saying at the table. I was so fascinated with the way you were speaking. So lively, so reassuring. I can't ever remember being drawn to someone like I felt myself being drawn to you."

He placed his hand on top of hers. "It's difficult to believe, Jennifer. You're so young and . . ."

"But surely you must be used to it? In your position?" She lowered her voice. "And you're a very attractive man."

Castleberry smiled, his confidence restored. "Really, it isn't something I notice. I mean, normally I would consider myself a happily married man. One can't be too careful in an exposed political position. The tabloid newspapers are like roaches. They slide underneath locked doors, and stamping on them doesn't help."

They were in North London now and the Minister began driving the Jag briskly as hormones dumped into his bloodstream. He easily beat a BMW away from the traffic lights.

"Ah," said Jennifer, "what a pity you're married."

Castleberry flicked the wheel to overtake a car. "Catherine and I are just good friends, really. Little more than that. She's a good sport."

Jennifer Montgomery moved her hand along the inside of the Minister's thigh, drawing little circles with her forefinger beneath his flies. She could feel a little wad of flesh there. Her palm rested on the overhanging fat.

The effect on Ian Castleberry was powerful. A tom-tom was struck in the back of his head and reverberated through his consciousness, wave upon wave, scattering his thoughts like autumn leaves. He realised that the feeling was terror! Never in his life had he met a woman like this. No one had ever been so sweetly aggressive. And he could hear her breathing heavily now. Yes, he liked it, but he was also completely terrified. He was tingling all over, yet could feel his sex retreating like a turtle's head.

Suddenly he swerved the big Jag, just missing a parked lorry, and realised that he was doing over seventy miles an hour. A jet combat pilot had replaced the boy racer. He slowed down, trying to concentrate on what he was doing, but only became more aware of Jennifer's heavy breathing.

And Jennifer was thinking that she was in danger of hyperventilating. It was certainly having an effect on Ian Castleberry, however, and the car drunkenly swung from one lane to another. Horns were blowing. A taxi driver leaned from his window and unleashed an unbroken stream of abuse. She pretended that she didn't notice all this. She pretended a lot of things. She pretended that this pompous little ass was arousing her with his corpulent, unattractive body, and she pretended that she wanted to make love to him – something which would revolt her if she thought too much about it. But she didn't think about it. It wasn't acting, not really, but it was pretend. In fact she had nearly finished her shopping list for tomorrow.

"Damn," Castleberry said finally and pulled over to the kerb behind a line of parked cars.

And then Jennifer's soft arms were around him, around his neck. Her mouth met his, open.

"Oh, Ian," she whispered as she pulled slowly away from the kiss. "Exactly the right thing to do. I was going to die if I couldn't kiss you again soon."

Castleberry's mouth was still open from the kiss. It seemed as if he had turned to stone for a moment. Then, as if it had a mind of its own, his hand moved over and squeezed her breast. Just as she imagined he would squeeze an orange.

"Oh," she said again breathlessly and let herself sink back against her door.

Cars were passing in the road and she opened one eye briefly to check, but the windows were smoked. Slowly she raised one leg and placed the heel on the edge of her seat. Her dress folded up to her waist.

Castleberry's eyes, at first transfixed on her face, slowly lowered, following the arrow, to the view unfolding below. This night was so unexpected for him. Everything was catching him by surprise. First there was the news about The Monastery. The Monastery, my god, he thought. Then there was this extraordinarily beautiful girl who fell into his arms from heaven. And now he was involved in a scene like those in the pornographic videos he watched secretly in his study. She was turned towards him, leaning against the door moaning, and she had raised one knee, unconsciously exposing the most gorgeous legs leading, in stockings and flesh, to a pair of very brief white silk knickers. His heart was pounding. Now it was like kettle drums in his head – first the gong and now the drums. Tentatively he reached down and touched her. Her body arched like a bow, and one of her hands clasped his to her.

She held his hand there, trapped for a moment as she lowered her leg and sat up. What on earth was he doing with his fingers, she wondered. They seemed to be twitching, as though he were fingering a guitar. So she moaned again. When she opened her eyes and looked at the Minister, his eyes were still wide, his mouth still open. His chin was wet and saliva dripped slowly on to his lapels. She pulled his hand away, took his handkerchief and dabbed at his chin lovingly.

"Thank you, Ian," she said softly, smiling up at him. "Let's go on. It's not far."

She returned his handkerchief to his pocket, folding it properly.

Ian Castleberry did as he was told, because he couldn't collect enough thoughts together to speak.

He pulled carefully away from the kerb and drove slowly to Willoughby Road like an automaton. He didn't speak once. Nor did she. Instead she leaned her head on his shoulder and put her hand back on the top of his leg. When they arrived at Willoughby Road, he found a parking place, locked the car and followed the woman in white to her house.

Jennifer Montgomery closed the door behind her, switched on the hall light and turned to Ian Castleberry. The horrible little fat man was standing like a statue, staring at her, and she wondered briefly if she should slow down a little, give him a rest, offer him a cup of tea. After all, she had no idea of his medical condition. Instead she held his eyes and unzipped her dress, which she let fall at her feet. She walked towards him, her naked breasts trembling with each step, her eyes fixed on his. Were they misty enough? she wondered. She put her arms around his neck and her lips moved towards his mouth, which was open again. His hands, trembling and a little cold now, reached around and gripped her buttocks like a pair of cabbages.

Chapter Two

Jennifer Montgomery was bored, and her legs ached. But she had another fifteen minutes on the bicycle before moving on to the stepping machine. Then the worst would be out of the way. Five mornings a week she was at the Tufnell Park gym, pretentiously called Body Experience, from ten until eleven fifteen. This morning she had forgotten her Walkman, so she was bored.

She was so bored that she started watching the other end of the gym where three men were heaving great lumps of weight off their chests. Two were black, one white, and all three were heavily muscled and glowing with sweat. They came in four days a week and trained hard, joking amongst themselves as they moved from set to set, exercise to exercise. Otherwise the gym was nearly vacant. Which was why she came in the mornings. The evenings were unbearable. It was hot and crowded with a number of show-offs, and you had to queue for the bike, the steps, the adductors, everything. Mornings were nice and peaceful, except for the three who usually stayed at the other end, training with impossible-looking weights. All three had tried to chat her up, no doubt as part of their macho routine, but she hated the looks of bodybuilders. The men she liked were thin and moody. If she liked men at all, that is.

She knew their names though and they seemed to know hers – probably checked through their mate at reception. The tall black was called One Time for some reason and the shorter one was named Keef. The white man was an American, who she guessed was from the Southern states or Texas from the sound of his accent. His name was something that sounded like Howg. 'How' with a 'g'. He was bald, with a pony tail formed from his remaining fringe, and was a little too fat for a real bodybuilder. He was a little under six feet tall and wide in the shoulders, but under the heavy looking chest was a bit of a belly, probably from too much beer. In short, he was ugly. One Time the best-looking – a trendy dresser with smooth features and closely cropped hair. Keef, the other black, was a brutal looking fellow with a shadowy goatee. She guessed that both of them were West Indian. They all looked in her direction from time to time, but

she was used to that. She soon cooled off the heat of their approaches
with her distant-and-frosty act. Long ago she had learned how to
handle men, beginning in the school of hard knocks with her own
father. She looked again at the three of them. While waiting his turn,
the American was staring frankly at her. She looked away, not even
pretending that she wasn't bored.

"The ice lady. You ain't gonna get her tangled up inside your
Mini," Joe Wayne Haug drawled to One Time. "One look from her
and your balls would freeze to your ass."

One Time Griffin was spotting an incline bench press for Keef.
He laughed.

"It's all right . . . it's all right. You gotta understand. I'm comin'
back."

One Time didn't make a lot of sense unless you could see him,
because he was about three-quarters body language.

Keef Sams slid out from under the bar. "You gotta bin there first,
'fore you come back," he growled.

Keef had very little body language, except for his forefinger, and
he only used that when he was mad. He had a hooded malevolent
look and scars at his hairline from head butts.

One Time slid under the bar for his turn. Haug helped him lift the
bar off the rack.

"One time," said One Time. "Right now."

He pushed the heavy bar easily, smoothly. Even his lifting had
style.

Joe Wayne Haug helped reseat the bar. "You c'n see he's comin'
back, Keef. He's clawed his way into third place in our school."

Both the black men laughed.

"'S all right," said One Time. "You forget who I am."

It was Haug's turn and Keef handed him the bar. He took the
eight reps slowly, making himself strain and fight, controlling the bar.
Then he swung off the bench and wiped his forehead with the
Guinness bar towel he carried in his kit.

"*That's* how it's done, asshole. Power."

It was a good partnership. They had been training together for
years and had become close friends. When Haug first met them, he
asked what they did for a living. 'Security.' That was the answer
both of them gave, and it made Haug laugh. It was the answer you
often got in gyms from the big lads. They made their livings

bouncing or as bodyguards, dedicating most of their lives to sweating with the weights.

Haug himself was just trying to fight off encroaching middle age. He was forty-four years old and beginning to feel it. He had been in London for sixteen years and had taken up weight training again in the early half of his thirties. It was a sport he had picked up in his early teens to build himself up for football, which he thought was going to be his career. He made it for one year in the pros. Those guys were just too big and too mean. If he had been born six foot eight, maybe things would have been different. After that he joined the 82nd Airborne Division, the paratroopers, based at Fort Bragg in his home state. He had started reading for the first time really later, while he was serving in Vietnam, a time he didn't like to think about. Once he started, he couldn't stop. His tastes started to change, and he no longer liked some of the things he had done in the army. When he got out, he used his GI Bill to go back to the university where he had flunked out when he was twenty, and got a degree in English Literature. He came to England with half a mind to continue his studies and found out that he had to get married to stay. That didn't work out, so he got unmarried and looked for something to do. Like his black friends, he drifted into 'security' and worked for a couple of Greeks in a collection agency. And that, he thought, was how he wandered into the private detective business.

But it wasn't exactly like Raymond Chandler, especially here in London. Chasing people who disappeared, that was the bulk of his work. They mostly disappeared to avoid payments on bank loans or hire purchase or alimony. He just tracked them down using common sense, mostly. Then there was the divorce business, which he hated. Pictures of wives and boyfriends or husbands and girlfriends, hours spent in parking lots or in front of houses or below flats. It was lucky that he still liked to read. It was about as exciting as a knob of grease, but it was money. He had his own little agency now and could come and go as he pleased. That left him time to pluck at the keys of his little PC. He was writing a kind of journal, especially about his experiences in Vietnam and what happened later in the States when he sent his medals back. And for that reason he probably wouldn't get it published. But he enjoyed playing at being a writer. It gave him a purpose in life.

They were doing arms now, having finished chest and back. Haug was bushed and knew that he wasn't quite as fit as Keef or One Time, but even his buddies had damp patches down the backs of their sweatshirts. He looked over at Jennifer, who was on the stepping machine. Now that was one good-looking broad, he thought. Jesus. She had on black lycra bottoms and a tight white top worn over, with just a thong separating the buttocks. He couldn't help looking at her. She was nice with a capital 'N'. And she trained hard too, every day as far as he knew. Too bad she had an attitude problem.

Keef sat down beside him, breathing hard. "You bin lookin' so hard, you gonna look her skin off, Haug."

"I'd tell you what I'd like," Haug said. "I'd like to just have her on a dinner table, covered with fresh cream and cherries. Then I'd just lick her till she was all gone. Goddam'."

One Time finished his set of curls. "You wouldn't know what to do with that woman, man." He moved his body fluidly into a kind of pose, head down, one finger in the air. "One time. All it would take. One time. Then she spoil for everyone else."

Haug laughed. "One time is about all you can do, isn't it?" He grabbed the bar.

One Time threw his gloves in his bag. "That's it, man. Gotta go. Quarter to twelve. Woman waitin' for me. Can't keep her waitin'."

"If you want to see her ag'in", Haug said, "you better wear a mask. Yer face is ugly enough to back a dog off a meat truck."

One Time laughed as he turned away, holding up one black finger. He watched him stop at the stepping machine and saw his mouth move. Jennifer ignored him, leaning her elbows on the top of the bars, her head down.

"He keeps tryin', Keef. You got to hand him that."

"Yeah," said Keef, banging the bar back into the A-frame. "Yeah, that's what we all do. Keep tryin'. Let's go have a shower, man."

Haug had parked his Chevvy pickup in front of the gym. It always looked huge parked in a row of European cars, huge and out of place. But that was part of the image, he thought. Besides, he had always liked pickups. There was a lot he still loved about the South. It was still a beautiful place, despite all the troubles there, despite all the bigots. He adjusted his Harley dozer cap and then wondered if he'd got his keys from the locker. He put his kit bag down on the hood – bonnet, they called it here – to dig in his pockets. He looked up just as the lovely Jennifer came out of the gym and he watched her out of the corner of his eye. She walked in front of his pickup, slowing to check the traffic, then stepped out into the road.

It was one of those things which happened so fast that there wasn't time to think. There was a squeal of rubber as a sporty black Escort swerved out of the line of parked cars behind the pickup. One glance told Haug what was happening and by that time he was already moving. He reached Jennifer in two giant steps, grabbed her training jacket with one hand and pulled as hard as he could as he passed. He caught a glimpse of her face as she turned towards the roaring Escort, only a few feet away. It was frozen in shock. The force of Haug's pull took Jennifer Montgomery off her feet, and she went rolling towards the pavement on the other side of the road. Haug somehow kept his balance as the car swept by and he managed to kick the side of the vehicle, caving in the rear panel.

"You son-of-a-bitch!" he screamed.

The Escort rocked from side to side, ran the red light at the junction and turned left up Dartmouth Park Hill. He picked up Jennifer's bag, which had been run over by the accelerating Escort.

She was lying like a bundle of rags against the frontage of the estate agency. People had stopped on the pavement and were looking at them. Chris, the manager of the gym, was standing outside and shouted at him.

"Haug! You OK? You need any help?"

Haug waved him away.

Joe Wayne Haug had been trained in medics when he was seconded to the Special Forces. He looked at her closely. She was breathing, her eyes closed. He put the back of his hand on the pulse in her throat, and it was strong. But she was pale, the blood drained from her face. As he pulled his hand away, her eyes opened and stared straight ahead.

"Can you hear me, Jennifer?" he asked softly.

She nodded slightly.

"OK," he said, "now move your head a little more. Tell me if there's any pain."

She shook her head. "No."

"Move your arms and legs. They OK?"

Again she nodded.

"Now I'm gonna pick you up. If you feel any pain, you just tell me and I'll put you back down."

He found his keys in his jacket pocket and put them in his mouth. Then he leaned over and gently picked her up in his arms. She held on tightly with one hand to the lapel of his coat and hid her face, trembling.

He carried her to his pickup, opened the passenger door and placed the woman gently in the seat. For a moment she wouldn't let go of his lapel.

He talked softly to her.

"'S all right, darlin'. The bad man's gone. And you're OK. You're just in shock, and I'm gonna get in the other side and take you home. Or to the doc, if you want. You just tell me where to go. OK?"

She released him, and he went round and slid into his seat, which was on the left. He had imported the pickup from America. Jennifer was slumped against her door and then she began to cry. He tried to comfort her by patting her shoulder and then he realised that she was laughing. Her window moved down a few inches then back up.

"The Yanks," she said without moving. "God. Power windows in a truck."

Haug smiled. "Got air conditionin' as well. Year round temperature control. 454 cubic inch engine, power steering and brakes. And a hi-fi."

She stopped laughing and began trembling. It was the beginning of May but still a little chilly. And also he knew that she would be in shock – probably light, but you never knew. He started the engine and made sure that the heater was on.

"You tell me your address and I'll take you on home," he said. "You need to get laid down so some blood'll slop back into your head."

She turned her head slightly towards him. "I'd rather get a taxi, if you don't mind. Don't want you bragging to your mates about getting me into bed . . ."

That made Haug angry.

"OK, lady, you can get a taxi or you can walk or go fuck yourself. Somebody just tried to kill your ass and I managed to jerk you outta the way. And for your information, I don't have to prove anythang to my friends, and furthermore I'm one of those folks who waits to be asked before I crawl all over a woman . . ."

Jennifer Montgomery turned in her seat and looked at Haug. He locked eyes with her.

"I'm sorry," she said sincerely. She looked down at her hands. "Willoughby Road, Hampstead. And thank you, Mr Haug. You saved my life. I, uh . . . my thoughts are a bit of a jumble. Sorry."

He smiled easily and put the pickup in gear. The heater was already beginning to work.

"That's all right. Don't you worry about a thang. What you got is a mild case of shock, and in shock all the blood drains outta the head and legs and into your vitals. So don't expect the head to work all that good for a little while."

He pulled out and turned left at the lights, following the path of the Escort, and drove towards Hampstead. Except for her directions, they didn't speak again until he was parked near her house.

Haug turned to her. "Now, you want me to carry you in? I don't mind."

"No, I think I'm all right now." She opened the door, grabbed her crushed kit bag, then stopped, turning to him. "I can offer you a cup of tea, Mr Haug. It's not much in the way of saying thanks, but . . ."

Haug thought for a moment. "Yeah. I'd like a cup a tea, if it's no trouble."

She was still feeling a little unsteady as she walked to her door and opened it. She held it as the big man came in, taking off his cap, then showed him to the sitting room. On the way to the kitchen she tossed the bag into a closet.

Filling the electric kettle, she noticed how much her hands were trembling and felt a wave of nausea pass through her. While waiting for the water to boil, Jennifer Montgomery risked a look in the mirror. A frightened, pale face stared back at her.

She collapsed in a chair at the breakfast table as she remembered the face behind the wheel of the car, a face she didn't recognise, a swarthy face wearing sunglasses, but it was looking right at her. It was no accident. She was the target and there was doubt of it. A man she had never seen before had tried to kill her. Another wave of nausea seemed to turn her whole stomach over and she just made it to the basin before vomiting. Wave upon wave passed though her and it appeared for a moment as if all her organs were going to follow – her stomach, her liver, her guts, her heart. As she stood up she heard the kitchen door open quietly, and then she started to fall and the room tilted on its axis.

When she opened her eyes, she was lying on the sofa under her duvet. No one else was in the room, but two mugs of tea stood on the table along with a wet flannel. She was cold and her body trembled. In her mind she saw the man at the wheel again, his lips pulled tight across his teeth in determination. The sitting room door opened. It was Haug with a hot water bottle.

He handed it to her. "Here you are, ma'am. Put it wherever it does the most good."

He sat down on the chair opposite, taking a mug of tea with him.

"Now, I apologise. I had to go into your bedroom, which I finally found, to get the duvet. And I had to dig around in the bathroom for the hot water bottle. But I haven't touched anythang else. You fainted in the kitchen. I heard you heavin' up. Oh . . . and I sort of cleaned up your mouth a little bit with that wash rag. I hope I haven't been outta line or anythang . . ."

Jennifer waved weakly, clutching the hot water bottle with her other arm. "No . . . no. It's OK. Thanks very much for your help."

Haug took a sip of tea.

"You got any relatives or a friend or a boyfriend or somebody I can call? You know, somebody to look after you for a while?"

She started to say something and bit her lip. Despite her best efforts, she felt her eyes filling with tears. A feeling of overwhelming loneliness crashed over her consciousness, a feeling worse than the nausea.

'No,' she said to herself, 'not a fucking person.' She felt so lonely, like a little girl. One moment she was a grown up, taking care of her own life – no, taking *control* of her life. The finance, the decisions, everything. And in one instant it was all gone and she wished desperately for a friend, someone to just hold her hand, comfort her. She fought off a nearly irresistible urge to put her thumb in her mouth and curl into a tight ball. She heard Haug asking for her telephone number and she gave it to him weakly.

"Mind if I use your phone?" he asked.

She nodded OK, and he picked up the receiver and dialled his office. His part-time secretary answered.

"Lizzy, I'm gonna be at this number for a little while if anythang urgent comes through." He gave her the number and hung up, turning back to the woman on the sofa. He studied her for a few moments before speaking, keeping his voice low and steady.

"Now, I know I might be takin' liberties here, miss. So I'm gonna let you be the boss, OK? Any time you wanna see the end of me, well, I'll just pick up my cap and jacket and leave. But what I reckon is this: you haven't got a friend to call right now. So I'm gonna be your friend for a while. And I *mean* friend. I come from the Southern part of America where *friend*'s got a whole different meaning. For however long you want it, it means that your battle's *my* battle, your enemy's *my* enemy, your friends're *my* friends. It also means that your wishes are my wishes. Now I *think* it's gonna do some good if I come over there and hold your hand for a few minutes. And I mean just hold your hand. Nothin' else in it. You can say no, if you want, or you can say leggo if you're fed up. I'm just doin' what I think will help you. OK?"

Jennifer Montgomery did not react – she just lay still on the sofa. So Haug moved his chair closer to her, found her hand and held it gently between his, warming it.

"Now somethin' awful queer has happened", he said, "and I'd like it a whole lot if you could tell me somethin' about it. Some asshole has tried to run you down in the road. He meant to do it. He was tryin' to hit you. Now, I'd like to ask you if you recognised him, if you knew him. Like, was it a . . .boyfriend, somethin' like that?"

He waited for a moment, but she didn't answer. She just stared straight ahead, her eyes still rimmed with tears.

Haug could feel her hand warming a little, but it was still lifeless.

"Now lissen. This is not just bein' nosy. I reckon I might possibly be able to help you. My business is . . ." He stopped for a minute, thinking how corny this was sounding. "Well, I'm a . . . a . . . private investigator. Which doesn't mean much, nothin' fancy. I chase after loose husbands or loose wives mostly. But I know how to find folks and ask 'em a few questions. And I got a waya shakin' the questions outta them if they're a little too shy to answer. I got some experience with heavier kinds of stuff, but that was a long time ago, in Vietnam. Now, I guess that this asshole is some boyfriend you elbowed or somethin' like that, and I guess it because ninety-nine times outta hundred, *that's* what it is."

Haug waited for a minute.

"Was it somebody you knew?"

Jennifer Montgomery understood only some of the words spoken in the soft, deep voice. She was looking at a tattoo on his forearm. It was a parachute between a pair of wings, and she wondered why some men had to have tattoos. Anyway, she didn't know what it was supposed to mean. Maybe it meant that he was tough or something. A signal to other men. What was he saying now? Then she heard him repeat his question. She shook her head, then made a great effort.

"No. I've never seen him before."

Haug sucked some air. "You got a good look at him?"

She nodded.

"And you don't know him? Well . . ."

He scratched his ear and then re-covered her hand. "Well, that plunks you in the one per cent all right. Makes thangs a lot harder. Now, two thangs occur to me. Either somebody has paid somebody else to try to kill you, or some feller has twisted himself into an emotional corkscrew thinkin' about you. If it's this last kinda feller, you know, somebody whose neurons aren't earthed properly, got a coupla wires danglin' loose . . . if it's this kind of guy, you probably woulda had some other indications, like dirty phone calls or phone calls with no one there or a sense of bein' followed at nights, that sorta thang . . ."

Her hand was squeezing his now, squeezing hard. And she was crying. Haug wasn't sure what to do.

Jennifer Montgomery sat up slowly, still holding hard to Haug's hand. She noticed that he had placed a box of tissues by the sofa and she took several, holding them to her face, trying to dry her eyes. She looked at him through tears and tried to smile. He had an honest, warm kind of face, and she could see genuine concern in his eyes. There was an intelligence there too, belying his heavy dialect. And strength as well. Not just in his body, but from within. Could she take a chance and trust this man? After all, she might as well. There was certainly no one else of whom she could think that she trusted. One thing was clear. She knew that she was going to have to do something to try and protect herself. From what or whom, she didn't know. She pulled her hand away from his, collected some more tissues and blew her nose.

"I have no idea who tried to kill me," she said, putting the hot water bottle aside and wrapping the duvet round her shoulders. "Or why."

"You're an actress, aren't you?" Haug asked.

She was suddenly alert, not knowing how long she had been unconscious. "What made you ask?"

Haug nodded behind him. "Saw your bookshelves. Always fascinated by bookshelves. While you were out cold, I sat here suckin' on my tea, and noticed there's a lotta copies of plays and books on acting technique. Elementary, my dear Miz Watson. Besides, you got looks that would knock the shine off a brass door knob. Which is one reason you might attract some guy twisted like a corkscrew who figgers he hasn't got a chance but wants to make sure nobody else . . ."

"No. I don't think so." Jennifer Montgomery relaxed slightly, a little amused by Haug's colourful figures of speech. "Tell me why I should trust you."

Haug rubbed a hand over his bald head and sighed. "Well, I'm not gonna do a sales pitch or lay out my wares. That's somethin' you gotta judge for yourself, lady. Now if it was me, like if the situation was reversed, and I was sittin' there and you here, I think what I'd do is let out a little bit at a time but try not to tell any outright lies and see if that big dumb-lookin' ox can help me without runnin' his mouth off or standin' on his dick or tryin' to get me in the bedroom evertime I smile at him. But I don't think I would play any games, not when I know somebody just tried to kill me. That's what I'd do, anyway."

"You have an unusual way of expressing yourself," she said.

"I say what I think. I don't see any reason for diggin' a hole and stuffin' my feelin's in there, then sittin' down on top of it. I figger the sooner somebody knows who I am and what I think, the more time we're gonna save."

"It's a point of view. For all I know, it might even be a healthy point of view." She was feeling a lot better now. Or a lot less bad. "Yes, I'm an actress."

Haug laughed. "Dang, just shows you my powers of deduction, doesn't it?"

"You're a real detective?"

"Depends on what you mean by real. I'm not a swanky feller with a briefcase and shiny shoes. And I don't use a bent pipe and magnifyin' glass or talk a lot about inference or deductive reasonin'. But I reckon I can tell if somebody's stepped in a flower bed to git through a winder."

Jennifer picked up her mug of tea, now gone tepid, and had a sip. "Well, I suppose I could use some help. Or at least somebody to talk to." She stared at her mug for a moment. "On the other hand, I don't know what to say."

"Well, let me ask you some questions then, just so that we can get our feet in the right part of the river. Have you split up with some feller recently?"

"No, I told you it wasn't that."

"OK," he said, "fair enough. Boyfriends, husbands, that sort of varmint, is out. The next thang is family—"

"I don't have any family," she interrupted.

"None at all?"

"No."

"That's awful hard to believe, Jennifer. Now, I was the only child in my family, but the cousins and aunts and uncles on both sides would probably make a fair-sized theatre audience for you to act in front of—"

"I don't have any family," she said, emphasising every word.

"Lemme try and translate what you're sayin'. Either you're an orphan and really don't know, or you have a family but don't want to talk about it. Which one is it?"

She sighed. "I don't want to talk about it."

"But you have one?"

"I have a father. Mother deceased. A couple of aunts and a few cousins whom I haven't seen or heard from for many years."

"I'm just askin' you to be square with me," he said firmly. "You don't have to talk about thangs you don't want to talk about. Everbody's got stuff in their heads they don't want to lay out in front of strangers. That's OK. But what you *do* lay out, I want it to be the truth. Otherwise we're wastin' our time. Now, would your father have any reason at all for wantin' you dead?"

She paused for a long while, thinking. "I don't know. When I left home, I stole some money from him—"

"A lot?"

"It seemed a lot then. Nearly £3,000. He doesn't know where I live. I haven't seen him since and don't want to. Ever."

Haug nodded. "OK. That's good. We'll put down Daddy as a possible and I'll get his address from you later."

Jennifer looked alarmed. "Now, don't—"

"I won't say a word to the man," Haug broke in. "Not without your permission. Now let's move on. You say there were no lovers—"

"I didn't say that. I said there was no romance, no boyfriends. Of course I have occasion to go out with various people, a number of people, but there are no living-in arrangements, no . . . steady affairs. You know what I mean."

"Right," said Haug. "I see. You got any reason to suspect any of these folks?"

"No."

"Would you mind makin' me a list?"

"Yes, I would."

Haug got up and turned towards the bookcases, thinking.

"Well, this makes it kinda tough, doesn't it? You got a father you don't want me to talk to, you got friends you don't want me to know."

Jennifer put the cold mug of tea on the table, leaned back on the sofa and closed her eyes.

"I can't give you their names because . . . I can't. That's all. I'm being as honest with you as I can, Mr Haug."

He turned back to Jennifer Montgomery. "Nobody ever calls me 'mister'. My full name's Joe Wayne Haug, and most people call me Haug. The English seem a little uncomfortable with double first names, however much they like double last ones.

"OK, the situation is this, the way I see it. You cain't think of anybody who'd wanna kill you. I cain't approach anybody who's got anythang to do with you either because you don't trust me enough yet or some other reason you cain't tell me. So let's take somethin' I can deal with. 'Cause there's another possibility here – the possibility of a mistake by the asshole in the car. I think it's a little unlikely on account of the fact that you were the only broad in the gym at that time, and the guy had a good view of the entrance and plenty of time. But, let's face it, there's some awful ignorant bastards on the face of this earth, and this guy coulda been given the address of some place south of the river and the target coulda been a short, fat, black-headed woman, sixty-five years old. And this guy shows up in Tufnell Park and tries to run *you* over. That kinda thang happens in real life.

There are folks around – and I've met some of 'em – who couldn't find their ass with both hands and a flashlight.

"So what I suggest is this: I'll watch you, follow you around for a week, make sure this character doesn't try it again. I'll do days and Keef will spell me nights. After a week, if nothin's happened, we'll talk it over, see where we are then."

Jennifer bit her lip. "I'm not sure . . . Haug. It's so bloody confusing. Why? *Why*? I haven't harmed anyone, done anything. Must be a mistake. Must be. And I don't want . . . I mean, it's awfully sweet of you to offer to try and look after me, but I can hardly bear the idea of being followed around all day. Yet . . . I *am* frightened. I don't know why, but maybe someone is . . . trying to . . . for some reason. It's ridiculous. I don't know what to do. I can't ask you to . . ."

"How you fixed for money?"

"Why?"

"Well," said Haug, "seein' as how we're temporary friends, I'll do the week for nothin'. Or rather I'll add up just what I spend, call it my expenses and we'll talk about it at the end of the week. But I cain't afford to pay Keef, who'll want about £40 a night to stay, up front. He's always broke, doesn't have much money. I'll need £280 by the end of the week. That OK?"

Jennifer pressed her fingers to her head. "This is ridiculous."

"It's up to you, lady. I'll talk to Keef. He may take a little less—"

She shook her head. "It isn't the money. That's all right, very cheap, very nice of you. It's just . . . ridiculous."

"You can call it off any time, startin' now."

She stood up, feeling a little light-hearted for a moment. "All right. What do I do?"

"Well," said Haug, "what kind of security you got in the back?"

She picked up the mugs and led him to the rear of the house, dropping the mugs in the kitchen. For insurance reasons the ground floor had bars on the windows and garden door. Haug went out and had a look. When he came back in, he was carrying a ladder he found lying near the flower bed. He laid it along the hallway, shut the door, locked it, gave Jennifer the key from the lock and moved a large heavy cupboard in front of the door.

Jennifer watched all this mutely.

As he was adjusting the cupboard she said, "Isn't that a little unnecessary?"

"We cain't watch both the front and the back, ma'am."

"But there is a separate barred door. No one can get through that, surely."

Haug stretched his back. "No problem to a real professional. He'd wait till you went out, shag around here with a hacksaw or portable Black and Decker, saw through the bars, then put 'em back with a little glue, just enough to hold 'em in place. Then, late at night, he comes back, an' plunk, plunk, he's in. Is there an alarm?"

She nodded. "All the windows, and sensors under the carpet."

"Well, that's a help. Won't stop a man that's good enough, but killers aren't always good burglars. Now, I saw you got a lock on some of the doors inside. You got keys?"

She shrugged her shoulders. "Somewhere. I can find them, I think."

"You got your bedroom in the back. For this week I want you to sleep in the front bedroom where we can see your light. If you're not gonna use the back rooms much, keep 'em locked. Any sounds, anythang suspicious, you just push the buzzer."

Jennifer looked puzzled. "*What* buzzer?"

Haug held up his hand. "I'm gonna give you one later. Carry it with you everwhere. In your pocket, not your purse. Under your pillow at night. You mash that button and mine goes off. You won't hear anythang from yours. Half a minute later, I'll be comin' through like a train. Me or Keef. I'll need your front door key."

Haug pulled out his wallet. "If we somehow get separated, call my office number and leave a message."

He gave her his card.

Jennifer Montgomery watched through the window as Haug climbed into his pickup and drove away. She had a lot of misgivings. The man seemed warm and good-hearted but a little simple. Like a big brown bear. He told her when he left that he was going to swap vehicles for one less conspicuous than the pickup and bring her the emergency buzzer.

She could see the beginnings of a depression darkening the edges of consciousness, like a storm cloud on the horizon. The negative thoughts were beginning to fall like the first drops of rain. She had no friends because she hadn't wanted any. Stupid. There was no one to call, no one to turn to. And deeper inside she knew that someone had really tried to kill her. It wasn't a mistake. She didn't know why, but she knew. She *knew*. Maybe it wouldn't be so bad having a bear around, even if he was stupid.

Chapter Three

Ian Castleberry sat at the desk in his office at the Department of Trade and Industry and stirred the sweeteners thoughtfully into his tea. He was determined to keep to his new diet and get some weight off. Which meant no sugar and no sweets, and that was why he had asked Sir Jonathan Mainwaring to keep the chocolate biscuits on his side of the desk. Sir Jonathan was his Permanent Secretary and had been making light conversation for the past ten minutes. He knew Sir Jonathan well enough to know that it was a bad omen. It meant that he had something on his mind, and light conversation was his idea of a pawn move to distract the Minister before he struck with bishop or rook. In fact he understood that his Permanent Secretary was a strong chess player. He could be a tricky man, that was for certain. Castleberry waited for the thrust.

Sir Jonathan Mainwaring bit into a chocolate biscuit and chewed thoughtfully, knowing that the Minister loved them. He studied the highly polished toe of his shoe and took a sip of tea.

"Oh, I meant to congratulate you on the wonderful news about old Penhaligon and The Monastery."

Castleberry brightened.

"Yes. You heard. It was a bit of luck, and it's hard to believe that the sale is going through with no difficulties. Solicitors on both sides have been instructed."

The Minister beamed at his Permanent Secretary, who was leaning back in his chair holding a biscuit delicately between two fingers and a thumb. Mainwaring was tall, well over six feet, and lean with large marsupial eyes. His face, in fact, was shaped like a skull with little flesh to spare for cavities and hollows. His hair was charcoal with flecks of grey at the sides, receding but pulled straight back and it looked as though it had been sprayed on to the top of his head. A hand with long slender fingers reached again for his teacup. Mainwaring was immaculately dressed in the only style and colour the Minister had ever seen him wear: the darkest of blue pinstriped serge, elegantly cut – an exquisite fit for such a tall bony man.

"Well," said Mainwaring, "one has reason for surprise, doesn't one?" He pursed his lips together and returned his teacup once more to its saucer. "I would have given it about as much chance as that of finding a pot of gold at the end of a rainbow."

"Oh, so would I," Castleberry agreed, his mind finally off the chocolate biscuits. "I have no idea why the old bastard finally let go of the title. Can't be short of money. Wouldn't do it for that reason anyway. Penhaligon is as stubborn as a bull terrier – and about as intelligent, I might add. Impossible to tell, Sir Jonathan, impossible to tell. Could be something religious, having seen the light on the road to Bognor Regis with the Lord telling him it was time to put an end to the old feud. I'm afraid we'll never know."

The Minister knew that there was no reason to tell Mainwaring the truth of the matter. He had been in politics a long time and knew that cards are best kept in the safety of one's hand and always played to one's advantage, if played at all.

Sir Jonathan Mainwaring smiled thinly, finishing his biscuit.

"I'm sure that Penhaligon would think it not unusual for the Almighty to contact him directly instead of routeing his advice through the Pope."

Castleberry laughed. "Well, after all, from Sir Benjamin's point of view, they are equals."

"Indeed, yes."

Mainwaring took a final sip of tea as he unfolded his frame and stood up. Then it appeared that he was struck by a thought.

"Ah, Minister, the Biblical reference reminds me. MATTHEW MARK. Are you quite *certain* you want the Department to approve the sale?"

"Of course I do!" Castleberry replied testily and realised at once that he had made a mistake.

He knew in an instant that Mainwaring had trapped him and cursed the cleverness of the man. Even forewarned, a fork on queen and king could not be avoided. He had brought up the subject of the unexpected sale of The Monastery and immediately bracketed it with MATTHEW MARK, letting Castleberry know that he knew – or suspected – that the two were related. As they, of course, were. And the Minister had responded emotionally, confirming what his Permanent Secretary knew or guessed. MATTHEW MARK was buying a large order of arms, including a number of mobile hi-tech anti-aircraft missiles, light armoured vehicles, a dozen up-to-the-minute attack helicopters with laser guidance systems and two hundred accompanying air-to-ground missiles. A large quantity of small arms with night-fighting capability was also involved. The largest shareholder in MATTHEW MARK was Michael Regis.

Mainwaring carefully sat back down in his chair and equally carefully tented his fingers.

"It is my responsibility, Minister, to draw your attention to certain disquieting aspects of the matter. Of course MATTHEW MARK is a perfectly respectable company—"

"And is Saudi Arabia not a respectable country, Sir Jonathan?" Castleberry asked in a slightly condescending voice.

Again Mainwaring smiled thinly. Perhaps it was the only way he was capable of smiling.

"Of course the Saudis are important trading partners, and the EU has endorsed such trade. What worries me is the involvement of WORLDWIDE. It's certainly a little out of the ordinary."

"The facts of the matter are these, Sir Jonathan. As far as HM's Government is concerned, the End User is Saudi Arabia and WORLDWIDE's involvement is a problem for Saudi Arabia and *not* for us. I understand that the Saudis are simply using WORLDWIDE in order to facilitate contractual arrangements and for trading and currency reasons. WORLDWIDE will merely provide an agent or agents at the port of entry as the weapons pass into Saudi hands," Castleberry ended emphatically, implying that the matter was closed.

The Permanent Secretary remained in his chair, his fingers still tented.

"Hmmm, yes," said Mainwaring, looking thoughtful. "I was having luncheon with Jeremy Evans at the club the other day and he mentioned WORLDWIDE in another context. He said that there was reason to suspect WORLDWIDE of supplying arms to a number of doubtful causes in Africa and the Middle East. If we accept this unusual routeing of arms, it will create a precedent and ensure WORLDWIDE a respectability they perhaps do not deserve. I am bound to add – though this is not strictly my department – that it could rebound severely if anything were not as it seemed."

He was not being completely truthful here. It was what he had extrapolated from Evans, a little pimple of a man.

"Are you suggesting that we cancel the order when HM's Government is needy of every penny from export sales? When there is a politically unacceptable level of unemployment?"

Castleberry was entering his favourite mode of dismissive sarcasm, particularly useful in disembowelling Opposition spokesmen.

"The competition for arms is the fiercest in the world market and we as a nation have steadily been losing ground to the Americans, the Russians – even the French – and now the Germans. I might remind you that the sale of the equipment is only a part of the final total. There are spares and maintenance, for instance. Re-supply for practice and mock battles. And I might add that Defence are delighted with all details of the sale. I have no intention of standing in the way of good sound business and, quite frankly, I wish that we had more companies with the cutting edge of MATTHEW MARK."

Sir Jonathan Mainwaring unfolded his limbs languidly as he stood again. "Jeremy Evans has promised to forward me further details of WORLDWIDE, and I will bring them to your attention upon receipt, Minister."

Again he smiled thinly before moving silently to the door, where he turned. "And let me congratulate you again on your good fortune regarding your purchase of The Monastery."

He closed the door quietly as he left.

Ian Castleberry nearly spat in frustration. He had had only two sips from his tea and it was cold.

"Fuck," he said out loud, as he got up and went to the drinks cabinet, glancing at the clock.

Eleven forty-five. Well, he thought, one before lunch won't hurt. A small one. He poured a finger from the whisky decanter and returned to his desk.

He desperately wished that he wouldn't let Mainwaring get at him like that. After all, he was Minister. If only he could remain detached and calm. Instead he felt rage multiplying like a cancer just underneath the smooth carpet of his exterior. On the one hand he knew that his Perm. Sec. was only doing his job – and doing it well for that matter. On the other he didn't like his nose pushed into the toilet.

"Well, that is the way things work," he said out loud, startling himself. There wasn't any *real* connection between Michael Regis helping him out and his assistance to MATTHEW MARK in the Saudi affair. Very likely the whole thing would have gone through in any case without so much as an eyebrow's being raised. Politics was the real world – and in the real world that is how things worked. We have goods for sale and there are buyers. As a salesman, how was he to know that the man who purchased a camcorder intended to make pornographic movies with it?

"Why should *I* care?" he said again out loud.

Yet he also knew that Mainwaring was trying to warn him as subtly as he could that he might be sailing a little close to the wind. Which meant that, if things went wrong – wrong enough for this sale to be dragged into the public domain and be endlessly examined by the Press – accusations could be made regarding inducements.

But that was ridiculous. Castleberry snorted. Unlikely. Impossible. He felt the whisky warm him and a kind of glow spread above his shoulders. He turned his mind away for a moment. He thought about The Monastery and immediately a kind of serenity settled over him. He smiled and shook his head, enjoying the feeling of pleasure spreading through him. Such beautiful unspoilt land, six hundred acres of it. Now it was his – or nearly his. In a few days perhaps, it would be his and his family's for ever. He was instructing his solicitors in the making of a will which would ensure that the two parts would never again be separated. Or parted with.

He then tried to recall some of the legend, a stupid matter really. It had something to do with an early Penhaligon's daughter who had married unwisely – a tinker or travelling musician. The father banished her to the furthest corner of his estates, cursing her, her husband and their offspring for eternity, or so it seemed.

'Well,' thought Castleberry, 'to hell with her father and old Penhaligon.' The Minister hardly considered the money at all, though it was plenty. It didn't matter. He would have stolen or begged the cash if necessary. So would his father or his sons. Nearly six hundred and fifty acres of the most beautiful part of England. Free from motorways and cars and the noises of the city. A place to go, a little paradise on earth.

If only he could take Jennifer there. Perhaps he could. Jennifer. How he had loved exploring her flesh, so young and firm, like a blossom just opened. Their lovemaking had not really worked. He had been too nervous, too excited. She had been excited too, but told him not to worry. He remembered rolling off her on to his back, so much wanting to be inside her, so frustrated at not being able to maintain his erection long enough to enter between those gorgeous thighs. She had worn her stockings and sandals to bed. So few women realised just how erotic that was, just a little bit of clothing, those electric changes of texture as your hand explored slowly. Catherine had never been like that. Naked and in the dark, always the missionary position. His thoughts returned to Jennifer and he could feel himself move inside his trousers. He had been lying on his back and he felt the lightest of tickles at the bottom of his stomach. He looked down. It was her hair as she bent over to take his penis into her mouth. Extraordinary. He nearly fainted with pleasure. Never, ever had Catherine done that. He had only experienced it at all with prostitutes, but that was mechanical. And he could tell that Jennifer was doing it with tenderness, maybe even love . . .

He had called her twice and the second time she returned his call, leaving a message that she was working and would be in touch very soon. Ian Castleberry sincerely hoped that it would be soon. The sooner the better. He finished his whisky and reached out for the remaining chocolate biscuit.

Michael Regis sat in Harvey Gillmore's office looking at a Blue Marlin on the wall. The office was part of his penthouse suite at the top of what had once been his newspaper building in Fleet Street. He had moved the newspaper to much cheaper property, fired half the staff as a frightener, cut the pay of the rest of them, hired a sizzling Cockney with buckles on his shoes as an editor. But he kept the building, leasing out everything but the penthouse to an insurance company who were paying more than the new property cost him. So, in a sense, the penthouse was free.

Regis assumed that the Blue Marlin had been caught somewhere on the high seas and sent to a taxidermist instead of being more sensibly eaten. Underneath the Marlin was a large model of a yacht called *Matilda*. On the wall over the desk were two crossed flags – one Australian, one British – and under the flags was a huge oil painting of a man who Regis could only assume was Gillmore's father. They had the same broad, flat faces with sunken, morose, humourless eyes. The nose and mouth were different. The wall facing the Blue Marlin was mostly window covered by vertical blinds. The window was certainly necessary because everything else in the room, bar the fish, the boat, the flags and painting, was dark. The carpet was very thick, very expensive, but black. Dark walnut or mahogany panelling covered the walls and the desk was also mahogany and larger than a billiard table. At the desk sat Harvey Gillmore, his lank dark hair falling across his forehead.

Gillmore used the spread fingers of one hand to push the hair back in place and scratch his head, and Michael Regis watched him frown. He tried to recall if he had ever seen him smile. The Australian baron was fifty-two years old, and gravity had pulled his features into a permanent mask of gloom. A bit like Richard Nixon. And, like Nixon, he always looked as though he needed a shave. He was not fat. He was a normal weight for his short stature but over the years he seemed to be collapsing gradually inwards and downwards. He was dwarfed by the huge desk, highly polished and clear of everything but a telephone, a glass of mineral water and a large model of Red Shadow, his beloved horse. He toyed with an expensive-looking pen.

"Have you ever thought about Christ?" Gillmore asked in his strong Australian accent.

Regis was taken aback. "I *beg* your pardon?"

Gillmore went silent again, morosely examining his pen as Regis tried to comprehend the *non sequitur*. They were meeting to discuss the timetable for delivery to WORLDWIDE. Harvey Gillmore was WORLDWIDE. WORLDWIDE was a very large holding company registered in the Cayman Islands and it provided an umbrella for Gillmore's many interests in the UK, Australia, Europe and America. During the good years the company had grown fabulously wealthy and Harvey Gillmore must have been one of the wealthiest men alive. During the bad years though, WORLDWIDE had experienced a gradual but cumulative and chronic cash flow problem. The present operation was an effort to solve a portion of that problem. Regis had opened the meeting with a proposal to make the arms delivery in stages over a period of six months and Gillmore objected. He wanted it sooner and all in one lump. Then, suddenly, he mentioned Christ.

Regis poured a little more Perrier into his glass. "Do you mean the symbolic Christ or the historical figure?"

Gillmore didn't move and continued to finger his pen. "I mean Christ the Living God."

Regis smiled indulgently. "I'm afraid that I've given little thought to religion for many years. I've left that to others more highly qualified."

He waited a moment, taking a sip of his Perrier. He was a little impatient to return to the subject because his time was limited. "However, I understand that earlier delivery will be extremely difficult under the circumstances. Since the small arms and some of the ordnance are more or less available now, why not take advantage—"

"I've been thinking for a long time about the state of my soul."

Harvey Gillmore's voice was always soft, but now it was almost inaudible.

"Indeed," said his visitor. "But perhaps I am not the right agent to take your confession."

Gillmore suddenly glared at him. "Oh, don't drag in all that Roman Catholic crap. I'm talking about being born again in Christ."

"Harvey," said Michael Regis with a smile, "I'm at a slight disadvantage here. I am certainly no expert in the world's religions, nor do I have even a passing interest in the subject. Ideally you should choose to talk this over with someone whose opinion is of more consequence than mine. In any case I am here now to try and reach some preliminary agreement on delivery dates."

"I am an Australian," Gillmore said redundantly as he got up from his large leather chair. "I find doing business in Britain really discouraging sometimes. It makes me depressed. I've brought new methods into the companies I own here. Well . . . not really *new* methods. They're old methods. I pay money for labour and I want labour in return. I don't want tea breaks and breaks for boozing in the pub or yakking in the office or pinching the arse of some sheila. I don't want people doing their *own* work on my time, time I buy with my money."

Gillmore was now leaning on his desk with both arms, looking directly at Michael Regis like a preacher and his forelock had again drifted down on his forehead.

"The Brits can be fine people, don't get me wrong. But this attitude has built up over years and years of having it easy, living off the resources of other countries. Now they just want to go into work like into a social club, spend two or three hours out of eight actually doing something for the boss, scratching their dicks for the rest of the

44

time, catching up on gossip, doing crosswords. For this they want high wages, short working weeks, long holidays, big pensions. They want smart houses, nice new cars, all the household conveniences with enough left over to drink their way through the weekends." He paused for effect. "But that is not Harvey Gillmore's way. If you are due at nine o'clock, you are in the office working at nine o'clock, not ten minutes after. And that goes for everybody, from the cleaner to the managing director or editor. I don't have unions and anybody who mentions unions to me gets his arse kicked out the front door pronto, right down the bloody steps. We don't have time and a half for overtime. We work to get the job out and when the job's finished we go home. And not before. That philosophy, old though it might be, is what put us in front and on top – and that philosophy keeps us there. Anyone who thinks differently gets fired. Simple as that."

Michael Regis stifled a sigh. Harvey Gillmore had always been a difficult person, but lately he was becoming even more eccentric. He had always felt a sense of pity for anyone who actually had to work for the man. How he had survived without being murdered was something of a mystery. He supposed that years spent sitting on the top of a mountain of cash, being able to afford anything money could buy, corrodes the intellectually vulnerable. Particularly if you are something of an ascetic as well. Gillmore did not drink or smoke and it was rumoured that he was vegetarian. He did have a yacht and an expensive house in expensive grounds, but the house was in atrocious taste, even for an Australian. In contrast to his office, everything was white and chrome and open-plan and split-level. The carpets were white, the sofas were white, the curtains, the wallpaper, the furniture, the fittings – all were white and chrome, scrubbed and bleached. Regis couldn't recall seeing a single book, never mind a bookcase, or a musical instrument. But he knew that Gillmore was not a genuine puritan because he also knew something of his sex life. He was one of Jennifer's regular customers.

Gillmore was still staring at him, waiting for him to agree or disagree. Michael Regis remained silent.

"If other companies were run like mine, England wouldn't be such a dump. Now, Michael, I want you to do whatever is necessary to get those lazy, worthless, union-ridden companies off their arses and on their feet. I want that order completed and on its way in sixty days. Maximum."

Michael Regis smiled easily. "You know I'll do what I can, Harvey. As always. The helicopters will be the real problem, though. I'm meeting with Lincoln of ASSOCIATED AERODYNAMICS in two days. Perhaps I can build a fire. He owes me a favour or two. In the meanwhile perhaps you could give a little thought to your own requirements, meet with your respondents, see if you could gain a little more flexibility—"

"Impossible."

"As I'm sure you well know, in business *nothing* is impossible – it only costs a little more."

"That too is impossible," Gillmore said softly as he picked up his pen and stared towards the ceiling.

Michael Regis rose and moved to the window, parting the blinds to look out towards St Paul's.

"Even in your remarkable world, Harvey, business is never an exact science. The Germans, even the Japanese, are no strangers to inaccuracies, delay, underpricing, bad timing or occasional poor quality. In other words, whatever the pressure, some things just may not be within human or mechanical capability. If it takes three months to build them and two months to test them—"

"They don't need testing," Gillmore interrupted again.

"On the other hand," Regis went on agreeably, "it may be possible to obtain four or six or even eight aircraft in two months, with the balance to be delivered a bit later. Helicopters are not the same kind of commodity as sprouts – to be ordered by the pound from the corner shop."

"It's the fucking Brits," Gillmore grumbled. "It's an attitude. I should be able to place the order, show them the cash, tell them when I want it, and then they die trying to get it to me on time."

He pointed his finger menacingly at Regis. "I'd understand it if they *died* working twenty-four hours on the assembly line. I'd say, 'OK, now I've seen you have worked your butts off, you can have a two-day delay.' But no, they want to go home and kick off their shoes and watch crap TV and wash their cars and water their lawns. And another thing: I didn't like giving up that horse. I love that horse. That old man will slobber all over him, spoil him . . ."

There were times when Michael Regis felt that he had earned every penny he made, and this was one of those times. To his knowledge the Australian had no friends, only business associates who were forced to indulge him, employees who were paid to hang on every word, wag their tails, roll over and beg. And then there was his wife, Mary. Mary was seldom seen by associates or employees and certainly not by the Press. They had been married for nearly thirty years, and he imagined Mary to be a kind of actress with a script for entrances and exits. She was occasionally seen at dinner parties but she only spoke quietly when spoken to, offered no opinions, smiled when it was expected, and finally disappeared to other duties when the men began talking business. She would appear again when everyone was leaving, to smile and nod. It must be a strange life, Regis mused as he looked at Gillmore speculatively. It had turned him into a little unbalanced bully who didn't even feel the need to order his thoughts before he spoke. Or maybe he had always been that way. It was a fine example of why money alone should never be the key to power. Yet this man had acquired far too much of both.

Gillmore broke the silence. "What are you looking at?"

"St Paul's," said Regis. "I find it restful. I don't know if it's the proportions or the whole. If we had any sense, we would flatten all these other buildings so that it could be seen properly, from a distance."

"You just told me you were not religious."

"Oh," said Regis, letting go of the blind and turning to Gillmore, "I think it has less to do with religion than standing in awe of something so beautiful."

"Just a building," Gillmore replied. "Like any other building. You don't need buildings to find the true Christ."

"I should think that Christ, wherever he might be, would find some comfort in St Paul's."

Gillmore shook his head. "Doesn't want comfort. Wants your soul."

"Well, he's welcome to it when I've finished with it."

The little man approached Regis and reached out for his arm, which he clamped in his hand.

"Let me tell you about Christ, Michael. You'll thank me for it."

His eyes were intense, his voice a whisper.

"Perhaps another time, Harvey."

He glanced at his watch, at the same time removing Gillmore's hand. "I have rather a lot on my plate at the moment, and—"

The Australian abruptly turned away and clapped his hands suddenly.

"I don't know why I went into this. Nothing goes right, not with your side or the other one. I've lost a tape. Somewhere. Fell out of my pocket."

Regis feigned interest. "Audio or video?"

"Audio. In negotiations I'm careful. Tape everything. This one was important. I remember putting it into my overcoat pocket to file when I got home and it wasn't there when I arrived. Things don't fall out of pockets, do they? They're taken out. Isn't that right?"

Without waiting for an answer, Gillmore went on. "I wouldn't want anything on that tape to reach any ears but mine."

Regis glanced at his watch again. "If it was a recording of a telephone conversation, it couldn't have been too sensitive."

"This was the secure line."

Michael Regis raised an eyebrow. Secure lines were granted to a very limited number of people. He knew of only about a dozen in existence.

"You taped a secure line?"

"I must have if I was talking on one," Gillmore said, as if to a child.

"Taping rather defeats the purpose of security, doesn't it?"

"I was talking to another party involved in this."

"The Saudis?"

"No. This was—"

Regis held up his hand. "I want to hear no more, Harvey. And, if I were you, I would ensure that the tape is recovered as soon as possible."

Gillmore nodded. "I've informed the other party so he can cover tracks if necessary. It's one of the reasons I need early delivery."

"There will be *no* delivery", said Regis, "if we are compromised in any way. I must make that clear before we go any further. My understanding is that the arms are for the Saudis with you acting as their agent."

"Oh, come off it, Regis. You know every bloody detail, so don't come on high and mighty and know-nothing-British to me, trying to keep your arse covered and pushing me out in the open. We wouldn't be getting top dollar if there wasn't a twist in it somewhere."

Michael Regis knew all the details of the 'twist', but he wasn't about to admit it in an environment which he was certain was audio taped. Previous conversations had taken place at the Regis residence, either in the garden or his study. Any visitor passing through his study door passed through a very strong electromagnetic current, guaranteed to jumble the filings on any magnetic tape. Unlike Gillmore, he wasn't the sort of person who wanted or kept evidence of his dealings or meetings. Many things he talked about were best filed once between his ears and stored there. The exterior world was not a dependable one. Friends changed over time – and so did enemies, for that matter. Occasionally friend and enemy swapped places. Wives and lovers changed too and were best left out of the picture altogether. Regis was a man whose cards could not get closer to his chest. He found that time relentlessly passed. Leaves fell from trees, machines became rusty and out of date, people were born, then aged and died. Given enough time, even the largest mountains changed their form.

In those terms 'legal' was a funny animal. 'Legal' had quite rapid cycles of moulting, and you were never really sure what sort of beast you had at any stage. Particularly when you operated on the periphery; and, if you were seriously interested in making money, the periphery was the only place to operate. It was the true twilight zone where nothing is ever what it seems. It was an amoral land with no good and no evil. The strong stole from the weak and the clever from the strong. There was much to lose and everything to gain. Michael Regis was a natural player in the twilight zone and for that reason he didn't want anyone in the sunlit zones of reality to look too long or closely at the legality of what he sometimes did. In his own mind he was convinced that they were legal in some sense of the word of many senses. And that was all which mattered. Meanwhile it was time to play safety shots.

"Well?" asked the Australian impatiently.

"I do apologise. My mind was elsewhere." Regis glanced at his watch once more. "I'm running behind schedule at the moment, so I'm afraid that we're going to have to continue this another time. If you feel uneasy about the arrangements, perhaps you could call by later tonight, after nine, and we can discuss it further."

He fetched his briefcase from behind the chair.

"Cover your arse, you Pom bastard." Gillmore had raised his voice to normal conversational level, but it sounded loud. "I know what happens when I walk through your bloody doorway. I don't know which doorway, but it's one of them. You don't fool me. I was playing this game when your mum was wiping shit off your arse."

Michael Regis had his hand on the doorknob.

"In the end, Harvey, I see no reason why we can't get your horse back for you." He smiled sincerely. "See you another time."

Harvey Gillmore stood watching the closed door for some while, a look of dark menace on his face. Then he went over to the window and looked out at St Paul's for a little longer.

"Crappy building," he muttered softly as he turned away.

Chapter Four

It was Friday, the fourth day after the near-lethal incident in front of the gym. Haug and Jennifer sat together in the little Greek café round the corner, two mugs of tea between them. It was the first time they had talked in any detail since Haug had begun watching her house. They came separately for training, with Haug following her taxi in the little yellow ex-telephone company van he had been using for surveillance. He had converted it three years ago to make things easier for himself. The back of the van was fitted with two-inch foam cut to size and covered. Three old sofa cushions could be arranged to form a comfortable *chaise longue* for easy watching from the disguised ports he had cut in both sides of the van. A purpose-built locker contained his photographic equipment, including a telescopic lens, a powerful telescope and a very expensive night vision scope. The back windows of the van were blacked out and a darkroom curtain could be drawn, separating the front seats from the rear. So Haug could also read to pass the time, with the aid of a little light mounted on a flexible arm attached to the roof. Just like home, except that he couldn't listen to music. It wasn't necessary to keep your eyes glued to the port, but you did have to keep your ears open for odd sounds.

Haug had kept watch from 7 a.m. to 7 p.m., and Keef had taken the night shift.

Keef often helped him out on a freelance basis. When he told him about the job, the Jamaican had grinned from ear to ear, saying that if it was Jennifer, that's the shift he wanted . . . man. Haug had pretended to be stern, telling him that it was a no-touch, no-approach situation. Lie back and watch, unless something happened or the buzzer sounded. Keef already knew that of course and his grin had broadened. Tell her, he said, not to bother drawing her curtains at night and he would watch her real close. But Keef was only joking. He was a good man. He was hard, but diplomatic and didn't lose his head when something unexpected happened. If there was trouble of course, Keef could probably stop anything but a cannonball.

Haug used Keef in this case because One Time couldn't be trusted around women. Anything else and he was straight as a die. You could give him a million pounds in a suitcase and he would never touch it. But a woman? The sight of an attractive female would open elemental hormonal gates somewhere in the depths of his being and his consciousness would be flooded, his groin engorged, his vision tunnelled, his ethics compromised and all other thoughts dashed to pieces. He would be over the garden wall and into the window as silently as an old black tomcat. No, it had to be Keef, not One Time, on this one.

And nothing had happened. Nothing at all. No one visited – not one person. Jennifer only went out to the local shops and the gym. She said that there had been no dodgy telephone calls, not even wrong numbers. Coming out of the gym, she was always watched by Haug on one side of the street and Keef on the other. Nothing abnormal happened at all. One Time would call a taxi for her and vainly try to chat to her while she waited. She would get in and Haug followed her back home.

"I'm beginning to wonder", she said, "if anything really happened at all last Monday. Today it seems a little like a dream – a nightmare I've nearly forgotten. It must have been very boring for you."

Haug grinned. "Naw, I'm used to it. A long time ago I thought I'd lead a real excitin' life, drinkin', raisin' hell, hoppin' from one adventure to another, travellin' the world with a romance in every port of call. But that's not the way the world is. For me the world is sittin' in an old yeller van readin' my book and watchin' somebody's winder. In this case, nothin' happenin' is the best thang that coulda happened."

Jennifer took a sip of tea. She had not been in the café before but knew that Haug was a regular. It was a small place with too many tables and chairs, so it would be a tight squeeze if crowded. Today it was almost empty, and the Irish woman behind the till was sounding bright and breezy as she harassed the inarticulate Greek cook.

"I think it would be a good idea to finish today. Whatever happened must have been some kind of awful mistake—"

"And I think a deal's a deal. I'm not makin' anythang outta this, but we said a week, and I think it should be a week. To be on the safe side, should be longer. Should be a month. But we'll take a chance and call it quits after a week."

Jennifer Montgomery shrugged her shoulders. "OK. Fine. In the meanwhile I'm going out to the West End this afternoon. I have a casting. My agent called me yesterday afternoon. Unfortunately it's for a commercial, which gives you about one chance in a hundred, if that. There'll be about thirty women who look exactly like me sitting in the waiting room."

"I find that hard to believe."

"What?"

"That there are thirty women in London who look like you."

Jennifer smiled warmly. "Thanks for the flattery, Haug, but I'm afraid the truth is that the competition is fierce and my chances slim. Anyway, I don't know if you want to be bothered following me, but—"

"I'll get one of the bikes," Haug interrupted. "Better for the traffic. I got a Harley and a Triumph, and I guess the Triumph is a little less conspicuous."

"All the usual male toys. Motorcycles as well. Aren't they American and English? I thought everyone bought Japanese these days."

"I'd rather eat shit than ride a Jap bike," Haug said.

"What a charming man."

"I'll be sittin' right behind you. On my male toy." He grinned at the double meaning.

Jennifer was not amused and her eyes reflected some anger.

"Male chauvinism is something I find rather repellent."

"Well, now, tell me something. Would you like to write up a little script of what I should say and how I should act so I could be perfect company for you? And maybe I could do the same thang for you. Or would you rather we just relaxed and both just said what we felt like sayin'? Don't you think that'd be better in the long run? Now you, you interest me as a person, and I'd like to know a lot more about you. So I'd like for you to say what you really thought sometimes."

"I did."

"Which kind of made me a cardboard figger. A big hairy male – except for my head – who lifts weights, rides motorsickles and treats women like they only got one use."

She shrugged. "Well, don't you?"

"I just said that I was interested in you personally."

"That's what you say, Haug. That's what they *all* say."

He swirled the remains of his tea around in his mug. "I cain't say I don't find you attractive, but that's a two-way thang, 'cause you work at bein' attractive, don't you? You work at bein' for the male what the male says he wants. Chauvinism is a game we are both playin', and I was treatin' it like a game and makin' jokes. If you don't like jokes, or you don't like my jokes, then I'll be plain. If you offered me a piece of butt, I'd turn it down. Now, I won't pretend it wouldn't be hard. I reckon I'd sit on a stump and think about it for a couple of hours before I said no. You are too goddam' young and you are too complicated. But it's the complicated that interests me in you as a person. You see, you don't say much and aren't the friendliest gal I've ever met, but I lissen anyway. I lissen to what you're *not* sayin' as well as what you're sayin'. It's like music. You know? Some of the most excitin' thangs in a Beethoven slow movement are the silences."

She was genuinely surprised. "*Beethoven?*"

"There," he said with a smile. "Jumped right out of the cardboard figger, didn't I? You figgered me for a country music man, right?"

"Beethoven?" she repeated, laughing. "You're joking. Which Beethoven?"

"The opus one thirty-two string quartet, for instance. That has a fine slow movement." He hummed a few bars of the melody. "See? The silence between the notes. *Very* important."

"Well, you did it, Haug. I find that absolutely astonishing."

"You figgered me for a Willie Nelson man. I used to like him. Still do, if I'm in the mood. I like blues, jazz. Just cain't stand pop music. It don't scratch places that itch."

"What other little surprises do you have in front of that ridiculous pony tail?"

Haug laughed. "You'll just have to wait and find out. I might look like an ape, but that doesn't mean my knuckles drag on the ground. You didn't believe it when I said we'd be friends, at least for a week. But I mean what I say. Let's find some time to talk."

"Ah," she said, glancing at her watch. "Time. Yes, all right. We'll talk some time. Invite me out for a drink. Meanwhile I have to run. The appointment is at three and I've got to do my hair. And look like they want me to look," she added with a trace of self mockery.

"I'll give you a lift in the van. Be quicker. Shouldn't, but what the hell. Thangs've been quiet. Then I'll go pick up the bike."

Jennifer put her bag over her shoulder and watched as Haug paid for the tea. She had found herself hoping that he would ask her out for a drink. She turned and stared through the condensation of the café windows.

She was still thinking of Haug as she dressed. Her agent had told her to look like a secretary. What the hell did a secretary look like? she wondered. Anyway she had chosen a pleated blue skirt, a saffron blouse and some medium heels, then shrugged her shoulders.

Wouldn't get the job in any case – which was the wrong attitude. Commercials were cattle calls and casting directors called in everybody who would look remotely right to let the clients choose which cow – clients who knew as much about acting and cameras as they knew about astrophysics. Her agent was trying to push her for commercials because there was little else about. Jennifer knew that she wouldn't accept a theatre job out of London. Because of her other business. She had given herself another three years. Make as much as possible, save as much as she could. Then get out.

She looked again in the mirror, combing her hair and wondering why her thoughts returned to Haug. What *was* it? He was ugly. Well, not *ugly* really. Just odd, unusual-looking. But it wasn't his looks that made her think of him. She was trying to put her finger on something, trying to understand why she liked him. Last Monday, when he had brought her home, she had been terrified, falling apart inside. Yet she wasn't worried about Haug's presence. He seemed to reassure her. He didn't *threaten*. *That* was it. He looked threatening enough, but he was so relaxed, so sure of himself, that she almost trusted him. Well, she thought, that would be a first. Trusting a man. It was difficult keeping her defences up with him, he was so disarming. In the café she had actually found herself enjoying his company. And during the drive home in that smelly old van, he was full of fun, cracking jokes about other drivers or people they saw walking on the pavement. She had to admit it: she was comfortable sitting in a vehicle next to a man. He never seemed to sneak glances at her or try to twist the conversation round to her sex life or boyfriends – the probing, thrusting questions she inevitably associated with any male she was alone with. Except a gay of course. And she seriously doubted that Haug was gay. He just seemed . . . well, natural.

The other business. Jennifer looked at herself and sighed. Next week it began again. There were three appointments this week that she had rescheduled, and three was her maximum, the most she could stomach. The new one, Ian Castleberry, the fat minister, was sounding like a lovesick boy on the telephone. She had told Michael that it was best to tell the truth to clients, but no, he felt that this was the best way sometimes. Regis had assured her that he would break the news to Castleberry at the appropriate moment. In the meanwhile she had to pretend to be infatuated with an ageing lump of lard with a toad's charm. On the whole though, she preferred him to one of her other clients, Harvey Gillmore. A slimy bat-like creature who flapped wetly through her door, a man with eyes which could chill the blood. After Harvey Gillmore she had to soak a very long time in the bath for her circulation to return. She complained bitterly about Gillmore, but Michael insisted.

Michael. She looked at her watch, wondering where the taxi was, wanting something to do to take her mind off Michael. When she thought of Michael Regis, her thoughts were troubled, turbulent, contradictory. A darkness crept over her brow. It was understood that Michael did not pay. Nor did she ask him to pay. Or want him to. She had realised long ago that there was emotion involved with Michael, and she did not know why. OK, he was attractive. He was charming, even good company. Yet she knew that he would never want to be involved with her. Did she want him? Well, yes and no. Both yes and no screamed like demons, equally loud. What did that mean? she had asked herself again and again. And she enjoyed lovemaking with him – or at least moments of it. Yet she could never forget that he was in control. He made the rules and the decisions.

Look at it, she said to herself, face up to it. It was like a wife, wasn't it? A mistress. She was there to do as she was told, the very trap she desperately wanted to avoid. And there was no way to dent his armour, to wrest the tiller from his hand. Behind the mask of warmth was nothing but ice. Or stone. She looked out of the window for the taxi and could see Haug relaxing with his helmet off, smoking a cigar, leaning on the seat of his motorcycle. But she wasn't thinking of him now. Michael Regis had crept in and flooded her with dread.

With relief she saw the taxi draw up. Grabbing her coat and handbag, she checked her watch again and opened the door.

Haug saw her come out of the house and he threw the butt of his cigar in the gutter. He wore an open-faced helmet, leather jacket and engineers' boots with jeans on the outside. The English always tucked their jeans into their boots – more sensible but a little uncomfortable. He tickled the carbs and used the starter motor since the engine was warm. The Triumph was a T160, the later three-cylinder engine made by the firm just before it had folded in the 1970s. He hadn't ridden it for some time, despite being very fond of the old thing. It was still fast, even by today's standards, and handled like a dream. Haug thought British engineers the best in the world when they wanted to be – eccentric, but unbeatable. For years they had tormented the rest of the world by spending a fraction of the money laid out by their competitors, yet still winning races. A miracle frame was cobbled together in a Belfast garage which gave Norton twelve more years at the top despite using a 1930s engine. Engines were fettled by Yorkshiremen with flat caps, oily overalls and pencils behind their ears. Bold riders got on these machines and beat the world until the Japanese simply overwhelmed them. His T160 was an example of the last of the British machines to hold the line, still winning in the early 1970s on an engine basically designed in 1938.

He followed the taxi easily, enjoying the sound the bike made. It was overcast and cool but not raining, something he was always grateful for in England. It was no wonder that the English talked so much about the weather. It was so bloody changeable. Where he came from in North Carolina, if the sun came up one day it was likely to stay there until nightfall. Here you never could tell. He remembered one day a couple of years ago when it had started warm and sunny, then had hailed, snowed and ended up misty and freezing – and it could easily have been the other way around.

The taxi was heading for Soho. He always closed up when the taxi neared a set of lights, as the drivers were notorious for running through on red. But the traffic had thickened as they neared Oxford Street, so he mostly had to sit and wait, the Triumph lumpy on idle. Finally they crossed over and into Soho Square, around it to the west side, then into Dean Street. They stopped in front of a yellow door with flaking paint and Jennifer got out and paid the driver. She smiled briefly at Haug as he backed the bike between two illegally parked cars so that he could watch the door.

Jennifer Montgomery rang the intercom, and the door buzzed. She pushed it open and went inside. It was dark and gloomy as she looked for the name of the firm by the doorway. It was at the bottom. CLAPPERBOARD FILMS. First Floor. That was nice, she thought to herself. They were usually on the top floor. She went up the flight of stairs to a landing, pushed open a door to the hallway and looked through.

Another door on the left had a nameplate. CLAPPERBOARD FILMS. Underneath was a hand-written notice AUDITIONS, with an arrow below. Jennifer adjusted her blouse and smoothed down her skirt, then pushed open the office door and went in.

She was only dimly aware of the sound of the door slamming behind her, because at the same time she felt something pass over her head and instantly tighten around her neck. It was pulled even tighter until she could hardly breathe. Her hands went to her neck, desperately trying to get fingernails underneath the rope. Then she was aware of a voice, nearly a whisper, close to her ear.

"You won't be hurt", said the voice, "if you do *exactly* as you're told. Nod your head if you understand."

Instead Jennifer was trying to scream, but all that came out was a high-pitched squeal. Instantly the rope tightened and she felt as though she were going to pass out. Then it loosened slightly.

Again the voice spoke. "You will not try that again. Hold your face up, turn your face up towards the ceiling."

She heard the words only dimly and tried to do what the man asked. Her chin had been digging into her chest, trying to stop the rope from tightening. There was another man in front of her now, and she could feel her hair being pushed back behind her ears. Suddenly a large piece of tape was slapped roughly across her mouth and pressed firmly. Immediately the rope loosened a little, and the man behind her spoke again.

"Take your hands away from your throat and put your arms down."

She did as she was told, not knowing what else to do. She didn't even realise that her eyes were tightly closed until she opened them and stared crazily at a naked lamp hanging from the ceiling. Her whole body was rigid with terror, but she did not move a muscle because she didn't want to experience again the pain of the rope tightening around her throat accompanied by that awful feeling of not being able to breathe. She felt a belt of some sort being cinched at her waist. Then her wrists were shackled, one to each side of the belt. The rope was removed from her throat, and she started to lower her head when the lamp bulb suddenly disappeared. Someone behind her had placed a blindfold over her eyes and was tightening it. Two sets of arms suddenly lifted her up in the air and she was dropped heavily to the floor on her back. Her ankles were grabbed and she heard someone snigger. She felt her legs being pulled apart. There was another snigger as one of her ankles was released and a hand pawed at her crotch.

"Look at that," said the sniggerer.

A flood of anger overwhelmed her fear and she lashed out with her free leg as hard as she could. It struck something soft and she could feel the hand immediately let go of her other ankle. She flailed both legs, trying to hit something. Someone was groaning and cursing in a language she didn't understand. Both her legs were grabbed by many hands and forced together. She heard tape being peeled back, then felt her ankles being bound together with several layers of tape.

"Are you OK?" a voice inquired.

Another voice struggled for wind. "Bitch. Right in the gut."

"It was your fault," the other voice replied. "No time for that shit. Get her in the bag. Quickly. Piet!"

After a couple of moments a door opened.

"Everything OK outside?" asked the first voice.

"Yeah."

Or was it 'Ja'? A deep growl.

"Help us get her in the bag," said the first voice. "Then take her out to the van."

Jennifer felt someone grab her and she was lifted into the air and held there by two large hands. Slowly she was lowered to the floor again and she felt a heavy cloth bag being pulled up around her. She tried resisting, but her knees were immediately buckled by a blow, and a large hand pushed her down into a foetal position. She felt the bag being drawn up, then the end being tied. They were talking again, but she couldn't listen because she was trembling with a great rush of terror. Not just terror of the unknown, but claustrophobia, the most powerful feeling she had ever known. Not only did she want her limbs free, not only did she want out of the bag – she wanted to be outside her own skull. Suddenly she was aware of being lifted from the floor, then bouncing slightly against what must have been a man's back. Terror was raging inside her until it overflowed. She began screaming, the sound escaping through her nose. Screaming and screaming. Something hard hit her in the back of the head and she heard ringing in her ears.

"None of that." It was the first voice. "One peep, one sound and Piet will smash you against the wall of the building. Do not move, do not make one sound. You hear?"

Again she felt the thud at the back of her head. Again her ears rang. And she realised that she was glad of the blows because the insane terror was receding like a dark ocean, away from her, leaving her able to try and reassemble her scattered thoughts as they skittered like balls of water on a hot grill. The man was going down the stairs. She could feel the movement, hear the heavy footsteps. Haug, she thought frantically. Haug was out there. What could she do? How could she let him know? Let him see her, she willed. Please let him see her, understand what was happening. Haug! Haug! she screamed silently to herself. She heard the front door open. Haug!

Haug was leaning up against the building opposite, which advertised dirty videos, watching the pretty girls go by. There were such a lot of them in Soho and such a variety of dress. From those in sweat suits and combat boots to others in what he would call bedroom fantasy gear. Still others had holes in their tights and hair dyed green or purple. A strange but interesting menagerie.

The yellow door opposite opened and a very large, extremely tall postman, who reminded him of Frankenstein, left the building, a mailbag over his shoulder. He opened his van door and threw the bag inside. Haug's attention drifted to a man with shoulder-length white hair, his coat draped over his shoulders Italian-style, accompanied by a young well-dressed lady with red hair. He was talking to her with great animation as she listened attentively. He turned back to watch two men, one white, one swarthy, exit from the yellow door. One of them was combing his hair and both were laughing. Actors, he thought. Always tell them. They were too loud. He was only dimly aware that they too got into the van as he turned back to the old arty boy and what he guessed was his girlfriend. The van immediately pulled away and moved down the road. But something was wrong.

There were no markings on the van. It was red, but there were no postal markings. Haug raced over to the yellow door and pushed all the buzzers, one after the other. No reply. He didn't wait any longer. He put his shoulder to the door once, hard but testing. It held firm. He was aware that the arty man and the girl were looking at him. He backed off two paces and ran at the door. There was a sound of tearing timber as it gave way and bounced off the hall wall. A quick glance showed him there were no rooms on the ground floor, and he bounded up the stairs two at a time. It was a dingy place. He smashed open the landing door at the first floor. All the doors were closed. Nothing on them, not one. He kicked the first one open. Nothing. Two chairs and an old desk, flyspecked windows. He slammed it closed and was about to kick the second one open when he stopped. There was something familiar. Perfume. Her perfume. He knew the smell – very exotic, very subtle. It was in the first room. He went back and sniffed again. Yes? No? He wasn't sure. He knocked one of the chairs aside. Cigarette butts on the floor, fresh. And something else caught the corner of his eye, under the desk. He tipped the desk over with one brisk movement and picked up the little shoe. For a second he just stood there, frozen. Then he jammed the shoe in his back pocket.

"Asshole!" he shouted. He was referring to himself.

Haug went down the stairs like a boulder. The tall long-haired man was standing in the doorway.

"Excuse me," he said in a loud middle-class voice, "are you responsible for the damage to this door?"

Haug shouldered the man roughly aside.

"What the fuck has it got to do with you?" he asked, already putting on his helmet and digging for his keys as he headed for the bike.

The starter motor caught again, and the engine drowned out the long-haired man's voice. The long-haired man was shaking an umbrella at him and the red-haired girl had joined in the din.

Haug pulled out and simultaneously snapped the clutch and opened the throttle full bore. The big triple leapt away, the front wheel momentarily leaving the ground. Immediately he slowed to overtake the traffic queue. Which way, which street? Haug wondered. Old Compton Street or on to Shaftesbury Avenue?

In the back of his mind he knew that it was useless, but it was best to choose one direction, any direction, and eat up as much traffic as possible, hoping that the choice was right. The odds were worse than one roll of the dice bringing up snake eyes, but Haug was a devil's mix of anger, frustration, self-damnation and fear. The fear was hard to keep down because the fear was for Jennifer. Whom he had let down. Because he couldn't keep his mind on his business. Because he was an asshole. A fucking obvious scam like that! She was in the mailbag of course and the son of a bitch had dragged it right in front of his nose. They must be laughing their asses off. And what about Jennifer? Scared shitless, if she was still alive. But Haug immediately tore that thought out of his head.

He took the turn at Old Compton Street in his roll of the dice and barrelled off towards Charing Cross Road, nearly hitting a policeman, who shouted something as he went by. He sailed through the red light and slid into the northbound traffic, thinking that they would probably try and get out of the centre as soon as possible. Though it could be South London, and then they would be going the other way. He had to stop at Oxford Street because of the crossing traffic but roared on into Tottenham Court Road, one finger on the horn to try and clear pedestrians. He also switched his high beam on. Haug was a good motorcyclist. He had spent much of his youth scrambling in the back country with other good ole boys. Horns were blowing as he took chances, cutting between cars, criss-crossing, jumping lights, looking for the red van. Just a glimpse, that was all he needed. All he needed. Please, please, let it happen.

Then he added an afterthought through his teeth: "Asshole."

Jennifer was trying to hold her head off the floor so that it wouldn't bounce. She was desperately listening for the sound of a motorcycle. Several times she heard one, but it didn't sound right and soon passed by. The three men were all in the front seat, and she slid from side to side as they rounded corners and forward as they braked sharply. They seemed to be weaving in and out of streets, and occasionally she heard someone blow their horn. Finally Jennifer forced herself to stop thinking of Haug. She tried to squeeze out her fear in order to think clearly. It was necessary to think clearly for survival.

So. She was a prisoner – of whom or for what reason she had no idea. But it was a fact. There was little chance of escaping. One against at least three, maybe more when they arrived at wherever they were going, and she was bound like a battery hen. She felt herself sliding violently as the van swerved to the left. Her head banged the side and the terror returned in a rush. No, wait, wait, she screamed at herself. Think! You are not completely helpless, because you still have your wits! Think! What would happen when they arrived? Assuming that they arrived somewhere and they were not just going to toss her in the river. Again the fear, and again the struggle to make back it down with logic. No chance anyway if they throw me in the river. She had checked her bonds. Her wrists were at her sides in some sort of manacles attached to a belt – she remembered seeing something like it on prisoners being transferred from jail to jail, something on the news. No chance there. Her ankles were taped so tightly that she was beginning to lose feeling in her feet. Indeed she could hardly move at all and found herself trying to relax her leg muscles from little threats of cramp. OK. Assume they take me to a place. What then? Rape? Probably. Fight or not fight? Survive. Just lie there. Try and make it as lousy for them as possible. Question: who are they? She knew nothing, didn't even know what they looked like. But she did know that all three had accents. Two of them South African, maybe. White African anyway. The third she couldn't place at all. Middle East? Possibly. Question: what do they want? If they took her to a place, they must want something. If you give it to them – whatever it was – what would they do then? What *could* she do? What? Panic again. Somehow lead them to Haug or him to them. What could he do? Never mind, just make a plan, some kind of plan. Think. Keep thinking, she told herself over and over again as fear spread like an ink stain through her mind. Suddenly she was aware that the van had stopped. The men were getting out. The doors slammed.

The man didn't drop her on the floor but let down the bag carefully and the top was opened.

"Stand," a voice commanded.

It sounded like the man Jennifer mentally called 'First Voice'.

She tried to stand, but the muscles in her legs wouldn't respond, wouldn't move. Someone grabbed her hair and she stifled a scream by biting her lip, but a slight moan escaped through her nose. Pain surged through her thighs, and it felt as though her scalp were coming off.

The First Voice spoke again. "Cut her legs free, Piet."

She heard a deep grunt, and a moment later her ankles parted. Her shoes were gone, her feet were numb and she still couldn't stand. The pain from her scalp made her eyes fill with tears and she felt the blindfold begin to dampen.

"Stand, you bitch!" ordered First Voice.

"No blood in feet," growled Piet.

She felt her legs being slapped, and a slow tingling feeling signalled the fact she still had feet at the end of her legs. She could tell that there was carpet on the floor. She struggled to stand, if only to relieve the pain in her head.

Suddenly the man let go of her hair and Jennifer wobbled from side to side, her feet and knees throbbing. Someone steadied her by holding her by the arm this time. Someone else tugged at her dress, and there was a sound she immediately recognised as scissors. They were cutting her skirt off, and she could feel the cool air of the room on her body. Then her blouse was cut from the back, including her bra strap. There was no other sound except the snipping of the scissors and a few grunts. Her tights were partly cut, then torn away, her knickers clipped at the sides.

She was naked and realised that the room was quite cool, too cool. She began to shiver. It was very quiet, though Jennifer could hear the sound of traffic. The road was not far away. No one said anything, but she could hear the men breathing. They stood around her.

"What time is he coming?" asked Second Voice.

"Soon, he said on the phone," said First Voice. "Time enough. I'll go first. You and Piet flip for second."

Jennifer felt excruciating pain as the nipple on her left breast was grabbed and pulled roughly.

"Come on, you filthy little whore," he said, pulling her after him. "Now you going to find what a good fuck really is. And if you kick again, I smash your face in."

She felt herself being jerked along, and she tried her best to keep up with the man who was pulling her by the breast. They left one room and then she heard a door open and she was pulled across the threshold, turned around and pushed abruptly in the chest. She fell on to something soft. A bed. Her mind was numb, but she felt a growing cold anger and wished desperately that she could spit. Lying on the bed, she concentrated fiercely, making her whole body as limp as a flannel. She could hear the man taking off his trousers. Then his hands were on her, and he was laughing.

He stopped laughing.

"Get some life in you, slut. Raise your legs."

She felt herself being tugged now from the top. He was trying to get her whole body on the bed. Then he yanked at her legs and knees, which flopped from side to side lifelessly. She felt his breath on her face, then his weight on her body.

"OK, you bitch, you behave or I slap you like a dog."

She waited. He slapped, but it wasn't too hard and, as she heard him cursing, trying to find his way in, she managed to grin across clenched teeth. She realised to her delight that he was small. He approached again and she moved her hips just slightly, enough for him to fall out. He swore again, this time in another language.

I'll win, she thought. Somehow I'll find a way to win.

Chapter Five

AUS 1 slid silently out of the underground car park and into the traffic flowing towards St Paul's. The Rolls-Royce was long, new and black. The rear windows were smoked, and inside were Harvey Gillmore and the editor of his popular tabloid paper, *The News*, Colin Greenaway.

Greenaway was a Cockney made good. Well . . . in his eyes he had made good, the point being disputed in other circles. Greenaway felt that he was at the cutting edge of new technology, new aggressiveness and the new realism of the Modern Age. Some of his critics maintained that it was the Old Realism of the Stone Age. New or old, the fact of the matter was that high unemployment made it a buyer's market. The man who pays the piper calls the tune. And that bromide hung on the wall of Colin Greenaway's office in Times Roman for the edification of all employees who were in any doubt. To anyone barely sentient, the newspaper was a bad joke, but, as Greenaway claimed, it outsold every fucking rag on the market.

The running costs had been cut right down to the bone. The bones had been boiled and the both strained. Unions had been beheaded with bold and ferocious strokes and the scattered remnants pursued through the streets and then the courts relentlessly and mercilessly, until they were completely impotent, if not totally impoverished. Every father of chapel, every shop steward had been fired on the spot and many of them had been blacklisted and financially ruined. It had been time to teach a lesson to those arrogant enough to think that the company owed them a living. Greenaway had smashed some sense into the bastards, namely that the company giveth and the company taketh away. Punches to the head, knees to the balls, that's what people understood, then give 'em a good kicking when they were on the ground. A brutal hiding sticks in the memory. The same philosophy extended to competitors. There were no rules when winning was the prize. The old-style tabloids had been blown out of the water or holed below the waterline. Those that didn't sink joined the sleek new killers under the water, silently searching the wastes and sewers of life for anything edible. Tits, bums, legs and royals sell a lot of papers, and royals' tits, bums and legs sell most of all. Sleaze, sport and scandal formed the unholy trinity which made *The News* great.

Around his boss, however, Greenaway became a different person. On newspaper premises Greenaway strode through the corridors like a contemporary Kray twin, shoulders swaying in a snappy Saville Row suit, cuffs shot with heavy gold monogrammed cufflinks, side-buckled shoes snapping on the polished tiles, voice as loud and vulgar as a sergeant major. But when he was with Harvey Gillmore, the body language reversed itself and he magically became a parody of his own employees. The master promptly became a slave when confronted with the Almighty.

And, Greenaway thought, this was as it should be – the natural order of things in a much better ordered world than the one of recent memory. Those with power flaunted it over those with none. Those with more power still craved allegiance from those beneath them. The man sitting next to him in the car was the ultimate piper payer. Indeed, if ordered, he would be delighted to kiss his arse in the middle of Trafalgar Square at noon and tell him it smelled like roses. In fact he had already done that once in Harvey Gillmore's office, down on his knees when the boss lowered his trousers. And those beneath his position had better be prepared to do the same for him. What Gillmore wanted, Gillmore got. If he didn't get it from Greenaway, he would fire him and find someone else. Life was simple when you came right down to it.

Harvey Gillmore sat with his granny glasses perched on the end of his nose reading the next morning's lead story about some royal infidelity with an accompanying photograph of the relevant princess swimming topless on a private beach with some wing commander. The picture was probably taken from forty miles' distance by a photographer with a telescopic lens borrowed from Greenwich Observatory, one normally used for taking pictures of rocks on the moon.

"At the end of the day," said Greenaway unctuously, "the strategy is this. We run it tomorrow, Saturday. Basically speaking, the Palace won't be able to come back at us till Monday, by which time we'll have some war atrocity to bleed off the attention. If not, we'll print an apology on Tuesday accompanied by two more pictures."

He handed these to Gillmore who looked at one of them with a bored expression on his face.

"At the end of the day, Saturday is an ace time to run it. We don't have the commuters, but we'll do a full run and get a sell-out. And at this moment in time, the Palace *can't* do a thing about it . . ."

Gillmore picked up the second picture, shaking his head sadly. "When I was a kid, royalty meant something. And now?" He tossed the second picture back to Greenaway. "Just a bunch of degenerates. It makes you weep."

Greenaway nodded enthusiastically. "At this moment in time I think we're doing the country a service."

"Don't be so stupid, Greenaway," said Gillmore softly. "All we're doing is selling newspapers. This is news. And it sells. So we print it. It makes me sad to do it, but there it is."

His editor agreed immediately. "Yes, exactly. Just what I was trying to say. We don't approve of this kind of behaviour in any way, shape or form. Not from our royal family. But at the end of the day, if they do it, it's our duty to report it."

Gillmore seemed to ignore Greenaway's reply. He was studying two A4 pages typed by his secretary.

"Shove this in on Saturday in a good position. Draw it into the royal story by comparing the two issues – one good, one filthy. The Saudis have come through with a big order – well, big for these days. Shows how our industry hasn't lost its punch and can come up with the goods – and deliver them on time. Make sure that Ian Castleberry gets a good plug for his hard-headed, no-nonsense business acumen. Something like that."

He handed the pages to Greenaway, took off his glasses, folded them up and stuck them back in his top pocket.

"Howell," he said without raising his voice.

The chauffeur immediately cocked his head. "Sir?"

"Why are we taking so long?"

"Traffic, sir," the chauffeur replied. "Appears to be rather heavy. Friday afternoon. Everyone leaving early."

"It's the civil servants," sneered Gillmore to his editor. "Overpaid and underworked. Should be the other way around. Waste of the taxpayers' money."

"Yeah, a waste of the taxpayers' money," echoed Greenaway, nodding his head. "Basically speaking, they don't deserve a weekend."

Gillmore stared out of the window. "Who asked you for your opinion? Don't waste my time telling me what *you* think. Like the man said, it's not worth the paper it's written on."

Greenaway dipped his head cravenly. "I just thought—"

"I don't pay editors to think," Gillmore interrupted. "Not even Brady."

Norman Brady was editor of the prestigious *Sunday Sentinel*, acquired five years ago and decried in Parliament as a fundamental example of sharp dealing in newspaper publishing. The Opposition also made the accusation that the new owner was gaining too much influence for one man. Brady was doing a follow-up on the Saudi article with all the intellectual and economic trimmings for Sunday.

"If Brady's not allowed to think, why should you be?"

"Ah . . ." His editor was trapped in a verbal minefield. Any move he made might blow his leg off.

Gillmore turned to him. "Speak, Greenaway."

Greenaway shot his cuff and toyed with his heavy cufflink nervously.

"Well, of course I'm not supposed to think. I just forgot for a moment. Sorry."

"Howell," said Gillmore again without raising his voice.

"Sir?"

"Pull over to the kerb, Howell, and change places with this idiot."

"Yes, sir."

Howell immediately found a spot, put on the emergency flashers, opened his door and then opened Greenaway's door. Uncomfortably Colin Greenaway got out as Howell held the door.

"Give him your cap, Howell."

Looking miserable, Greenaway got into the driver's seat of the Rolls while Howell sat beside Harvey Gillmore as straight as a corporal, his eyes on the back of Greenaway's head.

"Where to, sir?" asked Greenaway from the front.

The cap was too small for his head.

Howell told him the name of Michael Regis's French restaurant in Victoria and the way there. He spoke briefly but graphically, without hesitation and without moving anything but his mouth.

When he finished, Gillmore looked at his editor as if waiting for something.

Finally he spoke, and his voice had a considerable edge to it. "Aren't you going to say 'thank you, sir' to Howell?"

"Thank you, sir."

"For right now", said Gillmore, "you are the excrement who drives my car. Meanwhile Howell has been promoted temporarily to gentleman. When we arrive, I want you to hop out smartly and open my door for me. Howell will then return to his duties and you can find your own way home."

"Yes sir," Greenaway said, adding through his teeth, "and I hope you rot in hell, you fucking Aussie cunt."

"What was that, Greenaway?" came the voice from the back.

"Nothing, sir. Traffic, sir."

"Then drive on, boy!" And the first smile of the week creased Gillmore's sour face. "You have to learn that I am a man breaker. I make 'em, and I break 'em, right, Howell?"

He returned to his papers.

"Yes, sir," said Howell.

Thomas Howell despised his employer. His hatred was very difficult to quantify, but his whole demeanour was carefully formed to protect this burning furnace, not unlike a nuclear plant with its core encased in reinforced concrete. He had fantasies of killing this man in the slowest possible way. Twelve years ago Howell had applied for the job of chauffeur with his wife, Beth, though the advertisement had been for driver only. After a long wait while references were checked, Gillmore had hired both of them, taking on Beth to help his wife, Mary, around the house. There was a small but nice cottage tied to the estate, not too far from the main house, and they fell in love with it. But what was idyllic in their dreams soon turned into a nightmare.

The original agreement was for Beth to help Mary on a part-time basis for six days a week, but this soon turned into a full-time job which included things like scrubbing floors and even the patio, which they insisted be done properly, namely on hands and knees. In short, Beth was becoming a household servant and that was not a part of the agreement. Howell himself was prepared to put up with the abuse that Gillmore gave him as a matter of course. He had this ability to put a distance between himself and his emotions. Others, no doubt, would soon feel like the piece of excrement Gillmore just mentioned, but Howell did not talk a lot, despite his Welsh background. And that gave Gillmore less opportunity to jump down his throat. He was not tall and was slightly built, but he was wiry, like a spring. He did his job well and he knew that he was good at it. So he confronted his employer about his wife's increasing hours – at no more pay, of course! He had brought the matter up after they had returned from the City. He remembered every word to this day.

Howell had just let Gillmore out of his door and said, "Excuse me, sir, may I have a quick word with you?"

But his employer had simply brushed past him, briefcase in hand, crunching on the gravel towards his doorway. So Howell caught up with him, suppressing a brief flash of anger, and grabbed his arm lightly.

"Excuse me, sir. I would very much appreciate it if I could speak to you for a moment."

Gillmore stopped dead, one foot on his doorstep, and turned his head slowly to look at the hand on his arm. Howell dropped his hand, mumbling an apology. Then Gillmore glared at him.

"What the fuck do you want, Howell? I am a very busy man."

Howell took a deep breath. "It's about my wife, sir. When we originally spoke about the job, you said it was only to be part-time, sir. And now it appears—"

His employer broke away and opened his front door. Then he turned back and said, "Come in, Howell."

Thomas Howell followed him through the immaculate white hallway to his office. Gillmore placed his briefcase beside his desk and sat down in the huge white leather chair, put on his granny glasses, more of an affectation than a necessity in those days, and opened one of the drawers. While he was looking in the drawer, he muttered, "Close the door."

Howell closed the office door and stood before his boss, who had drawn out a large manila envelope. Gillmore looked up at him over the tops of his glasses.

"Before employing you I took up references. But, you see, I always do more than that. I have to be very careful, as you can appreciate. So I dug around a bit in your past. In fact, Howell, I think I know more about you than you know about yourself, eh?"

The silence seemed to last for ever and Thomas Howell at first felt himself reddening, then, rapidly, all the blood drained from his face. He stared at the envelope, unable to speak.

After glaring at his employee for a few moments, Gillmore began tapping the envelope.

"It's all in here." He paused again. "Even pictures. Pictures, Howell. Remember when they were made? Eh? Remember what you were doing?"

Howell's mind was racing. Yes, he knew the pictures, and he even remembered what they were. They were also from a long time ago. He was only eighteen and he was living with a man, a man who had been on holiday in Anglesey when they met. Howell was then desperate to get away from home and the father he detested. But there was no work. He could not get a job and, if he couldn't get a job, he couldn't move out. This man offered him a place in London. He could stay with him and anyone could find work in London. Except that he didn't, not for a long time. Earnest Holmes, a respected columnist for an evening newspaper. He quickly found out that Earnest Holmes was a homosexual, and for a long time he thought that he was himself. Holmes bought driving lessons for him, let him drive his car. He bought clothes for him and presents. But there was no cash, no spending money and Howell gradually realised that he was trapped. There were parties with other older men, other young boys. And photographs were taken. Some of the things became too excruciating, too painful, so he ran away. The only way he knew how to earn a living was in Piccadilly, standing around in tight trousers, going with other men for money.

But he knew that he wasn't really homosexual. He felt no real excitement, and it was girls who always interested him. By whoring he got enough money together for a deposit for a flat, then gave it up. He took a chauffeur's course. He met normal women and went out with them. Finally he met Beth. She was small, like he was, with dark hair cut in a bob. She was unemployed, but by then he had a good job with a financial advisor in the City and he asked her to marry him. He had never told her of his past, nor had he planned to. The thought of doing so made him wonder whether he could.

He silently cursed himself. He had even returned to Earnest Holmes's flat three years later demanding all copies of the photographs, but Holmes assured him that they were destroyed. Well, obviously they hadn't been.

Howell was not going to give up without a fight. He returned Gillmore's stare.

"Obviously, then, I will have to break the news to Beth."

"Oh, I'm not going to tell your wife, Howell. I'm not a tell-tale. I'm going to fire you both and this is all going to become part of your CV. On your reference will go the fact that you are a poof and a drug addict—"

"I was never—" Howell shouted.

Gillmore slammed his hand down on the large desk, stopping him mid-sentence. "You were! I have testimony, I have proof! I am going to make sure that you never, ever work again, Howell. Not as a driver, not even as a street sweeper. The moment you walk from this door you are unemployable. Do you finally understand me, Howell? It will go in my newspapers, eh? Thomas Howell is a ginger beer, a pervert and a drug addict. Live that down, if you can!"

Gillmore stood up behind his desk and walked slowly around to stand directly in front of his driver.

"I'm going to fire you right now unless you drop your fucking trousers and lean over that desk for six of the bloody best. You have exactly six seconds to decide, boy."

Thomas Howell took the full six seconds, but he did it. He felt that he had to. Gillmore pulled his own belt from his trousers and beat him with it, then threw it at him. Howell had tears in his eyes. Not from the blows, though. He hardly felt them. As he was on his way out of the office, holding his trousers up with his left hand, his boss stopped him.

"That's what my dad did to me," said Gillmore condescendingly. "It's a lesson I always remembered. Never forgot it. You won't either. Now listen to me. This is my last word on the matter. You *and* your wife will do what duties you are told to do when you are told, and you will not come whining to me again. I come from the school where you work for your money. If you're working, you don't have time to complain. So see to it that that little layabout wife of yours understands this. While you are here on my property, you do what I tell you to do or you leave the premises pronto."

Howell turned wordlessly to go, but Gillmore stopped him again. "I may even fuck your wife, if it pleases me."

Howell opened the door angrily and Gillmore continued, "And if you were a gentleman, you would thank me, because *my* prick has never been up some poofter's arse."

And Gillmore did fuck Beth. Not immediately, because Howell and his wife were close. She became more and more resentful because she felt that he wouldn't stand up for himself and fight for the original agreement. And his growing bitterness accelerated their drift apart. He wanted to tell her the reason, but by then the atmosphere was already too cloudy. He did feel guilty about his past. He was ashamed. But he couldn't bring himself to confess, and the longer it went on, the more impossible it was. She felt that he was weak, and her respect drained away.

After six months Beth told her husband that Gillmore had asked her to do his filing, answer his telephone, make calls for him and operate his tape recorders. Beth wasn't his secretary because she could not type or take dictation, but she began calling herself his 'personal assistant'. She talked about Gillmore, one eye on Howell, searching for something, but he never said a thing. Her clothes changed and she began wearing tights and heels and smart dresses.

One night she didn't come back to the cottage, returning the next evening to find her husband angry and miserable. He finally shouted at her and tried to tell her something of his past, but it came out all wrong because emotion had twisted everything so badly. He even told her that he still loved her. She just stared at him, not saying a word, then got up and moved all her clothes into the tiny bedroom upstairs. They continued to have meals together – when she was there. He never brought up the subject again, and some nights she spent at the big house, while Howell gradually sank more into himself.

Once, near the very end, he was called to collect a delivery from Gillmore's office. When he entered, his employer was at his desk and Beth was behind him browsing in a filing cabinet. By now her hair had grown longer and was pulled back in a pony tail, showing earrings he had never seen before. She was wearing a new pink dress cut just above the knee with matching pink high-heeled shoes. In short, Howell thought she looked gorgeous, prettier than he had ever seen her. Gillmore ignored him as he came in but, as he approached the desk for the parcel, his boss casually swivelled around in his chair and ran his hand up Beth's thigh underneath her dress. She turned and looked directly at Howell, held his eyes, just stared at him. Howell knew immediately what she wanted. She was daring him to say something. But he remained standing, his cap under his arm, so his wife slid into Gillmore's lap and kissed him. Gillmore, still kissing, swivelled the chair round and threw the parcel to him. He caught it, turned and left. He could hear laughter as he closed the door. A week later Beth left, giving no explanation, and he later discovered that Gillmore had got her a job with one of his newspapers, setting her up in a flat near his office for convenience.

It was getting dark when they pulled up to Le Bonheur. Glancing from the side of his eye, Howell looked at his boss. Hatred throbbed like a drum. Some day, somehow he was going to kill that man. The right time and the right place would eventually come to hand and justice was going to be done. Howell was not a violent man, but there was one act of violence he dreamed about every night. The Rolls whispered to a stop, and Howell was immediately out of his door and around to open the door for his boss. While he waited, his hand on the handle, his boss took his time collecting his papers and putting them carefully into the briefcase which he had placed on the seat beside him after locking it.

As he was getting out, he glanced at Greenaway. "Give Howell his cap before you go."

Greenaway got out of the driver's seat and came round the car with a jaunty gait, dipping his shoulders, a phoney smile on his face.

"Well? Have I got the job?"

Gillmore looked at his editor with a sour expression. "You might, Greenaway. You just might."

He left the two men and entered the restaurant, adjusting the small microphone underneath his lapel.

Harvey Gillmore spent most of the meal sipping his Diet Pepsi and watching Sheikh Abdullah eat. The Saudi had insisted on eating before they talked. Abdullah was a fat man with heavy black hair which crept halfway down his forehead. It was combed straight back and oiled. The Saudi wore a Western business suit and spoke excellent English. He couldn't have been more than thirty-five, the son of one of the minor royal houses, and spent much of his time in London. He had a round face with wide-spaced eyes, a heavy well-trimmed moustache and a weak chin. Underneath his chin was another, larger, chin. His mouth, however, was quite small, made smaller still by the size of his moustache, and his lips had a tendency to pout. His hands, though, belied his bulk and were small and finely made, very expressive. Abdullah was just finishing a good-sized sea bass, cleaning the bones expertly of every trace of flesh. Two bottles of a white premier cru had helped wash the fish to its destination. Gillmore had long ago finished picking at his salad. Abruptly the Arab pushed away his plate and called for the waiter.

"And now a brandy. Yes?" He raised his eyebrows, looking at Gillmore.

"Not for me," he said; then added, "I thought your religion forbade strong drink."

Abdullah laughed heartily and gave his order to the waiter.

"Yes, drink. Surely Napoleon brandy is not *that* strong."

Again he laughed.

Gillmore looked serious. "I don't want to offend, Sheikh Abdullah, but have you ever read any of the writings of Jesus Christ?"

"I do not know your religion very well, but I thought that your Jesus was a speaker, not a writer."

"I meant 'of' like 'about'," said Gillmore morosely.

"Ah," smiled the Arab pleasantly, "perhaps I don't know the intricacies of your language. You must forgive me."

"Well, I was just going to say that I don't think our own religion would allow such liberal interpretations."

Abdullah laughed good-naturedly. "Oh, no? What about '*Do unto others as you would have them do unto you*'? Surely not a company motto of WORLDWIDE?"

Gillmore took a sip of Diet Pepsi as the waiter delivered a large brandy to his companion.

"I do unto others as I expect they would do unto me. And every company employee has a Bible in the top left drawer of his desk."

"So strict with yourself and your employees. Very impressive."

Gillmore settled back in his chair. "A tight ship. I run a tight ship."

His guest leaned across the table and smiled. "And so you have a tight companion. Yes?"

"Anyway," said the Australian, looking at his watch, "we had better get down to brass tacks here. I built a fire under Regis and I think the delivery dates can be brought forward. The quicker the better, I reckon."

Sheikh Abdullah was holding the brandy under his nose. He took a drink and carefully placed the glass back on the table.

"The delivery dates. Hmmm. Not a major worry. No. The reason I requested this meeting is merely to clarify a rumour which the winds brought to me. The rumour is that there is a tape recording of certain transactions, and that this tape is missing. I wonder if you know anything of this rumour."

Harvey Gillmore was prodding a slice of lemon with a toothpick. He said nothing, just followed the lemon round the edge of the side dish, then back again.

Abdullah watched his companion for a moment.

"Hmmm. You see, Mr Gillmore, this is a very delicate matter, as we discussed at length in the beginning. The Saudi Government must not be compromised in any way. In certain circumstances they are quite prepared to turn a blind eye, but, if mistakes are made and embarrassment ensues, then they will open that blind eye and turn to those who are causing these mistakes and this embarrassment. As you know, I am not an official of my government. I am doing this more as a favour to you for concessions we may have need of in the future. As any business deal is formed. We help each other. Yes?"

He paused for another swallow of brandy. "I understand that you tape your telephone conversations. This is very unwise."

Harvey Gillmore was annoyed. "I've done it all my life and it's paid handsomely in the past. Handsomely."

The sheikh swirled the remainder of his brandy in his palm. "Are you taping our conversation now?"

"Of course not," lied Gillmore.

"If you are, that is also unwise. If the wind should return any of this conversation to me, it could complicate life. We could find ourselves doing business in another trade."

"I only tape on the telephone. And the telephone is secure. I have never in my life lost a tape."

"Except this one?"

Gillmore was unaccustomed to this kind of pressure. He became truculent, looking at the sheikh from under his eyebrows. "It's nothing for you to worry about. It's *my* problem—"

"Someone else thinks it's his problem as well. The man you spoke to."

"Well, it's not. It's my tape and my telephone."

Abdullah smiled. "But it's *his* voice."

Gillmore smacked his hand on the table and hissed, "Even if the tape's . . . misplaced, no one could prove anything. No names were used. Who's to know what the devil we were talking about?"

"All the wrong ones would know. We Saudis. The British. The Americans. The Israelis." He paused for a moment. "And others."

"You know and I know that they already know." Gillmore was exasperated.

"Oh, they know individually, yes. But they do not know *politically*. That is important. It is knowledge and it is not knowledge. Something exists and does not exist in the same place at the same time. Contrary to Aristotle."

"Bugger Aristotle."

"Buggered is what our agreements are going to be if the tape cannot be recovered. And, as you know," he added ominously, "the identity of the speaker on the tape must not be known at all. To anyone but us."

"He didn't say his name."

Abdullah made a gesture with his open palm. "And while you search for it, I would be very grateful if you could hand over to me my own two conversations on your 'secure' telephone. The originals, no copies."

Gillmore nearly raised his voice. "Aw, come on, Sheikh! They are filed in a safe!"

"And I would be so much happier if they were filed in *my* safe, you see. When they are delivered, I will have sound engineers test the tapes to see if they have been copied. In transit, of course."

"Now listen—"

"You see," interrupted Sheikh Abdullah, "I am well aware of why you need this operation to go forward to completion. Your company has much money but no cash. Because of this little . . . misadventure, we would now like to hold half of your negotiable shares in WORLDWIDE until it is finalised."

"Impossible!" spluttered Gillmore, pushing his chair away from the table.

Sheikh Abdullah spread his hands, expressively accompanied by a shrug.

"That is my father's company! You don't know what it means to me! It's not mine to give!"

He pulled himself back from his explosion and regained some of his inner calm. "This is not business. It is blackmail."

"An ugly word, but one I am sure is not unfamiliar to you in your own trading."

Gillmore got up from the table and leaned across to his guest. "I will pretend that I didn't hear that. I will pretend that this conversation did not take place at all. For your information, in case you didn't know, I can make a lot of trouble for you and your country, much worse than the tape will ever make for anyone, me included. If you know me and my business so well, Sheikh, you will know I mean that."

The Arab smiled pleasantly. "I also know that threats are dangerous things, only effective if they are left unspoken."

"Well, I come from a place where they speak their minds, and I'm speaking mine now."

He was now leaning further over the table, his face close to Abdullah. "So let me make myself really clear. Neither you nor any of your towelhead friends or any other living person on this earth is going to touch my shares – not now, not ever."

"It's of course up to you," said Abdullah equitably, draining the last of the brandy from his glass. He pushed his own chair away from the table.

"And now, my good friend, I shall go to Kensington to pursue my other appetite. I am afraid I have already kept her waiting too long."

He placed his napkin on the table and got up.

"It is a great pleasure doing business with you, Mr Gillmore."

Harvey Gillmore followed the slow-moving bulk of Sheikh Abdullah to the front of the restaurant in a mood blacker than the water at the bottom of the sea.

Chapter Six

Jennifer Montgomery lay on the bed thinking. Or was she trying not to think? Well, she was trying not to think of what had happened, but she had to be ready for what happened next. She could hear the men talking and muttering somewhere outside the door. The other two men had become very angry when they hadn't been able to rape her as well. First Voice had quarrelled with them, some of it in what she guessed was Afrikaans. Someone was about to arrive and would be angry. They could do her later. Plenty of time. First Voice had come back in with a wet cloth to clean her roughly. He was full of invective because he had not managed to consummate the act inside her. It was a small victory, but a victory for her nevertheless. She held on to it.

She wouldn't survive by wasting time feeling sorry for herself. She gathered from what the men said that they were waiting for someone. Their boss? Well, another *man* anyway. Keep thinking, keep alert, watch for an opening. The chances must be slim, but, if there was any opportunity at all, she must play for it.

Reflexively she stiffened with fear as she heard noises in the front of the house. The front door was being opened. There were voices which moved away to another room. It will be soon, she thought. Soon. Relax. Be ready to jump in any direction.

Someone came into the room, and a hand tugged her by the belt to the end of the bed. Then she was helped to her feet. A man leaned close to her ear.

"You'd better be nice to this man. He can be very nasty."

It was First Voice and he laughed quietly, tugging her by the belt this time as he led her out of the room and down what she imagined was a hallway. They entered another room and immediately she smelled tobacco smoke.

"Ah," said a voice she had not heard before. "What a pretty little whore." It was a high-pitched but loud voice. Again, the accent. "Leave us alone. And close the door."

Jennifer heard the door close and for some reason began to tremble. She did not know what horror awaited her with this new man. Not being able to see made things so much worse, she was thinking, and at the same moment the man took off her blindfold.

He was a tall, heavily-built man of about fifty, maybe a little more. His hair had once been black but now was nearly grey, receding from the crown but swirled around in such a way as to try and disguise it. He had a round face with a moustache under his nose which had kept its colour. Beside the nose were two very light blue eyes, closely-set, which peered from the slits of the lids. He wore a business suit that looked expensive. Between two sausage fingers of his right hand was a black cheroot. This he put between very full lips to puff twice, inhaling sharply on the second puff.

"Well," he said, starting to walk around her, "not too bad at all."

He patted her bottom then moved back to her front, putting the cheroot in his mouth, and speculatively weighed one of her breasts with his right hand. The hand then moved down to her belly, which he rubbed gently before dropping to the pubic area. This, like her bottom, he patted.

He retrieved his cigar from his mouth.

"I am going to take that tape from your mouth in a moment. When I do, all I want is the truth. No evasion, no humming and hawing, no hesitation, no maybes. I do not want screams, any protesting. I want you to pay attention to me at all times. Do you understand? Because if you do not do these things, if you do not follow my exact orders, then I will introduce you to the sjambok. Do you know what is a sjambok?"

He did not wait for her to nod but went to the corner of the room where a tall, tapered, whippy instrument was propped. He picked it up, holding it by the handle.

"A sjambok. Made of rhinoceros hide. It is for men who misbehave, but it can also be for women. One stroke will burst the skin anywhere it strikes. The pain, I am told, is unbearable."

He swished the air viciously near Jennifer's body, then returned the sjambok to its corner. "You will get three strokes with the sjambok for each lie, for each time you hum-haw or refuse to answer my questions or do immediately what you are told."

He reached over and tore the tape from her mouth.

"Can you please also remove these handcuffs? I have cramps in my arms." Her voice was as steady as she could hold it.

The man studied her for a moment. "And let you run away?"

"I can hardly run anywhere, barefoot, naked."

The man sat down in an armchair. "Anyway, what do I care whether you have cramps or not? Besides, I ask the questions, you answer. Is that understood?"

"Yes."

She had tried to take the initiative, and her arms were uncomfortable. It was a great help to see. She was in a conventional sitting room. Heavy curtains were drawn across the windows and there were two standard lamps on, one by the sofa in front of the window and one beside the armchair. A TV sat on a table near the man and his ashtray was held by another small table under the lamp. It was a moderately large room with a high ceiling.

The man was puffing on his cigar, looking at her speculatively.

Finally he said, "I am Coetzee, which is all you will know about me. It is a common name, like Smith."

He took another draw from his cigar and flicked off the ash on the carpet. "Now I am going to ask you a question. One time. I want the answer and I want the truth. Understood?"

"Yes," she said, trying to free her mind to consider quickly, jump in the right direction.

"You have the tape?"

Tape? What tape?

"Yes," she said with only a short pause.

Coetzee smiled slightly. "Good. That was the truth. We know you have the tape. And you are keeping it. For blackmail?"

"Possibly." She answered quickly, then added, "Whatever brings the best offer."

He laughed, a dirty man's laugh. "You are quite a businesswoman, yes?"

"Are you making an offer?"

This time Coetzee laughed heartily. "I am in the position to *take* what I want – without payment."

He reached over, his paunch cramping him a little, and stroked her thigh. "Is that not true?"

Jennifer forced herself not to recoil from his clammy touch. She saw a fork in the road and chose one path. She smiled slightly, she hoped confidently. "Then perhaps we could form a partnership."

Coetzee fell back into his chair and roared again with laughter. "Ah! You impress me. You *are* a good businesswoman. Cut your

losses, bring in a partner. Share the profits, but that's better than
none at all, eh?"

"I'm not negotiating from a very strong position," she replied.
"But I'm willing to share what I know. Perhaps with your experience
we could double our profits. There would certainly be enough for
two. I know some important people. We could put what I know
together with what you know and use the tape as a foothold. And
when I am free—"

"Oh, but you're not going to be free, my little businesswoman,"
he interrupted. "After you tell me where the tape is, I was going to
kill you, you see. Now I am not so sure. You are very pretty. For
an English person, very. I may just keep you as my personal . . . pet.
How would you like that? Huh? No quick answer? No . . .
negotiating for fees? Yes, I have a house here. In the country. Very
nice. I could keep you on a long chain maybe. Then you could have
your hands free. *You* would not be free, but then you would be alive.
But we waste too much time, pretty one. The tape. *Where* is the
tape?"

"In my house."

She had not been listening to him but thinking. About Haug.
What would he have done after finding out what had happened?
Watch her house? Was he there? It was a chance she had to take, her
only chance. A slim one, she thought depressedly, as he didn't seem
the most competent man she had ever met. But perhaps they would
take her there, and maybe . . .

"Hmmm, yes, your house, of course. We *know* it is in your
house. But where, my dear? Exact instructions, please."

He wasn't going to take her, she thought. Fuck. But she was too
far in now. Where? Where could she have hidden this non-existent
tape?

His voice was menacing. "You have two more seconds to answer,
my dear. I would hate to use the sjambok on that beautiful flesh, but I
will. So?"

"It's taped behind the mirror which is a sliding door in the
bathroom cabinet. The upstairs bathroom." She exhaled the rest of
her breath sharply.

An actual smile spilled across Coetzee's face. He brightened.
"Good. Good. A good place. We would have found it anyway, but
it would have taken many hours, much time. And time is important to

me." He paused, lowering his head. "And I hope for your sake that you are not lying."

He got to his feet, looming over the woman in front of him, and placed his finger on her pubis.

"If you are, I will cut you from here," he drew his finger slowly up her belly to her throat, "to here, and I will leave you to die slowly with no throat to scream with."

He paused for a moment, staring at her with his near blue eyes emotionless.

Abruptly he turned towards the door. "Fanie!"

A moment later a man in jeans and tee-shirt entered. He was about thirty, tall and blond, with close-cropped hair. He too had a moustache, but it was so light that it could hardly be seen.

"Mr Coetzee?" he asked.

It was First Voice. Jennifer stared at him, memorising his features. If not soon, she was going to kill him one day.

Coetzee gave Fanie the instructions for finding the tape, then added, "If it is not where she says it is, telephone me immediately. And," he said, turning to Jennifer, "I will take a few moments to find out where it really is. She has yet to hear the song of the sjambok."

Fanie leered at her. "You will love this song. One verse and you tell everything."

"You have her keys?" asked Coetzee.

"Yes, boss." He put his hands in his pocket and brought out a ring of keys. "Must be on here. Got it from her handbag."

"Good," said Coetzee. "Don't take too long. We must hurry."

Fanie left, closing the door after him, and Coetzee sat back down in the armchair and tested his cigar, which had gone out. He put the butt into the ashtray and leaned back, looking at Jennifer.

"Come here," he said.

She moved a step in his direction, trying to control the raging fear which threatened to leave her in tears or terror.

"Closer."

Again she took a step. This brought her to the edge of the man's toes and, as her feet touched his toes, he moved his legs apart.

"Now you kneel."

She tried to keep her balance as she put first one knee down and then the other. Coetzee loosened the belt on his trousers, opened the button and unzipped himself, pulling down his trousers and underpants enough to expose an uncircumcised penis lying flaccidly atop two hairy testicles. His belly cast a shadow from the lamp over his genitalia. Jennifer Montgomery knew what was going to happen and began concentrating on the overpowering sense of nausea churning her insides. In a way, she would welcome death, even a slow one, in preference to much more of this. It was a nightmare – worse than a nightmare – and her depression was devouring her confidence. Then, suddenly, despite all her resolve, she began to cry.

Coetzee laughed softly.

"Ah, I like that. The tough businesswoman finally crumbles, eh? The hard-hearted whore begins to feel the pressure. I like it. I like my women soft and pliable. My wife is like that, you know. She does what she is bloody told. All this new nonsense, this feminism, is rubbish."

He moved his hand and softly wiped away her tears. Then he cupped her chin in the hand and held it while he moved his face close to hers.

She felt the smell of his face, the smell of tobacco and cheap shaving scent, and closed her eyes so that she wouldn't have to look at the man. She felt his lips on hers and instinctively pulled her head away. Immediately her ears rang and her cheek burned. He had slapped her. Hard. But she kept her eyes closed anyway, choking back her tears.

"Now you will kiss," he said, grabbing her by the throat roughly. "And you will mean it. Open your mouth. If I think you don't mean it, I will beat you now."

Jennifer let him kiss her and did her best not to gag as his tongue pushed into her mouth like a slug. Pretend, she screamed to herself. Pretend! Survive! Tomorrow will come! Despite her entreaties to her own sanity, despite holding on by her fingernails to the cliff edge, she felt herself slipping, falling.

Coetzee pulled away and leaned back on the chair.

"Not too bad, my dear, not too bad. I have kissed better, you understand? But now you have a chance to improve, don't you? So."

He picked up his penis with his hand. "I introduce you to my little man. Coetzee junior. What? What?"

He pretended to bend down to listen. "He says, 'Give me a nice suck, you fucking little whore.'"

The room, the time, what was happening to her, had become surreal. A nightmarish Dali painting. When she opened her eyes, the lamp was bending itself over and the shade had acquired laughing, mocking, leering features which she realised were her father's. Coetzee's face, illuminated by the spill of the undulating lamp, had changed into the snout of a great white shark with its teeth sunk into the remains of a swelled and rotting belly which had ruptured, the entrails of which hung below, putrescent. The little eyes in the shark's great head looked at her as coldly as death. Looking downwards from the horrible eyes, she passed over the hissing stomach and smelled the stench of the gas escaping from it and returned her gaze once more to the remains of bowels hanging close to her face. She was morbidly fascinated by the entrails, which had begun to move and writhe. She stared at them as they filled with pus and realised that the great white shark was shouting something. Jennifer Montgomery knew that she was sliding down somewhere, probably into Hell, as she leaned forward, opening her mouth to greet the slimy, bloated, rotting red finger now pointing directly at her.

Haug and Keef lay in the back of the van in front of Jennifer Montgomery's house on Willoughby Road. Keef was dozing, his head turned away. Haug was doing what he had been doing ever since he had lost Jennifer early that afternoon, obsessively going over every event, ticking it off, then on to the next one. When he came to the end, he immediately began all over again. It was like walking round and round a millstone. Nothing changed, except that the track he made around the millstone sank deeper into the earth. He knew that he was wasting his time, but it was like a catchy, obsessive tune. His mistake was lack of attention. He had allowed this because both of them had convinced themselves that nothing was going to happen. It was understandable for her, but Haug was supposed to know his job. Surveillance inevitably obeyed the laws of Sod: if anything happened, it *always* happened when you least expected it.

Like now, he thought. He had hardly taken his eye away from the observation port in the van since they parked. Haug had picked up the van and Keef, explaining to his friend through his teeth just what had happened. Keef was shocked but sympathetic, urging him to stop whipping himself and get on with it. Haug knew the danger of defining yourself by your mistakes. It would simply create more mistakes. Learn the lesson, however painful, and carry on as positively as you could. The other thoughts, the ones about what was happening to Jennifer, he shoved out into the twilight landscape of consciousness where he stored all his demons from Vietnam. He had closed off this landscape with double airlocks and miles of chain around the doors. He could not allow himself one little fragment of thought on that subject. If he did, fantasy would overpower him and he would just sit down and cry. One of the thoughts driven out to the twilight zone was his near certainty that she was already dead. After all, they had tried to kill her the first time. She may have already been dead when they put her in the postal van.

He swore out loud, and Keef stirred briefly as he shoved those thoughts violently back where they came from. No! He was going to make another mistake if he allowed that bilge to spill out. He returned to the job he was doing. Keef had agreed that their only chance was to watch the house. Someone might come or they might bring her back. Or she could return on her own. It was futile combing North London for a red van. There were nearly as many red as yellow ones. Instead they had decided to take watches in four hour shifts so that they would be less likely to doze.

Fat chance of that, thought Haug. He was already past the four hours of his shift, but he had hardly moved position since he put his eye to the port. He checked everyone, male and female. It was now after seven o'clock, so it was still quite active. End of the day, Friday in London. Cars pulling in, parking in drives or garages or as close to the house as possible. Horns blowing fruitlessly at empty cars blocking drives. Other tenants arrived by foot from the Underground, though Haug decided that anyone who could afford property this near the Heath would seldom use the Underground. How, he wondered idly, did Jennifer afford hers? A whole house, not split into flats or maisonettes. Semi-detached, as they said in this country. A garage built in, three floors. Must be cracking on for half a million, maybe more. Didn't sound as though her father would buy it for her, not if she had stolen money from him. And she didn't seem that busy as an actress. Maybe it all had something to do with this mess. Then again, maybe not. He shrugged his shoulders. How folks got their money was no concern of his. His guess was a rich boyfriend and, with looks like hers, she should be able to snare one of those.

He pulled his attention back to what he was doing. Since three o'clock there had been only one alarm. A new and expensive-looking Jaguar had pulled up, double-parking in front of the house. That was just after five and Keef was still awake. He had nudged the Jamaican with excitement. Keef eased over the front seat quietly, his hand on the door handle, ready to move. It was a short, squat man who glanced at the upstairs windows before moving to the door to ring the bell. He rang three times before looking at his wristwatch and returning to his car.

Haug shook his head at Keef and said, "Nope. A gentleman caller."

Keef had replied, "Could be her father."

Haug had told him what he knew of Jennifer's past.

Haug made a decision. "Nope. Cain't risk it. That guy doesn't know where she is, either. We gotta wait for somebody who does."

"Yeah, you right," Keef agreed, crawling back beside Haug.

Since then, nothing. The usual neighbours doing the usual things. He thought that he would go ahead and take two watches, let Keef get a little sleep. Haug had got him out of bed when he had rung him on the mobile phone. He was afraid to ask himself one question. How long? How many days would he be prepared to lie in this yellow van watching an empty house? If anything happened, he guessed that it would happen this weekend or not at all. But he was prepared to give it a week. Another week. After that, he would have to reassess the whole thing. Yeah, he thought, after the weekend I'll start talking to the gentlemen callers.

Haug was sure that he sensed it before he saw it. The sporty black Escort, headlights on, stopped in front of Jennifer's house. He slapped Keef awake and, without a word, the black man slid into the front seat like a python. The Escort was pulling slowly into the driveway.

Haug's voice sounded different when he spoke to Keef. "That's the car. Give it three beats after he's inside, then let's hit it."

They watched the blond man get out of the car.

"He's one of 'em," muttered Haug. "Not the one drivin' that thang on the day. But he was there this afternoon."

The tension rose in the van as the blond man looked around and then up at the windows. He dug in his jeans for keys and stepped up to the door. Haug made sure that he had his own key in his hand. It took the blond man a while to find the right one. Then he looked around once more and ducked inside.

On the third beat two doors of the van opened together, Keef in the front, Haug at the rear. Both men moved quietly and swiftly across the street. Two doors away a man was putting out his bins. He stared at the two men as they climbed three steps, opened the door and entered the house.

Haug carefully closed the door, listening. Keef was moving slowly along the wall, almost invisible in the dark. A floorboard upstairs creaked and together their heads turned upwards. Haug went up first, keeping to the side on the stairs, willing them not to creak. They could hear the blond fellow moving about, not making any effort to be quiet. Just as Haug's head drew level with the first floor, the man left the bathroom. He had a torch and Haug ducked below the floorlevel as it swept the wall opposite. The blond man opened Jennifer's bedroom door and went inside. Haug moved slowly up, feeling Keef behind him, and eased himself around to the bedroom door. Bracing himself in front of it, he kicked.

The torch was shining on a telephone. The receiver was off. That was all Haug saw before the torch blinded him. The next instant the room was flooded with light. Keef had found the switch. All three men stood frozen in their places. Haug was in the middle of the room. The blond man was beside the bed, the telephone receiver in one hand, the torch in the other. Keef stood near the wall.

"Drop the telephone," said Haug, his voice low.

Instead Fanie threw it at Haug, who ducked but didn't move.

"Well," said Fanie, "the motorcycle man and a kaffir."

"I heard what he called you, Keef," Haug said, without turning his head away from the blond man. "But you still gonna have to have seconds."

Fanie chucked aside the torch, and his hand went underneath his leather jacket. As his hand moved, so did Haug, covering the six or seven feet between them like a stag. One of Haug's large hands went around Fanie's neck while the other grabbed his right hand, just emerging with a small automatic pistol. His lunge took Fanie off his feet and the blond man's head hit the wall. Haug then grabbed the man's right arm with both hands and snapped the wrist with an audible crack. The gun clattered to the floor and Keef moved quickly to pick it up as Haug stifled Fanie's scream with a pillow he had grabbed from the bed as he straddled Fanie's writhing body on the floor. Haug worked his other hand under the pillow to the man's throat, then threw the pillow aside. Fanie had stopped screaming and his face was turning an odd-looking purple. Haug loosened his grip on the throat a little and Fanie's eyes snapped open, swimming in pain and terror.

"I don't think you know who you fuckin' with, bo," Haug said. "Last man who pulled a gun on me, I broke his back."

"You ain't leaving me any seconds," Keef complained.

"Oh, there's plenty more where this one came from," Haug replied. "Right, asshole?"

He eased off his grip on the throat a little more. "Right?"

"You fucking broke my wrist!" Fanie gasped in a whisper.

Haug leaned close to the man's face.

"I've only just started, bo," he said sincerely. "I'm gonna break ever bone in your body. Not just your wrist. Unless you start sayin' thangs I wanna hear. Thangs like Jennifer is alive. Thangs like where she is, and who else is there. And I ain't got any time to waste, bo. In about two minutes, you ain't gonna be fit to be used for anythang but a doorstop. Now start talkin'."

Haug waited, staring into the man's rolling eyes. Without moving, he said, "Keef, start breakin' the fingers on his good hand."

Keef came over, kicking the bed aside to make room. "You get all the fun things, and I just get to break the fingers."

Fanie looked sick.

"She's alive," he croaked finally.

Relief flooded through Haug so completely that he relaxed his grip and Fanie put all his strength into bucking the big man off. Haug immediately slammed his head back on to the floor. Keef sat on the edge of the bed, leaned over and grabbed Fanie's good hand.

Keef smiled at the man on the floor. "You thought he was joking, didn't you, white trash? Well, I want to tell you I'm looking forward to this."

Fanie was now panicking. "I told you! I told you! She's OK!"

"Where have they got her?" Haug asked

"I can't tell you that! They are my people!"

Haug used the pillow again to muffle the blood-curdling scream that came from Fanie when Keef snapped his little finger and ring finger together. After a few moments the screams became whimpers and Haug lifted the pillow. Fanie's face was contorted in agony.

"Where have they got her?" Haug asked again.

"I'll tell. OK. It's near Green Lanes. Corley Road—"

"I better tell you right now, bo," Haug said. "You goin' with us, so you better give us the *right* address. Or my friend and I are gonna sit in the back of my van to finish breakin' you up. Wrong address, you get the rest of those fingers broke, next address is wrong, the elbows. And so on. Am I communicatin' myself to you?"

"Number 47 Corley Road," Fanie muttered painfully. "It's the right one."

Keef went out and turned on the light for the stairs, then came back to help Haug with Fanie, who squealed as they pulled him upright. Haug and Keef worked as a team, wordlessly. They walked out of the room either side of Fanie, each with a hand on his belt. When they reached the stairs, Keef went down first, all the way to the bottom and waited as Haug came down behind their prisoner, who was trying to cradle both damaged arms against further movement. At the bottom Haug switched out the lights.

Before he opened the front door, Haug turned to Fanie.

"I don't think you're stupid enough to scream out there, though you're pretty stupid. But I want to warn you not to try and run. I cain't run worth a shit, but Keef here runs like a greyhound. Until he catches up. Then he's a Rottweiler."

"How the fuck can I run? I can't even walk," muttered Fanie as they opened the door and went outside.

Haug and Keef walked on either side of the injured man, who was holding his head back and grinding his teeth. When they got to the van, Haug opened the rear door. They lifted the man off the ground by his belt and threw him inside.

"You drive," Haug said over Fanie's screams as he handed Keef the keys. "You know where this place is?"

"I know Green Lanes," Keef replied as he went towards the front of the van. "I think I know where Corley Road is."

"Well, let's get there pronto. No tellin' what's happenin' to that gal."

"If", said Keef, "that prick is telling the truth."

Haug got into the back of the van. "He better be."

Keef did a quick three-point turn, then stomped on the throttle. In the back Haug unfastened a motorcycle shackle lock from the side, dug out a key and opened it. He put the shackle around Fanie's neck and snapped the lock to a metal brace. It forced his prisoner into a prone position on the floor.

"What did you do that for?" asked Fanie through his teeth. "I can't use my hands – I can't go anywhere."

"That's right, you cain't," replied Haug genially. "I thought about breakin' your leg, but I think I'll wait to see if you've told me a lie. Or tell me one now."

Haug leaned against the side and braced one of his feet against the other side. "How come you grabbed Jennifer Montgomery?"

"She's got a tape belongs to us," mumbled Fanie.

"A tape?" Haug was puzzled. "What kind of tape?"

"I don't know," Fanie moaned. Then, seeing Haug raise his eyebrows, he added hastily. "No, I don't. Honest. I got no idea. Just know it belongs to us."

"Us? Who's *us*?"

"I'm from South Africa."

"I figgered that already from the shitty accent. But I wanna know who *us* is."

Fanie tried in vain to make himself comfortable. "We were all in State Security."

"BOSS?"

"Yeah. BOSS. A kind of network of ex-employees. Got residents living here, got 'em in France, big one in Holland, several big European cities, couple in America – all over. I belong to this one. I live here. Married Englishwoman. I don't know anything else."

Haug grunted. "How many of these assholes gonna be in this house we're goin' to?"

Fanie was silent for a minute. Then he shrugged his shoulders. "Three. And the girl."

"I hope that's the truth you're tellin' me. I hope there's only three."

Haug stretched his other leg and reached inside his jacket, pulling out a small pouch. He opened it and bit off a piece from the plug of chewing tobacco which he pushed with his tongue to the side of his mouth.

"Did you fuck with her?"

"Huh?"

"You know what I'm talkin' about, South Africa. What did you do to her?"

Fanie looked even more miserable. "Nothing. Nothing much. Had a little play around."

"A little play around," Haug repeated. His voice was dangerously low.

"Aw, come on," whined Fanie. "She's only a whore, for fuck sake."

Without warning, Haug leaned over and grabbed the man's balls, hard. The South African screamed and writhed in agony, waving his damaged hands fruitlessly.

"I don't think I understood you right, bo. I coulda sworn you just said she was a whore."

"I can't talk, I can't talk!" Fanie's voice was a high-pitched squeak.

Haug loosened his grip a little. "I'm listenin'."

"Christ, I thought you knew it!" cried Fanie frantically. "That's what she does for a fucking living! Everybody seems to know that! A top drawer one. One for the rich folks and movie stars. But it's all the same, isn't it? Paying money for sex. It's prostitution."

Haug let go and leaned back against the van with a sigh. "So what did you do, asshole?"

Fanie was getting his breath back. He was now desperately holding his legs together. "I fucked her."

Haug's voice was distant. "Anybody else?"

"No. Piet and Chaim, they didn't have time."

Haug looked thoughtful. "Chaim. That a Boer name?"

"He's from Israel," said Fanie.

"Israel?" asked Haug incredulously.

"I don't know anything about it, man. I just know he's with us. A friend. Works with us. I don't know—"

"OK. Piet and Chaim. Who's the third man?"

"Coetzee. He's the boss, team leader. Four of us in a team. She'll be with him. She'll be with Coetzee."

"Where?"

"Front room, first floor, first door you come to. Or that's where they were when I left. Maybe in the fucking basement now for all I know."

Haug pulled the tobacco round with his tongue and chewed it ruminatively. Finally he said, "And you were lookin' for the tape when I found you, right? Did you find it?"

"No."

"And the telephone?"

"I was to call if it wasn't where it was supposed to be."

"Did you get through?"

"No." Fanie fought back another wave of pain.

"I hope you tellin' the truth, bo. For your sake."

Fanie groaned. "If I am, are you going to take me to the hospital?"

"Hospital my ass," Haug said. "You lucky to be alive, bo."

He felt the van slow down to a crawl and turn to the right.

"This is Corley Road, Haug," said Keef from the front.

Chapter Seven

As an area Green Lanes was one of the biggest melting pots in London. There were Greeks and Turks, Asians and Irish, many of them refugees from areas like Primrose Hill, Camden Town and Kentish Town as they inevitably became gentrified over the years. Shooed from spots closer to Central London, they settled in Haringey, around the artery of Green Lanes, itself a vibrant, throbbing street open every day of the week and late into the night of every day. As they settled once more in houses the middle class didn't yet want, they bought their dwellings with family savings, loans from relatives or as syndicates. Some borrowed money and immediately bought another house, filling it with tenants to pay the mortgage and provide a little income. Shops were found, businesses opened – newsagents, doner kebabs, cafés, off-licences, launderettes, fruit and veg stalls – keeping overheads low by only employing family. Green Lanes didn't smell like England and the people you met were seldom English.

They had parked well past number 47 and only the street lamps dimly lit the road. It had been difficult to find a parking space, because these days everyone had a car and tried to park it in front of the house. Hopeless if you got back too late.

Haug and Keef discussed briefly what they were going to do. Keef put on Haug's Harley dozer cap, turning it sideways, breakdancer style, and picked up a clipboard from under the dash. Both men got out of the van and Keef went on ahead a few paces, adopting a jaunty walk.

There was a low garden wall which ran unbroken along the terrace. As they approached number 47, Haug ducked down behind this wall as Keef walked through the gate, carefully leaving it open, and immediately rang the bell. No lights were showing in any of the windows and Haug was worried. He peeped around the corner, watching Keef as he rang the bell again, this time longer. Finally a light came on in the hall and Haug breathed a sigh of relief. Let it be them, he prayed silently to himself, let it be the right address. The door opened a crack.

It was on a security chain, and he could hear a muttered question. Keef immediately went into a patter, saying that he was doing a survey and could he ask the man how many people in the house listened to rap, man? A stream of profanity could be heard, some of it in a language that Haug didn't understand. Was it Hebrew? He could just see the outline of a man's head from the yellow light cast by the street lamp. Swarthy? He couldn't tell. Fuck it, he thought.

Keef stood back a moment before Haug arrived at the door, low and running. The man inside had just started to close the door when the American slammed his massive shoulder into it. The momentum snapped the chain and the door sprang back, sweeping the man behind it into the wall. Keef moved quickly through the door and closed it with a bang. Chaim was stunned but swung at Keef as though he knew what he was doing. The blow glanced off Keef's head, which was on its way into Chaim's nose.

Haug opened the door to the front room and was nearly overpowered by the smell of vomit. Turned towards him was a big man with his trousers off who looked like a pig. He held a long whiplike thing in his hand. Jennifer was on the floor, her face turned towards the door, her eyes transmitting terror.

Anger and hatred surged through Haug like molten lava.

"If you've hit her with that thang, I'm gonna kill you."

Coetzee raised the sjambok. "Come! Taste it yourself, fucker! Piet!" he screamed. "Piet!"

Suddenly Haug was a linebacker once more. Head low, eyes up, knees high, he drove across the room. He felt something hit his back just before the impact which carried Coetzee off his feet and into the partition wall. Haug was still driving when they hit and, as the big South African slid down, stunned, Haug grabbed his ears viciously and smashed the man's face into his knee. The face exploded and one ear came away in his hand with the force of the blow. He threw the ear on top of the sinking body and spun towards Jennifer.

Her face was smeared with vomit, her mouth was open, her eyes wide. There was a deafening commotion in the hall. The noise sounded like two water buffaloes fighting over a mud hole.

"Hang on one more minute, honey. Gotta go rescue the West Indies."

Haug stepped into the hall and turned towards the rear of the house in time to see Keef bringing down a four-foot portion of the stair handrail on top of a giant's head. The rail broke in the middle without much effect on the tall man, who swung a gigantic fist towards Keef's head. Keef ducked easily and counterpunched a blow to the man's ribs with all his bodyweight behind it. The smack would have terminally damaged a normal man, but it only winded the giant.

Haug turned back into the living-room and dashed to the window where he got his fingers under the side casing, which he then yanked away. He grabbed an exposed sash weight and pulled with all his might. One of the windows flew up and he could hear the glass shattering. But he had the weight free, a two-foot length of broken rope dangling from the end. He grabbed the rope and raced back to the hall.

Keef was losing ground slowly to his adversary ,who must have been just under seven feet tall. The black man was pounding him in the midriff, the pelvis, the groin, but nothing seemed to stop him. The South African looked like a blond Frankenstein's monster, impervious to pain. His head was nearly square and as big as a water melon. Large, angry eyes were sunk back into his head under a low, bony brow. It was the width of the giant which was handicapping him, because he nearly had to turn sideways in the hall. Keef's blows sounded like a two-by-four hitting a country ham. Haug was amazed that living flesh could take the sickening pounding that the Jamaican was giving him. It was a bit like a battleship taking a series of torpedoes. The frame sort of juddered and kept moving forwards.

Haug stood in the hall and swung the sash weight like a propeller.

"Keef!" he shouted. "Jump outta the way on two."

He swung harder on the weight, as hard as he could. "One. Two."

Keef jumped sideways into a doorway as Haug let the sash weight go, just after it passed eight o'clock. It was rising on nine and hit the Frankenstein amidships on ten. Haug was right behind the sash weight, his shoulders about a yard off the floor, his legs driving, his feet searching for balance in the rubble. The giant had just started to fold from his middle in a classic jack-knife when Haug hit him between knees and pelvis. The momentum carried them both down the hall and into the kitchen door which went flat down, as though it had been hit by a bus. A wooden table standing in the middle of the room was immediately matchsticked. The velocity and weight of the bodies tore on through the kitchen and into the garden door, which simply exploded outwards, taking the frame with it. The bodies continued to hurtle on into the garden itself. Then suddenly all the noise stopped.

Keef looked out into the hall and through the kitchen into the black hole of the garden. It looked for all the world as though a cruise missile had passed through the house. He followed the wreckage and stepped over the remains of the garden door to look outside. By the spill of the light he could just see Haug getting to his knees beside a bouncing Frankenstein's monster. And he *was* bouncing, slowly up and down.

Keef went closer and saw that the South African had his neck jammed into a fork of a branch of what appeared to be an apple tree.

Lights were coming on in the back windows of the terrace, people were looking out.

Keef helped Haug to his feet and said, "You OK, man?"

Haug got to his feet painfully. "Think so."

He was badly winded, trying to catch his breath. "Not the man I used to be, Keef. Fuckin' glad that was the last one."

"We got to get out of here, Haug. There are people hanging out of those windows."

"Yeah."

. Haug used Keef as a crutch to help him back into the house. His legs were killing him, and his back was burning.

"Check the Hebe in the hall, and I'll get Jennifer. You're right. We gotta haul ass."

The bedroom door was open and he turned on the light and grabbed a bedspread on his way. Jennifer had pushed herself into a sitting position, her back propped against the sofa, her legs up, head resting on her knees. She looked up when Haug entered and tried to speak, but nothing came out. Haug kneeled down and very gently put the bedspread around her, making reassuring noises. Using the end of the spread, he tried to clean the remaining vomit from her face, then he picked her up effortlessly and laid her on the sofa. The room was beginning to come back into focus for her. Coetzee was lying face down on the floor in a pool of blood, naked from the waist down.

Haug turned to look at the man on the floor and Jennifer noticed that Haug's shirt was torn open, a long gash stretching down his back.

"I'll give you somethin' to think about when you wake up."

98

He picked up the sjambok and pulled Coetzee into the middle of the room. Then, taking the handle, he began to force it into the South African's anus. The body stirred with a grunt and a moan.

Then Haug returned and lifted her into his arms like a child. She buried her head under his neck and began to cry as the American carried her out of the room.

Keef nodded at the figure crumpled on the floor of the hall.

"Started to come around, so I kicked him in the balls."

Opening the front door for them, he said to Jennifer, "Hang in there. It's all over now."

There were neighbours in their front gardens as they went out. Men in their undershirts standing on steps, women looking from doorways, children peeping from behind the women.

"Just a family argument, ma'am," Haug said in a loud voice to a woman with a shawl round her head. "Husband's a little abusive, so I'm takin' my daughter back home."

He turned to Keef. "Could you drive again, buddy? I gotta get these goddam' handcuffs off her."

Keef opened the back of the van and Haug sat down with Jennifer, then pulled his legs in. The Jamaican closed the door and went around to the front.

Jennifer still had her head buried in his shoulder. He was rocking her gently and patting her on the back. The motor started and the van began to move. She heard him speak.

"You got the keys to these thangs, asshole?"

"I don't believe it," said Fanie.

She stiffened. It was First Voice. She felt chaos again inside, her thoughts screaming silently. First Voice spoke again.

"You got out of there alive. I don't believe it. What about Piet? How did you get by Piet?"

"If'n you're talkin' about the big feller," Haug replied, "he's hangin' out in the backyard in an apple tree. Now answer my question. You got those keys?"

"In my right-hand pocket," sighed Fanie. "You'll have to get 'em."

Haug reached over, cradling Jennifer carefully, and yanked at the jeans pocket, which tore away, emptying coins and a bunch of keys on to the van floor. He picked up the keys.

"Which ones?"

Painfully Fanie pointed with his left hand, which had two fingers at odd angles, now puffy and swollen.

Haug was very careful not to let the bedspread fall open as he awkwardly found her wrists and fumbled for the keyhole. Suddenly her right hand was free and, painful as it was, she brought it up to Haug's neck, holding on to him like a koala.

"Woah, gal, we gotta get the other one off," he said, trying to dislodge her arm and shift around her body.

Finally he managed to get the key in and her other hand was free. This immediately went round his neck as well. He rocked her like a baby.

"Now tell me somethin': do you know this feller layin' here?"

Without turning or even moving Jennifer said, "First Voice."

"First Voice. Uh huh, I think I know what you mean. Well, now you got dealer's choice. What would you like for me to do to him?"

She held on to him even tighter.

"I don't want him in here. I don't want him in here. I don't want him in here—"

Haug interrupted her. "Well, now, that's the easiest thang of all."

He leaned back and flipped up the two door latches and turned the handle.

"I'm gonna have to put you down a minute on account of the fact that his head is locked to the floor."

He carefully placed her as far away from Fanie as possible and Jennifer clutched the bedspread tightly around her. She watched as he put the key in the shackle lock and pulled it away. Fanie screamed as Haug turned him roughly around, forcing his feet through the back doors.

Haug turned to Jennifer. "I reckon you oughta be offered the opportunity of spoilin' the local environment by dumpin' this garbage on the road."

The South African looked up, startled. "You're not going to stop?"

Jennifer looked at Fanie with hatred. "Won't he try and hang on?"

Haug grinned. "He hasn't got anythang to hang on with."

She pushed her feet out from under the bedspread, bracing her back against the front seat. As her feet touched the top of his head, she recoiled briefly, not even wanting to touch him.

"Please, please!" begged Fanie. "*Not* while he's moving! Wait till he slows down, wait for a set of lights."

"*Please*?" she asked, her voice incredulous. "Did I hear you say *please*?"

She pushed with all her might and heard her rapist scream as he left the van. Briefly she watched in fascination as the shape appeared to roll down the road before the van doors slammed shut.

"Man overboard!" Haug shouted to Keef.

"Tough luck," replied Keef. "This is a non-stop boat."

"Throw out an anchor when you get a chance, so that I can change the plates," Haug said.

A minute or so later, Keef found a place between two street lamps and pulled in. Haug hopped out and peeled off the sticker strip of false numbers he had placed over the normal registration numbers. He walked around to the front of the van and did the same, returning through the rear doors.

Keef pulled away, turning his head towards the back. "Where we going?"

Haug looked at Jennifer still huddled in the bedspread, her knees up. She was resting her chin on her knees, staring at the side of the van.

"I want to go home," she said.

"I don't think it's safe," said Keef from the front.

Jennifer looked up. "Why? Why isn't it safe? They can't do anything to us now, can they?"

"Well," Haug said, "it woulda caused a lotta trouble to kill 'em. And I reckon there's more where they came from anyway. You're wanted pretty bad by some pretty bad folks."

Tears were in her eyes. "But why? Why do they want *me*?"

"I don't have the slightest idea," Haug said as he leaned back against the doors.

He felt a shaft of burning pain. "Shit. What the fuck's wrong with my back?"

He turned around. Jennifer saw the cut made by the sjambok.

"Oh, God, I forgot about that. He hit you with that whip. It's an awful mess."

"Yeah," said Keef. "I saw that. It don't look nice."

"Well," Haug said, wincing. "I suppose it coulda been a lot worse, specially if they'd had time to get their hardware out."

He turned to Jennifer. "My advice is this. We go by your house and pick up some of your clothes, and then you spend a couple of days at my place. It's not much, but there's a spare room. I don't really want to let you outta my sight after my fuckup this afternoon."

Jennifer felt tired, very tired. The chaos of her mind had begun to settle and following in the wake of fear and helplessness came an overpowering desire just to sleep. To get clean and then sleep. For as long as it took to forget.

"Whatever," she said finally. "I just don't want you two to go away. I want to sleep and feel safe."

Keef leaned back again. "Trouble is, I got a wife and two kids to look after as well. They haven't been seein' much of me this week. Take it from me – Haug's worth about a squad of soldiers. You gonna be safe. And I'm only a phone call away."

She reached around painfully and touched his shoulder.

"Sorry I was so rude in the gym—"

Keef laughed. "Oh, I'm used to that, Jennifer. They all turn me down."

She left her hand on his shoulder. "I've just begun to realise that you both could have been killed, and you don't even know me."

"A pleasure," replied the black man. "First chance I ever had to get stuck into South Africans. But for a few minutes back there I thought I was going to lose the first fight I ever lost. I've always said, if I ever lose one, I'm quittin'."

"That was a big mother," Haug said. "Like an ox with the brain of a chicken. Hope they don't have any more like him."

Jennifer banged her head on her knees.

"But what do they want from me? They said that I had some kind of tape."

"I know," Haug replied. "We shook that outta First Voice. Didn't know what kinda tape, though."

"And why would South Africans want it? I don't know any South Africans. I don't know anybody who would do something like this."

Jennifer was shaking with emotion. Fear fell away to reveal anger.

"Fuck. Why? When they mentioned 'tape' to me, I pretended to know what they were talking about, hoping that you were watching the house when they went for it—"

"It was good thinking," said Keef.

"But I didn't even know what *kind* of tape. Tape *measure*? Video? Audio? I still don't know. It's like a horror story, not even knowing *why* someone wants to kill you and rape you and beat you. I haven't done anything to anyone. I haven't hurt anyone else . . ."

She started to sob silently, wiping the tears away with the back of her hand.

"Well," Haug said quietly, "we're gonna help you. We're gonna find out what this tape is and what the hell this is all about. Right now you're with friends—"

"And all I've got now is you two."

Keef shrugged. "I know it ain't much, but—"

"No, no," she said. "I meant that you're practically two strangers. Yet tonight, for no reason at all, you saved my life. And suddenly I depend on you for my life. I've never depended on anyone . . . anyone. Fuck 'em. Fuck 'em all. Men. Fucking men . . ."

Keef patted her hand, still on his shoulder. "I'm sorry, but we got no choice. Born that way."

"Naw," Haug said, rubbing his chin. "I know what she means, I think."

Jennifer Montgomery let herself cry again, cursing because she didn't want to cry, didn't want to be helpless, didn't want people looking after her, didn't want to be sitting in a van with two virtual strangers, practically naked, smelling of vomit. Nor did she want Haug or Keef to leave her. Somehow she just wanted someone to take care of things for a while, just until she rebuilt her own will, which now lay shattered and fragmented. And for a second her defences fell and some of the stomach-churning images of the day returned to her. *Helpless.* That's what those men in that house had made her. Easily, like the snap of a finger. She hadn't even been able to fight. Her wrists bound at her waist, tape over her mouth, naked. Her body had been her own body no more. It was *theirs*. Their property. Stand, sit, talk, shut up, fuck, say this, do that. Never again must that happen. Never. Never let them get control over you . . . ever, she thought. The tears came and were harder to stop. She felt Haug take her other hand in his, and, as the flood came, she held on to his hand tightly and as tightly to Keef's shoulder, crying long and bitterly into the already damp bedspread on her knees.

———

"You don't have to be a hero," she said severely. "You can yelp – or at least say ouch!"

"To be honest," Haug said, "I just use a little trick I learned a long time ago. I put my mind somewhere else. It's like my body's a long way away."

Jennifer was cleaning up the gash on Haug's back. He was sitting on a stool in the bathroom, looking into the mirror, and she could see his face when she looked up. She was wearing his terry-towelling bathrobe with the sleeves rolled up and her hair was still wet from the shower. She had chosen the shower because she was sure that she would fall asleep in the bath, and she knew that something had to be done about his back.

They had gone to her house on Willoughby Road and Haug went in alone to get her a selection of clothes and some of her gear from the bathroom. She didn't know what he had brought yet, but he assured her that anything missing could be replaced at Boots or Marks & Sparks the next day. Then they had dropped Keef off at his place on the way there.

Haug had a second floor flat on Junction Road, near the Archway. The ground floor was an Indian supermarket, a small, family-run grocery. On the first floor were several offices. A solicitor with a Greek name, a dentist, and Haug's one room office. He pointed it out on the way up. PHOENIX, it said on the Georgian glass of the door: "on account of the fact I'm always risin' from the ashes," he had said with a chuckle.

Further up the stairs, his own flat surprised her. It was small, but the feeling was warm and comfortable – a little like the feeling she experienced around Haug himself. The sitting room, bathroom and kitchen were at the front, with the bedroom in the back. There was an old red flag hanging on the wall of the hall, and books lined the sitting room walls. In the bedroom was an enormous king-sized bed with a bookcase on one of the walls and a large collection of CDs and audio tapes on the other. Below the tapes was a stack of complicated-looking stereo equipment, and there appeared to be speakers fixed to the walls of every room in the flat, including the bathroom. A well cared-for fig tree stood near the window, its top nearly reaching the ceiling. There were prints and paintings and one or two framed photographs, ranging from one of a motorcycle engine to a signed one of the President of the NUM. All the furniture was well chosen and comfortable. It wasn't really tidy, but it wasn't a desperate mess either. Strange, was her first thought on entering the flat, a little puzzling. Like the magazine rack near the toilet. When she finished her shower, she pulled out several magazines, expecting soft porn. Instead there were copies of *Classic Motorcycle* and *Scientific American*.

"I like your flat," Jennifer said.

"Thanks." Haug caught her eyes in the mirror, then winced sharply. "Ouch. How's that? Satisfied now?"

"You probably should see a doctor tomorrow. I was only a Girl Guide, so I'm just cleaning it up a bit, dousing it with antiseptic, and then I'll put a piece of gauze down the length held by some tape."

"That'll do fine," he replied.

There were three odd star-shaped scars on Haug's back. One was behind the shoulder and two were below the shoulder blade. She touched them with her finger.

"What are these?"

"Bullet holes. Where they went in the front, you can hardly see 'em. Made a mess in the back, though."

The tone of his voice made her decide to leave the subject.

"I've never been in a flat like this before, I think."

"I didn't really put it together for show."

She stopped and looked at him thoughtfully. "First of all, there's you. A bald head with a pony tail – late 60s hippy? And a face that's, well, homely."

"My mother liked it."

"No," she said quickly, "I don't mean to be rude. Then there are these shoulders that make you look like a wrestler. My God, they're huge! No, not a wrestler, a bear. A bald-headed bear. Big hands. A rather coarse appearance, on the whole."

Haug looked up at himself in the mirror, a worried expression on his brow.

"This is real disappointin'. And me on the way to Paris to become a male model." He pretended to sob. "Oh, the shame of it all."

She hit him on the head with the scissors. "Don't be silly. I'm trying to tell you something—"

"I think yer gettin' it across."

"No. I mean, you're you. You look one way, and the flat belies your looks, raises questions. Not knowing you, I would say a . . . a scholar lived here, or a . . . or a hermit librarian who . . . liked motorcycles. And maybe socialism. An *idealist*, that's it. Then I saw you tonight. You burst into the house, the room – like in an old Western, in the nick of time – then smashed everything and everybody up. The most outrageous violence I've ever witnessed.

"There," she said, placing the last strip of tape and patting him gently. "That will have to do for now."

"Get you a drink? I think we both need one. Mine is Jameson, but I got gin and tonic, vodka, beer . . ."

Haug got up and reached for a clean shirt. She looked at the front of his torso. He did have a little too much belly, but it still looked solid. There was a mat of brown hair running from the chest and disappearing into his trousers. His arms were bigger than most men's legs. The overpowering impression was powerful solidity.

"What you're having is fine. Plenty of it. Not too much water. Strong."

When he returned with the drinks, she was in the sitting room, curled up on the sofa, holding her head in her hands. She took the drink with a little smile.

"I cain't say I like the violence," Haug began. "Or put it this way: I cain't say I like myself bein' violent. I try not to. When it's thrust upon me, like tonight, I try and end it as soon as possible – and you never can end it with a smile and a bunch a flowers. If you don't get 'em quick, they gonna get you – simple as that. Tonight I got a little carried away on account of the fact you're my friend, and I could see right away that they'd been takin' advantage of you."

He sat down in an armchair opposite her. "But, there you are. I got violence in me, whether I like it or not. It fits in OK with the motorsickles, but not so much with the books or maybe the music. There's lots of other stuff you don't know about and lots of contradictions. But I don't worry about the contradictions. If it was all logical, we'd be some kind of computer, speakin' binary code. So I forget about logic and just suit myself, do what I like."

Jennifer looked past his head to the heavy red curtains on the windows. "I wish I could do that."

"What?"

"Do what I like."

"You can," Haug said. "You just do it."

"That's what I want to do," she said, wiping a tear from her cheek. "That's what I try to do. And it never comes out right, not like I planned. In the end I always seem to be doing it for someone else. Usually men. Starting with my father. The bastard. The fucking bastard. You see, my mother died early on, and my father . . . my father. . . Oh, shit, I *hate* crying and that must be the fourth time you've seen me . . ."

"Cryin' doesn't mean anythang. I always find it helps."

She looked at him, astonished. "You mean *you* cry?"

"Yeah, when I feel like it. Why shouldn't I? Am I not s'pposed to?"

"But . . . you're such a . . . you know, a man!"

Haug laughed softly. "That's all horseshit. I tell you one thang. If they'd done to me what they'd done to you today, I think I'da cried more'n you. And I'm not just sayin' that either. 'Cause they had you hog-tied, there were four of 'em, doin' I don't know how many disgustin' and awful and unspeakable thangs to you, thangs you won't get over for a long time. And you couldn't even hit 'em. Shit, you're brave, girl. How old are you?"

She took a long drink of whisky. "I'm twenty-four years old. Twenty-five soon."

He snorted. "Hell, when I was twenny-four I didn't know shit from shoe polish. I still wanted to be a goddam' football player."

She looked at him seriously. "Tell me the truth, now. Don't just say things to try and cheer me up. Don't say things you think I want to hear. Do you really cry?"

"Yep. I remember cryin' when I read *The Old Curiosity Shop*, when Little Nell died. I cry sometimes when I get too involved with some broad and all those mysterious thangs happen, and then she says bye-bye, and I'm left wantin' her and knowin' I cain't have her. I don't mind it, you see. You gotta do somethin' or you're liable to explode. Hell, watchin' you now, knowin' what you been through, seein' tears in your eyes . . . you haven't been lookin' close enough, or you'd see tears in my own eyes. When I let myself think about it."

It was so spontaneous that she couldn't help it. She put her drink down and rushed over to him, sat in his lap and threw both arms around his neck. She looked and found a tear moving slowly down the lines of his face. She kissed him on the cheek.

"You're daft as a brush. But I can't help liking you."

Haug put his arms around her, rocking gently. Occasionally he would reach over and take a sip of his whisky, then return his arm to its place around her shoulder.

Her blonde hair, still a little damp, fell over his other arm. All the make-up had been washed from her face, and her eyes were closed. Looking at her, Haug realised that she was one of the most beautiful women he had ever held. Not just pretty, but glowing somehow from the inside. Yet, despite her sophistication, he saw much that was still a little girl. Vulnerable and insecure on the one hand, apt to skip or hug a teddy bear or laugh suddenly on the other. He guessed that she was a little girl who'd had to grow up too fast and make too many big decisions on her own without any support. Proud of what she had done, but wishing that she had something else.

He wondered briefly about what Fanie had said about her and his heart felt sad. If that was anywhere near the truth, she must have a heavy weight inside her. He looked down at her again, feeling the warmth of her body and the great pleasure it gave him to hold her. Then he shook his head. Impossible. But the thought was there – the two thoughts, actually. He hoped like the devil that she would want him, and he hoped like hell that she wouldn't. Another contradiction. He got up and carefully placed her down on the chair.

"Where are you going?" she asked dozily.

"Well," he said, "this sofa bed is disguised as a sofa, and I thought I'd unmask it. You look like you could use a good sleep."

He pulled it out. It was already made, with clean sheets and two blankets, and he turned down the covers. Then he went over and picked her up again and laid her down on the bed, tucking the covers around her. He fetched a pillow from his own bed in the next room, lifted her head and slid it underneath.

She watched him without saying a word. When he finished, he collected his drink.

At the doorway he turned and smiled. "Good night, sweet thang."

Then he went into his bedroom.

Haug had got into his night-shirt, crawled under the duvet and was reading from Volume Four of Bernard Shaw's letters when Jennifer came in, still dressed in the terry-towelling robe, her hair now nearly dry. She got in the bed from the other side without a word and cuddled up to him.

"Do you mind?" she asked. "I just want you to hold me tonight. I don't want to sleep alone."

He put down his book and finished his drink in one swallow. One arm he placed under her head and drew her to him.

"Well, that's all I'm gonna do. Hold you. I kinda like it myself."

He felt her turn her back to him so that their bodies fitted together, and he adjusted the pillow so both his arms could go round her. Then he turned off the light.

Chapter Eight

It was one of those days which England can have in early spring after a nasty winter.

When they arrive unexpectedly, it is like a jailer opening the door of an underground cell. The sky is unforgettably blue, the wind as fresh as when you were a child. Colour ambushes you because a whole winter has made you forget the difference in shades and hues. The plants are more wary, not yet convinced that the frosts are finished, and they are right. More frosts may come, more wind, more rain, more cloudy, dull, wintry days. A day like this takes you so much by surprise that you can only watch it pass in astonishment. They can't be forecast, or everyone in England would be in the countryside on such a day.

Like Michael Regis and Jeremy Evans, who were surprised by the weather that morning on their way to The Monastery to meet Ian Castleberry, who was keen to show Regis the results of his kindness. Well, The Monastery wasn't exactly his yet, but contracts had been exchanged and the rest was simply a matter of time. Regis was driving his Range Rover, pleased that he might have the opportunity of taking his vehicle off the road for the first time since he had bought it two years ago. Vivaldi's *Four Seasons* was playing softly on the compact disc player. They had left at half past eight to avoid Saturday traffic as much as possible, and the splendid, wonderful early May morning opened like a bright flower just before nine thirty, perfectly timed as they cleared the London area.

Jeremy Evans was looking out of his window at the farmland and hedgerows, still green in places despite a long winter blanket of cloud. He was a small, trim man in his mid-forties and greying at his temples. Otherwise he looked quite youthful, with a tendency for his dark brown hair to fall over his forehead. Unlike many politicians and civil servants, he did not pomade his hair or spray it down rock solid. Perhaps that was because Jeremy Evans was unlikely to appear on TV or in the newspapers. Even if his photograph were accidentally taken, it would later be discreetly snipped from the roll of film and the negative destroyed. No one was supposed to know who he was.

Everyone did, of course, including the IRA. The Deputy Director of MI6 was unlike many deputies. True, he was legally second in command, but he was also much more than that. Deputy Director was a hands-on position, recently made more so by its incumbent who secretly imagined himself as a latter-day and real-life George Smiley – quiet, unassuming, thoughtful, manipulating people and events with the smallest of nudges. Indeed, he might have been all these things.

In his own mind, however, he was a much more advanced model of earlier and illustrious colleagues at MI6. Not only were technology and communications more up-to-date, but so were his ideas and ideals. The earlier days, however luminous, were blighted with traitors and defections, because they had recruited from the dark and infested landscape of Oxbridge in the 1930s. If they weren't outright left wingers, they were Labour supporters or, at best, Liberals. The 1980s had gone a long way to putting all that right, and, while the boom hadn't swept completely clean, key positions were now held by 'friends'. After all, it was well past time to get back to the real business of government following so many years of welfare with its free this and free that for every oddball group of men in sandals and lesbians with hairy legs. People had forgotten how to work, how to carve a living for themselves from the tired, lazy and socialist-infected flesh that was Britain in the years after the Second World War. Enterprise, invention, ideas – those were the three prongs of Britannia's new trident, now used to prick the backsides of the so-called unemployed, that army of unimaginative heathens who expected work to drop into their collective lap or, worse, anticipated sucking the lifeblood from the nation until the day they died, doing nothing but sitting on their arses collecting weekly dole. The 1980s had changed all that, though. And the changes would continue in the work done by the hands of the bright young men and women who had heard the call and came. They were in place and working, having displaced the socialists and woolly liberals, who had died off or were kicked out to pasture.

Jeremy Evans smiled to himself as he continued to gaze out of the window, tapping his forefinger to 'Spring' in the Vivaldi concerto. Michael Regis might have thought the smile a little smug if he could have seen it. True, he thought, they needed a lot more time to do the job properly. But it was getting there. The informal links and feedback were so important. In business, of course, but also the vital media, the arts, philosophy, economics and finally the bowels of education itself, rooting out those incubators and instigators of left-wing social and economic theory. Professors and lecturers had lost their tenure, their free meal ticket for life. Some of the really dangerous ones had been eased out already. Many were left, but all things take time. They said that the BBC was too big, that there was a Charter, that the arts were traditionally left-wing. Yet the BBC was bending slowly to the new direction of growth. They said that the National Health Service was invulnerable politically. Yet here we are today more than halfway to a proper pay-as-you-go system.

Evans's smile lingered as he thought of his own guru. Was that the right word these days? Dr Alexander Hinkley, now with the Adam Smith Institute. The majesty of the man and his vision still inspired him. Today, he hoped, he would continue with his work. A nudge here, a suggestion there – but always with an overview, the ultimate objective clearly in mind. The old buffers in MI6 had never had the benefit of this overview. Though, as Hinkley had pointed out many, many times, we were still heading in the right direction, even in the dosser years. Why? Interests. Interests. Hinkley used to draw out that word, *interests*, stressing the sibilants. After a long pause he would then say 'Economic Interests', leaving it hanging in mid-air, as though it were a self-evident truth. Which, indeed, it was. Economic interests would ensure, in the long run, that the right thing was done. They – their group – were only mechanics, easing the way, greasing the rails, oiling the machinery, replacing worn parts.

"Lost in thought?" asked Regis as Vivaldi ended.

"Never lost, Michael. At least not in thought." Evans combed back his wayward hair with his fingers. "I think that what we want today is reassurance. Sir Jonathan was pumping me one lunchtime about WORLDWIDE and this business. Too clever by half, that man. We must continue to try and dislodge him at Trade. Meanwhile he managed to unsettle Ian slightly, just flaking off that little bit of dirt with his mandarin fingernail on to the idea. People like him simply do not know what their interests really are. They're content to play their little games in the halls of power."

"Ian will be all right," said Regis.

Evans chuckled. "He certainly took the sexual bait hook, line and sinker."

"Jennifer is very good. You should indulge in her yourself, Jeremy. Keep you looking younger."

Evans smiled his little smile again. "Pam is quite adequate for me, thank you. I'm one of those who don't really think it is wise to step out of the family circle. There are unquestionable delights of course, as in the case, I am sure, of your whore. Besides, I know who did the decorating at her home. Our usual firm of builders. No, no. Pam may be a little boring, but there are other things which excite me a lot more than extra-marital excursions that prove far too dangerous."

"Ah," replied Regis, "you don't know what you're missing. Jennifer is a prime piece of the finest English lamb. And, to expand the bucolic analogy, useful as the depository of one's sperm . . . or for leaving innocently tethered at night to attract the tiger."

"Indeed. I am a little surprised that Castleberry didn't rumble the fact that you were tossing him a tart, all wrapped and paid for."

"Hmmm. Yes, I'm afraid that intelligence isn't Ian's strongest suit. Cunning; but not intelligent. He has even convinced himself that she is in love with him."

They both laughed at the idea.

"Would you mind selecting another disc? Something as smooth and crisp and even as the last one?"

Evans studied the rack of CDs. "A little Handel?"

"Yes," said Regis. "A little *Water Music*, I think."

"Isn't it gorgeous? Isn't it marvellous? Isn't it a wonderful day?"

Ian Castleberry spread his arms in a crucifix, appropriate to standing in the ruins of a monastery, and turned back to Regis and Evans, a smile of childish happiness upon his face.

"It *is* rather nice, Ian," Regis said. "Particularly the woodland, which is completely unspoilt."

"Nice?" replied Castleberry, who instantly replaced his smile with a serious face. "It is difficult to describe to someone who doesn't know the history, who hasn't lived it like I have, who never imagined that he would ever finally own it."

"Quite impressive," said Jeremy Evans, who was standing on the remnants of the East Wall, hands clasped behind his back, wind blowing his hair.

Ian Castleberry's own hair, what there was of it, stuck steadfastly to its owner's skull.

"Actually, I'm glad you came, Jeremy. My Perm. Sec. mentioned that he had lunch with you a few days ago."

Evans stepped down from the wall, unclasping his hands and rubbing them. "Yes. I'm afraid that Sir Jonathan may have given you the wrong impression. In fact we are not at all unhappy with the arrangements."

"Good, good." Castleberry's smile returned. "I'm glad to hear that. There were one or two other noises, you know, from the old guard, always complaining about everything and anything."

"Nevertheless", continued Evans, "we want you to play everything rather close to your chest. What we have here is the beginning of green shoots. One of the first of our projects on a much larger canvas."

"Ah." Castleberry stopped and thought a moment. "Then you are actually involved, not just scrutineers—"

Jeremy Evans held up his hand. "Let's not use the word 'involved' just now. I will try and fill in a bit more of the picture later."

"Yes, well," said Castleberry, "I have to admit that I had a few of my own doubts. Mainly because of WORLDWIDE. Harvey Gillmore is a crank. A nuisance. A bad penny."

Michael Regis was studying the layout of the old nave. "Harvey Gillmore and WORLDWIDE newsprint have been very valuable to the nation and to the Party."

"Very valuable," echoed Evans. "In fact, for WORLDWIDE, this is simply a kind of payment for service, if you know what I mean. They are having cash flow problems, principally due to the depressed state of world markets. Need a bit of an IV drip. Besides," he added with a knowing smile, "it is useful having an Australian crank exposed, should anything go amiss. Rather than British interests."

"Yes, of course. *I* should have thought of that," Castleberry laughed. "What is the bigger picture, the larger canvas?"

"Nothing so desperately world-shaking, Ian," said Evans. "Simply a continuation of what has always been our policy. Now, as in everything else, we are trying to implement a leaner, fitter, better-defined programme – indeed, a more rational one. Logic. Now, there is a subject, Ian. Because with logic there is clarity." Evans was quoting directly from his mentor, Alexander Hinkley. "There is trouble in Africa."

"Always trouble in bloody Africa," Castleberry retorted.

"Hmm, yes, of course," mused Evans. "We have to do our best to ensure that, after the dust settles, our interests and the interests of our partners are served. If there was no intervention at all, it would simply be a matter of the strongest winning the day. Things are going to continue to break up in southern Africa. The so-called popular movement is behind the ANC, which is, as you know, riddled from top to bottom with radicals. Your people", he said, nodding to Ian Castleberry, "apply political pressure to such a group to encourage change. This takes time, however, so, in the short run, it is necessary to supply arms to their enemies, tribal and otherwise. While you grind away at the top, we grind at the bottom. In the end, such organisations as the ANC become more . . . trustworthy. Look at the successes in Angola, for instance. Years ago it looked hopeless. Now . . ."

"Well, yes," said Castleberry, "I'm aware of the bare bones of this business. I wouldn't have put it in those exact words, of course, but naturally we have to encourage democracy to flourish and grow in backward countries. But the supply of arms is always a dangerous area in a finger-pointing world. I have to think about that sort of thing, you know, while you chappies hide the daggers in the cloaks. The fact that everybody does it is neither here nor there."

"Oh, no," replied Evans as he picked up a small stone and threw it idly. "It is very much *here*. Our industries need a boost, our products are good, and there is no reason we should not increase our share of the market. While at the same time having a beneficial effect on political tensions. You see, Ian, the products just need to be more directed. Like smart bombs—"

"Jeremy."

Michael Regis had been standing nearby, apparently not listening, engrossed in architectural study.

Evans took the hint. He was telling Castleberry more than he really needed to know.

"Anyway. That, in short, is a little of the bigger picture, Ian. We really came down to have a look at this fine piece of land you have acquired."

Castleberry, whose face had accumulated a little worry, brightened. "I've been spending far too much of my time out here. Catherine tells me I come back smelling like a shepherd."

As they walked back to the Range Rover, Michael Regis was thinking about Evans. Usually he could be counted upon to keep a tighter rein. But any time he got near his beloved topic of ideology, the reins were off and the horses ran pell-mell. He would much rather that Castleberry hadn't been told any details, because Castleberry was one of those political opportunists with a whole set of hats, one for every occasion. Right now he leaned in their direction because that was the way the wind was blowing. When the wind shifted, the hat would change. Castleberry and his sort would easily survive any revolution. Just learn the new slogans and get his tailors to change uniforms.

Castleberry got in the back of the Range Rover. As he adjusted his seat belt, a little worry drifted across his face again.

"Jeremy? Just how do the Saudis figure in this scheme?"

"Sorry to interrupt," Regis said quickly. "But I keep forgetting. Ian, how did you get along with my cousin?"

Again Castleberry brightened. "Oh, yes – what was her name?" He knew that he mustn't give anything away.

"Jennifer."

"Yes, of course, Jennifer. I was meaning to ask you, Michael, if you had seen her this week."

"No, I haven't," Regis replied. "But I will probably see her tomorrow, Sunday. Yes. Why?"

"Oh . . . she asked me if she could come and visit the Commons one day. In fact I called and left a message, but perhaps she is out of town."

"More likely to be a little work she's picked up. Hope so. Acting is such a dreadful profession."

Castleberry stared out the window at his property. "Delightful girl. Absolutely delightful."

The Range Rover rejoined the road, and Castleberry asked no more about the Saudis or the arms. He was a politician and knew how to take a hint. The less he knew, actually, the better. His mind drifted back to Jennifer and he settled down with his memories of that evening before having to face Catherine over tea.

———

Thomas Howell was holding the door of the Rolls for his boss, who was taking his time gathering papers into a briefcase. He was delivering him to his London address at the old newspaper building. Harvey Gillmore was staying in town that night.

Gillmore got out of the car. "Oh, by the way, Howell, I'm seeing Beth tonight. Your ex-wife. Any message?"

"No, sir," Howell said neutrally and without missing a beat. He closed the door. "Anything else, sir?"

"No," said Gillmore. "Ten o'clock tomorrow morning."

An internal smile spread just to the corners of his mouth as he walked away. He knew that Howell hated staying in London. He never said so, but Gillmore could sense it. He also sensed his driver's hatred of the converted linen cupboard, a tiny room without windows, which was included with the top floor. But it was near the garage and convenient so what the devil could the man complain about?

Gillmore stepped into the garage lift and turned to catch the chauffeur's eye.

"Goodnight, Howell," he said as the lift doors closed.

He sometimes marvelled to himself that there seemed no limit to what some people would take. Howell's cowardice revolted him. After all, the man could hit him. He was bigger. But then, they all just wanted the candy, didn't they? And Howell would lose more than his job. In fact he would never again find employment in this country. Or any other. Gillmore detested homosexuals. Vermin. Howell deserved everything he got.

He thought that mentioning Beth was a subtle dagger slipped between the man's ribs. He hadn't seen Beth since being introduced to Jennifer. But Jennifer wasn't available for some infernal reason, something he wanted to take up with that turd, Regis. He was going to insist that Jennifer carry a beeper so that when he wanted pussy he could have it. Why should he have to wait? Why should he have to use Beth? Mind you, Beth was free, while Jennifer insisted that he pay the whole fee, every time. Damn that girl. He was going to have to do something about her so that she behaved herself a little better.

Gillmore put the key into his door and opened it, laying the briefcase on the table near the umbrella stand. When he called Beth, she was surprised. Didn't want to come. But she soon realised what that would mean. At least she had a head on her shoulders and he didn't have to draw a picture. In fact, Gillmore thought, as he hung his jacket on a hanger and loosened his tie, he rather enjoyed getting people to do things they didn't want to do. Why have power if you don't use it? His father had told him that it was an advantage to encourage fear in those below. They worked harder, they complained less and no one dared try and backstab you. Revolt or argument was dealt with in the same way every time – a backhand across the room.

He got a Diet Pepsi from the fridge and poured it into a glass with some ice. This he took to his office and placed on the desk in front of him. He glanced at his watch and frowned. She was a little late. He turned on the lamp and twisted it to face the doorway and switched out the overhead. As he took a sip of his Pepsi, the doorbell rang. He pressed a button on the console and waited. A few moments later there was a tap at his door.

"Come in," he said quietly, taking another sip of Pepsi.

Beth Howell entered the office and immediately shielded her eyes from the glare of the light. She could just see the outline of Gillmore behind his desk.

"You're late," he said.

She bit her lip. "Sorry, Mr Gillmore. The taxi—"

"I told you to come as a whore. That's what I want tonight, a whore."

"Well," she said, "I did my best. I . . . don't really have the clothes, the kind I imagine—"

"Show me."

Beth undid the belt of her coat and opened it with a hopeful smile. She let it drop to the floor. A black strapless half bra just covered the nipples of her small breasts. A black suspender belt framed her pubic hair. The stockings were black as well, and she knew that he would like the shoes because he had bought them for her. She never wore them except for him because they were so uncomfortable. Four inch stilettos with open toes and a strap around the ankles. She stood in the light, shifting from one foot to the other.

"You've put on weight," he said from behind the light.

She bit her lip again. "Yes, maybe I have. I don't know—"

"Well," he interrupted her impatiently, "sell it to me."

"I'm sorry, Mr Gillmore, I don't quite understand—"

His hand smacked on the table angrily.

"I told you I wanted you to come as a whore. Which means you've got something to sell, haven't you? Do I have to draw a picture for every fucking employee for every fucking thing they do? I want to be excited, and I am not at all excited. You've got some merchandise there and I want you to sell it to me. We're all merchants in this world, you know, Beth. Tonight you are selling me pussy and at the moment I am not buying. OK, I liked the idea of you wearing that gear under the trenchcoat. That was fine. But now you're standing there about as sexy as a wombat looking for a place to shit."

Beth was frightened of the man. He had broken off their affair suddenly, and she had gone through an awful period of swinging between self-doubt and relief. For over two months now he had not called. Then today . . . She just wished somehow that she could get away from him, free from the fear. She thought of him often and the thought of him brought emotional turbulence, and the fear. And now his voice behind the light, like something from inside her – mocking, evil, terrible.

The hand slammed again on the table. "Well?"

She put her hands behind her head and gave Gillmore a big smile, opening her lips. Slowly she walked towards the desk, swaying her hips and pushing them forward.

"Mr Gillmore," she said in what she hoped was a sultry voice, "I've got something for you."

"What?" His voice was sneering.

She ran her hands down her body as she stopped three feet from the desk. With her painted nails she stroked her thighs.

"Some . . . pussy."

The word didn't sound right, but she ran her tongue around her lips and looked at the dark outline behind the desk from under her lashes.

Harvey Gillmore was becoming aroused, as much from his sense of power over the woman as from the sight of her gyrating in front of him. For a moment he tried to imagine exchanging places with her. Would he have come out in a taxi in high heels, nearly naked beneath a coat for the whim of an employer? Would he now be debasing himself in front of this employer and doing everything he asked? Well, certainly the answer was *no*. *He* had some sense of moral values, while this woman clearly did not.

He looked at her in detail. Her face was OK, and he even liked her blue eyes, and her hair, since she had grown it out, now framed her face with a dark border which billowed when she moved her head. Her mouth, hotly coloured red, was open, reminding him of what it mimicked, reminding him that he could plunge in there and invade down below as well. Her skin wasn't nearly as clear as Jennifer's, but then it was hardly fair to compare the two. Beth had put on weight at her waist and stomach, which now shook and trembled as she moved her hips, coming closer to the edge of the desk. The thighs were OK too and didn't bulge over the stocking tops like some he'd seen. As he looked up, he saw her taking off her bra to rub her nipples. He wished that she had left it on. It made her tits look bigger.

He thought about calling Howell on the intercom and telling him to come up and watch him fuck his wife. The thought helped arouse him more. But it was enough already. The man had probably seen her come in and knew that she was up here, so let his imagination burn into the night.

He hated faggots. They were weak, weaker than this woman in front of him waving her snatch in his face just because she was afraid of losing her job. And not getting another one. All these people, including Greenaway, his editor, were trashy sorts. They were afraid of him, afraid of what he could do, what he would do to them. He had a lot to thank his father for, God rest his holy soul. "Never be afraid of power," he had told him. "Use it. Because that way people *respect* you."

"Come this side of the desk, Beth," he said, and watched her vamp around the large black desk, as he followed her with the lamp like a spotlight. "Now come over here and give me a nice blow job."

She knelt down in front of his chair and began unbuckling his trousers, then unzipping his flies. Gillmore smiled to himself as she took out his penis. He had always been really proud of his dick. Though he was a small man physically, his dick was longer than average and quite wide. It was his revenge on the athletes in the shower room when he was in school. Beth took the head of it into her mouth and he saw a smear of lipstick on the shaft. It was a tight fit, even for her mouth, and he could feel the tingling scrape of her teeth on top and underneath. The lamplight was on her face, now engorged with Harvey Gillmore's penis.

"You don't do this because you love me, do you, Beth?" he asked in his whispering voice. "You do it because you're afraid of me. I liked to watch you scrubbing my floors, your arse in the air. Don't you want to go back to that? Is poverty so bad that you'd dress like a tart and suck my dick? Or do you just like a nice big dick to suck?"

Gillmore put his hand behind her head and pulled her towards him, causing her to gag. He held her there for a moment, then whispered into her ear, "Now get down on all fours."

He let her go. He noticed as she turned around that she didn't even have the spirit to meet his eyes.

He knelt down behind her, not even bothering to take off his trousers.

"I'm going to bet you a £10,000 rise in salary that you are already sopping wet. You know why, Beth? You know why? Because it *excites* you doing these things for me. It excites you being treated as a dog." He felt her vagina with his fingers. "Ah, just as I thought, a nice slimed-up sheila."

He patted her buttocks. "Remember when I used to spank you. Got wet then, too, eh?"

He put his penis into the lips of her vagina and pushed sharply, sneering when she gave a sharp cry.

"I never told you that I spanked him as well, did I? Your husband. I thrashed him and he took it. Thanked me for it. Did he see you come in tonight?"

"Yes," Beth hissed through her teeth. "He was cleaning the car. Just stared at me, stared at my shoes."

She was doing her best to hold back an orgasm. She could not believe it. Emotions wrestled inside her like demons. Gillmore's words were gauged to hurt, to confuse, and some invariably hit the target. She was afraid of him. She tried not to be, but she was. And tonight, what was it? Somehow she was getting off on the fear. And the self-loathing. Was she demented? Going insane? She couldn't possibly *like* what was happening to her tonight. Her mind flickered back over the evening, pausing madly on images and emotions. Yes, she had always wondered what it would be like going out naked except for a coat – that was her choice. But when she first came in, she had felt humiliated and had very nearly turned and left, and to hell with the consequences. For some reason, though, she had stayed. Then, when she was moving in front of his desk, exposed in the light, it seemed that she entered a kind of dream. There was a dark man behind the desk, a dark, evil man. And she was exposing herself for darkness and evil. Her mind flickered to the moment she had knelt in front of him. Yes, at that point she wanted him. Hated him and wanted him in the same breath – the conflict grappling inside her. Deep loathing and deep desire. Tears came to her eyes as she realised that she had wanted his prick in her mouth. She was weak, it made her weak, and with the weakness she felt the strength and power of desire. Now, on all fours, with his prick stretching the walls of her vagina, filling her with every evil thrust, it was . . .

It was unexpected and completely overpowering. Beth Howell came as she could never remember coming before. Wave after wave crashed with thundering force, loosening gigantic boulders which thundered down the slope of consciousness into the wild and darkly stormy seas at the centre of her being. Trees were whipped out of the ground, tumbling end over end as they dashed themselves to pieces. Flashes of dangerous lightning were followed by thunder so loud that it made her belly roll over. Beth only realised that she was screaming when the raging of the storm finally began to subside. What was happening to her?

"Harvey!" she screamed. "Oh, Harvey!"

She felt her head ring and didn't know what had happened. He had struck her with the flat of his hand.

"*Don't* call me Harvey! Never call me Harvey!" he said.

As she felt him coming, the waves began again, fresh and new and terrible. The skies were darker, blacker, oilier. It was nastier. It was awful. She felt two of her fingernails break off on the carpet. This time she didn't scream, but realised instead that she was crying like a child. She felt him leave her, but she didn't move, holding her head on her forearms. Her hair was wet from sweat and her face from tears. She felt something being pushed into her vagina and she didn't even care, so despicable had she become.

"There's five pounds," he said from above her. "And I reckon I got my money's worth."

Had he pushed a five pound note into her? She rolled on to her back and realised that the light was still on her. She could see him leaning on the desk and she opened her legs to him. With two fingers she felt for the five pounds and pushed it further up.

"I'll keep it there. To remind me, Mr Gillmore."

She was not crying now but instead felt cold, as though she were hovering over her own body. Her body was warm and wet and still heaving, but her mind was above. What was happening to her?

Gillmore looked at the woman lying on her back before him, her knees up, breathing heavily, her head now in shadow. In all his life he had never experienced a woman coming like that, and it had shaken him a little. Only a little, only until he recovered himself and realised what had happened. She had liked it. She had liked acting the prostitute and the stripper. Beth Howell had *wanted* him. He was always one to recognise power, and this was another kind of power. He reached around for his Pepsi and took a sip.

"Are you trying to tell me something?" he said. "Lying like that?"

"You overpaid me," she replied simply.

He swirled the rest of the Pepsi around with the ice. "I included a tip."

"I enjoyed it."

"I know."

She paused a moment, looking at the ceiling. "I want you now."

"I know."

"I feel dirty and filthy, and I still want you."

"Go get me another Pepsi," he said, draining the glass. "I'm thirsty."

Beth got to her feet without a word and picked up his glass, which she took to the kitchen, filled with ice and another Pepsi. When she returned, Gillmore was sitting at his desk going through several coloured folders, his glasses perched on his nose. She leaned over and put the glass beside him.

Gillmore looked up at her, then at the Pepsi, which he picked up. Suddenly he flung the contents at her.

"Always deliver a drink on a tray," he said mildly. "And around the other side. Now go and get me another one and clean up this mess."

She had screamed with surprise when the icy drink hit her. Then she stood for a full minute staring at Harvey Gillmore, who was now reading his file as though she were not there. The anger was dissipating, being replaced by the sewage of self-hatred. She unclenched her fists and picked up the empty glass on the desk, turned and went to the door.

His voice stopped her. "I like those shoes. I want you to wear them more often."

She opened the door and went to fetch another Pepsi. With a tray.

Chapter Nine

Haug and Jennifer sat at the table in his small kitchen. They had just finished breakfast, and Haug was waiting for the water to boil for the coffee. He had thrown on some trousers and a shirt, but was barefoot. Jennifer still wore the same terry-towelling robe in which she had slept. The plates were clean except for a small pile of white cereal on Jennifer's plate.

"Thanks for the breakfast," she said. "Hit the spot, as I believe you Yanks say."

Haug heard the water boiling and got up to pour it through the filter. "You didn't eat your grits."

"I'm sorry. I tried."

"Won't grow up big and strong like me if'n you don't eat your grits. I get a friend to send them to me special from North Carolina. That and a mess of chewin' tobacco."

She pulled a face. "Ugh. How disgusting."

"Better than suckin' it inta your lungs, I reckon."

He poured out the coffee, taking his black. She put a drop of milk in hers.

Jennifer looked at her coffee as she stirred it slowly. "You didn't touch me last night, Haug."

"I sure did. Slept with my arms wrapped around you till I woke up to take a piss."

"You know what I mean. You didn't even try once."

"Look here, Jennifer . . . can I call you Jenny?"

"I'd rather you didn't."

"Okeydoke, Jennifer. Now, answer me one thang. I'd be some kind of ratfuck pig if I started pawin' at you after the kind of day you had. Besides, I'd rather have your trust than a screw any day."

She looked up. "Say that again."

"You heard me the first time. I like you. I already told you that. I'm not about to go back on my word about bein' a friend."

"Well . . . there's a first time for everything. You're a strange man."

He smiled and took a sip of hot coffee. "You're not your average run-of-the-mill broad, either. But let's leave all the mutual compliments for later. We got some decidin' to do today. Like decidin' what the hell's goin' on and what we gonna do about it. Right?"

She took a sip of her coffee. "If I knew what was going on, I would tell you. I don't. It's a nightmare."

"Well, we know certain thangs, don't we? There are at least three South Africans and one Israeli who think you have a tape that they want. They knew your address, they knew your name, they knew your agent's name—"

"They would have got my agent's details from *Spotlight*," she said and then added, "It's an actors' directory."

"OK. They still know your name and believe you got somethin' that belongs to them. Somebody gave 'em your name. You got any candidates for that? Somebody who'd give your name and accuse you of havin' this tape."

"Candidates," she replied. "I suppose there are a number of candidates, as you call them."

She rose, holding her coffee mug, went to the window and leaned on the washing machine, looking out at the heavy traffic on the street below.

"You mentioned trust just now. There's something I'll have to trust you with – may as well be now as later. I'm going to tell you something which may make you hate me."

"I doubt it," he said quickly.

She turned to face him. "It's about how I make my living. I have . . . clients. I sleep with men for money."

Haug shrugged. "I already heard tell of that."

"You *knew*?"

"Didn't say I knew. Said I heard tell. One of the thangs First Voice came out with while we were breakin' pieces off him."

"Then why didn't you say something to me?"

Haug took another sip of coffee. "I figgered that if you *weren't*, it woulda been insultin', and if you *were*, you'd tell me when you felt like it. Which is what you just did."

"And?"

"And what?"

She looked exasperated. "Well, you can't possibly approve of it, can you?"

"What the hell does my approvin' or disapprovin' of anythang you do have to do with anythang? You got some more understandin' of me to get done before we go any further today."

She started to interrupt angrily.

"Now wait a minute, let me finish, 'cause I wanna go right back to the beginnin'. As your friend, I support you. If *you* disapprove of somethin', then quite likely I'll disapprove of it too, at least on your behalf. If you say *you* disapprove of this, then I'll see you're unhappy with somethin' and I'll say, yeah, yeah, I can see that, and then try and help as best I can to get you out of it. On the other hand, if you say you do somethin' a little unusual and you're not unhappy with it, then I'm pleased you're doin' it and hope you're makin' a good livin' at it."

"But, Haug, I've just told you I'm a *prostitute*."

"What do you want me to do? Turn white and faint?"

"It's hard to believe that you are real," she said. "Are you telling me that you are completely unmoved by my telling you my secret?"

"Now you're askin' me a completely different question. Of course it affects me emotionally. Inside. But I'm only a human bein', not some kinda god. Which means I cain't possibly sit here judgin' you, what you do, how you do it. That is up to you. You got a better picture than I got. A better view. I can only sit here and guess, and I'm modest enough to think guessin' is probably better'n ninety per cent wrong. But guessin' I *am* doin', judgin' I'm *not*, on account of the fact that I don't have the qualifications to be the Almighty."

Jennifer walked over to Haug and kissed him on the top of his bald head, then hugged it to her bosom.

"Is that the truth?" she asked in a quiet voice.

He pulled back a little so that he could look into her eyes. "One thang I do tell to the best of my ability is the truth. I think you'll find that out, if you don't know it already."

She pushed his head gently back and held it with her arms.

"The short story is this: Jennifer Montgomery is *not* my real name. I come from a little town in Derbyshire called Buxton, and, while my father is not poor, *I* am, since I had to leave home because of his constant sexual abuse. To add to my handicaps, I also want to be an actress. So I sat down one day and did my sums. I could be a waitress or barmaid in my spare time – and there are plenty of those jobs – or I could give up acting, or I could take up something like modelling, stripping or prostitution. Well, I decided that one is as bad as the other, but none of them quite so bad as waitressing and living on beans and lentils. Or marrying somebody rich. So I thought that I might as well go in at the top of the market. Which wasn't easy, but I did it. As soon as my house is paid for, I will quit. Then I will at least have a nice place to be poor in."

She paused for a moment, thinking. "It helped that I fucking hate men, with their power and money and swaggering pricks."

She pulled his head back, loosening her arms. "With the growing exception of you, Haug. You are just about the strangest man I've ever met. But I think I like you ever so much."

She leaned down and kissed him on the lips. When they parted, Haug looked at her.

"Now, Jennifer . . . by the way, what's your *real* name?"

"Sharon, I'm ashamed to say."

"Don't be ashamed of it. Not your fault."

"Anyway, I want to be called Jennifer."

"OK, Jennifer. One's as hard to say as the other, if you won't let me call you Jenny. Now, Jennifer. I want you to go sit right down in that chair and listen to me. OK?"

"Don't you like holding me?"

He pushed her gently towards her chair.

"The point is, I like it too much. And I liked the kiss too. It was just about the sweetest and nicest one I've had in over two years. I also detected a little bit of danger there. A crinkle and crackle of electricity. Which rings a great big gong right in the back of my head. You are in your twenties, and I've sworn off girls in their twenties. Not for just screwin'. Screwin's OK. But for gettin' in love with. Or whatever it's called. The tarbaby. You know – your hand sticks to it, then your other hand, your foot, your leg. And you, sweet thang, are not the screwin' kind. You're the lovin' kind. There is a difference. It's a big one."

She smiled. "It sounds like a compliment. At least one I haven't had before. Why are you prejudiced against women in their twenties?"

"On account of the fact that you don't know what you want yet. *I* do. More particularly because I made a mistake and got in love with another girl, and she was a year older than you and just as beautiful. She was a musician. Harpsichordist. We were both in love for maybe two years and then she started changin'. Now, I don't blame her. Hell, when I was twenty-five, I didn't know what the hell I wanted. I was grabbin' one girl and then another one – no, yeah, not this one, what's this, no, yeah, that's OK – just flippin' through the catalogue seein' if anythang fit or looked good on Wednesday or Friday. And I fucked a lot. I've had more women than you can shake a stick at. Nothin' else to prove. I got nothin' to prove to you or me and, frankly, I think too much of you right now to put on the dog and try and lure you back in the bedroom so I can add you to some kind of score sheet. That little kiss tells me that there's a lot percolatin' 'tween you and me. I got six horses pullin' me towards you and six holdin' me back. There's nothin' I'd like better'n kissin' you again and tastin' that place where your neck joins your shoulder, holdin' you to me, feelin' us grow together like magic. So right now I think I'll just sit on my hands for a spell. I think it's the right thang to do too. Now. Is that enough truth for you in one go?"

"Well, I suppose it'll have to do," she said good-humouredly. "Does it mean I don't get any more cuddles?"

"I'd be delighted to sleep with you any time or have any kind of cuddle. Just no complications. Not right now. Right now we gotta stop this mushy stuff anyway and get serious. So, clients. You got any ideas?"

"It could be any of them, yet it would surprise me if any of them were responsible."

"How many are there, all together?"

"Four on a semi-regular basis, with specials arranged by Michael."

"Michael?" he asked. "Who's Michael?"

"Michael Regis. I don't really know what he does, to be honest. But he's very important, very respected by top politicians, judges, military people. Seems to know everybody at the top of everything."

"Does your list include Regis?"

She got up and went back to the window, where she had left her coffee. It was cold now, but she drank some anyway. She stared again at the traffic below.

"I don't know. Michael is . . . yes, sometimes we have sex together, but he doesn't pay. Well, not directly. But he helped with the mortgage, setting it up, banks, all that stuff, arranged the builders and decorators—"

Haug interrupted her. "Did a lot need doing?"

"Well," she said slowly, "not really. Different wallpaper, maybe, different carpet, you know. But he insisted that it was replastered, lots of carpentry . . ."

"Replastered? And the plaster was OK?"

"Well, yes. But I've got to admit they did a marvellous job in the end. So I suppose it was worth it."

Haug scratched his nose, a little worried. "So this guy Regis sort of arranges thangs, does he? Lines folks up, introduces new people, that sort of thang?"

"Yes, that's right. And sometimes he comes by just to talk and have a drink or take me out, and we usually go to bed together. I didn't mean to get into that, but you have to know Michael. You just can't say no to him. He has this . . . charisma. Or this kind of persuasiveness. Very smooth. Very confident. Very good-looking, come to that."

"None of my business, but are you or were you in love with him?"

"No," she said hesitantly. "Or, if I have to be absolutely honest, I don't think so."

"Does he take a cut of the money?"

"No. The bit I most object to is his insistence that I take certain clients despite the fact I find them . . . repulsive."

"Can you give me an example?" asked Haug.

"The only one at the moment is the newspaper tycoon, Harvey Gillmore."

"Holy shit! That scumsuckin' pig fucker!"

"Do you know him, then?"

"Only by his fruits," said Haug. "Lookin' at the titles of his newspapers turns my stomach. God knows how you manage to crawl into bed with him. No offence, but – Jesus Christ! – I wouldn't touch the son of a bitch with my mule's dick for a brand new full dress Harley. If I had a mule."

"An unconventional way of putting it, perhaps. But not far from my own sentiments. I've told Michael that I don't want to see that misogynistic bastard any more. He makes me feel really filthy. He likes to play games, nothing straight—"

"If it's all the same to you", Haug said, pouring some dregs from the filter, "I'd rather not hear the details. I got a hard enough job imaginin' you with him."

"Listen, Haug," she said a little testily, "I'm not some delicate piece of china or porcelain. Nor am I some garden nymph with feathery wings and a little wand. I made a decision a few years ago to do what I do, but that doesn't stain my heart. Or my body, for that matter. I knew the risks, and that horrible little Harvey Gillmore is certainly one of the big risks. But I'm not apologising for anything."

"Yep. You're right. I hastily withdraw my last remark. So, what about Gillmore?"

"He's the slimiest, the creepiest. I suppose that if I had to point a finger, it would be towards him. Then there's Ian Castleberry—"

"Minister of Trade."

"Brilliant. What about Tennyson Tobias-Wyatt?"

"Bank of England."

"Lord Stourbridge."

"Lord Chief Justice."

"Well done!" Jennifer exclaimed. "For an American. Highly confidential, of course, which is part of the reason for the fifteen hundred pounds fee."

"Fifteen hundred! I can buy a good motorsickle for that!"

"Michael pays in most cases. For all of the above, save for Gillmore, who leaves a stinking cheque. You and Michael are the only people in the world who know those names. So be careful. Also there is the odd sheikh; a couple of Japanese businessmen; the head of De Beers twice; and an American *female* movie star, my only venture into that sort of thing. Yes, you *would* know her name. No, you wouldn't believe it. And no, I'm not going to tell."

"There's a kinda pattern, though, isn't there?" Haug mused. "I don't know what kind yet, but I would guess you're some kinda business favour. Sure is top drawer, though – you were right about that. And let me tell you, those names stop with me. Not even Lizzy will know."

"Lizzy?"

"My secretary. Speaking of whom – how do you like that for first class English? Speaking of whom, I think I hear her elegant and delicate movements downstairs. So I'd better go tell her it's time to piss on the fire and call the dogs. Come on down and meet her when you get dressed."

After pulling on his shoes and socks, Haug went downstairs and opened the office door. Lizzy was sitting behind the PC tapping away at the keyboard. She weighed over sixteen stone, came from Dublin, and Haug had found her serving pints of Guinness across the street at The Drum. He had also watched her beat three bus drivers from the local garage one night in arm-wrestling. Another time she had faced up to a drunk with a broken glass. The drunk finally threw down the glass and walked out of the door, tail between his legs, propelled by an unbroken stream of Irish-accented profanity.

Lizzy looked up from her work with a coy smile, then glanced at the ceiling. "Do I hear the patter of little feet, by chance?"

"Now Lizzy, it's not what you think. It's a client."

"You Americans come over here with your stockings and chewing gum, thinking that we're all dying to fall into bed with you. It's not another barmaid, is it? I feel kind of protective towards barmaids, you know."

"Listen, you great hog-rasslin' paddy, I'm tryin' to tell you somethin'. It's the one I told you about – Jennifer Montgomery. Last night Keef and I rescued her from a mess of South Africans who kidnapped and raped her. Which was my fault, 'cause they took her right from under my nose—"

"Oh, I'm sorry, Haug." Her face serious now. "Anything I can do? Want me to go up?"

"Naw, she's as right as she can be under the circumstances, though part of it is the English stiff upper lip act. Inside, I guess she's pretty torn up. Be worse later, I reckon."

He hooked over a chair with his foot and sat down beside his desk.

"Anyhow, I gotta get movin' on this thang before this gang of thieves catches up with us again and a lot worse happens to her."

He picked up the phone and dialled One Time's number.

"I'll get you a cup of tea."

"Thanks, Lizzy."

Someone finally answered the ringing telephone.

"Who's that?"

"Griffin, One Time. Right now," said a voice.

"I need to see you pronto, Kemosabe. Don't bother wearing your glitter threads, but bring your ghetto blaster."

"Right now." One Time rang off.

Lizzy set down the mug of tea, teabag string still hanging over the side. "I'd just boiled the kettle."

Haug pulled out the teabag and dropped it into the paper bin. "Real class you are, sweetheart."

"Thought you'd never notice."

She sat back down behind her PC, which was behind the desk. Which was Haug's seat. The smaller desk, which he had bought for her at the second-hand furniture store, she didn't like. She'd rather look out of the window, she said, than face the bloody wall like a plant. True, it was a small room, particularly for two large people. The rest of the space was taken up by an old red filing cabinet, a small ancient fridge and three chairs – one for Haug, one for Lizzy and one for the client. When they had a client. The two-seater sofa had become a little greasy when Haug had sat on it after working on the Harley one afternoon. So they always offered the client the second good chair. Which Haug sat on in front of his own desk.

Haug read an old newspaper and sipped his tea, thinking. Then he got up, threw down the paper and went back upstairs, carrying his mug with him. Jennifer was in the bathroom and the door was closed. He went to his front room. An article in the newspaper had reminded him that he had a book somewhere on the political situation in South Africa written by a member of the ANC. He had trouble finding the book, though. Nothing was ever where it was supposed to be. It was under a stack of papers, and he moved it to his bedside table in case he had a chance to do some reading. When he took another sip of tea, he realised that it was getting cold so he went back downstairs.

"How come you're in on Saturday?" he asked Lizzy, throwing the rest of the tea in the little basin.

"Couldn't make it yesterday, and I've got to get these begging letters out so that you can pay me."

Lizzy lived alone with her two girls, one of them deaf and dumb. Haug let her choose her own hours so that she could have time for her kids. She had booted her husband out a year ago, saying that he was worthless.

Haug rubbed his unshaven chin. "I reckon it's wise to expect a little trouble before too long. Could be heavy. Won't take a herd o' geniuses to find out who I am and where I stay."

He took out his tobacco pouch, opened it, and bit off a piece of plug.

"You're not going to spit that in the waste-paper bin, are you?" she asked menacingly.

"I'll spit it between your tits if you don't stop givin' me a hard time about it."

"Filthiest man I've ever worked for."

"When have you ever done any work? Wish I could pay you for your looks instead."

"You couldn't afford it, you fat American git."

"It's a mighty big pot callin' a handsome kettle like me black."

"Who's calling you black?" asked a voice behind them. "Somebody running down our race?"

"Took you long enough to get here."

Haug got up and shook One Time's hand. He had never ever been able to hear his friend come up the stairs. One Time was dressed in a black and white tracksuit with a zipper top and all the trendiest European logos etched back and front. New trainers were tied in the latest shoelace craze and on top of his close-cropped head was an rakishly tilted black beret.

"Couldn't you get a crease in those pants?" Haug added.

One Time held up a finger. "Right now."

He tilted the finger towards Haug's secretary. "Lizzy-girl. Save it for me. One time."

He had a big smile on his face.

Lizzy grinned. "You wouldn't be able to handle it, big boy."

"I'll hold her down for you," Haug said to One Time. "That way I can watch."

"Right now," said One Time, going over to the kettle and flipping the switch with a smooth movement. He spun the mug, and sank a tea bag from three feet away.

"Got a house for you," Haug said to his friend. "It's Jennifer's, and I don't want you fingerin' any of her underwear."

"Heyyy!" said One Time. "OK, you got it."

Haug gave him the key and the address on a piece of paper. "Have a good look around before you go in, make sure nobody's eyeballin' the joint. When you get inside, do a careful scan. I expect if anythang's there, it's well hid. Spend some time in the main bedroom – and I reckon I won't have to tell you how to find a bedroom, you dirty bastard. Look for sight as well as sound, you savvy?"

One Time stirred his tea and looked at the sofa with distaste. He sat on the arm.

"I'm tuned in, man. I'm receivin'. Keep tappin'."

"I don't expect any bandits, but I didn't expect any yesterday either. I'll look the other way if you want to tool up. These are heavy dudes so if you meet any of them, don't bother shakin' their hands. Call Keef if you want."

"Keef? Keef? Who's Keef? I don't know any Keef. Right now."

One Time was smiling. One Time and Keef were the best of friends and close competitors, except for women, where One Time was well ahead. He was telling Haug that he could handle it and not to worry. Haug was used to him.

"Did he tell you about last night?"

One Time sucked air through his teeth. "Bad medicine. Wish I'd been there."

He looked up at the ceiling. "OK?"

"Feelin' more'n she's showin'," Haug answered his question about Jennifer. "I'm gonna start pushin' some buttons to see what works, so we need to have a pow-wow over at The Drum tonight. I got an idea that I want to drag around and let you and Keef take bites out of. But gimme a call when you've checked out the house, yea or nay. If you find anythang, don't terminate, just put a ring around 'em."

"You got it."

One Time took another sip of his tea and got up, pointed his finger at Lizzy, his thumb at Haug, and moved across the floor to some internal music that only he could hear. Haug was always amazed how a sixteen stone man could move so smoothly and soundlessly. He was ex-SAS and had been trained in electronic surveillance. His 'ghetto blaster' would be in his car. It was an up-to-date micronic scanner, capable of sweeping all known bugs and viruses. At least all of those known to him. They bred like real bugs these days.

Lizzy watched Haug as he stared out of the window, frowning, slowly tapping the end of a pencil on the desk.

"Don't tell me that you're going to have to do some thinking on this one."

"There's not enough information to think about so far, but I got warnin' signals hummin' on the line from me to Memphis. Now why would a bunch a South Africans – let's forget about the Hebe so we don't complicate thangs – want a tape that mighta dropped outta somebody's pocket in Jennifer's house?"

He looked around at Lizzy.

"I'm just guessin' that that's what happened – that it dropped outta somebody's pocket. Or somebody said that he left it there. Why doesn't he ask for it back? OK, it might have somethin' dirty or otherwise important on it, but so what? I don't get it. Which means that I don't unnerstand it yet. But these guys last night, Lizzy, they were pros. I know when I'm takin' on pros. When they lifted Jennifer in the West End, they knew what they were doin' – had everthang organised down to a 'T'. They only made one mistake. They came back to the house. Hell, I don't even think they were worried about me for one minute. They didn't give a shit if I was still watchin' the place."

"I don't understand anything you said, Haug."

"Yeah. Well, I don't either – yet. Anyway, I got nothin' but hunches and feelin's and guesses at the moment."

Lizzy laughed. "That's about all you ever have to go on. At the best of times."

"Listen, honey, you lookin' at a human computer here. Truth and logic – the two rapier prongs of my boundless intellect."

"Your intellect couldn't bound over that pencil if it was lying flat," Lizzy snorted.

Haug spat into the waste-paper basket.

"I knew you were going to do that!" she shouted. "I have to empty that thing into a bin with my hands!"

Jennifer had just opened the door.

"Oh, I'm sorry," she said.

Lizzy got up with a smile. "It's OK. We go on like this all the time. It's a form of love."

"That's what you call it," Haug said.

"Let me get you a cup of tea," Lizzy said to Jennifer. "I hope you've learned not to listen to anything he says."

"Learnin' to listen is the first step towards wisdom. One of the many steps Lizzy has not yet made in life. Lizzy, Jennifer. Jennifer, Lizzy."

They smiled at each other as Lizzy waited for the water to boil.

"I'd ask you to make yourself comfortable, but Haug's using the good chair and has his feet propped up in the other one. The sofa is too filthy for anybody but an American to sit on."

Jennifer leaned on the desk. She immediately absorbed the warm feeling in the room, the relaxed atmosphere created by people who really liked each other. It was a change. It was nice. She was wearing jeans, sweatshirt and plimsolls.

"I managed to put together one ensemble from the clothes you chose last night. Do you really think I need an evening dress?"

"You never know," Haug replied. "We might go to a barn dance. Besides, it was purty. Love to see it on you sometime."

Lizzy brought her tea. "I didn't put sugar in. From the look of you, you don't use it. I'm only making the tea because Haug's thinking, which is a new experience for him. It's usually *his* job. I'm the one who does the work here."

"You're the one who lowers the cultural tone," Haug grumbled. "Still, that's what you get when you hire Irish help. Anyway, Lizzy baby, are you home to guests for about an hour or so this evening?"

Lizzy looked at Jennifer. "Do you want her to stay with me tonight? It's OK, the kids can double up."

"Naw," Haug said. "I don't want to draw you too far into it. Because of the kids. But it would be nice for Jennifer to have a place to park while I talk to Keef and One Time. You're just across the street from The Drum. Take a buzzer with you. Get any suspicions, hear anythang at all, just buzz and we'll be there."

"No problem," Lizzy said as she switched off the PC and reached for her coat on the back of the chair.

She opened the drawer and fetched out a pager, which she dropped into her pocket. She turned to Jennifer.

"I'll give you a decent meal. You'll get nothing from him but Southern fried chicken."

Jennifer laughed. "I had some – what are they called? – this morning."

"Grits," Haug said helpfully. "She didn't eat but one bite."

"Don't blame her," Lizzy said on the way to the door. "Wouldn't feed them to pigs. And, Haug," she added as she turned, hand on door handle, "empty that bin yourself. Before I come in on Monday."

The door slammed.

Haug smiled, looking at Jennifer. "One hell of a woman. Don't know what I would do without her."

Jennifer shook her head. "When I first came in, I thought you two were having a row."

"Naah, we go on like that. Like she said, it's a form of love."

Jennifer shrugged. "*I* wouldn't know."

"What?"

"What love is, never mind its various forms. For a while, I thought it was like passion, but that passes too quickly, doesn't it?"

"Well, love passes too, I reckon. At least it changes. Like everthang else, it changes. Most folks don't take change into account. They want somethin' permanent, like photographs. But photographs change as well, even photographs of memories."

"I'm treading water, Haug, and I feel like I'm sinking. I didn't like being alone upstairs and came down as soon as I could. I was thinking about last night, yesterday. First time I've let myself. You can't imagine . . . I can't tell you. But, for a woman, rape . . . God, I even hate the word. Rape is one of the worst things that can happen. I find it impossible to tell you, because men think rape is just something to get over, like a fight or a hangover. But it's . . . you see, it's terror, that's what it is. Helpless, powerless – nothing you can do, and you don't know what's going to happen. It's being totally in someone else's power, being invaded." She smacked her hand on the top of the desk. "It's as though everything has been taken away from you – everything – and everything is plundered. I don't even know how I can talk about it. I didn't want to talk about it . . ."

"Come sit in my lap, if you want," Haug said gently.

"No, I don't. I want to talk about it. Do you understand?"

Haug nodded as she went on.

"No, you're very sweet, and I didn't mean to hurt your feelings, but you're doing just what a man does, what he offers— No, no, let me finish. It's something I'm going to have to resolve somehow by myself. Somehow. I mean, no, I want to cuddle you, and last night you saved my life, not just the rescue, but holding me tight in bed and being honest and letting me trust you a little. And I love the feeling here in the office with you and Lizzy. It's a warmth I've never known. And I'm hungry for it but I don't know how to get there. But I want to get there. Because I don't want to live with this kind of poison inside, which is all I can remember, for my whole life. Those men, those pigs, last night, they called me a whore and because I was a whore they thought that they could do what they liked – poke me and pull me and fondle me and fuck me. Well, there's a lot to my story, and I don't think I am a whore. I am trying to manipulate the world a little to *my* advantage, that's all. That's *all*. My father pounced on me first, making his demands, making me feel like shit. When I started developing, I found that I could manipulate *him*. Why the hell not? Why should I feel guilty about that? My mother was dead. I had no other resources. I used them. It's the same today. And now suddenly I find that it's all slipping from my grasp again, with people I don't know raping me and trying to kill me. Is it going to follow me the rest of my life, this chaos? OK, whore maybe. But it's not as dishonest a way to live as some."

"As most," Haug added.

"And then there's you. God knows what I'm feeling about you. Yes, I want to sit in your lap now and have your warm body next to mine just so that I can feel safe for a few minutes. Do you know, Haug, I have not felt safe for one day since my mother died? Not one hour."

She hung her head and spat through her teeth. "I've done my fucking best. I have. I can't do any more."

A silence fell on the room. Haug didn't break it for what seemed a long time.

"That sounds like somethin' you haven't told many people, and I feel honoured for the confidence. I'm not goin' to try and answer any of your questions 'cause I don't feel they were really questions. We're kinda thrown together accidentally on this thang and we're likely to be spendin' a lot of time together. At least until we can get you outta danger. I wish we were spendin' time together by choice instead of by accident, but you can wish in one hand and spit in the other."

She came and sat in Haug's lap and he folded his arms around her. She buried her head in his chest and closed her eyes.

They were upstairs when One Time called later in the afternoon. After lunch Haug had stretched out on the sofa and, wordlessly, Jennifer curled into the nest of his body and had drifted into a light doze when the sound made her jump.

Haug reached out for the phone and picked it up. "Hello?"

"You got eyes and ears. Both. See and hear, man. One Time."

"Thanks," said Haug. "See you tonight."

He hung up and thought for a moment.

"Didn't you say that you were seein' this guy Regis tomorrow?"

He felt her nod.

"Mind if I come? Got somethin' I want to bring up with him."

Chapter Ten

Julian van der Bijl sat in a large comfortable chair looking out of a picture window on to Regent's Park. Piet and Chaim sat opposite Van der Bijl on a matching sofa. Piet was stony-faced, apparently unmarked from the previous night. Chaim wore a protective brace over his nose. Two of his front teeth were missing and his lower lip was cut all the way through. The stitches made the lip puffy. All three injuries combined to disfigure his speech pattern.

Another man sat to one side in an upright chair. He wore a pair of Ray Ban sunglasses on a hard-set face even though it was not a bright day. His hair was wiry, greying at the temples, but close-cropped. His neck was as wide as his head, hinting that the body dressed casually in clean denims was that of an athlete. Or maybe a soldier. In fact Sam Bernstein had been born in New York but from his early teens was raised in Haifa. Then he joined the army, training in the underwater commandos and fighting in two Arab-Israeli wars. He had transferred to Shin Bet and risen to the rank of major before retiring. Or being retired – for his over-enthusiastic pursuit of Arabs in the West Bank. Few knew more about him than those bare details because Sam Bernstein did not talk much about himself.

There was a long unbroken silence in the room. No one seemed prepared to break it. Finally Van der Bijl sighed heavily. He was a tall, trim man who wore spectacles and a business suit. His blond hair was neatly trimmed and combed. He looked very much like a fit accountant. Or possibly a shares trader in the City. His features were fine and he had a long slim nose terminating over stretched, thin lips. Grey eyes peered through the spectacles, unblinking as they looked longingly out at the green of the park.

Van der Bijl sucked a tooth. "I hope I understand this properly. I'm trying to. I want to. Fanie went back to the house and entered without even checking whether or not someone was watching?"

Chaim spoke slowly but couldn't help hissing sibilants. "The Yankee never seemed a problem. Just some big weight shuffler she knew from the gym who was playing the hero to get into her pants. He looks stupid as shit."

Chaim sounded a little like Daffy Duck.

"Well," said Van der Bijl mildly, "he was smart enough to outwit a group comically calling itself the A-team."

"More like out*fight*," said Chaim bitterly. "He is one *hell* of a fighter, and I've seen quite a few. The black too – he was good. But the Yankee took out Piet. We felt this guy was no problem. After all, Piet—"

"In all my life", rumbled Piet, "I have never – ever – lost a fight. Not once. Not even close. Six men, no sweat. Eight men one time. I break dem up – bones, everything. Not once has any man hit me dat hard."

"Took out the doors, everything," Chaim continued with difficulty. "Even brickwork around the garden door. Like a rhino, that man."

Van der Bijl looked unimpressed. "Fanie? Coetzee?"

"Fanie's been knocked around. Busted fingers, broken elbows, busted kneecap, concussion, swollen balls – but not as bad as mine – lost a lot of skin, won't be with us for a while. Coetzee?"

Chaim stopped to lick back the saliva which was trickling around his injured lip.

"Coetzee will live. Nose gone, ear gone, fractured skull, ruptured rectum – hell, that fucker rammed that sjambok up his ass about seven inches! We had to cut it off with a saw to get him in the ambulance! Went into emergency surgery, looked like shit this morning."

Sam Bernstein spoke for the first time. "The mistake was playing with the girl. You played with her, right?"

"She was fucking nice," protested Chaim. "You should have seen her. Gorgeous tits, legs up to here – perfect, like a fucking picture. Only Fanie got a fuck though and Coetzee was fucking around with her when the fucking house exploded."

Bernstein didn't move and his expression did not change. "You should have killed her, found the tape later. I've killed pretty girls before, no problem. If you want to fuck 'em, fuck 'em while they're still warm. But dead."

"There was no problem with time, Sam!" Chaim quacked angrily. "We had the whole fucking weekend to dick the woman. Ahead of schedule, we were. We had the time to fuck her ass off and then kill her. You would have done the same, I don't fucking care what you say now. Man, she walked right off the pages of a fuck book."

"Bullshit," Sam said with contempt and turned away.

"Well," said Van der Bijl, "from ahead of schedule we are now falling behind schedule."

"We got the rest of the weekend," said Chaim defensively.

"So . . . you're just going to go up and grab the rhino's horn again?"

"I'll drill him with a rifle from fifty yards, him and the cunt."

Van der Bijl shook his head and looked at Sam. "Where do you get them?"

Sam shrugged. "He is a good fighter. Not a thinker."

Van der Bijl turned back to Chaim. "The American's name is Joe Wayne Haug – I don't know how you pronounce that, but it sounds Dutch – and he is a small-time private investigator with a small-time office in North London. We don't know who the kaffir is but probably he's some sort of part-time help. Haug works on his own and has a secretary called Lizzy McGuire. He lives in a flat above the office, and that's where they are right now."

"Give me the address," Chaim said. "No problem."

The tall blond man smiled faintly.

"And what will you do? Get a big gun, shoot down two people on the streets? Newspapers, scandal, police, pressure, the Embassy rolls down its shutters, doesn't want to know, the Saudis likewise – the whole deal collapses. What should I then say? That *you* thought of that brilliant plan? No, no, Chaim. We're going to do this properly. Two teams are being called in – one from Brussels, one from Amsterdam. Sam will lead, you two will join as well and this time you will do as you are told. Haug and Montgomery will disappear without a trace, and the ground will be swept over with a clean broom. We will meet tomorrow with the team leaders, so no need for Chaim or Piet. Go heal your wounds. We will move next week."

Chaim and Piet got up – Chaim with difficulty – nodded to both seated men and left. Van der Bijl returned to his appraisal of Regent's Park and did not acknowledge their departure. The silence deepened as neither man spoke or moved.

Finally Van der Bijl asked, "The man watching the detective and girl – he is very good?"

"Oh, yes," Sam said quietly. "He won't be seen. He is already in place. So we will know where they are when we want them."

Harvey Gillmore was entertaining an exotic guest on Sunday morning, a man of whom he had heard but never before met. Professor Alexander Hinkley had just come through his door and was lowering his small frame into the black leather sofa in his office. Gillmore studied him carefully, another habit he had picked up from his father. Every stranger, particularly powerful ones, must be scrutinised for weaknesses. Weak chins, furtive eyes, apologetic body language, evasive speech. Discover the weak point and you have a way in. To disrupt and perhaps control. At the very least you have the advantage.

Well, Professor Alexander Hinkley was something of a surprise in that he seemed to embody all the weaknesses and very few strengths. He was small, no taller than Gillmore, about the same age and his head was a mass of ginger hair which made him look a little like Harpo Marx. He had a receding chin with an ill-grown tuft of goatee making it look worse. His eyes seemed to be colourless, giving you the impression that you were looking directly into the brain. And he *was* supposed to be smart, or so Gillmore had heard. Alexander Hinkley was the guru of the New Right who had alighted at head table in the Adam Smith Institute after creating near riots in the student body at Cambridge.

"Thank you for being able to see me at such short notice," said Hinkley in his squeaky voice.

"Not a problem, mate," replied Gillmore. "Glad to finally meet you. Read your book of course—"

"Which one?"

"Ahh, the one with the funny title. Never mind. Could I offer you some tea or coffee?"

"Tea would be nice."

Hinkley tucked one small leg underneath the knee of the other, which he then swung. He adjusted his polka dot bow tie, then tented his fingers and looked off into the distance profoundly.

Gillmore rang a little hand bell and a moment later Beth entered the room. Her black hair had been pulled on top of her head in a bun and was covered by a little white maid's cap. She was wearing a maid's dress as well, a black one with little white ruffles at the sleeves and hem. It was one of Harvey Gillmore's favourite costumes, which he ordered from a firm in South London. This one was quite short, revealing Beth's stocking tops and a flash of thigh as she walked.

When she reached Gillmore's chair, she curtsied.

"Yes, Mr Gillmore?"

Professor Alexander Hinkley's tented fingers collapsed into disarray, and his small mouth was agape. He no longer looked at all profound.

"A pot of tea. Two cups."

"Yes, Mr Gillmore."

She turned without another word and left the room.

Gillmore let the silence build uncomfortably. He was perfectly relaxed because he knew that he had succeeded in completely unsettling the professor. Thus he held an advantage.

"Ah, yes," Hinkley said finally. "Interesting. Very interesting indeed. Your . . . ah . . . servant."

"Beth. Yes," replied Gillmore. "She is interesting, eh? A concrete example of some of your theories, I guess."

Hinkley was puzzled. "Do you think so?"

"Yeah. Meanwhile, what can I do for you?"

"Well," he said, trying to regain his balance, "I'm intrigued rather about how your maid might illustrate my theories."

Hinkley had heard that Harvey Gillmore was weird, but he had not quite been prepared for events to unfold in just this way.

"Sure, glad to, cobber."

Gillmore was accentuating his Australian origins to contrast with Hinkley's academic prissiness. Of course he had not read any of his books, but he did remember an article or two about him in the *Sunday Sentinel*.

"I recall something about the desensitising of modern employees from their welfare past. Where they are looked after by their unions when in employment and by the government when out of it. Right?"

"Yes, approximately," conceded Hinkley. "I believe you are thinking of The Paradigm of Industrial Value—"

"Yeah, that's it," Gillmore interrupted. "Well, Beth is an employee of mine. Works as a filing clerk, does a bit of typing for one of the newspapers. Quite an advance for her, since she left home at fifteen and wound up marrying a poofter chauffeur of mine."

Hinkley nodded. "I see, but how—"

At that moment Beth re-entered carrying a silver tray with the tea. She put the tray down on the low table between the men, bending her knees. She appeared to be a little embarrassed, as she did not know Gillmore's guest, and turned to go.

"No, Beth, stay," Gillmore said. "We were just talking about you as a good example of Mr Hinkley's Industrial Value whatsit. You can pour the tea in a moment and this time there's no need to bend your knees. I'm sure Mr Hinkley has seen a woman's bottom before."

"Yes, Mr Gillmore."

She stood to one side, wondering what to do with her hands.

Gillmore smiled to himself as Hinkley became more and more confused. Using Beth to unsettle him was an inspiration.

"She was my mistress for a while and I paid for her flat. She owes nothing to the state and less than nothing to any union. Everything she has, she owes to me. Her job, her home, what she eats. And she knows that whatever I give I can take away. This creates fear. And we found out last night that fear is a little like love. It's addictive. Isn't it, Beth?"

"Well . . . yes, I think I see what you mean," stammered Hinkley. "I have mentioned fear as a tool to reshape the attitudes of working people. It is rightly a stimulus, which, when properly applied in a scientific behaviourist context, can encourage not only better performance from a worker, but also loyalty. Yes . . . I suppose that would apply. In a way."

"Pour the tea, Beth," Gillmore instructed.

"Yes, yes, in a way."

Hinkley did not know whether to pretend to avert his eyes or stare as Beth bent over from the waist to pour the tea. For him it was an amazing sight in the midst of what he had presumed was going to be a delicate and confidential chat. He could just see the woman's knickers revealed at the tops of her thighs. He was going to go on but forgot where he was. Instead he began to wonder whether he was in a madhouse.

Gillmore leaned back in his chair, comfortable. "I was having this practical investigation of your theories last night when I discovered something else about fear. There are some who get off on it. Beth finds it sexually arousing. And she also likes a little humiliation. Show the professor how fat you've got, Beth."

For a moment or two Beth hesitated, feeling her face burning with shame. Then she walked over to the funny little man and lifted her dress, letting her stomach droop over the top of her bikini underwear.

"I've put her on a diet today," she heard Gillmore say.

Then she felt the funny little man's clammy hand on her tummy, patting, hesitantly touching.

"Go ahead." Gillmore again. "Have a feel. Hell, she'll give you a fuck for five pounds."

"I say, may I?" The little man asked.

"Go on. Be my guest," Gillmore replied with a grin.

Beth felt the clammy little hand begin to explore, trembling now. It crept down her thigh to her stocking and back again, then furtively, tentatively, between her legs, where it rubbed. She accommodated him by opening her legs a little. She heard Gillmore laugh, the first time she had ever heard that sound.

In fact Beth felt that she couldn't stop now. At some point the night before, she had gone too far and plunged over the edge. At least that is what it felt like. A falling sensation. She was not enjoying it, but that was the whole point, wasn't it? The fear which fuelled the self-hatred which ignited her sexually which surprised her, leading to a new level of self-contempt, and the whole cycle began again with greater intensity. Gillmore had accidentally found a way into her and now would not let her go.

"Well . . . I don't think she's fat at all." The little man again.

He patted her stomach, then the little hand withdrew, so she lowered her dress.

"I say," said Hinkley, "is there a place where I might wash my hands?"

"Show him to the bathroom, Beth." Gillmore's face was radiant.

Beth walked over and held the door for Hinkley, then led him to the main bathroom. Again she opened the door for him, turning on the light.

He was trembling violently when he grabbed her. One of his little hands groped under her dress as the other reached up to mash her right breast. She let the door close behind them and gently pushed the funny man away, trying not to look at the demented eyes in the middle of a back-combed ginger bush. In her heels she was taller then he was.

It was a very large bathroom with a dressing-table in front of a mirror, two hand basins, a toilet, shower and jacuzzi. Beth quickly slipped her knickers off and lay down on the large rug in front of the jacuzzi.

"Quick, quick," the little man was saying as he hopped around like Rumpelstiltskin.

"God, I want you, God, oh, God . . . Jesus, that was so sexy in the office, *you* are so sexy."

He was mumbling and struggling with his zipper and trying to open his Y-fronts, but his hands were trembling too much and he was making a mess of it. Beth sat up and helped him get his penis out. Even with her help it was difficult because he was jumping around, sweating with excitement. She finally got hold of it, easing it from his trousers. Unlike Gillmore, the little man's penis was perfectly in proportion to his body. It looked like a short, pink felt tip pen. She pulled her dress clear of her hips and lay back, opening her legs for him. He was on her like a stoat, and she guided the pink felt tip pen to her vagina. On the third manic plunge he came, and paused on top of her only briefly before springing off. Her eyes were closed, but she heard the tap running in the basin as he washed his 'dirty' hands – and, presumably, the felt tip pen. A moment later he was standing over her. She opened her eyes. He reached into his jacket pocket and extracted a wallet.

"Five pounds, I believe?"

"Yes," she replied, closing her eyes again. "That's right."

She felt the note drop on her bare tummy and left it there. She heard the bathroom door open and whisper closed again. Her hand moved slowly to touch the note, then, against her will it moved further down, just above the place where the little man had marked her with his felt tip. The moment she touched herself, her neck arched and she was aware of the hardness of the tiles under her head. That was fifteen pounds now. Because Gillmore had fucked her again the night before. It was in the bathroom, here. He had told her to clean the floor and dry it off before he had his shower.

She wasn't wearing his little costume. That was laid out, later, for her to wear today. She was still nude except for her stockings, suspenders and shoes, but the stockings were wet and laddered from the floor. Earlier he had told her that he was going to put her on a diet and give her a little exercise. Each humiliation felt like another notch on a ratchet which pulled everything inside her tighter and tighter. At the beginning she could have said no, or maybe even resisted. She could have walked away from the job, the flat and his festering presence, knowing that she would survive one way or another. He was not an emperor or a god with absolute powers over her.

But she discovered that giving way to him once made it easier to give way again. The revelation was that the giving way gave her pleasure. Pleasure? Perhaps not. But it was intense sensation. Her husband, Thomas, was a weak man, and she saw it in many ways as his fault. If he had supported her at the beginning against Gillmore, none of this would have happened. That is all she had wanted Thomas to do. Say something, stand by her, resist. Instead he had let Gillmore find a painful, obscure and vulnerable spot which he twisted and tormented.

She had served Gillmore his salad and Diet Pepsi for dinner, then stood by and watched him eat it in silence, munching on the salad, reading early copies of the *Sunday Sentinel* and *The News*.

The shoes were making her feet swell and she could feel little cramps in her legs. But she said nothing. By now she was terrified to say anything, because she knew that if she complained he would only make things worse. When he had finished his salad, he placed the platter on the floor beside his foot without even taking his eyes from the newspaper. Without a word Beth got down and ate it like a dog, not even using her hands. She took her time because it gave her feet a rest.

As she finished the remains of the salad, she felt his hand grab a handful of her hair. He pulled, not hard, until she sat on her heels, and held her there, staring into her eyes.

"We should have found all this out a long time ago, eh, sheila?" His voice was quiet, almost soothing.

She said nothing in reply, just held his eyes. Her face was wet with salad dressing. Then he told her to scrub the bathroom floor, hands and knees, bucket and brush. He watched her from the doorway as she began, then went away. When he came back, she was nearly finished, having dried off the clean floor with a towel. Her back was to the door when he entered and she continued scrubbing. In a sense she knew what he was going to do a moment before he did it and so was not completely surprised when he used his foot to push over the bucket, flooding the floor with dirty water. She put her head down between her arms and waited.

Yes, she wanted him. The fire which raged in her skull should have been anger. Instead it was sexual, a raging, horrible, unpleasant thirst. Suddenly he was there, forcing his way inside her roughly, stinging and stretching at first. It took longer this time for Gillmore to come. She heard herself crying hoarsely as he forced her hips down so that she was flat on the floor in the muddy water. Her spasms became completely uncontrollable and she was helpless in the throes of the relentless plunge and withdrawal of his penis. She knew that she was screaming and crying, but she had no idea what she was saying or even if it had any meaning. It was like emptying her consciousness, much as she would later that evening empty her stomach by vomiting.

Then it was finished, and she lay heaving on her belly. But she could feel him still there, still standing behind her.

"Roll over," she heard him say simply.

Completely exhausted, she slowly forced herself on to her back. She opened her eyes, aware that wet hair streamed across her face. Gillmore was nude, holding his half flaccid penis with one hand. He kicked her legs open and stepped between them.

Then he began to pee, and she felt the warm splash on her belly and in her crotch.

Lying on the bathroom rug after the little stoat had gone, Beth thought of this moment as she came, her fingers working in furiously increasing tempo.

Meanwhile Professor Alexander Hinkley had recovered a little as he sat and talked to Harvey Gillmore. His host had said nothing to him when he re-entered the office. It was simply a 'He knows', and 'He knows You know He knows' situation. On a Sunday morning in the luxury flat owned by Gillmore on Fleet Street, the fastidious Professor of Philosophy had leapt on the household maid on the bathroom floor as she invited him to have coitus, an invitation he had eagerly accepted. It was totally unlike his usual behaviour. In fact he could think of no time in his life when such a thing had happened. He considered himself a shy, modest intellectual with a keen aesthetic sense, and what he had just done was simply too sordid for him to grasp properly. He was desperately trying to put it to the back of his mind as he led the conversation into the purpose of his visit.

"Mr Gillmore, I believe that you are to some extent aware of our work, the practical aspects as well as some of the theoretical projections. I have no intention of going into them too deeply here—"

"Oh, plunge away, cobber. Plunge away, deep as you like," Gillmore said as he clasped his hands behind his head and stared at the uncomfortable little professor. "I'll stop you if anything's going over my head."

"Well, of course, perhaps you know how Marx said that he was going to stand Hegel on his head. I, in my turn, am endeavouring to stand Marx on *his* head. In other words, turn him upside down. Or, again as he said of Hegel, to put him the right way up. With the emphasis on *right*," he added with a condescending smile. "You see, we have allowed history to be rather helter-skelter, higgledy-piggledy. Events unfold in unpredictable ways, causing much loss of time, money, resources and human effort. We have been looking into ways of controlling our movement forward in time. Controlling it, that is, for the free, democratic, enterprising countries of the world and simultaneously keeping it away from either autocratic or communistic pressures which would undermine the economic thrust that we must make to ensure the smooth progress of mankind. Many take Marx as a fool, but he was not. Not completely. His critique of capitalism was in some ways valid, particularly in relation to the wild fluctuations in the world's economy. In other words, boom times followed by recession or depression. We go forward three steps and fall back two. Why can't we go three steps and stay there? Or at worst, fall back only one step?

"In brief, we are looking at a *planned* economy. Yes, sounds Marxist, doesn't it? But it's not. For untold years separate countries have pursued their interests and clashed with others in pursuit of theirs. We are building up a worldwide cartel of economists, philosophers, industrialists and politicians so that the free, democratic world can pursue its interests as a whole, so that all the member countries can pull in one direction *together*. At the same time we are relentless within our own individual boundaries, re-knitting structures, re-gaining ground lost, re-staffing the civil service and, coming closer to your own speciality, re-forming the media. Notice that I said re-forming, not *reforming*. It must be re-formed into *our* image, the image of a free democracy. Such institutions as the BBC, for instance, have been infested with liberals and left wingers who have no idea of their direction or the consequences of their action as they stir up protest and unhappiness.

"Within the media, you, Mr Gillmore, are one of our true stars. You showed us something we did not know. You took a simple title, an underdeveloped little tabloid newspaper called *The News*, and transformed it into the hammer of history. To me, of course, it may be a tasteless, unpleasant little newspaper. But that is only because you have discovered the true language of the working class. They want diets of sport, sex and gossip to go with their chips and beans. They want small words that they can read. They want a newspaper which reflects their petty prejudices. Marx was totally at sea when he believed that the working class were capable of reflecting on their own condition. Of course they aren't! They are like children and need to be led. And you have provided a universal comic book for their simplicities. An act of genius, Mr Gillmore.

"It is why our group has fallen in behind you in Australia, in the UK, in America, in Europe. Finance has been provided, interest rates have remained low or at least competitive and likely newspapers, radio and television enterprises targeted. We hope that we have been of some small assistance to you."

"Yeah," said Gillmore, "but where does Christ come into this?"

Hinkley was stunned into silence for a moment. "I *beg* your pardon?"

"As you may know, I have been born again, so I'm a little upset at being approached to pander to heretics and savages. Japs, Pakis, Abos, never mind Catholics and countries crawling with Jews. Why should I? Why should I make an effort to print newspapers slanted towards these scum and their scummy religions? I think that we should bravely carry the banner as missionaries to drum some sense into these people. That's what I think."

"Ah, indeed." Hinkley tapped his tented fingers together reflectively. "Of course, I am personally an atheist—"

"A *what*!"

"An unbeliever. Though, I hasten to add, I see the utter usefulness of religion, particularly of Christianity. It gives hope to people who might otherwise be hopeless, and—"

Gillmore was incandescent.

"To my knowledge I have *never* had an atheist in my home! You mean, you deny the sanctity of Christ? You deny the Word of God? Let me tell you, Professor, I am a very religious man. If you weren't who you are, I would kick your arse down five flights of stairs.

That's exactly what philosophy does for you. You juggle words and ideas about until you don't believe in anything. You waste your time reading Hegel and Marx and shit like that when you only need to read one Book. I never thought I would see the day when I had an atheist in my home."

Gillmore turned half around and pointed at the picture of his father. "My father would not believe this. He certainly wouldn't allow it. But I am a lot more understanding than he was. I will just warn you not to take the holy name of God in vain while you are in my home."

"I, ah, have no intention of doing so, Mr Gillmore."

Alexander Hinkley was now convinced that Harvey Gillmore was a madman. He had been enticed into a lunatic asylum, assaulted by a nymphomaniac maid and was now being threatened by a religious fanatic who had a limited grasp of reality.

"If you will please pardon me, I did not intend to bring the subject up. I was really interested in discussing the background to your proposed purchase of the *Johannesburg Star*."

Gillmore reclasped his hands behind his head. "Yeah, well, we'll soon turn it around. Though I am *not* going to have columns by witch doctors or whatnot for the Abo readership—"

"We weren't suggesting that you do—"

Gillmore pointed to a nearly empty bookshelf. "I have books over there that *prove* that the Abo is subhuman."

"Uh, yes, of course." Hinkley was trying to humour his host in an effort to regain the safety of his profundity. "The African situation in general and the South African in particular continue to concern us. It is near the top of our agenda, with the collapse of the communist empire. Certain ideas have spread and are taking hold which are antithetical to us. We must make certain that these are weakened, that our friends are assisted, and that our enemies are undermined. You must be well aware that the arms in the deal we have allowed you to broker are going to friends of ours. Or rather friends of friends. Not to South Africa directly. But through Angola to the homelands." He paused for effect, as he did in the lecture theatre. "Socialism must not be allowed to take root and grow. Not in Africa. Not anywhere. It is nearly eradicated but, like a weed, needs constant control."

"You can count on me, mate, you know that."

"But what I must heavily stress is the need for discretion and security at all times. Our interest group has secured expansion in our own country, linking up with similar groups in many other countries. After all, the world is really just one large economic community now. Whatever you may think of racial issues, we must ensure that our ideas percolate through all layers of humanity. Everywhere. What we must not do is give our game plan away to the opposition.

"By 'opposition' I mean two principal groups. One is the old medieval conservative group who believe in looking after their flocks in various paternalistic ways. The other is the Left, from faint pink to bright red. Whatever you may think, they are not defeated. Not yet. Scattered. Disorganised. Leaderless. That is why we need to build faster and encourage links with friends everywhere. Before they regroup under new leaders, we must have hands joined under the table. We cannot control revolution, therefore we must be willing to fall upon it all together when it arises—"

Gillmore yawned. "Is this going to take *much* longer?"

Hinkley held up a hand. "I'm just coming to the point, Mr Gillmore. We arranged for you to have a secure telephone, because you are in our front lines, one of our key people—"

"I thought it was about that. The tapes."

"In . . . indeed. The tapes. I must warn you never to record or hold recordings of any conversations made on this telephone. Or with any of our personnel. Ever. Make notes, if you will. Then destroy the notes. Our enemies know we exist, but they have no proof that we are actually saturating the infrastructure of the economic and political world. To have such evidence as you hold is a weak link, Mr Gillmore. We trust you, of course. But we are aware that accidents can happen. Like the loss of a tape."

Gillmore got up and stretched. "I'm tired of hearing about that fucking tape. No one will know whose voice it is on the other end. No one can prove anything."

"With the greatest respect, Mr Gillmore, the correspondent on your tape is very upset indeed. His involvement does not have to be proven. Just hinted at. A finger pointed. Then all our years of groundwork go up in smoke."

Gillmore was dismissive. "I told him on the telephone. There is only one place it could be. The only place I stopped on the way home. A friend. I asked her if I left anything there and she said I didn't. Either she's lying or the damn thing is on a garbage dump somewhere. Anyway, it's harmless. We didn't say anything important. I have been trying to see my friend, but she has not returned my calls yet."

"The tape held by Miss Montgomery will be retrieved. But you must destroy all other tapes."

Harvey Gillmore was unaccustomed to being pushed on the defensive. His guest had got his legs back under him. It was time to distract him again. He picked up the little bell and rang it.

Professor Hinkley sprang from his seat.

"Well, I'm just a messenger really, and must be on my way – now that I have passed on the message."

Beth entered and Hinkley swung around to retrieve his coat from the back of the sofa, putting it on hastily.

"So. I must take leave of you and . . . your delightful maid. I will see myself out, thank you very much."

And with three bounds he was out of the door.

Gillmore stared darkly after him, leaning on the back of his chair. Beth stood in the centre of the room, waiting, her feet together, hair and make-up repaired. The atmosphere in the office was leaden but electric.

Harvey Gillmore did not often shout, but suddenly he stood up and shouted.

"You'd think that those people would at least respect private property! My tapes are *my* tapes! You understand? Do you understand?"

Beth curtsied. "Yes, Mr Gillmore."

Chapter Eleven

Michael Regis stood in the middle of Jennifer Montgomery's sitting room looking as though he had been thunderstruck. It was noon on Sunday, and Jennifer sat in her favourite wing armchair wearing jeans and the blue jumper. She had just narrated the events of Friday to her mentor, and he seemed to be completely at a loss for words.

When he had arrived that morning, she opened the door and it was as though she had been transported backwards in time. Michael Regis was as good-looking a man as she had known. The olive skin, thick black hair, deep and dark eyes, firm chin with a faint cleft, beautiful teeth. He always appeared to know everything and everybody and be completely at ease with any company. She felt a little surge of emotion as he entered and recognised the smell of his expensive aftershave lotion. She realised that she was glad to see him and felt reassured when he gave her a warm hug and kiss on the cheek. He had listened to her story without interruption, as if rooted to the spot.

"If true, this is an outrage," he said finally.

"It's true," she replied simply.

"I will leave no stone unturned until these men are hunted down and brought to justice. If you will allow me to use your telephone, I will call the head of Special Branch. I'm sure that they will want to interview you and take down details of this atrocity—"

"Michael. Please, no, not at the moment. I don't want the police brought in just yet."

"The police are the proper authorities to deal with the matter," he said. "You can't go around using some private detective when firearms are involved. And kidnap, rape, assault, false imprisonment—"

Jennifer held up her hand. "I don't want them involved just yet because I do not understand what is going on and because of . . . what I do."

"I assure you, Gordon will be extremely discreet."

"No. Not yet."

Regis moved smoothly to her chair. He took her hand.

"Jennifer, now that you've told me this awful tale, I have no alternative but to turn the matter over to the police. It is my duty, and in my position it would be impossible to suppress this information. Do you understand?"

"I think I unnerstand, Mr Regis," said a voice behind him.

Michael Regis turned around to face Haug, who stood in the doorway. Jennifer had asked him to give her thirty minutes with Regis, but this seemed a good note for an entrance. He had been waiting in the front bedroom but had easily overheard the voices.

"And you must be the American private investigator. Well," Regis said, turning to Jennifer, "I was not aware that you were here."

He turned back. "But I am glad you are. In the first instance, I would like to thank you, with heartfelt gratitude, for rescuing Jennifer, who is very, very dear to me. In the second instance, it will be helpful if you could give a statement to the police at the same time."

Haug leaned on the doorway and folded his arms. "I got a real strong feelin' that you won't be callin' the police or anybody else, Mr Regis, on account of the fact that they don't usually look kindly on pimps."

Jennifer was alarmed. "Haug, please."

Michael Regis did not even blink. "As much as I feel that I owe you for your assistance of Jennifer, I do take deep offence at your words, Mr Haug. And I insist that you withdraw them immediately."

Haug looked at him levelly. "Or *what*? Don't tell me you're gonna demand satisfaction?"

Regis lowered his voice. "Or you will regret it. Deeply."

"Aw, shit. I was lookin' forward to you slappin' me across the face with your glove."

"I can do better than that," Regis said, his face pale.

He took two quick steps across the room and swung a backhand at Haug's face. Haug caught Regis's wrist with his left hand and held it. The Englishman was surprisingly strong and nearly pulled his hand clear until Haug doubled the pressure. He could see the pain in the man's eyes.

"Well, you got guts, bo, I'll say that, but if you don't behave yourself until I finish talkin' to you, I'm gonna hit you so hard that your teeth'll march out your ass like little white soldiers."

Jennifer was on her feet. "Haug, what on earth are you doing? Let him go."

"And I advise you to listen to her," Regis said through his teeth.

"Now, let's get this the right way around," said Haug. "*She's* the one who's gonna listen to *you*, because you're the one who's gonna be doin' the explainin', asshole."

Haug backed Regis over to the sofa and pushed. The Englishman sat down heavily, resisting the urge to rub some blood back into his right hand.

Jennifer was looking at Haug, surprise slowly turning to anger.

"What's the matter with you? Why are you doing this? Michael has nothing to do with what happened."

"Maybe, maybe not," Haug replied. "But he's got somethin' to do with this."

He pulled a hooded torch from his pocket and flicked on the ultraviolet light. With it he scanned the wall until he came to a circle, invisible without the torchlight. It had been drawn by One Time on his visit the previous afternoon. He turned to Regis.

"Mind tellin' her what that is?"

Regis stared. "It's a circle drawn on the wall."

"Very good for the well-educated Limey. Now tell her why the circle is there."

Regis got to his feet, and Haug pushed him back down.

Regis pursed his lips angrily. "Even if I knew the answer – which I don't – I would refuse to reply to your questions under threats and intimidation. I have already warned you, Mr Haug. You are going to regret this deeply."

"Important feller, are you? Well, I thought I would dig away at that high-class varnish of yours and show Jennifer a little bit of the more profound, subliminal Michael Regis."

He pulled a pocket knife from his jeans and walked over to the wall. The circle was just above head height, and he began scratching with the blade of the knife. There was only a thin skin of plaster over the head of what looked a little like a large nail.

"Look familiar to you, Mr Regis?" he said over his shoulder as he dug the blade under the head of the nail and began levering it out.

Then he grasped it with his fingers and gave a tug. He took the nail over to the man on the sofa.

"Want a closer look, Mr Regis?"

158

Jennifer got up and came closer. "It looks like a nail. Just a nail."

"Yes, 'looks like'," said Haug. "But it's *not* a nail, is it Mr Regis?"

He turned to Jennifer, showing her the miniature transmitter. "It is designed to look like a nail so that folks like you won't know that it's really a microphone. A little bug. So that conversations in this room can be picked up and recorded, if necessary."

Regis appeared genuinely amazed. "Are you sure? A little thing like that?"

"Oh, there's more, and better, Mr Regis, as you well know."

Haug reached over and grabbed Regis by the coat and pulled him to his feet.

"I'm not used to being treated in this way!" shouted Regis.

Haug pulled him out of the sitting room. "Oh, it's somethin' that you can get the hang of, like most thangs. Millions of folks get treated like this all the time, and they get used to it. You've probably treated people like this yourself, and they never complain. It's 'cause they've got the hang of it."

They were at the foot of the stairs, and Haug turned to face Regis. "Now you can walk up there to Jennifer's bedroom or I can drag you. Your choice, bo."

Jennifer was following silently. Her face was white with fear and anger.

Regis pulled away from Haug and smoothed his coat, which had been torn. With as much dignity as he could manage, he walked up the stairs.

The telephone was still lying against the wall and the bedside table was smashed, but it was a nice room. Large, painted magnolia white, it contained a queen-sized divan bed, a dressing-table with large mirror, a hand wash basin, a large chest of drawers and one remaining bedside table. The curtains were still drawn, and Haug went to the double window and drew them back.

"Sorry about the mess", he said, "but this is where we caught First Voice."

He threw the pillow back on the bed and took out his torch, playing the beam on the walls and ceiling. The window had let in a lot of light, so he half closed the curtains before trying again.

"Now there's two of everthang in this room, this bein' a real important room where private thangs might take place. We got two cameras. One above the bed, which is disguised by the plaster mouldings surroundin' the light fixture, and we got another one high on the wall, again hidden in the hand-painted moulding pattern. These days you don't need much of an aperture, isn't that right, Mr Regis? If you got two films, you could even do some fancy editin', I think. But I don't know much about that end of it."

He continued to play the torch over the walls. "And we got another two mikes, one the same as this one here, the other a little more sophisticated, like a radio mike, probably in stereo."

Haug switched off the torch. "You got one more camera in the bathroom so you can watch everbody takin' a shit and a shower. There is one camera in the front bedroom and one mike. And there is a camera in the small third bedroom. Plus a mike. All the other rooms just have mikes, like the sitting room. So," he continued, turning to Jennifer, "you been on film for quite a while. If I were you, I'd get my agent to look into the contract here with a view to renegotiatin' your percentage. Oh, yeah. There's also a state-of-the-art recordin' machine disguised as an electrical transformer underneath the stairs. Which is where the video and audio have to be picked up and changed from time to time."

Haug stopped for a minute and put his hands in his pockets. Jennifer had her arms crossed over her chest and was looking at the floor. She was breathing heavily. Regis stood rigidly in the centre of the room, returning Haug's gaze without emotion.

"I hope you are not implying that I have anything at all to do with this," Regis said finally.

"Naw, I'm not implyin' such a thang, Mr Regis. I'm not the type to imply. I'm standin' here and outright accusin' you of buggin' this house, invadin' the privacy of my client and holdin' on to her property, namely the collection of what I would imagine are some pretty dirty tapes."

Regis turned to Jennifer. "I sincerely hope that you do not believe I could do such a thing. You have my word that I had nothing to do with it. I am as shocked as you are. I will deal with this animal here and his profane accusations in very short course. I will also find out who is responsible for this—"

Haug held up his hand. "Now, Mr Regis, I don't want you to go
to all that trouble of runnin' all over London to find somebody to
smear this shit on. I know you hired the builders who did this work,
and I also know somethin' about this firm of builders. They are
special. You don't get these builders unless you got pull. They don't
do a lot of ordinary work. They are special hi-tech builders for
special hi-tech jobs. They are known in my business. And they are
very expensive. Though," he added, looking around the bedroom, "I
think you can say you got your money's worth here. You hired 'em,
all right. The same man who checked out these bugs was in the army
with one of these builders. You even instructed them where to put the
tape machines, didn't you?"

Haug waited briefly for an answer, then went on. "And who else
but you would collect the little tapes from that thang hangin' on the
wall under the stairs? Regular visitor here, weren't you?"

Michael Regis looked relaxed and shot his cuffs. "I don't have to
answer any of your questions. I'm sure that Jennifer knows me well
enough to realise that your accusations are as wild as your
imagination. This will not be the end of the matter—"

Haug exploded. In one step he reached Regis and grabbed him by
the throat, propelling him across the room into the wall. He held him
there while he watched Regis's eyes drain of anger, to be replaced by
terror and pain.

"You bet your ass it's not the end of the matter, bo! You are a
pimp, a pornographer, a blackmailer an' a thief. Your friends in the
police may not put you in jail for all that, but you lissen to this: you
got exactly seven days to get every one of those tapes together and get
'em back to Jennifer, and she is gonna watch you burn 'em. If those
tapes ain't here in seven days, I'm gonna come lookin' for you. And I
don't care if you are up to your ass in bodyguards and cops – I'm
gonna find you and break every fuckin' bone in your body, you
scumbag. Now get your filthy, stinkin' ass outta here."

Haug pulled Regis off the wall and pushed him through the
doorway. As Regis staggered towards the stairs, he gave him a kick
which lifted him six inches off the floor. Regis landed on the stairs
and started to tumble.

Jennifer Montgomery was standing exactly where she had been
before, her arms folded, and she was still staring at the floor. Haug
sat on the edge of the bed, trying to control his anger.

"Are you sure it was him?" said the voice behind him. It was a flat voice, drained of emotion.

"There's only one candidate, Jennifer. Who else could it be? Who hired the builders? Who is a regular visitor? Who else has a key? Whose interest is served by the tapes? I suspect that Regis is not the only one, though. I'd guess that he's some sort of managin' director. This thing is beginnin' to look awfully complicated." He smacked his fist on the palm of his hand. "And I gotta watch my goddam' temper. I didn't mean to rough him up that much, but somebody who'd do somethin' like this to a nice person like you, well, that just burns me up. I mean, jerks like that will just use anybody to get what they want. They don't give a shit."

Haug got up, and Jennifer could see that his face was flushed with anger. His eyes flashed dangerously.

"They used me for a while once, so I know a little how you feel. Makes me want to throw up. It's not the cream that floats to the top. It's the fuckin' garbage."

Jennifer Montgomery had not spoken, but she was not looking at the floor any more. She was looking at him.

He stared at her. "And now I want to apologise for not tellin' you that I knew about this shit yesterday. One Time is an expert, and I gave him your key to check it over. I thought it was better to show you this way."

She looked up at the ceiling where he had pointed out the camera.

"In a way it's worse than the rape. It's my privacy. It's my life. It's just worthless, isn't it? Something to be used by other people. Like me. Like my cunt. At least I thought the *house* was mine. It really wasn't a big thing fucking those men. The money was good. I didn't have to live on the streets."

Haug stuffed his hands back into his pockets. "How much did you get? Fifteen hundred a trick? Well, that sounds like a shit pot of money to me. But one thang you can bet your hat and ass and three cords o' wood on, and that's the fact that Regis is gettin' at least ten times that amount in return. Maybe not in money, but in thangs he wants. You unnerstand?"

She sat on the edge of the bed.

"Oh, I understand all right, Haug. I am an expert at being used. Maybe I'm not your classic victim, because I fight back, I try to move my own goal posts. But I find myself outclassed sometimes. Outclassed and outplayed."

"Well," Haug growled, "now you brought the subject up, I better tell you that I'm probably outclassed as well. That asshole's right. He can probably generate some deep doo-doo, and I'm expectin' to be up to my nose in it pretty soon. I just wanna tell you the truth – that I'm probably not the best private eye in the world. Or in London, or even in North London for that matter. I don't think like Sherlock Holmes or Poirot or any of those dudes. This isn't outta modesty. But I'm concerned for your welfare, here. You got the dough to buy a lot better'n me. I expect that thangs are gonna get pretty rough from here on out. I hope I can pull you through, but I cain't promise. The only thang I can promise is that I will do my best. But I thought I'd tell you now. You just might need somebody with a little more class."

Jennifer laughed a funny little laugh and got up. "Oh, Haug, you make me want to cry sometimes."

She came over to him and looked into his face, started to say something, then just threw her arms around him and hugged him as hard as she could. She leaned back and put her arms around his neck.

"You're all I've got at the moment. And I wouldn't trade you for all the private detectives in the world. Unless I am completely mad, you are honest and you are good. There is just something honest and good about you, and I've never met anyone like that in my life." She shook her head. "And all you can do is just stand there with your hands in your pockets."

Haug removed his hands from his pockets and put his arms around her.

"I'm gonna kiss you once, Jennifer – goddam' it, why don't you let me call you Jenny? – and I know it's gonna be the fuckin' wrong thang to do."

As they kissed, Haug knew even more strongly how wrong it was, at least for this time and this place. But her lips were soft and the smell of her skin made his thoughts float like clouds. Her mouth opened and he tasted her tongue and underneath it. Moving his hands down her back was like following an electrical current, and he wanted her more than he could remember wanting anything or anybody. When she moved her hips against his, he realised that he was growing rampant, both sexually and emotionally. So he pulled away and looked into her face.

"Well, kiss my ass and call me Charlie. What're you tryin' to do? Make all the hair grow back on my head?"

"As I said, I like you just as you are."

"Then you better stop doin' what you're doin'. We both better stop. This is not the time or the place."

"Why not?"

"Because if you're gonna stick with me, then my advice is that we gotta get a move on. We got this Regis guy stirred up, and there's one more thang I wanna do. Once we knock over that hornet's nest, we can go rest for a while. And then if we haven't got good sense, we can try this again."

She pulled away and straightened her jumper. "Right, Sergeant Major. If you can wait, I can. So what do we do now?"

"Gillmore."

"Ugh. Well, that is a brutal way to suppress one's sexual appetite. Think of him."

"Where can we find him?"

Jennifer thought for a moment.

He's probably at his home in the country. Or out of the country. No, there were several messages from him on the answerphone. He also has an office in Fleet Street, a flash apartment."

"Let's try it."

"I've got the address somewhere downstairs. He tried to get me to visit there."

There was not much traffic as they drove to the City, and Haug didn't say much. Something was worrying him and he kept checking the rear-view mirror of the pickup. He could swear that he was being followed but, if true, it was a very professional job with at least two cars being used. Police?

He had felt as though he were being followed last night too, when he met Keef and One Time at the pub. But whoever was following would not risk coming into the pub. It was a very local local. Everyone knew everyone else – mostly Irish labourers and nearby residents. Keef and One Time had taken the precaution of coming separately at different times, and they had left the same way. Even if he wasn't being followed, he had to assume that he was. Just as he

164

always assumed that his telephone was being tapped. Safest in the long run. In the pub Haug had presented his plan. Such as it was. The important thing, though, was to try and keep one step ahead of whatever was unfolding and to pick a playing field that was a little more level. He pulled the pickup into the underground car park. A man was washing a Rolls-Royce. The number plate read AUS 1.

"I think we might be in luck," said Haug.

"Yes," she confirmed. "That's his car, and I think that's his driver."

Haug pulled into an empty space and got out of the pickup. He walked over to the chauffeur, who had stopped washing the Rolls and was watching him. Haug took a folded twenty-pound note from his shirt pocket, holding it between his second and third fingers.

"We want to speak to your boss for a couple of minutes."

Thomas Howell looked at the note then back to Haug. "Does he know you?"

Haug nodded to Jennifer in the cab of the pickup. "He knows her. I cain't say he's gonna be one hunnerd per cent delighted to see me, but you never know."

Thomas Howell thought for a moment. The big man with an American accent looked hard. He thought that he recognised the girl in the truck, a truly beautiful lady whom Gillmore visited at times. His guess was that she worked as a high-class prostitute. He sensed that the combination spelt some trouble for Gillmore. Ignoring the twenty-pound note, he picked up the bucket and chamois leather.

"I wasn't out here when you arrived," he said simply. "And you found the bell over there. There's a video camera, so perhaps the lady could show herself while you stand to one side. The lift is the only way up."

He turned and walked back to the entrance leading to his room, hoping that the American was some kind of hit man from New York.

Haug put the note back into his pocket, where he kept it for petty bribes, and walked back to the pickup.

"Must be the kinda man who inspires loyalty in his staff," he said to Jennifer as he opened the door for her.

Gillmore was very surprised to see Jennifer Montgomery on the screen. His guess was that Michael Regis had given her a good talking to. It could be an interesting afternoon. Two women together. Unlimited possibilities. Though he had intended getting through a backlog of urgent chores this afternoon, it was impossible to swim upstream against fate. On impulse, he told Beth to answer the doorbell and show the visitor through. He settled himself behind his desk and waited.

When Beth opened the office door, she was followed into the room by Jennifer and a rough-looking man he had never seen before. He levelled his most malevolent stare at the stranger, not blinking his eyes, not moving a muscle.

Jennifer spoke first. "I apologise, Mr Gillmore, for this unannounced visit on a Sunday afternoon, but I would like to assure you that it's an emergency."

She noticed the direction of Gillmore's gaze. "This is a close friend of mine, Mr Haug. He is helping me to find out why someone is trying to kill me."

Gillmore continued to stare without answering.

"I said, someone tried to kill me. It has something to do with a tape, a missing tape. I wanted to ask you if you knew anything about this."

Haug was returning Gillmore's stare and he waited a beat before speaking. "The lady just asked you a question. Are you gonna have the decency to answer?"

Gillmore's quiet voice was charged with venom. "I did not invite you here and I want you to leave. She can stay."

"Well," Haug replied, "you didn't invite me, but I'm here, and that's a fact. The quicker you answer the question, the quicker I get outta here. Place gives me the fuckin' creeps anyway."

"Do you realise who you are talking to?"

"I'm afraid I do. And I tell you honestly, Mr Gillmore, I'd rather be suckin' shit outta a boar's ass any day."

Gillmore ignored the comment. "If you know who I am, you must know what I can do to you if you don't immediately vacate the premises."

Haug walked easily over to the desk, planted both hands on it and leaned close to Gillmore, who did not move.

"Now, lissen, bo. That is the second time today some asshole dressed in fancy clothes has threatened me."

He stopped Gillmore from speaking with a raised hand.

"Lemme tell you somethin'. We can do this two ways. The easy way or the hard way. You might not like the easy way, but, I can tell you with a lot of confidence, you're gonna hate the hard way."

Gillmore spaced out his words. "Get your hands off my desk."

Haug grabbed the back of Gillmore's head and banged his face on the desk.

"Why don't folks lissen to me? Why do they make me do this?"

Gillmore was squirming, but Haug had a good grip of his hair. Blood began to trickle from his nose.

"That was just to get your attention, bo. Now answer the lady's question."

Gillmore was mumbling, his eyes closed in pain, hands flailing. When he opened his eyes and wiped his nose, he realised that he was bleeding.

"Oh, my God, it's blood!"

He reached for his bell and rang it as hard as he could.

When Beth came running in, Gillmore flailed at her. "Get me a towel! And some water! This bastard has just broken my nose!"

She turned immediately and ran out of the room.

"Let go of my head!"

Haug released his grip and put his forefinger in Gillmore's face.

"I'm gonna do it hard next time. I'm gonna push your face into that desk and juice it like a grapefruit."

Beth came back with a towel in a basin of water. Going behind the desk, she squeezed out the towel and dabbed at the blood on Gillmore's face.

Gillmore grabbed the towel out of her hands.

"It's hot, you stupid cow!"

He flung the towel at her face.

"Cold water, I want cold water!"

Flushed with anger, Haug grabbed his shirt front, pulling him half out of his chair.

"That's a human being you're talkin' to, not a fuckin' dog!"

"It's all right," said Beth. "Please let him go. Don't hurt him anymore. It was my fault." She looked at him imploringly. "Please. Don't hurt him. I'll be right back, Mr Gillmore."

Haug shoved the Australian back in his chair, a look of disgust on his face.

"For you, miss, I promise to leave him alone till you get back."

Gillmore was dabbing at his nose with a pocket handkerchief. He was rattled and couldn't collect his thoughts. But anger was boiling inside him in dark swirling red mists. He realised that he was grinding his teeth.

"Who did you say you were?"

"Haug. Call me Haug."

He drew over a notepad and reached for his pen. "Spell it."

"H-A-U-G."

Gillmore finished writing and looked up as Beth returned with a fresh basin of water.

"I'm going to look you up, Haug, and I'm going to spend some pleasurable time breaking you."

Beth was cleaning his face with the towel.

"I broke her. Didn't I, Beth?"

"Yes, Mr Gillmore."

"And you're wrong, Haug. She's not a human being. She's a dog."

He grabbed the towel and threw it across the room. "Fetch, Beth."

He turned back to Haug. "She's the wife of my chauffeur, Haug. While he's downstairs cleaning my car, I fuck her. Isn't that right, Beth?"

"Yes, Mr Gillmore."

She returned with the towel and rinsed it in the basin.

Gillmore leaned over and raised the hem of Beth's dress. "That's my pussy, there. For as long as I want it—"

"I can't take much more of this, Haug," said Jennifer. Her voice was hard, angry. "Let's go, let's get out of here."

"I gotta admit, Gillmore, that you just left me speechless for the first time I can remember."

Haug shook his head. "I'm just tryin' to control myself so I don't reach over there and yank your dick off, just to make sure that you don't have any children."

"Leave him, Haug," Jennifer said again. "I've got to go before I throw up."

"OK, asshole, a question. And you remember what happens when you don't answer. A tape. Do you know somethin' about a tape?"

Gillmore thought for a moment. "Ask her. Ask your whore."

With one swift movement Haug grabbed Gillmore, lifted him from his chair and dragged him across the desk.

"Lissen, cocksucker, that is *Miss Montgomery*. Would you like to rephrase your question quick before you lose your teeth?"

Beth was tugging desperately at Gillmore. "Please, Mr Haug, don't hit him . . ."

The words came from Gillmore in a whisper.

"Louder!" Haug snarled.

"Ask Miss Montgomery . . ."

"Thank you." Haug slung him back into his chair.

"Now, to answer your question, I have already asked Miss Montgomery and she tells me that you might think you left a tape there. Is that right?"

"I didn't go anywhere else," Gillmore muttered. "Just her place. For a fuck," he added with malice.

Haug was trying desperately to control his anger. "What was on the fuckin' tape?"

"Ask her!"

"*I'm asking you!*"

"A fucking telephone conversation," shouted Gillmore, losing control. "A fucking *private* telephone conversation!"

"With who?" Haug smacked the desk with the flat of his hand. "No, with *whom*. Ever time I get mad, my fuckin' grammar goes! With *whom*? Who with?"

Gillmore leaned over the desk like a black rat. "None of your fucking business!"

Haug grabbed his head and smacked his face down on the desk again.

"I'm makin' it my fuckin' business!"

Beth rushed around the front of the desk and pushed at Haug, who was purpling with rage, as Gillmore wailed and reached for the towel again.

"I'm begging you not to hurt him any more."

But Haug was transfixed by Gillmore and seemed about to launch himself across the desk. The tendons on his neck stood out like anchor ropes.

Beth went down on her knees. "Please. Please."

With the greatest difficulty, Haug tore his murderous gaze from the bloody face of Gillmore and looked down. Then, with a rush, everything seemed to fall away from him – his anger, his resolve, his will.

"Haug." It was Jennifer. Her voice was firm.

He leaned over and gently lifted Beth to her feet, noticing that she had on very high-heeled shoes with straps around the ankles. And, just as gently, he wiped the tears from her cheeks with the back of his hand.

"I sincerely wish that I could do somethin' for you, lady. But I cain't. The best thang for mankind would be to sling that worthless piece of shit outta the winder. But if you don't want me to, I won't do it."

He turned and put his arm around Jennifer, and they moved towards the door. He felt utterly defeated.

"I will find you and crush you, Haug!" Gillmore howled as they closed the door to his office.

They said nothing in the lift on the way down to the car park. When they got out at the bottom, Haug spat and leaned up against one of the columns.

The chauffeur was just finishing off the Rolls with a chamois leather.

"I don't think I can remember meetin' a man without a single redeemin' feature. That feller is evil from one end to the other. Australian, my ass. He came flappin' straight outta Transylvania."

"Honestly, Haug," Jennifer said as she leaned against him, "I feel physically ill."

"I cain't even think of how to get rid of the varmint without pollutin' the earth."

The chauffeur turned to them with a friendly smile. "I gather you've just met Mr Gillmore."

Haug walked over to Thomas Howell.

"Feller, I got a whole lot of sympathy for you. If that's your wife up there—"

"She's not my wife any longer. She was once. I can't stop her from doing what she wants."

Haug rather liked the chauffeur. "Do you mind me askin' a question? How can you stand to work for a man like that?"

Howell folded the chamois carefully. "I'll work for him until I find a way to get even."

"Well," said Haug, "good luck to you."

He turned back to Jennifer, who was standing by the pickup.

"At least we know the tape came from him," he said to her as he walked back. "Now we need to find the other party. Somehow."

"*I* have a tape," the chauffeur said behind him.

Haug stopped in his tracks and turned. "What kinda tape?"

"Found it on the floor in the back of the car."

"Was it after a visit to this lady here?" Haug asked.

"Yes," Howell replied. "I kept it. I dreamed that somehow it would help me get even. But there's not much on it."

Haug got out a pen and a piece of scrap paper, then scratched out an address leaning against a concrete column. He folded the paper and crossed to the chauffeur.

"This here's my box number at a post office in the West End. If you make a copy of that tape and send it there, I promise I'll do my goddamnedest to screw that son of a bitch right into the ground and then piss in the hole. I'm the only one who knows that address, so best memorise it and burn the paper. If that's the right tape, someone's already tried to kill this lady over it. So play safe and be careful, OK?"

Howell nodded and put the paper in his pocket. "Will it do a lot of harm?"

Haug shrugged. "I'm beginnin' to think that it might well."

"Then I'll send you a copy."

The chauffeur turned away, collecting the bucket and brushes. He did not look back as he went into the building.

Haug checked the car park before getting into the pickup. There was only one other car besides the Rolls and it had been there when he pulled in. He opened the door and climbed in beside Jennifer.

"What do you think?" she asked.

"Keep your fingers crossed. We need a break," he said, as he put the key in the ignition and started the engine.

Chapter Twelve

The pickup had left the M3 and was on the A303 moving past Salisbury Plain. They had left London early on Monday morning to avoid rush hour traffic.

The night before, Haug had been busy loading the pickup at the garage, carefully choosing things he might need for the journey. The garage was a large one situated in a mews off Regent's Park Road and cost Haug an arm and a leg in rental. But it had electricity and plenty of room.

The Triumph sat next to the Harley Davidson Electroglide. Both machines were chained through the frames to the concrete floor, and a locked cable connected one bike to the other. Motorcycles were easy to steal, and those two machines would be worth the effort for any burglar – particularly the Harley. Spares for Harleys were so expensive that the bikes were stolen and broken up to sell in bits. Thousands could be made on one bike alone. A worktable was fitted to the opposite wall holding the vice, lathe and drill press. Haug was not a first-class mechanic but he enjoyed tinkering with the machines and doing minor repairs.

At the back of the garage was a little camp bed he used occasionally. He had moved this here, together with the old rug underneath it. It had taken him a long time and great deal of effort to carve a hole in the back floor of the garage. The top to the hole was a piece of galvanised steel with a skin of concrete on the top. When it was fitted, you would certainly have to know what you were looking for to realise that there was a hole there.

He screwed a purpose-made L-bolt into a small opening normally covered by a shelving leg and lifted. The hole was lined with galvanised steel, like the lid, and was in fact a hidden safe. In there Haug kept things that he definitely did not want others to have, and from the safe he removed a wooden case which he placed under the seat of the cab in the pickup. Then he emptied a carpenter's locker of tools and filled it with various items he thought might be useful.

After locking the garage, he picked up Jennifer from Lizzy's house, but not before he was made to sit down and have a huge platter of fried chicken, roast potatoes and spinach, followed by a large glass of Jameson. Haug was pleased to see Jennifer laugh, and she seemed to enjoy the evening as Haug and Lizzy cut and thrust in mock verbal battle. They left later than he had planned and returned to his flat, where she again fell asleep in his arms.

"Are you going to tell me where we're going now?" Jennifer asked, breaking his reverie.

"A little holiday, like I said."

"Yes, a holiday. Good. In the West Country? A good guess? Devon? Cornwall? Getting close?"

"Well," said Haug, "it was gonna be a surprise, but you keep pickin' at it ever ten minutes, so I better let you in on the secret. You see, my Dad died a few years back and left me a few dollars. He had a decent job, not like me. What I did was, I bought this pickup truck, the Harley and this place we're goin' to. Paid cash for all of 'em on account of the fact that I hate mortgages and monthly payments. Took me a goddam' long time to find the place, 'cause I already knew what it looked like. Had a picture in my head. First off I tried the coasts of Suffolk and Norfolk. Nope. Not a thang. So I went south, startin' in Brighton and movin' west. Thought I was gonna run outta land before I found the place I was lookin' for. It's an old fishermen's place – not really a house. Where they used to bunk down, and they probably used the other rooms to dry or smoke fish, I dunno. But the thang's got two foot stone walls, is a crab apple's throw from the water, two up, two down, and you can only get there with a lot a difficulty. That house is a tale in itself, I tell you."

"Sounds isolated," she commented.

"'Bout as isolated as you can get and still be in England. A real hard place to find."

"Well, sounds just what I need, but is this the time to go for a holiday?"

"Perfect time. Spring of the year. Sun's startin' to shine, bees are hummin', women gettin' their short skirts out, fish are bitin' – hell, you couldn't pick a better time."

"Don't be difficult, Haug. You know what I mean."

"Thangs are afoot, Miz Watson, don't you worry. For instance, I finally got this guy spotted. First time since Friday night. Which means he is real good."

"What guy?"

"This one's been follerin' us around everwhere. Now what I'm gonna do is get rid of this son of a bitch, 'cause I don't want him on our holiday. He just doesn't fit into my plans."

"Someone has been following us?" she asked, starting to turn to look.

"Don't turn around, sweet thang. Don't you ever go to the movies? You gotta pretend that we haven't seen him. On the other hand he's laid so far back that it won't make the slightest little bit of difference. Now there should be some roadworks up here where they're carvin' another highway they don't need through some very nice landscape. We've just passed Stonehenge. Shouldn't be far."

"Are you sure you can lose him?"

Haug patted the steering wheel. "This here's my Batmobile. It cost me near about as much as that damn house. To start off with, I got a 454 cubic inch V-8 engine underneath the hood—"

"I don't know what that means."

"Well, it's a little over seven litres, nearly seven and a half. But that's not all. I ordered the engine, had it taken out and sent to one Mr R.C. Childress and his associates. Now Mr Childress and his associates tune engines for stock car racin'. The whole thang was taken apart, balanced and blueprinted. It's got tuned port fuel injection—"

She stopped him. "Haug, this is macho boy talk and I don't understand it."

"Sorry, I was gettin' carried away there. I don't know if horsepower means anythang to you, but this baby has been tested out at just over seven hundred brake."

"Is that a lot? Sounds like it."

He pointed to the car in front. "One of those little English cars has about a hundred. It will *haul ass*. Cost me a fortune, but it's somethin' I've always wanted to do, ever since I was a kid. Most men are still kids, you see, never do grow up."

She smiled. "I'm glad to see you're man enough to admit it."

"Anyway. I'm just tellin' you all this 'cause when I take off in a few minutes, I want you to hang on to your virginity. This guy behind me is in for a big surprise. He's so confident, you see, that he didn't even bother to fit a homin' device to my pickup. Checked for that this mornin'. Anyway, we might be off on some back roads for a while or even be goin' through a few cornfields. Cross your fingers that we don't run into any law. He's drivin' one of those BMW thangs, but I'm gonna show him the American Law of Cubic Inches."

They were just entering a stretch of dual carriageway, and Haug was glad to see that traffic was light. The roadworks were about five miles away and he waited until the fast lane was relatively free. At sixty-five miles an hour he shifted down from fifth to fourth to third.

"Here we go," he said to Jennifer.

The sensation was unbelievable, and Jennifer had never experienced anything like it before, except perhaps in the takeoff of an aeroplane. She heard the engine roar, and then her body was forced back into the seat. There was a scream from the rear wheels which did not stop as the scenery passed with increasing speed. Haug had the steering wheel in both hands, but he seemed alert and relaxed. He flashed his lights as a Granada started to pull into the lane and she just caught a look at the driver's astonished face as they shot past. The pickup continued to accelerate hard, with the wheels intermittently squealing, particularly as he shifted gear, when the rear end would fishtail slightly.

"Haug," she said, trying to remain calm, "how fast are we going?"

"One-forty and risin'," he answered as he shifted into fifth.

The wheels screamed again.

"My God! I think I'll close my eyes."

He laughed. "You'll miss all the purty scenery, honey. Hell, I've only opened her up like this about twice before."

They were fast approaching a sporty number in the fast lane. Haug had his lights on, but the car would not move over, so he stood on his brakes and had to wait until the sporty number overtook a lorry. The car still would not move, so Haug shifted down and went around on the left-hand side, honking his horn. One of the men in the front seat held up two fingers as the driver tried to keep up with the roaring pickup. A minute later another car pulled out to overtake slower traffic, and Haug had to brake again.

"Goddam' it, don't they ever check their rear-view mirrors?"

"Well, you are breaking the speed limit."

Haug checked his own rear-view. "He's still there, the bastard. Just a little speck, but I can see him."

Again he went round the car on the left. This time the other driver flashed his lights angrily. A long straight stretch opened up. The tyres squealed.

Haug grinned at Jennifer. "At about one-fifty the steerin' starts gettin' a little light, so I gotta be careful."

"Yes," she answered through clenched teeth, "you be careful."

As they cleared the top of a hill, Haug started braking. A queue of cars could be seen ahead, filtering into one lane marked by plastic cones. Haug pushed the pickup into the queue then squirted out on the hard shoulder on the other side. His lights were still on and he used his horn as well.

"Hell, they'll think I got an emergency. Maybe you can look a little sick."

"I don't have to act for that."

"Hell, we're only goin' about sixty now . . ."

Suddenly the cones ahead appeared on the hard shoulder as well, tunnelling the traffic into just the single lane, where cars were moving at a speed less than twenty miles an hour. Earth-moving equipment could be seen on a hill to the left where the foliage had been scoured away. Haug pulled the wheel to the left, only slowing a little as he left the asphalt and entered the actual building works. The surface was uneven, and the pickup bounced as the suspension tried to soak up the jolts. Jennifer became more and more alarmed as she braced herself against the side of the cab, putting her feet on the dashboard. Haug still looked relatively relaxed as he honked at the shouting excavation workers and pointed at Jennifer. He directed the truck up the side of the hill, and Jennifer could feel the wheels beginning to spin as they tried to bite the loose earth. At one point, just before they made the crest, the pickup slid to the side and Haug fought the steering wheel to bring it back around. Then they were over. More excavations were on the other side, including what was clearly another roadway elevated from two deep cuts on either side. Haug headed the pickup towards the primitive road, but, up ahead, Jennifer could see that it was partially blocked by a huge digger pulling great lumps of earth from the right shoulder. There wasn't much room on the other side of it.

Haug stood on the horn and headed for the gap, but the noise from the digging machine was too loud for the driver to hear much. The light pickup truck was bounding and bouncing through deep ruts made by the machinery. As they neared the gap, the giant digger began to reverse, the big wheels slowly biting backwards. The gap was closing, but Haug gunned the engine. The wheels whined, the rear end slewed around dangerously close to the right-hand edge, then caught. At the last minute Jennifer closed her eyes, certain that they were going to be hit and pushed over what looked like a nasty thirty foot drop on to tons of stacked bricks and building steel. Expecting to hear the crunch of metal as the digger collided, she heard Haug's voice instead.

"Another coat of paint on this thang, and we wouldn't have made it."

She re-opened her eyes as they left the earthworks for the new roadway and topped another little rise. A tarmac road curved away in front of them, separated only by a chainlink fence. Haug swore and swung the truck to the right to find an exit. There was an opening about fifty yards in front, but a dump of plastic cones blocked their way. Haug headed straight for the cones.

"Hope they don't have a pile of bricks underneath those thangs," he said, just before a blizzard of cones appeared.

Underneath the pickup, dragging between the wheels and arches, beneath the wheels, covering the windscreen – they were everywhere she looked. Then they were through, as Haug turned left for the gate where a plant road joined the tarmac. With a final jolt they were on a smooth surface. The tyres squealed as Haug accelerated again.

Haug opened his window. It was hot in the cab.

"We'll have to dodge around a little bit, but this road'll get us to the A30. We wanna pick that up and lay down a few miles between us and that BMW."

He glanced over his shoulder at the disappearing excavation site.

"He won't try to follow us. Even if he's got the guts, wouldn't be anythang left of that ole German piece of shit. And there's no other way out. Those roadworks go on for about three miles without a turn, without a crossin'. He's stuck there in that jam for at least thirty minutes. And then he doesn't know where we are. We coulda gone back the other way, up north, directly south. If he's got any sense, he'll give it up and call his boss."

Jennifer was just beginning to breathe again. "Haug. You're crazy. Barking."

He grinned. "Yeah, but that's because the world's crazy. I just try to survive and keep the other inmates from steppin' on my dick."

Jennifer shook her head. "No, you're dead bonkers. Nothing but luck got you through that . . . back there."

"Yeah, luck's got a little to do with it. But," he said, holding up a finger, "you gotta take a chance to find out if you're lucky. I reckoned that we had a purty good chance. Anyway we can back off a little bit now. That son of a bitch back there is gonna have to roll snake eyes twenty times in a row to catch us. In other words, we had the odds with us, and now he doesn't. We'll lay down a few miles then have ourselves a nice country lunch."

They found what looked like a nice pub on the other side of Yeovil. Haug had been looking for a place which had parking in the rear where his pickup couldn't be seen from the road. It was an old pub too, the kind he liked, the kind that made him feel comfortable. The ceiling inside was low, so anyone over six feet had to duck under the beams. Haug ordered a Guinness and Jennifer decided to have a white wine. They asked for a menu. He ordered plaice and chips and she said that she only wanted a sandwich.

Haug took a sip of Guinness and leaned on the bar.

"I've never found anybody who knows how to make a sandwich in this country," he said to her.

"Well," she smiled, "I'm a native. I'm used to them."

"Are you an American?" said a voice behind him.

Haug turned around to see two young men sitting on bar stools. They were obviously locals. One was a lean, good-looking fellow with the first two buttons of his shirt open. His friend was shorter, with a premature beer belly. The shorter one wore a flat cap.

Haug nodded. "I reckon I am."

"What part?" asked the lean man in a local accent.

"You've probably never heard of it," Haug said. "Place called North Carolina. Down South, despite the 'North'."

"Yes," answered the lean man. "I've been through there – travelled from New York to New Orleans to see the festival."

He grabbed his pint and leaned closer. "Now personally I like the South. Down there they know how to deal with the niggers."

Haug let out a breath then looked at the man from underneath his eyebrows.

"Now *that* is a word I do not like, feller, and I would be obliged if you never use it again around me."

The lean man backed off and coughed a little laugh. "You mean, you *like* niggers?"

Haug lowered his voice. "I like all kinds of people. What I don't like is assholes, black or white. Particularly assholes who think that because I'm white they can use the word 'nigger' around me."

Haug held up a warning finger as the short man turned on his stool and started to speak. His voice was still low.

"Now lemme tell you somethin', assholes. The South is a really beautiful place, and I like it a lot. But I won't live there because a lotta people use words like that and strike attitudes which are a lot worse. I've mighty near killed people down there who use that word around me. You unnerstand? Now I don't remember that word bein' used ten or twelve years ago when I first came here, and I didn't expect to hear it in a decent pub like this. Let me tell you right now, I will not tolerate it."

The short man held his empty pint glass as if he were about to break it. "Maybe you haven't noticed. There are two of us."

"What I see", said Haug, "is that one and one doesn't always make two."

With a swift movement he grabbed the wrist behind the glass, pulled and squeezed. The short man shouted with pain and dropped to his knees. The glass fell from his hand.

The publican rapped on the bar. "I'm afraid I'm going to have to ask you to leave."

Haug spotted a copy of Gillmore's tabloid, *The News*, lying on the bar between the two men. It had a front page picture of the wind blowing a princess's skirt halfway up her thigh. Haug grabbed the newspaper in his fist and turned on the landlord.

"This is part of the reason this country's goin' to hell." He jerked his thumb at the two men on his left. "These punks read this shit like it was true. A decent pub wouldn't allow one of these thangs in the house. I wouldn't wipe my ass with it."

He flung the paper at the publican and turned to Jennifer. "Come on, let's get outta here. Must be a good pub somewhere in this country that doesn't have trashy people swarmin' around the bar like horseflies."

The other customers in the pub watched in indignation as Haug and Jennifer left by the back door. The short man was still on the floor nursing his wrist.

"You cause trouble everywhere you go, don't you, Haug?" Jennifer asked after they got in the pickup.

"Cause?" he asked. "I *caused* that trouble? I asked him not to say that word, and he said it again. Lissen. Nobody would use that word, not in public, if everbody who hated it spoke up against it. The word would die, like it should. Naw, *he* was the cause, not me. Him and that fuckin' newspaper they read. Him and everbody else who won't speak up when they see somethin' bad or somethin' evil right in front of their noses. Like the rest of those folks in that pub. I bet about half of 'em agreed with me, but naw, I'm upsettin' their dinner or their little drink. Look, I've seen what happens when you let thangs like that get outta hand. In no time at all they're wrappin' barbed wire around boys and cuttin' their dicks off and burnin' down their homes and chasin' 'em away from their jobs, and generally just stompin' 'em right into the dirt for no reason except they got a different colour skin."

He turned to her in the cab. "Now, honey, I personally think that is evil, and I'll be goddamned if I'm gonna let it pass right under my nose without sayin' a goddam' word about it."

He started the pickup, reversed and moved out of the parking lot.

Jennifer Montgomery was quiet for a few moments. Then she smiled lightly.

"Never a dull moment with you. And that's the truth."

Haug pulled out a cassette of *The Creation* and bunged it into the player.

"Haydn's good for clearin' filth outta the head."

They moved west down the A30, this time well within the speed limit.

Sir Jonathan Mainwaring sat on a bench in St James's Park feeding the ducks. He enjoyed eating his lunch there when the weather allowed, when it wasn't too cold or wet. He always bought extra slices of bread for the ducks. And cheese. For some reason they liked cheese, and he often wondered why. Not a natural duck food, and they were not particularly well equipped to eat it. Possibly something to do with the milk base? One of the unknowns which would remain unknown for Mainwaring. In any case he wasn't thinking about the ducks today. Logically he was shuttling between the general and the particular. In fact the particular had led to the general. It was not an unusual topic for either Mainwaring or his countrymen. He echoed the words of Haug, a man he did not know, in a pub west of Yeovil. What, he thought, *is* the country coming to?

Mainwaring was not a bad man. He was a civil servant looking forward to retirement in seven years' time. He was getting older, but he wondered if that was really the problem. In his youth he remembered elders worrying about change and how many changes had seemed to be for the worse. Now here he was in his turn asking many of the same questions. But somehow he felt that there was a qualitative difference in this instance. The world seemed to be suddenly in a state of indecision. Things seemed to be about to happen, but they hadn't as yet happened. In the East, communism had collapsed, yet things were more uncertain there than ever. In the West, economic factors were unsettled and capitalism looked more and more the unlikely victor.

He slowly tore up his last slice of bread, heaving a great sigh. At least, he thought, they had finally got rid of that dreadful woman who had been prime minister for so long. It was with her that many of the troubles appeared to begin. It wasn't just that ministers became more and more incompetent. Perhaps they always were. It was the others, though, who slowly began to alarm him. The newer intakes of MPs, the junior ministers, the advisors – there seemed to be so many advisors these days, and they were young and sparky. But not bright, not intelligent, not the way Mainwaring understood intelligence. In their zeal they shared something with salvationists, missionaries, true believers. Scratch the thin coating of zeal from the surface and nothing was there. Nothing at all. Nothing except . . .

Mainwaring chuckled to himself as a large fat duck came boldly up and grabbed the largest piece of bread out of his hand. Then he frowned. Because he didn't like to use this word, even in thought. Except . . . corruption. But that was what it was, wasn't it? Was there another word for it? He dusted the crumbs from his hands and crossed his thin legs to look out on the lake. Water always relaxed him. Reminded him of his youth in Sussex. In short trousers. Reading Shelley beside the mill pond. Shelley also spoke of corruption. Was it the same kind of corruption then? Somehow it was different.

Mainwaring was not a radical or revolutionary. His father had been a Liberal, and he himself usually wasted his vote on what remained of the party. Mainwaring believed in certain things, had certain standards. He certainly did not see property as theft from the poor, but he did see regressive taxes as taking unfair advantage of people unable to speak for themselves. He even believed in privilege. But privilege always carried responsibility. *That* is what these new men of the Right could not see. They had the same mentality as football hooligans who smashed things up and took what they wanted, elbowing aside the infirm, the elderly, the underprivileged in their greed. It was distasteful to Mainwaring, and he thought it a change not worth having. He had been taught responsibility *with* privilege, because otherwise the tectonic plates of classes would become unstable. If their betters smashed and grabbed, who could blame the poor for doing likewise?

Ian Castleberry was a weak man, but he was not the only weak minister for whom he had worked. Neither was Castleberry a bad man. But his weakness left him open to corrosion and rust from those new acid waters rushing past him. Michael Regis, Jeremy Evans, Alexander Hinkley and their ilk. He was reluctant to admit that it had become a cabal. Power was like sand. If you tilted the room, sand would slowly shift to the other side. And the room was now being slowly but surely tilted to the right. There were fewer and fewer men such as Mainwaring, who held power responsibly, and more and more cynically using it to gain their objectives. Corners were cut, lies were told, promises broken, precedent laughed at. Advertising and presentation were everything, substance nothing. Or very little.

He hadn't approved of the sixties, when change was also in the air. It was a different kind of change, though. He remembered being unsettled then. The difference was that there was hope in the future. Change was going to be for the better. He thought that the young people were daft then. Now they were just . . . what? Resigned? Humour and lightness had gradually distorted into deep gloom.

Another annoying thing was that Britain was becoming more and more Americanised, something that Sir Jonathan Mainwaring hated intensely. He had nothing against the USA, but why on earth should *his* country change to become like another one? Burger joints crept across the face of England like acne. People were asking for 'fries' instead of 'chips'. TV was full of American programmes and, increasingly, radio announcers aped the frantic, vacuous, American stream-of-consciousness delivery. Even Radio Three now had American-style programmes in the mornings and early evenings with snatches of this piece of music and snatches of that one and useless news updates every few minutes. Cricketers were now wearing advertising. Soon, no doubt, they would have baseball caps and knickerbockers, lighted scoreboards paid for by Coca Cola, popcorn and hot dogs and American beer served by shouting youths. America and Japan now owned their car industry. Shop assistants were frequently saying 'Have a nice day' – a phrase which never failed to set his teeth on edge. I'll damn well choose the type of day I'm going to have, because that is virtually all that is left for me to choose. That was what he thought. But he never said it. He was too English, too polite.

Politics had filled with sharp and slippery people. The sort who used to become car salesmen or bookies or estate agents.

Sir Jonathan Mainwaring took his glasses off and wiped them with a clean handkerchief which he folded carefully before replacing it in his pocket. He still had a problem that he could not solve – what to do about the Saudi deal. Except that he knew perfectly well that those arms had little to do with the Saudis. The arms were being illegally sold to one of several African nationalist or right-wing groups. The Saudis were being bribed to act as middlemen, though they would never actually touch the goods. It was not just this transaction to which he objected. Enough information had passed through his hands for him to reason that this sale was part of a larger strategy. New channels were being established to supply targeted groups all over the world. And not just in the Third World. Small caches of arms were secreted in places all over Europe for use by certain groups under certain conditions. Mainwaring knew little about this, but he knew enough to know that it was going on.

What did this mean? Why was he so uneasy? After all, there was plenty of historical precedent for supplying friends in foreign parts with arms and support to overthrow unfriendly governments. Because – and this was the crucial factor – because they were political decisions taken outside Parliament or Cabinet. In fact, they were made in spite of Cabinet. A transnational network had gradually emerged from somewhere – probably, thought Mainwaring with a frown, from the USA. This network was very real indeed. He did not know its name, but there was a name for it. Conspiracy. It conspired to subvert the British democratic process. Within this network, no one who was elected to government was answerable for what happened. It was a little surprising just how easy it was, really. Corruption was a series of very small things, in themselves not wrong. Or not very wrong. When added together though, it was a different story.

Mainwaring had been naming some awful things in his mind. He knew it. His own minister, Ian Castleberry, had been successfully bribed to do something that was not in itself too wrong. However, it had established a channel, a pattern and a precedent. The network would continue to grow as it had grown. No one would know anything or say anything. The civil service would once have been a defence against such a virus, but the civil service had been reseeded and replanted throughout the Thatcher years. Mainwaring could count on the fingers of one hand senior civil servants with whom he had talked this matter over. Too few. Too late.

He had actually considered approaching the Press. But what Press? Of course, there were some responsible journalists – good people, who would fight with their lives to prevent this kind of thing happening. But they also had editors, and the editors answered to owners. There was WORLDWIDE and Harvey Gillmore slithering through the British Press, buying up key newspapers and putting pressure on independents to fight with his methods. No, he could not trust journalists until he had a complete folio of evidence. And by then it would be too late. That was Mainwaring's dilemma. To whom could he turn? The Prime Minister? A weak man. The whole Cabinet was weak. Not a man there with the guts, the dignity, the pride to stand in Parliament against all the shifting sand in the world and state the truth. That, thought Mainwaring, would be a truly British thing to do. A decent man not afraid to stand for decency, even if the whole world should cry against him.

It was a great loss, he thought with deep regret. He refocused on the little lake in front of him. A group of Japanese tourists was being led around the other side, and Sir Jonathan Mainwaring felt like a near extinct animal at a zoo being examined by visitors with newer and more modern genes. The tourists were all neatly dressed, each with an expensive camera, for all the world like little automatons run by circuit boards printed without souls.   He was only a curious relic being captured on camera as proof that they had really seen an Old-Fashioned Englishman, a patriot who thought that his country should do things its own way and speak with its own unique voice, faint though it might be in these changing days.

Sir Jonathan Mainwaring got up from the bench, smoothing the seat of his trousers, and he retrieved his rolled umbrella from its place on the back of the bench.   With his left hand he picked up his briefcase and stood up proudly.

The Japanese tourists had made their way round to his side of the pond and advanced towards him, clicking away with their cameras. Looking neither to the left nor the right, Mainwaring walked towards the visitors, keeping to the centre of the path.   His bowler hat added height to his already towering frame.   The umbrella, as always, was used as a cane in a rhythmical pattern with his long stride.   He was upon them in short order and the Japanese scattered in disarray and something like admiration as the tall, thin, pinstriped gentleman marched through them to the sound of his own dying drum.

Chapter Thirteen

Haug sat on his favourite rock looking out across the water. It was warm and seemed almost like summer. This could be a lucky year, he thought. When England finally decided to have a real spring, it was more beautiful than spring anywhere in the world. The last one had been wet, the one before cold and windy and wet. If he could afford it, he would spend much more time down here. Across the bay he could just see Fowey through the haze. Fowey was a lovely little seaside town, but this was about as close as he wanted to be to any settlement. Some day he would find a way to live out the rest of his life here. Nothing could be heard except the wind and the sound of the sea. The nearest house was almost a mile away and it was unlikely that anyone would build any closer because of the nature of the coastline.

He heard Jennifer approaching behind. She had wanted to have a wash and change her clothes.

"It's gorgeous," she said as she sat down beside him. "Breathtaking. You're very lucky."

Haug was sitting on his leather jacket. He wore jeans, one of his check shirts and a leather waistcoat. And he had on his Harley dozer cap.

"Cain't tell you how long it took me to find it. There's only two ways to get here. By sea or the way we came in."

Behind the house was a steep slope and there was a narrow path winding down from the top. The descent had taken nearly twenty minutes. They had parked the pickup at the end of the tarmac. Haug carried Jennifer's suitcase and the wooden case he had tucked underneath the driver's seat in the garage the night before. She had asked him what was in the little wooden chest and he had told her to mind her own business.

"And it has a lovely little bay. Is it deep enough for boats with a keel?" she asked.

He chuckled. "Yeah, that's a lovely little bay all right. I dug it out myself."

"You're joking. With a *shovel*?"

"A shovel of sorts. A mechanical shovel. What you Limeys call a JCB. You see that raft over there?" He pointed at a pontoon raft pulled up on the rocks on the other side of the little bay. "That's what I floated it across on, all the way from Fowey. All your locals were laughin' at me and shakin' their heads and suckin' air through their teeth. Said it couldn't be done, not out on the open sea. Tried to rent a JCB, but nobody would insure the damn thang, so I finally just bought one. Bought that raft in sections, lashed the JCB to it and bought her over one night when it was calm. I bet everbody in that town was out watchin' me, shakin' their heads and suckin' air. I floated it over here, I dug the son of a bitch out by myself, and I floated it back to Fowey. Nearly lost it about three times, but I did it. Sold the goddam' JCB for more'n I paid for it. If Hemingway hadda been here, he woulda written a story about it."

She turned to him. "Have you always been like this, Haug?"

"Like what?"

"Well . . . you sort of do things your way, come what may. No matter what anyone thinks."

"I don't think you're right there. Not come what may. I just sort of go on my judgement. If I reckon I'm right, well, I do it. I take advice about thangs I don't know about. But when I do know about somethin', it's my opinion against theirs."

She was quiet for a minute. "You were in Vietnam, you said."

He threw a small rock at the sea. "I don't talk about that."

"I just wondered if it had anything to do with the . . . violence in you. I've never witnessed anything like it in my life. It's like an unstoppable force. Or an immovable object maybe, I don't know. It's so elemental. So frightening. Yet you are soft as a brush at other times. Sensitive, intelligent, literate. So I wondered if you were a nice, studious boy from the rural South who has been turned into some kind of monster by military experiences."

Haug laughed ironically and leaned back, his hands behind his head, staring at the sky. "It's more or less right, but the wrong way around."

"The army made you sensitive? Surely not."

"After the war, after the army, I had my Pauline conversion. You know – Paul on the way to Damascus, the bright light. To be honest, it started *in* the army. I started readin' stories. Know what I read? Dickens. Dickens," he repeated with a smile. "I think I read nearly all of Dickens. Gradually, as I kept readin', I talked to other kinds of people, different folks from those I'd been used to."

Haug sat up suddenly, then stood up. "But before that – I'm gonna tell you the truth – I was a killer."

Jennifer leaned over on her elbow, using Haug's jacket. "All soldiers are killers, aren't they?"

Haug hadn't moved. "Yeah, maybe, but I was a different kind of killer. I didn't mind it, was sort of good at it. I worked with a group of three other men mostly. Sometimes we had an objective, like an assassination for instance or blowin' bridges, burnin' villages, but mostly these objectives were fuckups. Some great plan of some great general, thinkin' that we were Rambos . . ."

He breathed out and folded his arms on his chest. "Aw, shit, I'm not gonna talk about this crap. I haven't before and I don't see why I should now. I just wanted to tell you that I've killed a lot of people. I didn't feel bad about it at the time, on account of the fact that I was young and I thought my country was right and I was doin' the right thang. They said, kill these people, and I did. We did. They were the enemy. I killed men, women and children, 'cause when you're shootin' in a village and folks are shootin' back you just lay down fire, and anythang in the way is dead."

Haug turned to face Jennifer. "Now, the whole point is, I now know those people I killed were my friends. They were the good guys. I was fightin' with the bad guys and didn't know it. I'm not apologisin', 'cause I didn't know any better. But I was one violent son of a bitch. Before I went into the army and while I was there. I still got it in me. Didn't just go away. But it's not like it was before. I don't do it for fun any more. I was just full of shit, that's all; fulla the shit they feed you in the newspapers and on TV and standin' aroun' the local drugstore."

Haug turned back to the sea and squatted down. "I've never told anybody even that much before, and I don't know why I told you. I guess I thought it was fair sharin' a confidence after you told me about your old man abusin' you and what you do to make a livin' and all the crap you've gone through. Anyway, to complete the little bit of biography, I got outta the army, took up the GI Bill and went to college. Played football, majored in English Lit. I was good in football and gradually became better at English. Met some people made me think. Started wonderin' about thangs, began to realise what a shitass I was. Wasn't all at once, in a flash. Hell, I played a year of pro ball after college. Then I quit because I wanted to study some more. Which is why I came over here. And after all that, I wind up in a business that's still violent sometimes. But one day I hope to come and live here, maybe bang out my life story on the old typewriter and sit out here and catch fish."

He looked back at Jennifer. "Now, why cain't I call you Jenny?"

She couldn't help laughing. "You can call me Jenny if it'll make you feel happier. On one condition. Do you have a nickname? If I have to use one, so do you."

He grinned. "Back home people used to call me Hoggy. Or Hog. Think it had somethin' to do with the way I hit fullbacks head on and rooted 'em into the backfield."

"OK, Hoggy, you're on."

"Jenny. Like it a lot better'n Jennifer. Anyway, what I want you to do is this. When we go back to the house, I want you to call up Michael Regis and tell him we got the tape—"

"But we don't. Not yet. We don't even know if the chauffeur's sent it."

"Yeah, but just tell him we got it. Tell him we want a hundred grand for it. Give him the telephone number and tell him to call back yes or no. That's all. Don't argue with him, don't discuss thangs."

She sat up. "But why? For what reason? He probably doesn't even want it. Nothing to do with him."

Haug stood up again. His knees were getting stiff.

"I cain't tell you any more right now. I got a couple of hunches, and if I told you ever' hunch I had, it'd drive you crazy." He pretended to cast with rod and reel. "It's like throwin' out a line, see. You sort of put a little bait on the end and hope it catches what you want. I could tell you that I'm lookin' for a marlin or a tuna and come back with a minnow or a crab or an old boot. But I'll let you know if I get a real strike."

She got up and put her arm through his. "All right, Hoggy. Right now I'm just glad we're here. It's so beautiful, so quiet, so peaceful. Thank you for telling me that awful story. Maybe you could tell me more later."

"You don't wanna hear any more, not any more of the 'Nam stuff. It was a long time ago, and I was a whole lot different."

Instinctively she hugged him.

"It's just that I want to know more about you, Haug. You seemed to fall out of the sky into my life, and I find that I care about you. I think it's caring I feel, because I've never cared for anyone before."

"You're gonna be real disappointed in me, Jenny. I'm really an awful old romantic at heart. Readin' all that Dickens shoulda given you a clue. I kinda had a picture of us standin' together like this on this old rock when I suggested we come down here."

"Did you have a picture of anything else?"

"Nope," he said. "I stopped it right there and stuck 'The End' on it."

"Last night when I curled up beside you, I wanted you. You went to sleep."

Haug moved around to look into her face. Then he hugged her, holding her gently. She put her arms around him.

"You gonna wind up breakin' my heart, sweet thang."

"No, I won't," she whispered. "Promise."

She turned her head up to him and they kissed deeply, bodies pressed together and beginning, as such bodies do, to move as one. A duet becoming a solo. It was a body with four arms and four legs perfectly co-ordinated.

It would be difficult to say just how long the kiss lasted, but it seemed that the electrical discharge had teased the elements. Low clouds covered the sun and the wind had picked up, blowing from the sea past them, past the house and up the steep hill and over it. But they continued to kiss and move as one, their eyes closed to what the wind and clouds were doing.

Haug opened his eyes and looked at Jennifer. Then he broke away and took off his hat.

"All right, goddammit, let's fuck!"

He threw the hat, which was caught by the wind and blew past the house.

She was laughing. "Right now! Right here!"

She pulled her jumper over her head and threw it in the air. Her nipples hardened, erect against the cool wind.

Haug threw off his waistcoat, unsnapped his shirt and threw it as well. "You're fuckin' beautiful!"

She had kicked off her plimsolls and was unzipping her jeans, which she pulled down with her knickers.

"So are you, Hoggy!"

He was hopping around pulling off his boots. His trousers were already around his ankles. He managed to tear the boots off, throwing them into the air like mortar rounds. Before he could get his right leg out of his jeans, Jennifer had landed on his hips, clutching him like a koala bear, her breasts pressed into his face, muffling his voice as Haug danced round and round on the rock.

Jennifer's head was thrown back in laughter.

"What?" she screamed. "What are you saying? Can't hear you!"

His head broke free. "I said, you got the prettiest goddam' knockers in the world, and I'm tryin' to get 'em both in my mouth."

"Well, it should be big enough!" she shouted as his face disappeared again, and she felt his tongue searching for her nipples.

Her ankles were locked around his back and she held his head with both arms, kissing and licking the smooth crown. Haug was dancing close to the edge of the rock at times, but she didn't care. Falling was one of the things which didn't matter any more. All that mattered was the closeness of their bodies and the closeness of a world she had never seen before. She was aware that he had stopped dancing, and at the same time she loosened the grip of her legs, letting her body slide slowly down until she felt the tip of his penis. He was holding the base of it with his hand, moving it gently against her outer lips. An instant later he was inside her, slowly moving up. Slowly and inevitably, and she wanted the sensation to last for ever. Then suddenly he was in, and she arched back to get the deepest possible penetration while he held on to her. Her arms thrashed wildly at the air as they began to move rhythmically together, and Haug began to dance again. He was shouting and she dimly wondered what he was saying. Then she realised that she was shouting too and didn't know what she was saying either.

Jennifer had her eyes closed, but somehow she could feel the distortion of the world, which was warping and bending around her. Time, it seemed, was fornicating with space. The thought struck her as hilarious and she heard herself scream with laughter.

Haug felt the laughter too and began to laugh himself, as he was sure that he knew what she was laughing about. But as he laughed he realised that he was being ambushed by an orgasm which he could no more stop than he could stop the waves below in the sea. He knew that she was with him though. He knew that they were together. He had stopped dancing, and he was aware of something coming from below and from within like lava forcing itself through the mantle of the earth. It was hot, and steam whistled through his body moments before the eruption. The steam blew through every pore of his skin as he felt the lava rushing from his belly. He began to bellow like a buffalo.

It was irresistible for Jennifer as well. She took great gulps of air and let them out in an increasing crescendo of sound which echoed the waves roaring through her pelvis and rushing with her blood like the sea beneath her. It was a tide which overwhelmed her, and she was thrown, end over end, into the shore.

They opened their eyes together. Or maybe they just thought that they did. But they were looking at each other, appearing as two, disappearing as one, dissolving and resolving until at last they were two again, two people pressed together. Haug's arms were trembling, but he didn't want to let go of her. And she wanted to stay there, attached, for ever.

He felt weaker and weaker and searched behind him for his jacket. He tried to lie down and keep inside her, but as he squatted he felt himself slip out.

"Ohhhh," she said in comic petulance.

He leaned back on the jacket. "Toothpaste is all gone outta the tube anyway. Best throw the thang away now."

She reached around and tried to stuff it back in, managing only to get the head inside her lips. She sat on it and leaned back on his bent legs.

"Well, Hoggy, you're full of surprises."

"You took the words outta my mouth. I cain't recall bein' fucked ever quite like that before."

He reached up and massaged both her breasts. "Now I'm gonna find it hard to keep my hands off you."

She sat up and let her hands wander up his stomach, across his chest, around his shoulders. "Muscles everywhere. Isn't it boring being the strongest man on earth?"

He chuckled. "Plenty stronger'n I am, but very few meaner."

She touched some scar tissue just below his shoulder. "What's this?"

"Where one of the bullets went in."

"You cold?" she asked.

"Gettin' that way."

"Sun's gone in, gone away. Want to race me to the house?"

He grinned. "For kids, isn't it? Not for old plough mules like me."

She jumped up, then leaned over, pouting her lips, and cupped her breasts in her hands.

"Catch me and you can have another fuck."

Then she turned and ran.

Haug got up, wincing a little with stiffness, and started after her.

"I'm gonna have a goddam' drink first," he yelled after her. "I'm not a twenny-year-old stud any more!"

She reached the door first and turned to block his way. "You lost. But you can still have a fuck if you want."

He leaned down and pulled her nose into his mouth, sucking. "I think I'll have you for supper. Just lick you like an ice cream."

She put her hand under his genitals and closed her fingers softly around them. "OK. And I think I'll have a banana and a couple of plums."

"You taste good," he said, licking around her mouth and chin. "Want some white lightnin'?"

"Thought I just had some of that out on the rock."

"I wanna get you drunk so I can have some fun with you."

"Good idea," she said as she turned to open the door. "I'll have a large one, whatever it is."

He reached around her with one hand to catch her breast and leaned in to nibble her ear. "But first, my little flower, I want you to make a phone call."

She stopped halfway through the door. "Oh, that. I'd forgotten. It will bring me right down talking to that swine."

"My moonshine will pick you back up. It's stronger than horse piss with the foam farted off. Gotta be done. Then we can relax. I'll build a roarin' fire and throw a blanket in front of it."

He closed the door behind them. It was getting dark and he found the light switch. She raised her arms then dropped them.

"OK. Let's get it over with. Where's the phone?"

Tuesday was even warmer than Monday and Sir Jonathan Mainwaring found a place by the pond in St James's Park that was not shaded by trees. He even took off his bowler and laid it on the bench beside him.

Sarah, his wife, had made another delicious smoked salmon sandwich, cut into little triangles. The salmon had been left over from the weekend. The Saturday before, he had gone all the way to a fishmonger in Islington to fetch the salmon. It was the finest and cleanest fishmonger in London and his salmon was marvellous. It melted in the mouth when sliced very, very thinly. She had put just a drop of lemon on each triangle. Today he could have eaten two. He sighed and instead poured himself a cup of tea from the lovely flask his daughter had given him for his birthday last year. He had a fine family which remained close, even though both his son and daughter were now married and had moved away from home and from Guildford, where he still lived with Sarah.

Mainwaring had not lived an exciting life, but he had never expected to. He had gone directly from Cambridge to the fast lane of the civil service, and he achieved the rank he had expected to achieve when he set out. There were only two excesses he allowed himself. His collection of antique tea caddies and the Morgan motor car he had bought in 1964 and still owned. He smiled as he thought of the Morgan. It wasn't the fact that it was a quintessentially British vehicle. He would never call himself a chauvinist. It was simply that the car expressed something individual to the maker, and that individuality fitted Mainwaring like a glove. He didn't drive the old car much any longer. Perhaps three times a year he would take it out for a run to Littlehampton, with Sarah complaining about the wind. But every year it was serviced by the same mechanics, and anything worn would be replaced.

Mainwaring looked up to see Stuart Easton approaching in the distance. Easton was a dapper, slender man who carried himself erect and had a taste for light-coloured suits. The suits were always off the peg but nevertheless fitted well. He had a full head of hair, which had once been sandy brown but now was well sprinkled with grey. The wind was lifting it as he walked towards Mainwaring's bench. Stuart Easton was a Labour MP for Sheffield, a Yorkshireman who still spoke with the broad bluntness of the county.

Mainwaring did not like Easton's politics very much and never had. In Parliament he was a maverick, but a maverick with a sharp tongue who usually gave better than he received in any heated

exchange with the Government or his own front bench. Mainwaring
reluctantly conceded that Easton was intelligent. Not conventionally
intelligent, not the intelligence that Mainwaring really admired. A
craftsman with ideas and words, that was how he put it. Stuart Easton
was an old-fashioned class warrior who saw himself better than no
man and bettered by none. Some Tories feared him as the incarnation
of Satan as he scattered them in the corridors with caustic wit and
intellectual barbs. He still called lunch 'dinner' and dinner 'tea', not
in the least ashamed of his working-class manners and background.
Easton had been a miner until he was twenty-eight and had won his
seat with sponsorship by the NUM.

Why had Mainwaring asked to meet him in the park today?
Mainwaring was still asking himself that question as Easton
approached. But he had been through a long list of people, some of
them friends, many of them colleagues, one of them an ex-prime
minister. But for one reason or another he had rejected most of them.
He didn't like Easton personally, but he respected him deeply. When
he had to make a decision, he forced himself to be honest. He could
not think of a better man. No one in the country would question
Easton's integrity. He actually lived on a miner's wages, donating the
remainder of his salary as an MP to the miners' union. He lived in a
council flat in Sheffield and had rented rooms in London when
Parliament was sitting. Unlike most other MPs he treated his
parliamentary duties as a job of work. Unless seriously ill, he
attended. He fought in the House like a tiger for what he believed in,
and he was ferocious in attacking privilege and hypocrisy. And, as a
Yorkshireman, his word was truly his bond. Mainwaring was certain
that a confidence could not be teased from Easton with offers of the
crown jewels or by white-hot tongs.

Easton sat down on the end of the bench.

"What do you want?" he asked bluntly.

Mainwaring was tearing up three slices of bread for the ducks
which had already gathered like a choir near his feet.

"Obviously I wish to talk with you or I wouldn't have asked you to
join me here."

"What about? I'm busy today and haven't got time to chat about
country clubs or debutante balls or whatever you gits talk about when
you sit on park benches with your handmade briefcases full of
sandwiches."

Mainwaring pursed his lips. The man really could be tiresome.

"I know what I want to say", he replied finally, "but I just haven't decided yet how to say it. Or whether I will say it."

Easton got up abruptly. "When you decide what to say and how to say it, give me another call."

"Sit down, Stuart. There's no need to be unpleasant."

Easton turned and looked at the pond.

"You've asked me out here for a private chat, and any time one of your sort does that I expect some sort of offer I'm going to have to report to an ethics committee."

Mainwaring smiled. "You know me better than that, don't you, Stuart?"

Easton sat back down on the end of the bench. "I'll admit you're one of the few I've got any respect for at all. But if it's not a bribe or inducement, what the devil could it be?"

Again the fat duck got the biggest pieces and was waiting for his cheese. Mainwaring opened another linen napkin and extracted a chunk of stale cheddar.

"I have come to the conclusion that there is an imminent danger to this country and to Parliament from a group of people who serve interests outside this country: in short, a conspiracy."

He threw the rest of the crumbled cheese to the choir.

Stuart Easton sat silently for few moments, his legs stretched out comfortably in front of him. If anyone else had given him the same information, he would have taken it with a pinch of salt, considered it a slight exaggeration or possibly agreed with what was meant as a general sentiment. Coming from Sir Jonathan Mainwaring, however, it had a different kind of meaning. He would not have said it if he did not believe it to be true and, if he *did* believe it was true, then it was a little frightening.

"Are you talking about a coup?" he asked finally.

Mainwaring crossed his thin legs. "Before I say anything further, I want your word that any action on any information shall be decided jointly, between you and me. Furthermore I want your word that you will repeat nothing to anyone – and I do mean *anyone* – without prior agreement from me."

"You *are* serious, aren't you?" Easton muttered.

"I wouldn't have asked you here if I weren't."

Stuart Easton was silent again.

"I don't like to promise things like this, and I don't have to explain why, do I? You know me well enough to know what I think by now. Decisions made in cosy clubs, in fancy restaurants, in common rooms and even on park benches are part of what I've fought against all my life. Decisions which affect other people, and usually at their expense. I don't know. Maybe you'd better choose somebody else, Jonathan."

Mainwaring smiled, knowing immediately that he had chosen the right man. Far too many in this world – people who should know better – would promise anything for important information. The easiness of the promises also indicated their worth.

"Quite frankly, Stuart, I can't think of anyone else. No one I can really trust. Most are probably all right, but I know you are. I can't say that I am an enthusiast either of your ideas or your politics. I am, however, an admirer of you personally. I know that you are a patriot, a democrat, a detester of hypocrisy and, most importantly, a sworn enemy of those whom I consider to be my own enemies. Either you give me your word or the information remains with me. And the danger increases."

Easton laughed shortly. "You're not trying to tell me that we're the *only* two honest people in Britain?"

"Oh, no. And I don't think it either. But one must begin somewhere. And I need an ally."

"You know," said Easton, "it sounds to me like an officer who needs an enlisted man to dig the latrines, peel the spuds and do the fighting for him."

Mainwaring sighed. "If it will make you feel any better, I do wish that I could have found someone. . . from my own. . ."

"Class."

"I loathe that word."

"Of course you do, and for a good reason too. If you admit class, you have to admit the rest of the argument as well."

"As you wish." Mainwaring was finding it difficult, as he had known he would. "But for one thing, if I were discussing this with a colleague, then we would not have to wade through this very predictable preamble before joining forces. You waste so much time on what you insist on calling the class war that the ramparts are overrun and the castle falls. As a personal favour to my eccentricity, would you please agree to a little truce?"

Easton pondered for a moment.

"I suppose I'm going to have to agree to this promise, Jonathan. But I want you to know something first. If the information is truly seditious, I'm not going to just sit on it. I'm quite clear on what my duty is."

Mainwaring nodded.

"As I am. Which is the principal reason I am talking to you and not to a dozen others. I spent this weekend trying to decide exactly what my duty was and to whom it was due. The former was easier than the latter because normally, as a civil servant, the chain of command is quite clear. Normally also, it is not for me to make any judgement or institute action outside the civil service framework – those concerning the legislative or judicial spheres, for instance. However, I find myself thwarted. What I would normally do is not possible because the chain of command has been corrupted. Important links are untrustworthy. Much has happened to the civil service during the past twelve years. And I would further point out that changes have occurred elsewhere as well.

"Changes are all very well. Happen all the time. But these changes have developed a pattern. As replacements were made in the civil service, the judiciary, Parliament, the armed forces, the police and security services, they were of a certain type."

Mainwaring stopped for a moment to wipe his glasses. Easton still had his legs stretched out, hands in his pockets, looking out over the pond.

"Not, as you may think, all of a certain ideology. But some were. Others were weak or shallow people."

He replaced his glasses and folded his handkerchief carefully.

"In the early days I often thought of it as simply poor judgement. In the past three years, though, other events have begun to unfold."

"You've said nothing that surprises me so far," said Easton.

"I am dealing with a matter just now which, in itself, is of little importance. It concerns a sale of arms to Saudi Arabia, who have signed the End User Certificate. The arms are going elsewhere, of course. Nothing terribly unusual in this, as politicians have for centuries been supplying those they consider to be their friends in foreign parts. The interesting thing here is that the decisions are being made, not by any elected or appointed officials of the government, but by another source. The government is merely supplying a rubber

stamp facility as a result of what I would call bribery. There have
been other corrupt acts more heinous than this in the past – that, too,
is true. But I have gathered a copy of documentation over the past
few years which shows similar routeing, particularly in the sale of
former public companies. And you may have noted how key
segments of the media are now controlled by companies with interests
which lie elsewhere. There is pressure to erode or dismantle the BBC
and the NHS—"

"I never suspected that you would some day sound like a socialist,
Jonathan."

"Absolutely nothing to do with socialism, Stuart. The point I am
making is that the entire *structure* of the country is no longer owned
by the people of the country. And this is the important factor: our
lives are no longer determined by the democratic processes evolved
over hundreds of years. As you can imagine, this is partly due to the
unprecedented success of one political party remaining in office for
fourteen years. One particular faction of that party, I might add.
This coincided with a very similar period of like people in the United
States. Natural alliances were formed. Then they congealed. And
they have become extremely formidable. They are now expanding
rapidly. The arms network is becoming alarming, if not critical.
They are supplied exclusively to other ideologically similar groups to
undermine by fair means or foul of whatever governments they
disapprove."

Easton turned towards Mainwaring, drawing one leg under the
other. "Who is behind this network?"

Mainwaring thought for a moment. "I don't believe there is a
Mr Big, a Mr Bad – a Dr No, if you wish. It's more like a series of
committees, study groups, so-called 'think tanks'. But it is without
doubt subversive. It is becoming more overt. It is becoming
downright dangerous."

Mainwaring smiled thinly as he turned to the Labour MP. "You
see, Stuart, we were told that the menace was on the Left, so we all
ran to the trenches and turned our artillery *à gauche*. And the lunatics
from the Right have simply walked in and altered all the deeds and
leases. We now find that we don't even own the trenches we were
defending so righteously."

Easton nodded. "It is a coup, isn't it?"

"Hmmm. Yes. Not a shot was fired."

"You have documentation? Can I see it?"

Mainwaring shook his head. "No. Not yet. I think we need to move with great caution. I would like to decide with you the composition of a committee of our own. But I suggest that we must both completely agree on every name on that committee."

"To be honest with you, I don't think I can come up with many. Not many that I fully trust. A devil of a thing to say, isn't it?"

Mainwaring tented his fingers cautiously. "I think we must never use the telephone. Only word of mouth. Nothing on paper. As for the committee, we need as broad a spread of specialist talent as is possible. So, think in those terms."

Easton smiled ironically. "Sounds like a conspiracy."

"It is," agreed Mainwaring. "A conspiracy to restore democracy. Meet here again next week?"

Easton got up from the bench. "All right, Jonathan. I'll go along on your word alone. Because in my bones I feel that you're right."

They shook hands without another word. Stuart Easton walked briskly away, his hair blowing in the wind, as Mainwaring picked up his bowler, adjusted it carefully, picked up his briefcase and umbrella and set off at a brisk pace down the centre of the path by the pond.

Chapter Fourteen

In the north of London two other men sat on a bench in Regent's Park, but neither of them was feeding ducks. Sam Bernstein had just joined Julian van der Bijl, who had been waiting for him. Bernstein wore a tracksuit and trainers and looked as though he had been running. Van der Bijl wore an expensive leather jacket over casual clothes and looked cool and comfortable.

"Living in England makes you want to sit in the sun," said Van der Bijl to his colleague.

When Bernstein didn't answer he went on, "They've been found."

"Good," said Bernstein simply. "Where?"

"Cornwall. Near some little town called Fowey. I don't know much about it yet, but it sounds ideal. Isolated, apparently. I can't find out much more by telephone."

Bernstein thought for a moment. "I'll go down myself. Today. Find a suitable hotel. Send the men under business cover. Suits and briefcases, nothing casual. Is this place near the sea?"

"Right on it."

"Easier to clean up, then. I still don't see how Erik lost them in the first place."

Van der Bijl smiled. "They lost Erik, to be precise. Perhaps you are underrating this man."

Bernstein snorted. "A punk. I know I could take him myself. But I'll do it by the book. Overkill is better than no kill."

"Excellent. I don't want to hear any bad news on the television. Or the telephone, for that matter. There is pressure to get this settled yesterday. Or the day before."

"It'll be settled pronto. I get down there tonight, send the men tomorrow. By the time they arrive I'll know where it is and have a map and assault plan. Don't worry. They are dead. Yesterday. Or the day before."

———

There was a structural beam running the length of Thomas Howell's small bedroom under the old newspaper offices. It was clad in reinforced concrete and appeared quite massive. It was from this beam that they found Howell hanging by his neck on Tuesday morning. A chair had been kicked over underneath his feet. When the police spoke to his employer in his office later, they confided to him that, even though their investigations were by no means complete, all signs pointed towards suicide. The only unusual feature of the case was that the room had been completely vandalised, as if in a frenzy. The mattress was torn open, the drawers emptied in the middle of the floor, the linings of suits cut open, a portable radio/tape player was smashed open and various pre-recorded tapes had been unwound and dumped in the middle of the mess. Their initial reaction was that the man had been in a depressive rage which culminated in suicide. The rope was one kept in the boot of the Rolls-Royce by Howell for emergencies. Of course, the police could only surmise at this point because fingerprinting was not yet complete and there was much sifting of evidence yet to be done.

It was at this point that Gillmore asked to speak with the detective inspector alone. When the two accompanying constables had left the room, the Australian confided that he knew his chauffeur to be homosexual, though at the time of initial employment he had been married to a woman who subsequently had come to work for him. The detective inspector nodded, taking all the details down in a notebook, muttering helpful sounds from time to time. He informed Gillmore that quite a number of people who took their own lives were found to be from the gay community. He congratulated Gillmore on being a liberal employer and left the office with a little bow, as though he had just left an audience with a king. He didn't even ask why the Australian had a plaster across his nose. That, after all, was his business.

During the police interview Beth remained in the bedroom where Gillmore had installed her. She was sitting on the bed staring at the wall and had not moved for over an hour. Her mind was not really blank, but she would have said it was. Mainly because of the lack of feeling, the absence of emotion. The only thing she felt was hunger. Gillmore was feeding her literally on bread and water. And occasionally he let her have the remains of his salads. The kitchen door was locked at night.

She no longer really knew why she was here, why she was doing what she was doing. One night – when was it? – she had had a dream of an endless spiral staircase. She was looking down and the staircase wound on for infinity. Beth was not educated, and she couldn't even say that she knew herself very well, but the downward spiral seemed to make sense. What appalled her, though, was that she didn't care. Which was one of the reasons she sat on her bed looking at the wall.

Thomas had killed himself, probably because of her, and she didn't even care. At least there were no pounding emotions, no guilt, no regrets. No regrets? Well, maybe. But what were regrets? Just fantasies, memories of things in the past, constructions of things which might have been. As she descended the spiral, Beth was aware that she was becoming more and more obsessed with Gillmore. It wasn't just that she wanted him sexually. No, that was only a part of it. She wanted – *craved*, that was the word – she *craved* his scorn and abuse. Was that the real hunger she felt inside? But why? Because I don't care, she told herself.

She held her feet up and looked at the shoes Gillmore liked so much. Her feet were swollen and they hurt. She had hardly had them off since Saturday except to change her stockings or for an occasional wash. Her fingernails were broken from scrubbing. Why did she want long fingernails anyway? She got up wearily and sat down again in front of her mirror. From her bag she took a file and bottle of fingernail polish. Bright red. He liked bright red. Carefully she filed her nails and applied the polish, thinking of nothing, just concentrating on what she was doing. Afterwards she fanned them dry whilst looking in the mirror and realised that she had been crying. She dried her face and repaired her eyeliner. As she was putting on fresh lipstick the door opened suddenly.

Gillmore stood and looked at her for a few moments. "You're a disgusting tart. Your husband has just topped himself and you're fixing your make-up. You ought to be ashamed of yourself."

Beth didn't reply. She sat frozen in front of the mirror, the tube of lipstick still in her hand. The fear returned when he entered her room. He had not come in before. He had always buzzed when he wanted her. But the fear also brought the excitement too. The feeling of emptiness disappeared when he entered – she was aware of that.

He came up behind her and she watched in the mirror as he yanked off her little hat and grabbed her hair, pulling her head back. He looked down into her face.

"I said, you ought to be ashamed of yourself."

"Yes," she replied, afraid to look into his eyes.

"You only want one thing, don't you?"

"Yes," she said again.

"Well," he said, "I'm tired of fucking you. From now on, it's something you've got to earn. Nothing in this world is free. My father told me that, you know. Have you ever prayed?"

"What?" she asked, confused.

"Don't say 'what' to me. Have you ever prayed? On your knees? To your Lord and Saviour, Jesus Christ?"

He still had hold of her hair, and she didn't know what to say. "I don't know. Yes. When I was a little girl, I think I did."

He let go of her hair suddenly and went towards the door. "Follow me."

Beth got up and walked behind Gillmore, who led her down the long hall and into his office, and she watched as he pulled a black curtain back from a section of the wall by a rope. A large safe was hidden behind the curtain, fixed into the wall, and he twirled the combination deftly. Pulling the door open, he reached inside to pull out a willow cane. A box of tapes fell to the floor.

Gillmore laughed as he picked up the box, hooking the cane over his wrist.

"One of the most valuable things I've got. Just a bunch of tapes. But if anyone ever tries to nail my arse to the floor, I'll squeeze 'em like a lemon. I've even got a tape of you in here, Beth. Squalling and asking for more. Want to hear it some time? I like to keep records."

He placed the box back in the safe and opened a drawer of his desk and took out a Bible which had satin markers in many places. He opened the book and quickly found what he was looking for.

"Pull your knickers down to your ankles and bend over the front of the desk, Beth," he said quietly.

She did as she was told, and he placed the Bible in front of her.

"Now read to me the marked passage. It's from Matthew, chapter 25, verse 29." His voice was kindly and patronising.

Beth raised her head, licked her lips and found the verse. "*Unto everyone that hath shall be given and he shall have abundance: but from him that hath not shall be taken away even that which he hath.*"

"Read it again, Beth," he said. "Louder. Except where it says 'he', you say 'she', and change 'him' for 'her'. Read it, Beth."

"Unto everyone that hath shall be given and she shall have abundance: but from her that hath not shall be taken away even that which she hath."

Tears were streaming down her face as she read it the second time.

"And what hath you, Beth?"

"Nothing," she whimpered.

Gillmore leaned over and whispered in her ear. "Oh, you are wrong, Beth. Wrong. I saw you making up in front of a mirror. You hath vanity. And you only think of yourself, don't you? You want me to fuck you right now, isn't that true?"

"Yes," she cried, "it's true."

It wasn't, but she said it anyway. She was too scared to want anything. Her whole mind was tingling with fear, every nerve screaming.

He was still at her ear, and she could feel his breath. "On the other hand, Beth, I hath much and the more that I hath, the more is given. Because I am a Christian, a believer in Jesus Christ, our Lord and Saviour. And I'm going to help you. I'm going to take away even that which you hath."

He closed the Bible and placed it back into the drawer, then returned to the safe inside which he opened a small door. He pulled out a set of handcuffs which he placed on her wrists. They had a piece of nylon cord attached to the middle. This he drew underneath the desk and tied to her ankles. He then pulled up the back of her dress and tucked it into her apron.

"My father was a great believer in corporal punishment, Beth," he remarked as he brought the cane down with force on her bottom.

Beth could not believe the pain. It was so much sharper than she had anticipated that her whole body arched up and she opened her mouth and screamed.

"No!" she shouted. "No, no, no no!"

The voice behind her was measured. "Count for me, Beth. That was one of twelve. If you miss a count, I'll add it to the end. My father always did that. Focuses your mind. Count."

She tried to look around, catch his eyes, but he was standing back.

"Please. Please, not so hard!"

"It's thirteen now, Beth. So start again, from one."

The cane struck again.

Beth screamed again, then in complete panic yelled, "One!" at the top of her voice. It was an ordeal which became nightmarishly timeless as the blows struck her again and again, and each one seemed harder, worse than the last. Towards the end she felt as though her heart was going to burst, and her body just sagged on to the desk. She stopped struggling for the last three strokes, dully counting just above a whisper. She could not remember such pain, not even in the dentist's chair, not even when she had broken her forearm when she was thirteen. It was far too much to bear. But it was finally over, and she was struck by the silence, how quiet it had suddenly become. The pain in her bottom was making her nauseous and she choked back the burning fluid from her stomach.

Gillmore came around behind his desk and lifted Beth's head by the hair.

"That is a picture of my father, there on the wall. He was a saintly man. A God-fearing man. I loved him more than anyone in the world, Beth."

He put his own face close to hers. "Do you love me, Beth?"

"Oh, yes, I do!" she heard herself say faintly. "I don't know why, I don't know, I don't know . . . but I do."

He lowered her head to the desk and patted it.

"Then learn also to love the Lord, Beth. There is a Bible in your bedside table. Read it every night, and tell me what you've read the next day."

He put the key in the handcuffs and turned it, first one and then the other. "Now free your legs and stand up. No whimpering. You're a big girl."

It took her several minutes to undo the knot because her whole body was trembling. She realised that a small amount of blood was running down the backs of her thighs. Her misery was deeper than at any time she could remember. She took off her knickers and used them to swab at her thighs, then, painfully, she stood, clutching the knickers in her right hand, making them into a ball.

Gillmore sat down in his chair and swung it around to look up at the portrait of his father.

"I can't tell you how many times he did that to me, and I'm none the worse for it, eh? My wife, Mary, got the same, and now she's right as rain. I believe in it."

He swung back around to Beth. "Now go make me some lunch, and don't forget the Diet Pepsi. While I'm eating, I want you to start on the woodwork in here – scrub top to bottom, right round the windows and doors. I want it finished by this afternoon. But first," he said, pointing at the cane, "that stuff goes back in the safe."

He watched her painfully gather up the handcuffs and cane and replace them. "Now close the door and spin the dial for me."

When she turned around, he was signalling her silently with his finger to come over. Then he put his hand beneath her dress and touched her between the legs. It was nearly as painful as the throb from behind. She felt his finger slide inside and her knees began trembling.

"I've got a way with women, sheila. I know how to treat 'em."

He pulled his finger out and wiped it on a handkerchief.

"Now go fetch me a nice salad and a Pepsi. I'll eat it here, as I've got some phone calls to make."

He picked up the receiver and dialled. Since the police left he had not thought once about his chauffeur, who was at that moment being opened from gut to gullet for an autopsy.

Sheikh Abdullah opened the door of his Eaton Square flat for his visitor himself, as his butler was busy in the kitchen supervising a special dinner for the evening, a dinner to which he looked forward with relaxed anticipation. Michael Regis had introduced him to a charming young lady who lived off the King's Road, Glenda Howard. Glenda was exactly the sort of English girl he liked best. Dark red – nearly auburn – hair surrounding rosy cheeks and very milky white skin. The girl had very large breasts and Abdullah was extremely fond of large breasts. The bigger the better. Regis had told him that Glenda loved krugerrands.

But first it was business, and Sheikh Abdullah showed Julian van der Bijl into the reception room. Van der Bijl still wore the leather jacket he had worn that morning when he spoke to Sam Bernstein.

Van der Bijl refused Abdullah's offer of a drink.

"No, I shan't be long," he said as he sat in the comfortable leather armchair. "I am happy to say that I am a messenger of good news today."

Abdullah clasped his hands over his stomach and smiled. "Ah, excellent. I love good news. It soothes me."

"The tape has been recovered. And destroyed. So you can inform your shy and retiring friend that he can relax."

"Hmmm," Abdullah mused. "And the girl, Miss—"

"Interestingly," said Van der Bijl, "the tape was held by Harvey Gillmore's chauffeur, not, as your friend believed, by Miss Montgomery. However, to be on the safe side, her silence will be guaranteed."

The Sheikh frowned slightly. "*Will* be?"

"It is being attended to this week."

The Saudi sighed. "Then it is not all . . . quite . . . good news."

"Oh, yes," said Van der Bijl confidently. "It was necessary to entice her out of London to a suitable location where she will be interviewed shortly."

"How shortly?"

"By the end of the week."

"Hmmm." Abdullah sounded unconvinced. "This is already a week longer than you first promised, Julian. My friend is extremely worried and remains very exposed through the indiscretions of the Australian lunatic. Truly a loose cannon about whom we must do something. My brothers and I are proposing moves to hobble WORLDWIDE so that Gillmore can be properly controlled. A useful man, but also extremely dangerous. Meanwhile I think we are going to have to give thought to retrieving a number of other tapes he has made which can be considered compromising. Do you know any . . . burglars? By any chance? Someone who might be able to help us in this matter?"

On a notepad in front of him Harvey Gillmore had written: *J.W. Haug, 230c Junction Road, N19.* There was also a telephone number, and he was talking on the telephone to Ian Castleberry.

"I should think", Castleberry was saying, "that it is really a matter for the police, Harvey. You say that he actually attacked you? In your office? How on earth did he get in?"

"He was with that whore of Regis's."

There was a change in Castleberry's voice. "Which . . . whore?"

"Jennifer Montgomery, the bitch. She's hired him as a private detective, but I think there's more to it than that. I think she fancies the bastard."

Gillmore waited a few moments, idly watching Beth scrub woodwork at the window.

"Ian, are you still there?"

"Yes. Of course," Castleberry said, distractedly. "Michael uses her as a prostitute, you say?"

"Sure, everybody knows that. I dicked her, Regis dicks her. And all his mates. Sometimes he even pays for his mates. But not for me," said Gillmore testily. "I'm not a good enough friend. Fifteen hundred quid a fuck – now that is the most I've ever parted with for nookie. But she was the best in town, cobber."

"I see." Castleberry's voice was low.

"Anyway, Ian, I want this guy closed down. His licence revoked, whatever. He's not going to make a living in the UK, not while I'm still alive. I'm going to buy the building he's living in as well. My solicitors tell me it's owned by some Paki."

"Harvey, please!" said Castleberry in an exasperated tone of voice. "The profanity is bad enough. But I simply cannot allow the language of bigotry. After all, I am a member of HM's government, and as her minister I represent the interests of *all* the people, not just some of them."

Gillmore laughed. "What about abo, then? Or wog? Do you get the same kind of campaign contributions from the wogs that you get from me? Or editorial support? Check your bread for the buttered side, mate."

The Minister's voice was sharp. "Listen, Harvey, I promise to do what I can, make a few enquiries about Mr . . . er, Haug and his agency, but I really can't promise anything—"

"Call Adrian at the Home Office," Gillmore interrupted. "See if there's any way of deporting the bastard."

"I will speak to Adrian as well," he promised.

"If we can't do anything officially, then I'm going to go unofficial, Ian. I'll hire East Enders with pickaxe handles. I'd prefer to do it the other way," he said as Castleberry started to protest, "but I'm going to hound that man into his grave, an early one. I'll make sure of that. He is going to wish that he'd never been born. No one who has ever crossed me hasn't eaten sulphur in the pits of Hell."

"Yes, Harvey. Yes, Harvey. I must run. Urgent meeting."

Ian Castleberry hung up the telephone quickly, cursing himself silently for having to be pleasant to a man like that. But somehow Harvey Gillmore delivered votes, and the word was to give him anything he wanted. His mind was, however, elsewhere.

Jennifer. The moment Gillmore mentioned it, he knew that it was true. Had to be. Of course. It was the humiliation of it all, though. To be taken in by Michael like that. The man had probably laughed his head off. And the whore, Jennifer. It actually hurt to think of her selling her body. She had been so beautiful, so convincing.

'Well,' he thought as he leaned back in his chair, 'fifteen hundred pounds, eh? That's what you get for that kind of money. Serves you right for being romantic at your age, and with a family as well.'

His thoughts were interrupted by Sir Jonathan Mainwaring, who tapped on the door and entered. He was carrying a manila folder.

"Have a read of this when you get a chance, Ian. Some information the staff have put together on WORLDWIDE with all the usual projected pitfalls."

Castleberry tossed the folder to the corner of his desk. "The devil with WORLDWIDE. I've just been talking to the insufferable owner."

"The cultivated Mr Gillmore?"

"Yes. Because he's who he is, he calls the bloody Department of Trade and Industry for what is basically a police matter. He is being hounded by some American private investigator who apparently burst into his office and attacked him on Sunday."

"Good Lord," said Mainwaring. "But unfortunately he survived?"

"I'm reading between the lines", said Castleberry with a sigh, "but I gather it has something to do with the Saudi business you keep warning me about. Or perhaps he's just paranoid, I don't know. Anyway, it's just a bloody headache. I've got so much to do and little time to do it in. Everyone's nagging me. The PM nags me, you're nagging me, and now Gillmore calls and wants to revoke someone's licence. It's like the little straw that broke the camel's back, Jonathan."

Mainwaring smiled gently. "Yes, perhaps I should be helping a bit more instead of hindering, Ian. Give me the details on this private investigator, and I'll drift them on downstream so that you can say something is being done."

"Good. Excellent."

210

He tore off a sheet from his pad and handed it to his Permanent Secretary. "You deal with it. Get it out of my sight."

The telephone rang and Castleberry picked it up, nodding goodbye to Mainwaring, who carried the sheet of paper between thin thumb and forefinger as he left the room.

In his own office Sir Jonathan Mainwaring sat behind his neatly ordered desk and thought deeply. Finally he opened the piece of paper and studied the contents, wondering idly how the family name was pronounced. Mainwaring didn't altogether trust feelings and couldn't understand why he had such a strong feeling about this incident mentioned by the Minister. An attack on Harvey Gillmore was completely understandable, and it surprised him that the man had survived this long. Gillmore had more enemies than anyone he knew, living or dead. A detestable man.

Mainwaring looked at the note again. An American private investigator, he thought with slight distaste. That conjured up one of two images. A wise cracking busybody in a fedora. Or a gum-chewing, sweaty, balding man who scratched his privates in public. And why American? Are they taking over everything, even the seedier ends of life here? Most of all, why was he even interested in Mr J.W. Haug?

Then again, he thought, leaning back, perhaps it wasn't just a feeling. He considered chess. Not the best analogy, but it would do. Quite often, after analysing the board in a particular position, one had a strong feeling for a move or strategy of moves. Feelings which arise in such circumstances are often more than just feelings. They are a result of analysis. There is a weakness on the king side which is developing rather than evident, so you 'feel' that your attack must build in that direction.

Suddenly he decided that he had wasted enough time, so he refolded the note and placed it carefully inside his wallet.

———

Beth was still studying the name on Gillmore's pad, but she didn't know why she was staring at it. She remembered the big man with the bald head who had grown so angry with her boss. And the pretty woman who was with him.

Beth was very, very tired and realised that she had been standing and staring at the desk for a long time. Gillmore had gone out without saying where he was going or when he was coming back. She had risked taking her shoes off to give her feet and legs some relief. They were hurting more than her bottom. She held her shoes in her hand and looked down at his chair, suddenly shocked with a sense of danger. Carefully and a little painfully, she lowered herself into the chair, listening for any sound of a door opening. Her heart began to pound and her breathing became deeper. One moment she felt dead, and next moment she was alive again. And her body welcomed the cool comfort of the chair. It wasn't comfort she sought though. What was it she sought? What was it? It was driving her crazy.

She reached over and touched the model of his horse which he always kept on his desk. It seemed to be made of metal and was heavy. Her hand glided from the horse and across the smooth, clean, black surface of the desk to the telephone, which she picked up, every nerve alert and straining. Slowly she dialled the number on the notepad. The number rang several times. Then a woman answered; an Irish voice?

Quickly Beth hung up the telephone and stared at it, alarmed at what she had done. She picked up her cloth and wiped what she imagined were fingerprints off the phone and the horse, and started to get up. But she didn't want to and sat down again, leaning back this time. Every muscle was tired, and every joint. Her dress stuck to her body, and the leather was cool to her back. She was worried that she was going insane. What was it like to be insane? She must be insane to love him. Thomas had been kind to her. Oh, Thomas, what had happened to him? And the big bald man, he had been kind to her too.

But it was his touch she craved. And his curses. Before he left he had stopped and watched her for a couple of minutes.

He had said, "I like to see a sweaty woman working for me."

Then he had left.

She got up wearily and washed her cloth in the pail.

Sam Bernstein registered in a modern hotel outside Fowey near St Austell under the name of Ralph Cotton, Sales Director, UDS Software, Wilmington, Delaware. He carried a passport and driving licence in that name, with which he had hired a Jaguar XJ12 in London.

Bernstein carried his two bags into the single bedroom on the
second floor and dumped them on the bed before calling Van der Bijl
with the address and telephone number of the hotel. Then he spread
the Ordnance Survey map over the bed, studying it carefully. He had
obtained general instructions on the address from a petrol station in
Fowey. After plotting his route, he opened both bags. From one he
took a full bottle of Wild Turkey, opened it and poured one finger in a
glass. Then he laid out a pair of black jeans, a black jumper and
trainers.

From the other bag he took out a shoulder holster, unwrapped a
small 9mm automatic, checked the breech and inserted a loaded clip.
There was an Uzi wrapped in oiled paper at the bottom, but he left
that where it was. He then changed his clothes, strapped on the pistol
and covered it with the windbreaker.

From the bag which had held the pistol he extracted another
smaller bag. He opened it and checked the contents carefully. There
were a number of items inside – a powerful torch, a night compass,
infra-red binoculars, a penlight, Swiss Army knife, a sheath knife,
pens, matches and survival paraphernalia. He put everything back
inside and zipped the small bag closed. The other two bags he also
closed and locked, placing one underneath the bed.

Bernstein checked his watch. Nearly six o'clock. He would find
the place while it was still light, park nearby and wait for dusk.
Looking at the Ordnance Survey map had cheered him up. It was
across the bay from Fowey, perfectly isolated. He couldn't have
asked for better. Already a plan was beginning to form. As he
reached for the Wild Turkey, he found himself looking forward to
putting a bullet between the eyes of this jack-off who was playing out
of his league. And no fooling around this time with the girl. Maybe
she was pretty, but that didn't make a fucking bit of difference to Sam
Bernstein. He remembered an Arab girl in the Strip with gorgeous
big black eyes who couldn't have been more than seventeen.
Bernstein dropped her with a head shot when two of the others had
hesitated because she was so beautiful. Ten minutes later Bernstein
was eating a sandwich. He couldn't have cared less. Arabs were
Arabs. Arabs were enemies. If more people in the Service would
realise that, they could clean out the whole nest of them in no time at
all. That's the only thing they understood – fucking bullets.

But no, they told Bernstein, he was too wild. He was eased out with a lot of clucking tongues and asshole officers talking about politics and about how Arabs were human beings. Arabs were sub-human garbage. Didn't even make decent servants. Anyway, that was his career fucked. Kept his pension.

Then, three years ago, he had been approached by Van der Bijl and the South Africans. They had met in Tel Aviv some time ago when the South African was negotiating for arms supply. Suddenly he had another job. Training South Africans to operate in tight groups of three. He tried to place one experienced Israeli in each group, but he couldn't always find good men. And he never used anybody he didn't know personally.

"I'm one of the best," Bernstein said out loud, sitting on the edge of the bed. "And here I am at a turkey shoot. Some fucking redneck."

He finished his drink, checked his watch again, got up and zipped his jacket. He was ready to go.

Chapter Fifteen

At noon on Tuesday Haug sat in a canvas chair near the end of the pier and cast a line into the sea. He wore a pair of flowered shorts and his dozer cap. Jennifer lay on a beach towel nearby wearing only a pair of sunglasses. It was a warm day and even the breeze from the sea had lost its edge since the morning.

"Almost like summer," Haug said. "Unusual, this time of the year, even for Cornwall."

Jennifer turned on to her stomach. "You didn't bring my swimming costume."

"Don't need one here."

"You've got those shorts on," she complained. "Dreadful things. Where did you get them?"

"Cain't remember. Had 'em for years. Thought they looked high-class."

"All the king's horses and all the king's men couldn't make you look high-class, Haug."

"Aw, shit, don't say thangs like that. You don't know how sensitive I am."

He put the rod under his foot, grabbed a can of beer and pulled the tab.

"Funny bugger," she said. "I'm hungover. What did you call that stuff we were drinking last night?"

"White lightnin'. Or moonshine. Feller who makes it calls it grape brandy, but it don't taste like grapes or brandy. Good moonshine, though. Comes from Harnett County, North Carolina."

"You seem to have a lot of it. How on earth do you get it into the UK?"

"He sends it over in these cases of O'Connell's Fireball Barbecue Sauce. Never been opened by Customs yet."

Jennifer laughed. "I'm sure you're winding me up with all these stories of yours. Trying to make me believe that there are cartoon characters with hillbilly accents and banjos followed around by hound dogs covered in flies and ticks."

"Not hillbilly. You wouldn't unnerstand that accent, not if we got back in there. But the South . . . the South is colourful. Beautiful place. I miss it a lot. But I'm not hillbilly. I come from the foothills. Hell, I grew up thinkin' all that stuff I been tellin' you was normal. It was only when I left that I started to appreciate the place. 'Cept for the goddam' racial attitudes. It's improved, but it's still fuckin' bad. And I was one of 'em once. Maybe that's why I hate it so much. 'Cause I unnerstand it. That makes you really hate it when you unnerstand it."

"You promised to tell me about your conversion on the road to Damascus."

Haug chuckled and picked up the rod, thinking that there was a pull on the line.

"I made it a little overdramatic. Didn't happen all at once, of course. I started readin' these books while I was in 'Nam. I tell you, everthang was so crazy over there I just about went nuts. It was Dickens, like I said. I may have read him in high school, I don't know, but when I read him this time I'd done a lot more livin'. And a lotta killin'. Then I started askin', you know, other guys I saw readin', what they were readin' and why. That was the first bit. Readin' made me start thinkin' for the first time in my life. Second bit came when I met César Chavez. Ever heard of him?"

"I don't think so," she answered. "Spanish?"

"Mexican American. I got outta the army in California and went whorin', hell-raisin' and fightin' down across the border. Wrecked my car and had to come back by bus. Anyway, I was sittin' in this seat on the bus with a cracked head and busted knuckles and I started talkin' to the guy sittin' next to me. And he was César Chavez. I didn't know his name then either. He was the head of the United Farm Workers Union. Now, Jenny, I've met a lotta folks in my life, but that guy impressed me more than any of 'em. I don't think there's such a thang as a good person, but if there were, he would be one of 'em. Kind, gentle, intelligent, but with iron in his gut. D'ya know what I mean? He invited me to stay at his home for a day or two till my head felt better, and I did. That's when I started learnin' somethin' about politics and what some people'll do to get money. Do to other people. You hear about all kinds of union barons and all that crap, but Chavez never owned a car in his life and only drew union wages. When you saw him, he looked like a poor man, but when he walked down the street, hell, now that was an experience. When he walked down the street, he had *respect*. Not like a dook or king or prince or even rich folks. Not like any other kind of respect I've seen. He was a quiet, natural person. But lemme tell you, if he saw evil, he would stand in its way. It wouldn't pass unless it passed over his dead body. They came after his workers with pickaxe handles, and he would stand up to them unarmed, just calm and quiet and . . . good. I wound up stayin' there and workin' for nothin' for three months. In those three months I learned more than I ever learned in my life – includin' university, where I went next."

Haug took a drink from his can. "Racism. It's one of those thangs certain groups of people, certain governments encourage to keep the poor whites from linkin' up with the poor blacks or the poor Mexicans. Get 'em all together pushin' against what is really wrong and the rich folks got big trouble."

"Well, you can't say that you haven't led an eventful life, Haug."

"If I had to live it again, I wish I could do somethin' useful, like Chavez. Maybe I could even learn to do it without violence . . ."

"I've got to admit that that frightens me."

"It's a violent goddam' world. Ever since I can remember there's been some country where people are hackin' each other to pieces. Or countries. Everwhere. Even here or the States, so-called civilised countries, fulla violence. There's the head-bustin' kind, which is what I think you're objectin' to, but there's also the violence of society against people. Closin' down a factory, a pit, a mill destroys the whole community. Shops close, nobody can pay the rent or mortgage, so they move away – thousands of lives wrecked. To wreck lives, that's violence, Jenny. When I first came here, I hardly ever saw a beggar, 'cept the odd drunk. Now I'm up to my ass in beggars ever time I move around in London. Beggars, cripples, the insane, folks without anythang, no hope. All they got is a sign hangin' around their neck with their life story written in pencil. That's civilised? Hell, Jenny, I don't go out and stir up violence. I don't go huntin' it with a gun and deerstalker hat. It comes up and smacks me in the nose. I don't hit the weak, I hit the strong. I have not got the inner resources of somebody like César Chavez. I go ape shit. Paid and trained by the US Army, remember."

She leaned on her elbow and looked at him. "There's that, I suppose. But you got out of bed this morning and trained with weights. I could not believe it. You train for violence, Hoggy."

He put the rod under his foot again and turned to her. "Yeah, you got somethin' there, I reckon. I've always worked out. Doesn't feel right to miss many days. A habit."

"It's a holiday. So far, the most beautiful one I can remember. With a beautiful man I can relax with, talk to, touch . . . without the thought that I'm going to regret it tomorrow or the next day. And there you are, lifting barbells."

He got up, bringing the rod with him, and lay down beside her. Then he stuck the rod under his foot again. He grinned.

"Usually I don't respond very well to criticism about my habits. That's the way I am, take it or leave it. Usually. But in this one case I think you got a point. But, hell, I thought you were asleep anyway."

"Just pretending. I was feeling so relaxed, and it was so quiet except for the sea and the birds. I just wanted to lie there and feel you nearby. But no. To my utter amazement I hear grunt, sweat, push, ugh . . ."

"You didn't complain last night when we were gruntin' and sweatin' and pushin'."

"Listen, Haug, I don't know what it is, but sex is fucking fantastic with you. I have never really *liked* it before. Not really. It was just something you do. Tingles occasionally. Occasionally there's a kind of orgasm, I suppose. But when you touch me it's really nice. I really, really want to do it. What's the secret?"

He leaned over and put his hand gently on her tummy. "The secret is . . . chemical. Or electrical. Chemistry makes good lovers of us all. We hum together. You just haven't picked the right fellers."

"OK, so you've had it lots of times, right? This chemistry?" she asked petulantly.

"Well, quite a few. But I tell you right now, I haven't had quite a few who hit the bell like you did. You in a category of your own."

She took off her sunglasses. "Do you mean that?"

"Course I do. Did you think I was puttin' on an act roarin' like a lion and bayin' like a dog who's treed a possum? I was hummin' in places I didn't even know I had places. My mind was reelin' like I bit into the best piece of angel food cake I ever tasted, whoopin' like a crane, chewin' pieces of the rug up and spittin' out wool bullets, draggin' my fingernails across the floor like a yard rake, my eyeballs spinnin' in their sockets like pinballs when you hit the jackpot. Holy shit, honeypot, I've had just about the best fuckin' I can remember in my life, and you're thinkin' I got some sort of secret recipe I use on 'em all. I wish the hell I did. We just twang together, that's all. But what a goddam twang!"

"Well, I reckon that's one of the sweetest thangs I ever did hear," she said, mimicking his accent. "Wanna do it again?"

"Hell, cain't you see I'm fishin'?"

He leaned over and kissed her breast, sucking the nipple into his mouth and caressing it with his tongue.

"Have you got the right rod and tackle?"

She slid her hand underneath his shorts, along his belly, and found his penis which was still half soft.

"Not going to catch much with that."

"Hgmmgh," he said.

"Pardon?"

Haug lifted his head. "My mammy told me not to talk with my mouth full. I sure hope I don't wear these thangs out suckin' on 'em."

He lowered his head and pulled as much of her breast as possible into his mouth, letting his hand drift down to her pubis.

"I feel absolutely wanton lying here at midday, out in the open, naked, making love," she murmured as she raised one leg to let his fingers into her.

His penis was stirring, hardening under her caresses.

"Take these ridiculous shorts off."

Haug struggled out of the boxers and the two of them lay close, touching and kissing. Clutching each other, they rolled off the towel. Jennifer was on top. She sat up.

"You can be on the bottom this time. I don't want any splinters in *my* arse."

"What about a two by four?" asked Haug.

"You flatter yourself." She raised her hips and used her hand to guide him into her.

"Ah," he said as he felt himself slowly disappear. "You got the sweetest-feelin' snatch in the world."

"That sounds like a compliment. Not sure I like the word 'snatch'. A little coarse."

"I ain't nothin' but trailer trash, honey. Only my shorts got any class, and you don't like 'em."

She was moving slowly up and down, leaning forward. "It's nice fucking out of doors. Feels naughty."

"I'm in the mood for somethin' slow after all that frenzy last night."

Jennifer sat up, pulling her knees under her, and moved her hips in a circular motion.

"Hmmm. Hoggy. There's a boat out there with two men. They're watching us."

Haug raised himself enough to have a look then lay back down.

"Local fisherfolk. Simple. Hardworkin'. Salt of the earth. Wave to 'em like a good neighbour."

She waved.

"One of them is waving back."

The younger man in the boat turned to the other one. "Now that's what *I* would like to be doing."

The older one had grey hair which was rucked up by the wind. He had throttled the engine back and was squinting towards the shore.

"Wish my eyes were better."

"Want me to describe it to you?"

The older man scratched his head. "No, better not. Won't be good for me."

"They're really going at it now."

"Is she waving again?"

"Don't think so," said the younger one. "Think she might just be getting a little overexcited. Want to drift in a little closer?"

The older one watched for a moment then spat into the water. He opened the throttle.

"Better leave them to it. We've got a living to make. Anyway they shouldn't be doing it out in the open like that. Bad for people."

"It's not doing me any harm," said the young man. "Rather be at it than watching it, though. Who is the fellow?"

The older man turned the boat back out to sea. "American, I'm told. Watched him float that JCB over on the raft, lost ten pounds to my cousin. Crazy American."

"Who is she?"

"No idea. He's quite a jack the lad, though. Likes the ladies."

"I can see that."

"Too many tourists around here nowadays," the older man said, turning his back on the shore.

Haug and Jennifer lay side by side. His arm cradled her head.

"They're all different, aren't they?" he asked.

"Hmmm. Love the sound of the sea. How long are we staying?"

"Don't know. Few days, maybe a week. Did Regis ever introduce you to any South Africans?"

She thought for a moment. "No. I don't even think I ever met a South African before. African, yes. But not South African."

"African? You mean black?"

"Yes. Nice man, really. Very polite, quite kind. A gentleman, I suppose."

"Are you sure he wasn't a black South African?"

"No, I remember he said he was Nigerian. And that's where Michael said he was from. Nigeria. A businessman, I think. Not tall, I'd say late forties, well-built, not fat, soft-spoken, well-spoken, smiled a lot. Clothes weren't terribly expensive. No dangly gold. Clean. That's all I can remember."

"Well, it was a thought," said Haug. "What about Israelis?"

"No. At least none I'm aware of."

"Gotta be some connection somewhere. What was Regis's reaction when you told him about the tape?"

"I told you."

"I mean, how did he sound? The tone of voice?"

She raised herself up on an elbow.

"Cold at first. But when I asked for money he was angry. First time I can remember him losing his temper. Called me a bloody whore, a blackmailer, said he wasn't interested in the bloody tape anyway – just blathered really. Usually he's so self contained."

"And after you gave him the telephone number?"

"Cold again. Got his feet back under him. Like I told you, he said not to expect to hear from him again. Not to get in touch with him ever. Then he hung up."

Haug sucked a tooth. "Give my right ball to know who he called next."

"I doubt if he called anyone," she said. "He's the sort of man other people call."

"Oh, he called somebody. I'd *bet* my right ball on that."

"You're awfully extravagant with your right ball."

"That's 'cause I only use my left one. If I used both of 'em, I'da blown you into the ocean."

She leaned over and grabbed his testicles. "Next time I want you to prove it, you big hog."

"Careful," he said. "That could go off in your hand."

She shook her head. "I don't think so somehow. I bet there aren't any bullets left."

"Yeah, well, it takes us old sweats a while to reload."

She leaned back.

"Haug. May I ask you something? You don't seem too upset about what I do. What I did."

"The way I see it, you're another person and I've got no right to judge. If I hadda had your problems, your life, your range of choices, I'm sure I woulda done the same thang. But I don't think that's what you're askin' me, is it? If I were in love with you, I'm sure that jealousy would start oozing up through the cracks."

"You aren't in love with me." She said it as a statement.

Haug looked off at the headland of the cove, watching the gulls.

"I hear all the alarms ringin', so I know there's a fire. Just don't know right now whether to throw water on it or petrol. Too goddam' soon anyway. You've just been kicked up and down the stairway of life a few days ago. I'm surprised you even want to touch a man any more."

She was pensive for a moment.

"It seems a lifetime ago. I sealed it off, you see. There's a place inside, a kind of sub-basement. I learned the trick of shoving all the nightmares down there and sealing it like a tomb. A magic door. They can go in, but they can't come back out."

She paused, thinking. "Except sometimes. I can look at it now because I'm a little happy. But I don't want to because it makes me sad. Angry."

Suddenly she slapped her hand down on the wooden deck. "Fuck you, Haug. Why did you have to bring it up?"

"I tell you one thang, Jenny. You got an impressive strength in you. Anybody else woulda been in a mental home the next day, and I wouldn't'a blamed 'em a bit."

"I've had a lot of practice. I grew up with it, remember? There was no one else to call on, not when you were an only child, your mother is gone, and your father comes creeping into your bed and puts his hands under your nightie. And you don't know what to do. It's a man, but it's also your father. Your mind splits into two halves and those two halves shatter into millions of tiny fragments, each reflecting little pieces of reality. You can't call for help, can you? Your father is already there. Who else does a girl of thirteen ask? A policeman? When you're full to the brim with shame and confusion, and you're sure that it's not right but not sure that it's completely wrong because, after all, that man is your father. Your parent. The person you trusted. You have to trust because that's all there is. I wasn't an adult. I was a child. I knew a little about sex, and I was very interested. But very embarrassed, too. That bastard spoiled everything for me – that's the way I see it."

"And for what?"

She turned on to her back and grabbed her breasts. "Is the female body so overpowering that men can't be normal? Can't control themselves? Can't let us be, when we don't want them? It can't be just sex, can it? That only lasts for a few minutes, and you can't do it all the time – it's not possible. No, it's not just sex. I'll answer my own question. You want to dominate us all the time. Possess us, like furniture or a pickup truck to sit in or lie on or drive any time you want, and meanwhile clean your house, buy and cook your food and serve it, swell up and pop open with children from time to time until we're old and then you boot us out and find someone younger. Right?"

"I'm listenin'," he said.

"How could he do it – my father? That's what I keep asking myself. Was it worth it to him? He's not stupid. How could he dare break the trust between himself and a child? To have such a little thing, he gave up such a lot! He could have had my love and trust for the rest of his life. Can you answer that question?"

"No, I cain't. I only know that reason is only a part of any person, and maybe it's just a small part, however dominant we think it is. And even reason is loaded, isn't it? It's not objective, somethin' you can balance on a scale. My guess is that reason didn't have a damn thang to do with why your dad abused you. You say he gave up a lot, and he certainly did. But he never looked at it that way, I guess. In his reasoning, he got what he thought he wanted. Or needed. And that's the important bit. Selfishness. Self-interest. Someone wants somethin', he grabs it. Reckons he needs it, has the power, grabs - fuck you and your problems. And I think you're right. Men got the power, so they want and grab. They figger - if they figger at all - that you'd do the same thang if you had the power and they didn't."

"But that can't be right, Haug, if everybody just takes what they want."

"No, it's not right. That's how power works, though."

"You're different, aren't you?"

Haug laughed. "Only one way am I kinda different. I just don't want thangs that bad. Yeah, I wanted you, for instance. I wanted you in the gym. Hell, we used to joke about you, how pretty you were, how you had your nose in the air, what we'd like to do to you - usual stuff. But I can recognise that as a fantasy. When I knew more about you, I wanted you in a different way, a real one. I didn't know if it was the right thang or not. Still don't. Now the only unusual bit as far as I can see is that at any point I can turn around and walk away from it. If you tell me right now to fuck off, I'm not gonna plead with you or beg you or grab you. I might wanna know why, but I can walk away from this thang right now. Or the pickup truck. Or that house over there. I been with 'em, I been without 'em. Doesn't make me any different, one way or the other. Sometimes you hurt for a little while, but that soon passes.

"What beats me is how you drag the kinda weight you got behind you, without a family, without a friend, and you bein' so young."

Jennifer turned back on her stomach and put her sunglasses on.

"I decided I wanted to survive. Not like I sat down and made a big decision. But over a period of time. My father took me to a play when I was about ten. At that time I thought he had his arm around me because he loved me as a daughter. It was a Noel Coward play, *Blithe Spirit*. It was so funny, so witty. And the actors - what they were doing! I knew what I wanted to be. I said, that is me. That is what I want. He did let me go and see plays, my father. Gave me the

224

money. So I had that beacon in front of me. You see? That's all I really wanted to do, be in the theatre.

"When I started developing – my tits grew, I filled out a bit – I started using my father. Baiting him. Making him pay for it. I couldn't escape at first, but I could pretend to be ill or having my period. Other times I would come on to him. When I wanted something. Clothes, money, West End tickets, travel. You may think that's a little calculating, whorish. . . ″

"I don't."

". . . but it was about power. For once I had a little power. The first time in my life. When the time came, I stole his money and left him there. The penny had dropped though. The one advantage I have is looks. And talent. I'm a bloody good actress! But this power business is illusory. I thought I had more than I do in fact. All the while, Michael is pulling the strings, making more from me than he is paying. Probably a lot more."

"You're right there," Haug agreed. "You're makin' a lot of money, but you're spendin' it. He's usin' you to invest in more and more power. When you put all that down on the balance sheet, you gonna be short-changed in a big way."

"It's not fair. It's not fair."

"It was never *fair* from the beginnin'. It starts unfair, and it continues that way until the end. We're all in the shit, but some people have boats."

"Haug, I'm going to tell you what I was thinking last Friday at that house, wherever they took me. I thought only about how I could survive, get out of there alive. Or that's what I tried to do, but I failed. The terror finally overcame me, although I was struggling to hang on. And I gave up. I felt myself give up. For the first time."

Haug rolled on his side and put an arm around her shoulders.

"Lissen. I don't know anybody who wouldn't face a hail of bullets than be hog-tied, helpless and tormented like a wingless fly. Anybody would go in time, most of 'em long before you went. You cain't whip yourself for bein' a human bein'."

"You wouldn't have broken, Haug. You would have hung on, I know it." She was struggling to keep her voice steady.

"Don't believe it," he said. "I don't know what I'd do, and you cain't know until you've been there. I know enough about myself to know that I can be as weak as any person on earth."

"What it feels like inside now is that I've lost something valuable. Whatever it was . . . my willpower or purpose in life or sense of self. Whatever it was seemed to snap. That's when I felt helpless. I felt sick. Why did they do that to me? Why did they have to do that to me? They didn't care what I was feeling. They just wanted to torture me."

"That's not quite right. They cared what you were feelin', all right. That's why they were doin' what they did. The more frightened you got, the more terrified you were, the better they liked it. I've known people like that. Find a lot of 'em in armies."

She grabbed hold of his hand.

"Do you know what the worst thing was? I mean that was the first time I'd ever been raped. You see, men have got it wrong when they think that rape is nothing, just someone forcing you to have sex. Because the sex didn't have a lot to do with it. It's because you have no power. You're physically unable to stop the person having sex with you. Therefore you know you can't stop him doing *anything* to you. I didn't know whether I was going to die or be cut or mutilated or beaten or left so that I couldn't walk again. Your imagination goes wild when you're terrified, Haug. And that man, the fat one, was the worst. I knew that he was going to kill me, I just knew it. And I didn't want to die. I didn't. I didn't. I worked so hard to live in that room with him, but in the end I just broke."

She turned her head away from him and he could feel her sobbing. He held on to her, rocking her body gently, like a baby. Struggling, she turned back towards him, her face wet with tears. Her sunglasses were gone.

"You don't know what it feels like – I can't tell you what it feels like – to be totally alone in the world, but that's what I am. OK, I thought I was tough, I thought I could take it. I was going to hammer out my life like a blacksmith, make it something in spite of everything and everyone. But, God, in that house – no, in the back of the van on the way to the house – I felt so lonely. I wanted a friend. Someone to come, do something, hold me, take me away, wipe away my tears, let me be weak, not try and take everything away, let me trust them. Oh, I wanted all that, Haug. And I wanted to wake up and find that my past had all been a nightmare, and I could turn to my father and he would take me back in. Do you know what I am saying? Oh, God, this is *so* hard . . ."

Haug held to her. "Do you think it's a bad thang to feel vulnerable?"

"Yes, I do," she said. "When I'm vulnerable, *that's* when people hurt me most."

"Well, I cain't promise never to hurt you because I cain't see the future. But what you've said to me is a secret between us. And, anyway, you got one friend now. You can come and cry and talk or laugh. You can be just how you feel and I'm not gonna turn it back against you. Even if we drift away in other ways, you can always come back and prop your feet in front of my fire."

"I wish I could tell you what that means to me," she said. "I hope it's the truth."

"You can trust me."

She raised her head. "I don't know how. Don't you understand that? I have never trusted anyone in my life."

"Yes, you do. You know how. Trouble is, you don't know if you should. And I don't blame you a bit."

She sat up and reached for the towel, which she wrapped around her.

"It surprised me that I could have sex with you so soon after that . . . horror."

"Me too."

"It surprised me even more that I wanted to. But I did. I do. So I suppose you're right. I do trust you. Just a little, maybe."

Haug sat up as well. He reached for the fishing rod.

"I reckon the fish don't like my bait."

She wrapped her arm around his waist.

"Why don't you lose that bit of stomach you've got. It's not much."

Haug was reeling in the line. "You want to know the truth? Because I kinda like it like this. It feels me, it feels comfortable. I'm not a bodybuilder. I don't even think those guys with little waists are attractive. Looks stupid havin' a big pyramid balanced on its tip. Like I said, I just suit myself."

She laughed softly, drying her face on the towel.

"Yes, it is you. Wouldn't look right. Wouldn't look like a big bear any more. It's what I need to do. Think more of myself, not give a fuck what other people think."

"It saves a lot of inner stress, it really does."

"Hard to do. Hard to really do. You can say you don't care, but somewhere inside you do."

"That's right, Jenny. Truth is, there are thangs I care about. Don't wanna say thangs that hurt people I like, for instance. Or shit on somebody else's lawn. But I think it's where you draw the line. A guy's got a right to complain about me standin' on his foot, but no right at all to tell me what kinda shirt I wear. It's good to have a social conscience, what's right and wrong about gettin' along with people, but everbody from governments to neighbours gets tempted to tell you what side of your pants to wear your balls on. And speakin' of pants, where did you throw mine?"

"In the sea, I hope."

Haug saw them at the end of the pier. "Damn near."

He got up and walked down to get them. "Trouble with you, you got no class."

He put them on. "Bought these at J.C. Penny's in America. Ever heard of 'em?"

"No."

"More exclusive than Harrods. Movie stars buy all their stuff there."

"It's complicated, though," she said, "where you draw the line. Obviously people have to live together without killing each other."

"That's the theory anyway. Theory on account of the fact we don't do it very well. Even in a so-called civilised society. In a small community, there's less of a problem. But stack folks into cities like London and you run into trouble. And stack all these cities into a state and all these states into a world, it must be some sorta geometrical progression of problems. Damn near an impossibility, when you look at it. It was industrialisation and capitalism that bought people into the cities. They didn't go there naturally to live in a honeycomb like bees. I mean, how the fuck can you have a family in a big city? You cain't, not really. Even if you got a big house. Kids don't see the natural world: animals, corn growin', rabbits fuckin', thangs growin' old and dyin'. Instead they gotta worry about bein' run over by a bus or gettin' mugged and have to go a long way to be able to play in an open field. A city's fulla shops with their winders fulla thangs you cain't afford. Most of all, a city's fulla strangers, even though y'all live in the same town. It's somethin' we just haven't had time to adjust to."

228

She got up, refolding the towel around her, tucking it in at the top.

"Well, I suppose we're not going to have fish for lunch, right?"

"Can if you want. I got some in the deep freeze."

"Are you hungry?" she asked. "I sure am."

"I could eat a ham or two. But I think you're overdressed, if we're gonna eat."

"Bollocks."

"I'll cook. Would you like some genuine North Carolina barbecue?"

"With O'Connell's whatsit sauce?"

"That's right. Fireball Barbecue Sauce."

"Just the ticket," she said, putting her arm through his as they walked back towards the house.

Jennifer really liked the barbecue. Haug explained to her that Carolina barbecue was made by shredding pork, then mixing it with a special hot sauce. It could then be served on a plate or on a hamburger bun. They had theirs on a plate with coleslaw and hush puppies. Hush puppies were sweet cornbread deep-fried in oil, light and delicious if properly made. They ate so much that they decided to have a nap afterwards.

The sound of the telephone woke them about half past six, and Haug reached over to the bedside table and picked up the receiver.

It was Keef.

"That bill you were worried about has arrived. You want me to pay it?"

"Naw," said Haug. "Just keep an eye on it for me. That the only one?"

"So far."

"I expect there'll be more. We'll wait till we got a bundle of 'em, pay 'em all at the same time. What about the rest of the staff?"

"Yeah," answered Keef. "All paid, waiting for instructions."

"Try to keep Andy off the streets."

"Yeah. One Time gave him a bone to chew."

"Speak to you later."

Haug hung up and stared at the ceiling.

"Anyone I know?" Jennifer asked.

"It was Keef. Told me we got company due. And we've got a lot to do first, on account of the fact that I wanna make sure they get a good welcome."

She could tell by the tone of his voice that he was not talking about friends. "Is there something you should tell me, Haug?"

"Yeah. Your friend Regis is somehow tied in with the gang that kidnapped you."

"You're joking! No, he *can't* be. How?"

"I don't know yet," Haug replied. "But I aim to find out. Outside of my friends, Regis is the *only* one who knows we're here. Which is why I wanted you to give him my telephone number. Whole reason for the phone call you made to him. I was actually tryin' to eliminate him as a suspect, but he's gone and traced the number and given the address to unfriendly folk. One of 'em has just arrived. I expect more."

"Oh God," she said. "I should have known that this wasn't a holiday, a little piece of bliss, an escape. Haug, we're trapped here now. There's the sea at the front and hills at the back and sides. No way out."

"I'm hopin' like hell that they're thinkin' the same thang. It's a trap all right and we're sure enough the bait. And I'm hopin' I'm gonna catch me a couple of skunks. No, lissen," he said to her. "Don't worry too much. Nothin's gonna happen tonight, but we got to get ready. Keef and One Time and Nightmare Andy are providin' backup. Part of the trap."

"Nightmare Andy?"

"Yeah, I don't use him very much, as he's a little hard to control sometimes. Awful good though when you got a real nasty situation."

"I wish you had told me, Haug, I really do."

"It was best not to," he said. "And I didn't know for certain about Regis – just had my doubts. If he hadn't been involved, we woulda just had a nice holiday. So blame him, not me. Anyway, we gotta solve this thang, get these goddam sons of bitches off our backs."

He got up, pulled on his jeans and grabbed a shirt.

"Come on, Jenny. We gotta lotta work to do."

Chapter Sixteen

On Wednesday afternoon a mini van pulled into the parking lot at the red-brick hotel near St Austell called The Crossroads, and eight businessmen emerged with briefcases and overnight bags. All of them had company name tags pinned to their lapels.

The businessmen did not notice an old yellow telephone van parked in the corner of the lot and, even if they had noticed it, they would have seen that it was empty.

They did not speak together when they approached the registration desk, they merely stated their names and collected their keys. The assistant manageress at the desk scarcely noted that the men did not look like the typical businessmen whose bookings the hotel encouraged for seasonal conferences. But then she wasn't really looking at the faces. Except for the very tall man who stood towards the back. She did do a double-take on Piet because, even dressed in a suit, he looked out of place and as inelegant as a dockworker in a debutantes' ballroom. She noted his huge jaw and the simian overhang of his bow and shuddered involuntarily. The rest of the men she might have described as fit. There were certainly no fat ones. The telephone rang as they ascended the stairs and a few moments later she had forgotten all about the new guests at the hotel.

An hour after they arrived they were sitting in folding chairs in a business conference room that Sam Bernstein had booked the day before. All still wore business suits and name tags and all still carried their briefcases. When the last man arrived, Bernstein stood up and looked at each man.

"Piet, Chaim, Ferdi, Louis, Ilya, Jan, Schlomo, Andries. And you all know me. I'm Sam. First name use at all times on the operation. Here at the hotel, I am Ralph Cotton, and you are . . . who you are."

He walked over to a chart board and placed on it a high-definition, large-scale survey map. "Move your chairs around so that you can see this thing."

He waited for them to settle.

"Now there's no reason this shouldn't be straightforward, but never look at anything, even this, as a piece of cake. The house is located here, small, compact, but with heavy walls. First floor and second floor. Or, as they say in this country, ground and first. There are two subjects, male and female. I have no reason to suspect that they are armed, but they might be, so assume it. Both subjects are to be terminated, head shots, and I want to confirm both kills personally."

Bernstein turned back to the map. "Location is excellent. No neighbours. At the rear is a winding path, steep grade, fifteen minutes' descent from assembly area. That will be Team A. Team B will approach from the sea in an inflatable, row in for last two hundred metres. Team B will land first and signal by handset. Team A will then proceed from assembly area and signal Team B when in place. I will lead Team B from the sea, Chaim will lead A. A will act as backup and B will carry out assault on the house."

Bernstein leaned against the chart board. "Minimum use of firearms, silencers, and I want all shell cases accounted for. They have a small boat. At the end, Team B will place the bodies in this boat, weight it, tow it well away from the shore and sink it. Meanwhile Team A will houseclean. No garbage. I want a neat and clean picnic site. OK? Team B will return, boat deflated, packed, and A and B will ascend path to assembly point. OK, that's the general picture."

He picked up eight envelopes and handed them out. Each envelope had a first name on the front.

"These are your individual assignments, with a repeat of everything I've said, and individual maps. Normally I'd want you all to have a look at the place in daylight first, but we've got an express delivery on this one. A little pressure. Anyway, I don't think there will be any hitches, if we all concentrate. No grabass and farting around. After the operation we break camp and leave for London. There are two flights booked at Heathrow tomorrow morning for Brussels and Amsterdam. OK. Any questions?"

———

Haug had taken the call from One Time, who was still inside the little yellow van. He returned to the kitchen where Keef and Nightmare Andy sat on either side of the refectory table with mugs of tea. Haug had made barbecue and ham sandwiches, which were piled on a platter in the middle of the table. Jennifer leaned against the sink, holding her cup of tea. It had been another bright day, though the sun was hazier, and it was not as warm as Tuesday.

Nightmare Andy had a profound effect on Jennifer, who had been quiet since their arrival nearly an hour ago. Nightmare Andy had a profound effect on everybody who met him, including Haug three years ago at the gym.

Haug saw him first at the reception desk, when he came out of the dressing-rooms, and thought for a moment that the man must have stepped out of the film *Tarus Bulba*, because he looked like a medieval heathen from the wild steppes of the East, an eater of babies, a defiler of women, a sacker of churches, a scarcely human savage used in the vanguard by marauding armies to panic and scatter their enemies. This strong first impression wasn't far off the mark either.

Nightmare Andy was a Greek Cypriot who had fought against the Turks during their invasion of the island. Haug did not know many details, but it was all apparently the stuff of legend. A small band of Greek irregulars had retreated to the hills and fell upon Turkish patrols, leaving little but entrails and odd body parts at the sites of the ambushes. Isolated Turkish villages were attacked and those inhabitants who did not flee in terror were butchered, their houses and belongings torn to pieces and burned. In the end the small band was cornered by a battalion of Turks, and Nightmare Andy was the lone survivor. According to the tale, Andy had staggered into a small Greek fishing village at dawn, naked, covered in blood, still gripping the head of a Turkish captain in his right hand, his fingers locked into the empty eye sockets. There were other stories about his escape first to Greece, then to England, but Haug expected that they were embellished by the flourishes undergone by any legend passing from mouth to mouth.

In a straight fight with Nightmare Andy, Haug knew that he would lose. The vital difference was that, as far as he could see, Andy had no empathy at all with his fellow man. Andy was one of those men who would do anything to win and do it with a controlled ferocity which would leave his opponent, if he survived at all, crippled and disfigured. He was big, at over six feet and eighteen stone and strong – Haug saw him once do a chin to a bar with another man hanging on his waist – but he had a chilling lack of conscience and a roaring inner furnace of hate. Haug suspected that this came from his experiences in Cyprus, but Andy was not a man to talk a lot about his past, nor was he given to much self-examination.

Jennifer thought that he looked like the personification of evil and actually felt the blood drain from her face when she opened the door. Andy's head was shaven except for a scalp lock at the back and he wore a large earring, like a pirate. At the back of his neck the flesh was forced into folds by bunched muscle. He wore a heavy moustache over a ragged goatee. But it was his eyes which froze the blood. They were small, like the eyes of a pig, and totally without expression. If indeed his eyes were the windows of his soul, the shutters were drawn. From such a man you would expect a deep, bellowing voice. But Andy's voice was high – not squeaky, but high and light. Something had twisted this man, either genetically or historically or both. He only had to enter a bar to clear it.

"There are more than I counted on," Haug said as he sat down at the table. "I must have made an impression in round one."

"How many?" Keef's voice was grave.

"Nine, countin' the chief honcho."

"Fuck," said Keef.

Nightmare Andy didn't move. "Don't worry. No problem."

"Which makes it nine to five," Haug muttered.

"Who's the fifth?" asked Andy.

"Jenny."

Andy snorted and took a bite of ham sandwich. Haug leaned back in the chair.

"They will probably split into two parties, which gives us a better chance."

"Why is that?" Jennifer asked.

"Well," said Haug, "they're military. Or ex-military. The ones at the house certainly were. You can tell. I know the bastards, the way they think."

Keef sucked a tooth. "One group probably by boat, the other one down the hill behind. A trap, no way out."

"Right," Haug replied. "Got to be. Which means it will be two groups of four and five. You two and One Time need to jump the group comin' down the hill, and we'll hold off the other ones till you get here. All we can do, basically. There's a place on that path comin' down which I'll show you. They'll be comin' into it blind.

Now I expect that they'll all have tools, so don't fuck around or you'll get hurt. The idea is not to kill 'em, but to bust 'em up, but it's gonna be dark and they're armed, so you're just gonna have to go for it and hope for the best."

Haug turned to Andy. "Now there's a big fucker who will be here, One Time tells me. I reckon it's the feller that Keef and I know already. I gotta tell you that he's one strong, mad son of a bitch. Must be near seven foot tall and as pretty as Frankenstein's monster. A bolt straight through his neck and a brain the size of a chicken. I want you to try and draw that card outta the deck, 'cause I'm gonna worry as long as he's still lumberin' around frightenin' children."

Andy grinned, still chewing on his sandwich. "No problem."

Keef got up and plugged the kettle back in.

"But listen, man, how long can you hold the house? I'm going to worry till we get down here back to back with the wagons circled."

"Don't worry 'bout us. Just get down as soon as you can. But split up. You and One Time on one side of the house, Andy on the other."

"Push 'em into the sea," Andy laughed. "Hold 'em under the water until there are no more bubbles."

He grabbed another sandwich. "I'm hungry."

He winked at Jennifer, who looked away, and took a big bite.

Keef found the teabags and put one in his mug. "I hope you don't mind me saying this, but I think the best idea is for Jennifer to get out of here. Use the boat, go into Fowey."

"No," said Jennifer firmly.

"My idea as well," Haug said, "but she won't have it, and I'm not forcin' anybody."

Jennifer unfolded her arms and used her hands as a prop on the sink.

"Look. I'm going to admit that I'm scared to death, but I'm not letting anyone fight my battles. It's not you they want, it's me. If I went over to Fowey tonight and came back to find you all dead, how do you think I'd feel? What do you think I'd do then? No, I'm just grateful you're here. The only question in my mind is why you'd bother wasting your lives for me."

"No lives are going to be wasted," said Keef.

"There are a lot of them – I just heard you," she replied. "Accidents can happen."

"Accidents happen to other people," said Andy with a shrug. "Look, could I trouble you for some milk? Those sandwiches made me thirsty."

"I don't know how you can eat," she said, going to the fridge.

"Yeah," said Haug. "She's been as nervous as a long-tailed cat in a room fulla rockin' chairs."

"Don't worry, lady," Andy said, taking the pint of milk and flipping the top off. "They'll only get to you over my dead body."

He drank off half the pint and wiped his mouth with the back of his hand. "Where'd you say these guys come from?"

Keef came back to the table with his tea. "South Africa. Israel. So far."

"Shame they ain't Turks." He finished the rest of the pint.

The lean-to kitchen was in the back of the house and Haug pointed at the window.

"Jenny and I spent yesterday nailin' chickenwire around the downstairs windows. No tellin' what might be comin' through."

"Yeah," said Keef. "I spotted that. Gas grenades?"

Haug took another sip of tea. It was cold.

"If it was me goin' in, I wouldn't bother with gas. One concussion, smash the door, two partners comin' in layin' down fire, one to each side."

"What stumps me", said Keef, "is why they're coming in so heavy. Why so many? Like you say, if they're pros, it would only take two. If they knew what they were doing."

Haug scratched the top of his head and looked at his fingernail.

"Yeah. That's what I been sittin' here wonderin'. I mean, I'm not exactly superman. And if I wasn't expectin' anythang, two'd be plenty. I'd be sittin' here with my dick in my hand and a hole in my head. This thang's beginnin' to worry me."

"I'm glad you're finally worried," Jennifer said. "My teeth have been chattering all day."

Haug stood up and went to the window. He reached into his rear pocket for his tobacco pouch and broke off a piece.

"Naw, I'm not so worried about these assholes tonight. It's the size, the scale of this business."

He turned to Jennifer as he put the tobacco in his mouth. "Whatever you're supposed to have must be pretty damn' big. I mean, like atomic secrets or somethin'. They wouldn't bother this much otherwise. And I'm thinkin' that it might not be just the tape."

"What else could it be?" she asked.

"Somethin' you know. Maybe some*body* you know. Shit, whatever it is, it must be big. And who the hell are these guys? South Africans? Jesus. Well, I aim to find out tonight. If I cain't shake the information outta one of 'em, Andy sure can."

He opened the outside door and spat.

Jennifer winced. "That's a dreadful habit."

"Now," Haug said, closing the door. "Afterwards. Assumin' all goes well. There's gonna be a lotta racket at some point, so we wanna haul ass outta here. In case somebody comes to investigate. But let's try and clear up, so nothin's obvious. I hope there won't be any dead, but if there are, they gotta be chucked somewhere in the ocean with rocks around 'em. These guys will probably be as worried as we are about that."

He turned to Keef. "You still got that gun?"

Keef raised his jumper and pulled out the small automatic they had taken from Fanie on Friday.

"I won't use it unless something goes wrong, Haug. I got a pickaxe handle for the main business."

Haug turned to Andy. "What have you got? Louisville Slugger?"

Andy opened his holdall and pulled out a baseball bat and machete, then he replaced them.

"What about you?"

"Don't worry about me," Haug said. "Now I better take you up and show you that place for the ambush. I think it's probably best if you two hide there and leave One Time to follow down behind 'em. He'll give you a buzz as they're startin' down so that you can dust off home plate."

Downstairs there was a sitting room and smaller room that Haug used as a gym and office. The lean-to kitchen led from the dining-room and a toilet from the office. Upstairs were two bedrooms and a small bath. Haug spent most of the rest of the afternoon studying the house from the sea, pacing off and timing the distance from the water. He had his hands in his back pockets, lost in thought.

Jennifer sat on the doorstep watching him. She really did not know what to expect, and the unknown is more terrifying than the known. Haug seemed calm, not nervous at all, just concentrating on what he was doing. Finally she called out to him.

"I'm lonely. And I'm scared."

He walked back towards her, his hands still in his back pockets. "Sorry. I was miles away."

"How do you prepare for something like this? It's worse than a first night."

"I don't like it either. Nightmare Andy is the only one who likes it."

"He's frightening."

"That's why they call him Nightmare. He's lookin' forward to it, like a kid."

"I don't understand that," she said. "How people can like danger and gore and horror. Crippled minds."

"Don't be too hasty to judge, Jenny. You don't know what the man's seen in his life. Not everone grows up goin' to a school and havin' decent neighbours and local shops and hope for the future. I mean, what you went through with your dad was pretty fuckin' bad, but it's got a perspective. I heard that Andy's family was bayoneted, his sisters raped and gutted. Don't know whether it's true or not. But I've seen thangs too. Kids with no legs, no eyes, no dicks. A woman carryin' her guts in a dishpan, tryin' to find a medic while pigs are eating her dead husband."

"I don't think that's fair, Haug," she said bitterly.

"There's no god to make thangs fair. We just got to do our best with what we got. When you step in shit, it's hard to get it off your foot. Some people are liable to track it around the rest of their lives."

"Sounds like crackerbarrel philosophy, you know."

"I don't give a fuck what you call it. It's true. Look, I'm tryin' to help, not hinder. You're scared now, and I wanna get you out of it. And the way you get on top of these thangs is to keep climbin'. Don't look back, don't look down. You decide to do somethin' and you do it, the best you can. Nobody can ask more than that."

"I know," she said, "but this is not even my fault. It doesn't have anything to do with me. And I've been kidnapped, terrorised, raped . . . and now they're trying to kill me. I don't even know why."

"I'm tryin' to find out why."

"And if you're killed? Or I'm killed? Or both of us?"

She turned away, not looking at him.

"We don't find out why if we're killed. We don't find out if we don't try either. And we might be killed anyway, whether we try or not. The choice is clear. We're gonna try, you and me both."

"There are all kinds of choices, Haug. We could run – go to Europe, go to America, even Scotland, change our names. There are all kinds of things to do. But no, you want to have a big battle so that you and the other mastodons can clash and slash and kill and maim."

He sat down beside her and his voice had a gentle tone. "With those kinds of folks behind you, runnin' is the worst thang you can do. Even if you get clean away, you can never sleep right or stop lookin' over your shoulder. Best to meet 'em head on. Like mastodons, if you want. That's the sorta thang they unnerstand and I know a lot about it. And I wouldn't be draggin' you through this if I didn't think we were gonna make it out alive. You gotta believe that."

She was still looking away. "For a while, yesterday, I thought I might even be in love."

She laughed ironically. "I didn't know you had all this planned."

He nodded and looked away too. "I didn't know for sure that Regis would trace the number and give it to the bad guys. But I thought it was best to be prepared if he did. So I got together with my friends last Saturday, and we made some plans. Now tonight we're gonna grab the tail of the dragon and hold on. That's the only way we can find the goddam' head. Once we find the head, maybe we can find out some answers. Then, and only then, will you be safe."

"Will I?" she murmured.

"You're lookin' down. You're not climbin'. Lissen, we all get dealt a hand of cards and you gotta play 'em as they're dealt. And not whimper about the man at the next table who's got a better hand, or waste time wishin' you had four aces. And so far, you've done just fine. You got to remember that. You survived your father—"

" Did I?"

"Yes! You were dealt that card and you played it. A lotta people got better ones and fucked up. Some got worse. You hurt a lot, but you still managed to get away from home, audition for the top drama school, graduate and do what you wanted to do. Despite everthang. Now you're in another fix. You've been dealt another bad card that you didn't ask for. But you're gonna play that one just as strong as you played the others."

She turned and looked at him, smiling faintly. "You *are* trying to help, aren't you? I'm sorry. When you're walking through a minefield, you sometimes just get tired. You know what I mean? Fed up. Want to give up. Like at the house with those men. And tonight. What if it happens again? What if I lose my nerve? Want to quit? Run?"

"What if you break a leg? Or it rains? Or they shell the shoreline in a battleship? You got to deal with it as it unfolds, one event at a time. That's how you keep your mind clear. That's how you concentrate. Those nine men tonight will be quite enough to fight without also tryin' to fight a headful of demons as well."

"Is that why you aren't afraid?"

"I *am* afraid. But I got an advantage. I've been in these situations before. I know what to expect. Hell, you're afraid when you go out on stage, aren't you?"

"Stark terror."

"But the reason that you're able to say your lines and be a character is because you've been there before and you know you can do it, right? But push me out on stage and I'd just stand there, a quiverin' wreck, while everybody laughed at me or yelled at me to go home. Horses for courses, as you say in England, and this is my course. I think you're holdin' up awful well myself. If I was waitin' in the wings to go on stage, I wouldn't be half as good."

She leaned against him. "You're very sweet. Reassuring. Wish some of it would trickle down and keep my stomach from turning over."

Haug pointed at the long shadows. "It's gonna be dark before long. And I want us inside and ready the moment the sun goes out. They could come any time from then to midnight."

"How will you know?" she asked, getting up.

"One Time will call."

He stood up and brushed off his trousers.

Jennifer went into the kitchen to fill the kettle while Haug went upstairs. She didn't know what else to do. When in doubt, have a cup of tea. Haug returned with the wooden case he had carried from the pickup and a small canvas bag. He put them on the refectory table and opened it. Inside was some kind of gun, and she stared at it.

"Now, you won't see these thangs in this country," he said as he took out the gun. "Very illegal. I smuggled it in a piece at a time, hopin' I'd never have to use it. Very nearly illegal in the States. It's called a Streetsweeper. Basically," he said, pointing to various bits, "it's a twelve-gauge shotgun, but it's got an eighteen-inch barrel and two pistol grips. One in back and one in front of the drum. This drum – it's like the old Al Capone tommyguns – holds twelve rounds, pushed through spring-loaded."

He held up another piece. "And this is a spare drum. Another twelve shots. Fast as you can pull 'em off."

"Oh, God," she said. "I thought you didn't want to kill anybody, Haug."

"Don't. Eighteen-inch barrel gives you a spray at about twenty yards. Much closer and you start to get bigger holes. Loaded with double-ought buckshot, thangs about the size of BBs."

"I don't know what a BB is, but it looks wicked."

"Well, that's the word for it. Wicked. 'S why you call it a Streetsweeper. Sweeps the streets. Great for urban crime. Drug dealers have started usin' 'em in the big cities. The Cubans in Miami love 'em."

He opened the canvas bag and pulled out a pistol with a huge barrel. "Now, this is all I got for you. It's actually legal. A flare gun."

She held up her hands. "No, I don't want anything to do with it."

He looked sharply at her. "Get ahold of yourself, Jenny. This isn't a game. You do what you got to do, whether you like it or not. Now, you're takin' this flare gun and you're keepin' it with you until it's over. Keep your eyes open when thangs start to happen. Concentrate. If we get separated and if somebody comes at you, point this thang at him and pull the trigger. Just point it and pull. Don't think. That's the way you do it. You might go down, but you don't go down helpless."

She stared at the awful things on the table. "I'll try."

Haug heard the kettle boiling and got up to fill the mugs.

"Good. You'll do fine. You're a strong girl. Remember: one event at a time. Thangs don't happen all at once – they just seem to. Use your ears and your eyes. We got a big surprise for those sons of bitches, 'cause they don't know who they're fuckin' with."

She looked up and caught his eyes. There was something in his expression that she didn't recognise, something which made her recoil inside.

"Who *are* they fucking with, Haug?" she asked quietly. "I wonder if I know."

He turned away without answering to get the milk. It was getting dark. After handing Jennifer a mug and putting his down on the table, Haug walked through to the sitting room, drew all the curtains and turned on the lights. He went into the office and did the same, except that he did not turn on the lights. The kitchen had no curtains and he sat down opposite her and took a drink.

"After we get the call, we'll move into the office. No talkin' from then, because I wanna lissen and get used to what thangs sound like so that I can tell when they don't sound right. When I make a sign to you, I want you to get down behind that stuffed chair and stay there. Keep the flare gun with you. Don't call out or shout for me. I may have to leave the house, but I'll be back. And remember: Keef, One Time and Andy will be comin' down from the back. Thangs are likely to get confused, but don't panic and run. Worst thang to do. Stay right where you are. They'll be more confused than we are because we know somethin' that they don't."

Sam Bernstein was glad that Ilya and Schlomo were with him in the boat. Both were in their early thirties, and he knew Ilya's parents. They had been in his unit, so there was a certain understanding between them. Unlike the South Africans, whom he usually found either dumb or arrogant or both. Jan and Andries sat sullenly on the other side of the inflatable. Ilya and Schlomo were sitting opposite them joking quietly in Hebrew. Bernstein listened to them as he steered the small outboard engine from the stern. Ilya was talking about the blow job he had received in Amsterdam the night before they left. He said that he had met a girl in a bar and taken her into the men's toilet, locking the door. She was drunk and couldn't wait to get his cock out, gobbled the whole thing and had to throw up in the toilet while he took her from the rear. Schlomo was laughing and said that that was a good way to wipe it off.

Bernstein didn't mind their joking. They were pros, they were relaxed. When it was time to go to work, they knew their business and he could count on them. He wasn't so sure about Jan and Andries, who had their collars up and looked cold. The wind off the sea was cool but by no means freezing. There were swells in the water and it wasn't too choppy. For that he was grateful. It was only a small inflatable, not a proper military one. There hadn't been time. He had to grab what he could get. In fact he didn't like the speed forced on him by Van der Bijl. Even on a small operation like this, he preferred a carefully planned and rehearsed script.

After all, that's what made the Israelis the best in the world. That's why the South Africans came to them in the first place, looking for ex-army, ex-Shin Bet men. Bernstein didn't give a shit for whom he was working so long as the pay was good and it was interesting. And the pay was fucking good.

So. What did he feel about this gig? Poor preparation; no rehearsals for a start. The men had had no time to blend, know each other, learn to work as a team. On the other hand, he had helped train them all personally. The weaker men he placed in the backup team. When he thought about Piet, he just shook his head. The man was so stupid that he probably tied his shoelaces together in the mornings. Big, yes; strong, yes. Big and strong meant little and thinking meant the most. Being able to think and act while confusing things were happening, that was the key. The one time when Piet might have been useful, he had failed. Chaim was good but a little hot-headed. Ferdi and Louis? Well, they were South Africans, weren't they? Boers. Like Germans without the intelligence.

Bernstein kept checking the compass strapped to his knee and adjusting course. It hardly seemed as if they were moving at all as the little outboard chugged away. But they were making progress. They would get there. Mustn't be impatient. One thing at a time. Easy does it. For some reason he was nervous though. It was a simple operation yet he was nervous. That bothered him. He wasn't a believer in sixth senses, but he remembered other times when he had felt nervous, and invariably there had been some kind of fuckup. How could there be a fuckup? Ah. How could it rain? How could the sun shine? There was something nagging at the back of his mind, some detail which wouldn't surface. Maybe that was what was making him nervous.

Was it last night when he had been scouting? It had been simple. He found his way down the path easily enough. No problem, even in the dark. He had got closer to the house than he had intended and could see two figures moving behind the curtains. Hell, he could have done it then. Just knock on the goddam' door, bang, bang. But this way was safest, the surest. There was simply no way they could get out, no escape. If he had made an approach last night, for instance, there was some chance, however remote, that one could have escaped. Or the man might have been such a moose that he could take a hit and keep coming. After all, he had had only a small calibre weapon.

He saw the flicker of a light and checked his compass again. Dead on, dead ahead.

"OK," he said just loud enough to be heard above the engine. "No talking from here on. And grab those oars. You're gonna need to warm up before we land."

He watched the men moving carefully around in position, then he looked back at the light. It was hard to judge the coastline in the Stygian darkness which surrounded them. Bernstein found himself changing his mind. That wasn't a good sign. He suddenly decided that it was better to get a little closer than two hundred metres. A hundred should be plenty. He checked his watch. Nearly half past ten. Over twenty minutes later than he planned. Team A would already be in place waiting for his signal to begin their descent. OK, a hundred metres. The fucker wouldn't be able to hear the engine cut out at that distance. Hell, last night they had been playing music. Some kind of classical shit. Why was he nervous? He cut the engine.

It took another twenty minutes to reach the pier and they sat still on the water for five minutes, listening. Bernstein peered at the house. Lights were on in one room downstairs. Upstairs was dark, but they could be up there fucking. No music tonight. He pulled out his handset from his jacket and pressed the buzzer.

Chaim answered. "Where have you been?"

"Crossing delay," whispered Bernstein. "Everything OK with A Team?"

"Fine," said Chaim. "Dying of boredom, that's all."

"Right," answered Bernstein, checking his watch. "I'll give you fifteen minutes. Go."

"Roger."

The set went dead and Bernstein replaced it in his jacket. He motioned to the others to get out of the boat on to the pier. Then he carefully pulled himself up, sitting on the edge, his legs dangling. He pulled the waterproof gun case from inside his jacket. The silencer was already fitted but he checked the clip, then loaded one round into the chamber, clicking the safety catch on. As arranged, the other men had spread out in a perimeter from the pier and he could just see their shapes as they crouched low.

It was when Bernstein got up to join them that the thought struck him. Yellow van. Why yellow van? Where did that thought come from? He stopped. There was a yellow van in the parking lot of the hotel. So what? There was something about a yellow van that he was desperately trying to dig out. He was staring at the house, frozen to the spot. He must have stood like a statue for over five minutes. Then finally he remembered.

It was something that Chaim had said after the disaster on Friday. Haug, the Yank. *The Yank had a yellow van.*

Chapter Seventeen

Chaim led the group in single file down the path. Piet was directly behind him, Ferdi and Louis followed. As they passed out of sight someone else stepped on to the path, but no one watching would have been likely to see him because he was dressed completely in black, with a black wool cap pulled down over his ears and black gloves on his hands. His face was nearly invisible too except when he opened his eyes wide. He had no weapon other than a short nylon rope between two toggles of wood. After listening carefully and consulting his watch, One Time silently followed the men down the path.

Chaim was thinking about his nose, which was beginning to throb, and thinking about his nose made him think also of his front teeth. Or lack of front teeth. Chaim had been bought up in the eye-for-an-eye school of social thought, and, no matter what Bernstein had to say on the matter, he was going to spend some time tracking down the black bastard who had smashed his face. He incidentally hoped that Bernstein would leave him a piece of the big Yank, though he didn't remember him at all. He would, however, never forget the black bastard – the mean face, the little shitty goatee, the woolly head which had smacked into him like a bowling ball. They said that you couldn't tell them apart, but he would remember this one until the day he found him again. Chaim didn't consider himself a racist, but, after all, a black man was no better than an Arab. The fact that he had been beaten by one irritated him like a patch of itchy skin under a plaster cast. After all, he had been a corporal in the Israeli army, a squad leader, a veteran. No one had ever taken him out like that. A fucking head butt. Thinking again about what happened made him angry, which made him a little bit careless. He was making too much noise and he was getting too far ahead of Piet, who did not have a torch.

It was a special pencil torch, Israeli Army issue, with a very tight beam for about three or four feet. After that it was useless. But it was very difficult for the enemy to detect, so long as you used it sparingly. Chaim could already see the light reflecting off the ocean, but the house was not yet in view.

Anyway, he thought glumly, it would be all over by the time he got to the house. He had to admit that Bernstein was good. A vicious, deadly man, but a good one to have on your side when the going got tough. A real evil bastard. He had a hell of a reputation in Shin Bet and his nickname was The Footman. This came from his very successful method of interrogating Arab suspects. He heated a thin filleting knife and used it to lift strips of flesh from the bottom of the subject's feet. Chaim grinned and that made his nose throb again. He was going to lie awake dreaming about filleting the shit who had bust it. He flicked the light on again and saw a sharp bend in the steep path. He slowed down and glanced behind. He couldn't see him, but he could hear Piet coming as his head swept the tree branches.

As Chaim rounded the bend he again met the man who occupied his thoughts. Or, to be more exact, he met the pickaxe handle which was being swung by that man. His nose was instantly rebroken, but that was the least of Chaim's worries – if he had been conscious and capable of worrying – because his face simply broke like a vase hit with a hammer. His upper jaw, the maxilla, collapsed in fragments and the lower jaw was broken and dislocated and swept back into his throat. His tongue was torn and most of his remaining teeth were shattered. The force of the blow actually drove Chaim a couple of steps back uphill, and blood spattered into Piet's chest as he emerged round the bend.

One Time heard the crack, which reminded him of the sound of summer in Barbados, a cricket ball on a bat. Immediately he moved forward down the path like a wraith, making little noise, pausing momentarily at a turn before rushing smoothly on. He too could now see the light on the water, and it was by this light that he saw the man called Louis, a pistol in his hand. Because now there was more noise, sounds that he had never heard before, not in Barbados, nor in Northern Ireland, where he had served two tours of duty. If anything, it was a jungle sound, the sound of a big cat and a buffalo. A frightening, horrible, chilling sound. It was enough to freeze the South African in front of him to the spot and make him crouch low, pushing his pistol in front of him.

The man called Louis had just begun to move cautiously forward when, in an instant, there was a whisper of something, a night creature, like a bat. It was just a flickering thought cut short by a sharp, suffocating pain in his neck. Louis suddenly couldn't breathe and couldn't speak as his brain briefly searched in panic for a reason before he blacked out completely.

One Time held the man with the garrotte until he felt him go limp, pushed him on to his back, put one knee across both knees of his adversary and pulled both his ankles sharply upwards. He knew that the man would not walk again for a while as he reached for the silenced pistol that the man called Louis had dropped in front of him. He pushed into the pistol in his belt and again moved ahead with feline grace.

The sound that One Time had heard a minute before came from Nightmare Andy and Piet. Piet had rushed forward, stepping over the body of Chaim, as Keef withdrew. The big South African had his arms up, reaching for Keef, and thus it was his ribs which were broken instead of his arm as Andy's Louisville Slugger slammed into him. But Piet was an unusual man with very heavy bones, more like the bones of a horse or donkey. Three ribs fractured but they didn't break right off and sheer into his soft organs. The pain didn't even reach his brain. But rage did. He grabbed the bat and pulled, expecting it to come away from the snarling bald man with pig eyes who held it. Instead, the pig-eyed man came with the bat when he pulled.

Nightmare Andy landed on Piet like a grizzly bear on an elk. With a roar, he seemed to climb the tall South African until their heads were level. He then sank his teeth around the base of the giant's nose and bit as hard as he could. The nose came away in his mouth as Piet howled and staggered backwards, stumbling into the trunk of a tree. The enraged Greek was pounding Piet's body with his fists and elbows and knees before remembering to spit out the nose, which was still in his mouth. Piet could not see for the blood streaming into his eyes and was flailing his arms wildly.

One of his huge fists finally found Nightmare Andy's head, but to Piet it felt as though he had hit a stone. All he heard was a high-pitched scream immediately before he felt a force which he had never before experienced. He was actually being pinned by another man. Or maybe not a man. An animal, more dangerous than any he had ever before faced. He was aware of a crushing, terrible weight as the pig-eyed man beat and screamed and gnawed his way through his big arms to his chest. Piet still could not see, but he felt the relentless pressure, as if driven by hydraulics. Fingers grabbed and gouged his eyes. He roared for the last time as he felt teeth on his neck.

Blood fountained from the ripped and torn throat of Piet's body as Nightmare Andy stood up and drew his machete. Keef stood in stunned silence and it was a moment before he was aware that his jaw had fallen open. In earlier days a great saga would have been written about such events. It had been like Beowulf and Grendel. The big Greek looked like some fiend from hell, belched on to the surface of the earth by an underworld that found him impossible to digest. In the darkness he shone from head to foot, and his clothes were torn and dark with blood. It was one of those moments that Keef experienced in slow motion because he was mesmerised by what he was seeing.

A few feet up the path was another man, who was drawing a gun from a holster. It was like an elaborate choreography. Slowly the gun came up and, just as slowly, Andy turned towards the man, his machete raised above his head, his mouth open in a bloody grimace, from which came an ear-rupturing shriek. Andy seemed not so much to move as to explode towards the crouching man, and the machete came down in a long powerful arc, taking away the gun and half the arm. Keef was not even aware whether or not the gun had actually fired. It all happened within a split second, but it seemed to Keef as though hours had passed. Keef was a hard man, but never in his hard life had he ever witnessed such stomach-churning ferocity. Finally, with heavy legs, he began to move forward because Nightmare Andy was about to kill the man.

It was One Time who stopped Andy by stepping between him and the body of the screaming man on the ground. He calmly held up both palms to the crouching Greek who held the machete like some primeval savage crazed beyond redemption. Andy's chest heaved, his eyes were wild, and empty of every emotion but rage. Keef came up behind the man with the machete talking soothingly, as you would talk to a child. Andy half turned, his back to the hillside, the machete still drawn back to threaten both black men.

It was the sound of gunfire from below which broke the spell. Without a word, Nightmare Andy seemed finally to understand where he was and what he was doing. After applying a quick tourniquet to the amputee, One Time led the way down as swiftly as he could with the other two following behind.

The yellow van, Bernstein thought. That could mean only one thing if it was the Yank's van: a trap. Of some sort. He shoved the screaming questions about why and how roughly to one side and cocked an ear. Sounds were coming from above and there shouldn't be sounds from above. Backup party was being ambushed. Time to move. Time to make a quick change in plans.

He motioned for the four men in front to return to the pier and they quickly gathered in front, crouching low.

"Team A is being attacked, so we can't count on them. If they're fucked, we could have enemy unknown, number unknown on top of us. I want Jan and Andries to go in first, instead of Ilya and Schlomo. Ilya I want on the left, Schlomo on the right, I'll take centre. As they hit the door, we start moving in. The two flankers make sure that there's no movement out the back."

As he was talking, Bernstein was replacing the pistol in its holster. He then took off his heavy jacket and from the inside pocket he pulled out an Uzi which was unmuffled. This was a time for firepower. He'd worry about the noise later. He threw the jacket behind him and gave the signal for Jan and Andries to go.

Haug heard the noise on the hill too as he crouched in the shadows of the dark office, holding the Streetsweeper in front of him. The front door opened directly into the office, and the sitting room led off through an archway. Haug had his foot on a barbell loaded with two twenty-kilo plates. He glanced back at the overturned chair behind him where Jennifer was hiding. Then he quickly rechecked the arrangement of everything in the room. Any minute, he thought.

As the time had grown nearer, Haug felt an old and unwelcome feeling spreading through his insides. Something he thought had gone for ever. What had frightened Jennifer about Nightmare Andy, Haug also recognised in himself, a discovery he had made long ago in Vietnam. Then he was proud of it, felt it made him a man. It was only later he discovered that it was instead a form of pathology. Because Haug found himself looking forward to this. He wanted it to happen. He wanted to fight. He wanted the danger, the flying bullets, the tangle of the unexpected. He realised that he had even subconsciously engineered it so that he faced the best of the attack by himself. Those making the actual assault were bound to be the better team. They didn't really need One Time up on the hill. He was sure that Andy and Keef could handle a good ambush. Having One Time with him would have given Haug an advantage. By himself it was going to be a struggle.

Why had he done this? It endangered Jennifer; it even endangered those on the hill. And he knew *why*. Because only at the edge of death did he feel most alive. He was at last in his element. Where other men froze with fright or became hyperactive, not knowing what they were doing, Haug saw things more and more clearly. Ancient anger inside him was turned into laser-like purpose. He saw everything, smelt everything, heard everything. Every sense was peeled back and exposed to air. It was as though he could feel the touch of light particles on his skin or the draught from someone breathing a hundred yards away or the sound of a feather lightly touching the ground. Haug felt alive, gloriously alive. Gloriously happy! The really disgusting thought was that he also liked to kill. Or was that the right way to put it? It was more like this: 'kill' floated in the air, linked with 'death'. The end of Haug was linked with the end of another man. With the death of the other man, the 'kill', his death also evaporated. During such a fight, with all his senses exposed, time warped and stretched itself, folding over and twisting. When you entered this world, it was an eternity, without beginning or end, a different universe with huge unfamiliar leaves and flowers, an awful landscape shaded by a giant red sun, low in the sky. Once experienced, this world, this strange universe, was addictive. You wanted back, you wanted to return. Just once more. Haug ground his teeth, his eyes alight. This would be the last time. The last time. And this time he must try not to kill. Only to maim, only to show those sons of bitches who they were fucking with.

He heard the running footsteps first, even as they began. Then the window of the sitting room broke as the grenade hit the chicken wire. Immediately he knew from the hiss that it was gas – the stupid bastards. Worried about the noise and choosing second-best. A clue which he noted as he braced himself.

The door came right off the hinges as the two men hit it. Two, as he had guessed. That left three behind. The two men hurtled into the room – to Haug it seemed as though they were in slow motion – firing towards the light. The moment they appeared, Haug kicked the barbell with all his might towards the advancing bodies. The first man had got off two shots, and the second man one before they were scythed to the floor by the thundering barbell. Before Jan hit the floor, while he was still in the air, Haug's boot made contact with his head. Again, he put everything behind it. You had to. In a fight, you must give one hundred per cent. Jan's body actually turned 180 degrees before landing. Andries was already on the floor, turning back towards him, his pistol elongated by an ugly silencer. With both knees, Haug dropped in the middle of his back and, hearing a crack like a breaking staff, realised that he had probably killed the man.

This gave him extra fuel as he slid to the front door on his belly, his shoulders just feeling the cool outside air. He started on his left in an arc, firing the Streetsweeper. After the fourth round he was aware of a light, a small flickering light in the centre. And he felt the wind of bullets passing close, hitting the wall, chips of rock and mortar spraying and stinging. In a split second he shifted the Streetsweeper and poured five rounds towards the centre and the flickering light stopped. Another light on his right and around the shotgun went, three more rounds of double-ought buck. The moment he fired the last round, he rolled back inside the door, ejecting the empty drum, reaching inside his shirt for the spare, his ears still ringing.

Everything Haug did was clinical and efficient. Every movement was exact. He had forgotten nothing. While he was reloading, he checked the two bodies lying nearby, but there was no sign of life. Good, he thought. Sons of bitches. Then he heard Jennifer's voice, frightened and low.

"Haug. Are you all right?"

. "Two down, three to go," he murmured, more to himself than to her.

Then he raised his voice. "Bet your ass I'm OK. Now stay quiet."

Bernstein was lying painfully on his right side silently swearing to himself. A fucking shotgun of some sort, a fucking cannon – what the fuck was it? He now wished that he had kept on the heavy waterproof jacket. He had caught a load of shot down his left side, at least one load, maybe more. His shoulder, his arm, hip and leg were all warm and wet. He had been in a crouch with the Uzi when the fucking cannon started firing and had got off five or six shots before he was hit, that's all. Just as well, though. He didn't have a spare clip for the Uzi. Fuck. Lack of fucking preparation, one of the fucking basics.

He stared at the empty doorway, trying to see, looking over the sights of his gun. And underestimation, he thought. Another basic. That fucker was good. Whoever he fucking was, he was fucking good. A pro. A real pro. And here I am, sucking on the shit end of the stick. He wasn't worried too much about his wounds. Painful but superficial. Got into the muscle, but he didn't think the shot had hit any arteries. No, couldn't have. Bound to know it.

Bernstein couldn't see any movement on the right or left, so he didn't know whether Ilya and Schlomo had been hit or how badly.

He shouted in Hebrew, "Who's got trouble? Schlomo?"

From his right he heard a cry. There was pain in the voice.

"Alive. Got my legs. And my fucking dick, I think."

"Can you walk?" asked Bernstein.

"Don't think so. Bleeding like fuck. Still shoot though. Cover?"

Bernstein called to the left, "Ilya?"

"I'm all right," said Ilya. "Jacket stopped a lot of it, whatever the fuck it was. Shotgun? Bleeding a bit, superficial. How about you, Bernstein?"

"Hit but all right. I want you to move, Ilya. Around the back. You have one minute, starting now. Wait till you hear me fire, then hit it. And we may have trouble coming down the hill any time."

Bernstein had noted that the noise up there had stopped and he had an ominous feeling in the pit of his stomach. A feeling which told him that the wrong side had won.

"Who *is* that guy?" It was Schlomo.

Bernstein ignored the question. His mind also twisted away from his own pain. He was going to disregard it. If he did not, he knew that he was dead. He checked his watch and started to move slowly, quietly forward on his stomach.

He called out to Schlomo, "Cover me. Going in."

Haug was leaning against the doorway listening to the conversation. He was still breathing heavily.

"What's happening?" asked Jennifer in a stage whisper.

Haug waited until one of the men outside spoke.

"Not another word, no matter what happens. Silence."

Because he was listening. And he knew that the other men would be listening. They were talking in another language, probably

Hebrew. Haug couldn't even speak French, though he had studied it for three years in school. But he could hear tones of voices. One injured. The other two sounded all right. One in front, one on the right. They would stay split, the two good ones. One on either side or one in front and one going around to the back. The one in the middle was *the* man. That's the one he wanted. As long as he stayed still and silent he knew that they would have to come to him. And come soon. They must know that it was an ambush by now, that their squad on the hill had been attacked, that they might now be outnumbered and outgunned. The only thing that worried him was the possibility of more grenades. The door was open, and he and Jennifer were vulnerable. But they would have to get closer for that. Then he heard something. A faint sound, a little clicking noise. It came from around the back. So they had split front and rear. Haug hooked the barbell with his foot and dragged it slowly towards him across the carpet. He was going to try and use it for cover when he rolled back into the doorway to nail the man in the middle when he made his move.

But he had already made his move. A split second after Haug heard the pounding footsteps there was the sound of a machine-gun, and the doorway was suddenly aswarm with bullets and ricochets. Instinctively Haug rolled away from the danger, trying to bring his gun up in time to catch the man coming through. But the man was good, he realised that, because he was already in.

He had come in low and fast, holding the Uzi in his right hand, assuming correctly that Haug would be on the darkest side of the doorway. Indeed, Haug would have been a dead man if the Israeli had not tripped over the barbell. The man was coming in so fast that he hit the contraption and slid head first to the other side of the room. Haug saw the Uzi clatter into the darkness of the kitchen, by which time he was rising from his position. His own gun, the Streetsweeper, he slid along the wall towards the back of the overturned chair, hoping that Jennifer would take the hint.

Because he now wanted this man alive. This was the man who was going to answer some questions for him. But the moment he released the Streetsweeper he regretted it, because the Israeli had recovered his wits by the time he hit the far wall and was up on one knee, his hand at his waist. Haug was moving by then, though, and by the time the pistol was out he was on the man.

Bernstein was surprised by how quickly the big Yank moved. He tried to roll to his left as he drew the pistol, but the damned silencer made the thing awkward, and then the Yank was on him and he felt the gun being wrenched out of his hand. Bernstein made a knife of his left hand and chopped with all his strength at the back of the Yank's neck. This was immediately followed by two karate punches to the ribs. His left leg came up hard, searching for kidneys. Then suddenly his right hand was free as the Yank relaxed his grip and Bernstein was on his feet like a steel spring. The Yank was up on one knee. Perfect, as he aimed a vicious kick at the head. But unexpectedly the Yank's arm swept up under his leg, pushing upwards. Bernstein felt his other leg come up from under him and landed on his back heavily. As he landed he was already rolling to the side as a big foot stomped the floor where he had fallen. Bernstein was back on his feet. And so was the big Yank.

They stood four feet apart, and the light from the sitting room illuminated the two men in a long rectangle, not unlike a boxing ring. They stood for a moment staring at each other, breathing heavily. Both men's gazes were steady though, as their eyes locked.

"OK, asshole," said Haug. "Looks like it's back to basics here. So let's see who's second-best."

In answer Bernstein danced forward, leaned away and kicked. The blow caught Haug in the chest, and he reeled back from the force of the blow. Another kick followed, then two punches in rapid sequence.

Haug was hurt and alarmed at the speed of his opponent. Instead of collapsing with the pain though, Haug grew instantaneously more alert. Where other men's heads would fog with such blows, his cleared. The man danced forward again, and again the foot was up and snapped at him like a whip. The man was very, very fast. Haug had tried to catch the foot and missed. A sharp edge of the Israeli's hand caught him on the side of the neck, and then he danced briefly out of range.

"Well, motherfucker," said Bernstein. "Now we know who's second-best. I don't give a fuck *how* I kill you."

As he danced forward again Haug suddenly moved towards the expected blow and, as the leg came around, he caught it and lifted. The Israeli's other foot came off the floor and Haug felt a hard kick behind his shoulders. He realised that he was fighting for consciousness. With all the strength in his body he gripped the man's upper thigh with one hand and his ankle with the other. Bernstein was in the air, whipping with his free foot and striking with elbows and fists when he could. Haug dropped to one knee, bringing the Israeli's leg down with as much force as he could muster. He felt, rather than heard, the man's leg break across his knee.

Bernstein yelled but did not scream as he rolled on to his back and tried to bring the other leg up for another kick. If he could only get the Yank's head, just one blow, one chance . . . His fucking leg was fucking broken, but that did not matter. You never stopped, never, not if you wanted to live. Then out of the corner of his eye he spotted a pistol lying underneath a chair. The Yank couldn't see it, not possible. Maybe eighteen inches away, less than two feet. Bracing himself for the pain, he flipped over on his stomach. He nearly passed out but did not cry out. He was nearly there. He reached – had it! With a swift movement he brought the gun around ready to fire the moment he saw the Yank.

But Haug caught the hand with his own and smashed the arm to the floor and held it there. He grabbed Bernstein by the neck with his other hand. The Israeli swung with his free arm, aiming towards the head.

Haug avoided the blow easily and tightened the grip on his neck.

"I gotta say that I hate to kill a man like you on account of the fact that you gave me the best fight I can remember havin'. So I'll give you a choice. You tell me who sent you here, and I'll leave it at a broken leg. Call it a day."

"You haven't won yet, cocksucker," Bernstein spat at him.

"You right, I haven't," Haug said and grabbed the pistol. "There's unfinished business here. You can make yourself useful."

Haug put the pistol in his belt and hauled the Israeli to his feet with one hand. He passed his left arm underneath Bernstein's chin in a half nelson. His broken leg dangled out at an odd angle, and the man's face was contorted with pain. He didn't make a sound though. Holding Bernstein's body close to him, Haug realised that he felt a strange kinship with him. His courage was phenomenal. His will to live, to win, was so close to his own. Even now, he realised that the Israeli was thinking, looking at real possibilities, waiting for a slip, for something unusual to happen, any advantage at all. Haug knew that if he gave him the slightest break, he would slip away and Haug himself would be dead. He had a basic primeval admiration for his captive. Was it still there after all these thousands of years? The instinct of the jungle warriors?

Haug dragged his man to the doorway, drawing his pistol and using Bernstein's shoulder as a rest. Then he stepped outside, moving away quickly from the frame. He was looking for the man on the left, but his eyes had not adjusted to the darkness.

"I got your boss," he shouted. "Throw your gun out and you follow it, on hands and knees."

Bernstein struggled and tried to say something in Hebrew, but Haug tightened his grip on his neck and the words died in his throat. He began to move forward slowly, making his prisoner hop on one foot.

Jennifer, still crouched behind the chair, was clutching the shotgun Haug had shoved towards her in the mêlée. She had watched the fight, wondering if she should risk a shot and decided that she shouldn't. She didn't even know how to make the thing work. But she had found the trigger and assumed that, if she pulled it, something would happen. What, she was not entirely sure. Never in her life had she held a gun in her hands. It was heavy and cold and she found it remote and disgusting.

She tensed as she heard the back door to the kitchen open. She looked over the top of the chair, bracing herself.

"Anybody home?" It was Nightmare Andy's voice.

Jennifer recognised it and emerged from behind the chair. "I'm coming. In a minute."

As she turned the corner carefully into the kitchen she saw such an awful sight that she would never be able to forget it. Nightmare Andy stood there, still dripping blood. He looked like some satanic animal which had been feeding on carrion, tearing at the entrails and stuffing them into his mouth. He still held the machete in his hand, and he was smiling.

"Hey," he said. "What's for dinner? I'm hungry."

Suddenly Jennifer raised the Streetsweeper towards Andy, her eyes wide and crazed.

"Hey, wait a minute—" Andy had time to say before Jennifer fired the shotgun.

The force of the recoil drove her back through the door and she staggered into the office.

The blast missed Nightmare Andy completely and blew a hole in the kitchen window. In a rage Andy charged into the office and snatched the shotgun from Jennifer's trembling hands.

"What the fuck do you think you're doing, woman? It's Andy, you stupid fucker! Andy, right? I came to save your arse and you try to blow my fucking head fucking off. I ought to smack you into next week—"

Andy's voice was peaking in a high squeak.

"Back off, Andy." It was Keef's bass voice from the kitchen.

Andy whirled to face the Jamaican. "What the fuck's it got to do with you?"

Without saying a word, Keef motioned Andy to come outside. When Andy stepped through the door, Keef pointed to a figure on the ground.

"Now you just go back inside and apologise to the lady. She just saved your life. This cunt was about to put a bullet in that thick skull of yours."

Andy raised both hands over his head, a huge grisly smile spreading over his face. "Heyyyy! Heyyyy!"

He raced back into the kitchen. "Jennifer, juniper! Lemme give you a big kiss! You saved the best-looking Greek in England!"

Jennifer was still standing near the doorway of the office, arms crossed on her chest, trembling. She backed away from Andy in alarm as he came rushing into the room. Elaborately, he grabbed one of her hands and bowed low to kiss it.

"Give you a bigger one after I wash," he said gaily.

Keef had darted past to the open front door and was looking out.

"Grab one of those pistols, Andy. We better give him some cover."

———

Haug approached the injured man cautiously. He had not answered him, and Haug had pressed slowly forward. As his eyes became accustomed to the dark he could see better. He had heard the shot from the house, but the voices of Jennifer, Keef and Andy reassured him that whatever happened had been taken dealt with. Haug had not pinpointed the man's position yet, and he was beginning to wonder about the wisdom of this manoeuvre. Bernstein was a dead weight and Haug was beginning to sweat heavily.

Then he heard something. Someone moved, off to his left. Awkwardly, he tried to adjust himself.

"One Time!" shouted a voice from the darkness.

"Have you got him?" Haug shouted back.

"Right now!" One Time answered.

"Don't kill him. Bring him in."

Haug relaxed his grip on Bernstein's throat and started back towards the house.

The kitchen had been turned into a makeshift prison and infirmary. Ferdi, Louis and Chaim had been collected from the hill and bought down. Haug decided to leave Piet where he was, wrapping his body in a tarpaulin and pulling it off to the side of the path. Chaim was still unconscious, his face an ugly pulp, but he was breathing. Louis's legs were broken, and Ferdi had lost half his arm. One Time's tourniquet had worked, but the man had still lost a lot of blood.

There were three survivors from Team B. Andries had died when Haug broke his spine, and Ilya had lost half his head when Jennifer shot him through the window. Jan was still unconscious, Bernstein had a broken leg, and Schlomo had leg and groin injuries. The kitchen looked like a battle station. Haug supervised first aid for the injured, and everyone mucked in to try and clear up the mess.

After a great deal of thought Haug decided that it would be useless to question Bernstein. He knew instinctively that the Israeli would not talk. Bernstein was made of a fibre that Haug recognised, even respected. That fibre would bend a little, but it would not break.

So Haug chose one of the South Africans – Louis, whose knees had been dislocated by One Time. Haug had pushed the bones back into the joints himself while Keef and Andy held the screaming man down. After applying splints, Louis was carried into the sitting room where the furniture was eerily undisturbed by the evening's events. Haug made sure that he was comfortable, got his name and sat down in an armchair.

"Now, Louis," he began. "You know about the good cop and the bad cop?"

When Louis didn't answer, he went on.

"Or some people call it the soft glove and the hard glove. You know what I'm talkin' about, Louis? I think you do. Now I'm as busy as a one-legged man in an ass kickin' contest right now, so I don't have time to fuck around with you. I'm the good cop, you unnerstand? I'm not gonna hurt you. But when I leave this room, I'm gonna send in Nightmare Andy. He's the bad cop. He likes hurtin' people. You behave yourself and tell me what I wanna know and in six weeks you'll be walkin' around, drinkin' and fuckin'. If I let Andy in here, you won't be fuckin' any more. 'Cause he's gonna cut your balls off with that big knife. OK? Got the picture? You got ten seconds to start talkin', or I'm gonna walk outta here and you don't get a second chance. We just drag somebody else in, that's all."

But Louis had already made up his mind. Both teams had been smashed like bugs by these people, and even Bernstein was prisoner. Louis believed what Haug told him.

"I don't know much," he mumbled. "None of us do, except Bernstein, and you won't get a fucking thing out of him. We work in cells, learned from the commies – three men, four men only. I was in Amsterdam when they called—"

"Who? Who called?"

"It's the only name I know, I swear to God, and I wouldn't know that if we hadn't been called to London. Don't know the Christian name. Van der Bijl—"

"Spell that."

Louis spelled it for him and gave him the address where they had met before coming down to Cornwall. "That is all I know. I don't even have a telephone number – nothing."

Haug was thoughtful. "What kind of cells are these?"

"We just get calls sometimes and activate."

"Like what?" asked Haug. "Give me an example."

Louis was quiet for a moment.

"Bomb under an embassy car, don't know which one, don't care. Followed a man out of a hotel, dumped him in a canal. Oh yeah, once we even did a bank job, you know, and dropped some left-wing stuff, like it was accidental. Rest of it is not very interesting. Leaned on some union officers, gave them money, that sort of thing."

He pointed at his knees. "Broke some legs, like this."

"And what's the connection between Israel and South Africa?"

"The Israelis are good. They train us. Part of some deal. I was recruited out of the army in Pretoria. You got all I know now. I'm a foot soldier, not a general."

Without another word, Haug got up and left the room.

When he returned to the kitchen, he looked around. "Where's Andy?"

"Said he was going for a swim," Keef said with a shrug.

"A swim?" Haug asked, incredulous.

"To get all that blood and shit off him, I guess."

Keef was sitting at the refectory table and had been trying to comfort Jennifer, who was very withdrawn.

"What the hell did he do to that big guy?"

Keef nodded towards Jennifer, who had her head in her hands. "Tell you later."

Haug shook his head. "Looked like Frankenstein met Dracula."

―――――――――

The fishing boat chugged closer to the shore and the older man peered towards the light of the house, listening. They had heard something out on the water that night, something that sounded like backfiring. Or gunfire. But it couldn't have been gunfire. Still, he thought that he'd better check, just to be sure. The younger man said that he was tired and wanted to get back home, but there was a tradition around here. If people were in trouble, you always gave a hand. That's the way of folks who lived near the sea. Not like Londoners or farmers inland. People down here looked after each other. Always have, always will. Even if they were bloody foreigners.

"There's something in the water!" the younger man shouted.

"What is it?"

"Can't see," the young man answered, shining his torch. "Looks like a jellyfish."

"Good evening," said Nightmare Andy, turning towards the light. "Want to join the party?"

The sight of the man in the water alarmed the young man. "Are you all right? We heard some noise."

"It's a party," Andy replied in his high-pitched voice. "Plenty of women to go around. I told them to turn down the music. I could hear it all the way out here. Don't want to disturb you folks."

The older man stared down at the odd-looking face in the water. It seemed Oriental. With pig eyes.

"Just checking to see if everything was all right."

"Ah, fine," Andy said, starting to swim away. "Think everybody's fucking now. Better get back."

The older man returned to the helm and opened the throttle, turning the boat towards Fowey. He shook his head sadly.

"And they ask what's happened to the morals of this country. Foreigners, that's what's happened. Foreigners, tourists. Wasn't like this years ago, not in my father's day."

Chapter Eighteen

On Wednesday evening Beth Howell was kneeling on the black carpet in Harvey Gillmore's office surrounded by mechanical clockwork toys. There was a tin elephant which raised and lowered its trunk. A monkey was beating a tambourine and jiggling his legs. Another monkey climbed a pole and slid back down. A large yellow duck flapped around in circles quacking. A Disney Pluto wagged its tail and nodded its head, and there was a crocodile nearby opening and closing its tin jaws. A tiger nodded its head back and forth menacingly. There were several tin soldiers, but only a large one would march properly on the thick carpet, so three were walking around on the top of Gillmore's desk. There was also a toy train on the desk top. Just a cheap toy train with an oval track and a wind-up engine pulling a tender. A Spitfire was also going around in circles on one of its wheels, the propeller spinning wildly. There were a number of toy cars manufactured in the 1940s, some of them with a friction mechanism. The noise was nearly surreal, with quacks and whirrs and clattering and bangs and snappings, with some toys running into others and falling, their legs or heads still walking or nodding as they lay on their sides, helpless.

Beth wound up each toy as it ran down, as she had been doing for over an hour. Gillmore was in his dressing-gown playing with one of the cars on the desk. He made engine noises for the car and squeals when it braked to a stop. He was totally absorbed in what he was doing, only hissing at her when he spotted one of the toys not moving.

"You know, Beth," he said finally, "I used to pay a boy threepence an hour to do what you're doing. He wanted sixpence, I gave him three. Poor kid, son of my father's maid. I think his mother took the money and the little bastard didn't even get to buy any sweets."

He was playing with an old Bentley, a replica of the one which had won at Le Mans.

"Errrrrrrruuuh . . . eeeeeek. E.e.e.e.e. . . e.eeee . . .rrrrrrruh. Anyway, I'd pay him to keep all my toys wound up when I was playing with them. What's the point of having toys just sitting around idle? I like to see them working. Errruuuuuuh . . . er. . . er . . . er eeeeeek. I couldn't wind the toys *and* play with them, could I? So . . . I delegated responsibility. Like I always do. But, Beth, I always keep in control. That's the secret. Keeping in control. The elephant, Beth, not moving . . ."

Beth turned and picked up the elephant and began rewinding it. Her fingers and wrists were tired, but she didn't know if she cared any longer. She replaced the elephant and started re-winding the soldiers on the desk. Then the train. The Spitfire. The tiger, the monkeys, the croc, the dog. It went on and on endlessly. When was it she had arrived? She didn't even remember any more. What had happened? It was all a jumble.

It had been this afternoon when the man he called Michael visited. A good-looking man, dark, a little mysterious. They had an argument – more like a row – over some arms deal. The man Michael was insisting that Gillmore release shares to the Arabs or the deal would not proceed. And the subject of those tapes came up again, with a threat to take Gillmore's telephone away from him. Why would they do that? How? It didn't make much sense. Neither man was in a good mood. The man Michael said Gillmore had caused no end of trouble with his bloody tapes, and they were having great difficulties fetching one back. And there was mention of Thomas, when they had both looked at her and stopped talking.

Thomas. She didn't think about him. Not because she didn't want to, but because she couldn't. Harvey Gillmore had pushed everything else out, and her mind seemed to her like an empty house through which she walked in a daze. You needed furniture in a house for memories, with things in the drawers and pictures on the wall.

She shrugged and wound up another toy. Gillmore had offered her to Michael, but the man refused. Gillmore said that she was a better whore than Michael's and a lot cheaper at five pounds. There hadn't been a lot of sex in the last few days. But there had been a lot of work. Every inch of the flat had been cleaned, even the walls. She was exhausted, but at least she had stopped being so hungry. And she was losing some weight. She felt it. Maybe the fat on her belly would stop wobbling soon and maybe that would make him happy.

Did that matter? Making him happy? She didn't know, but she missed him when he left the flat. She didn't know what to do and often became confused. Once she had picked up the telephone and

called Australia. One of his newspapers there. Like the times before,
though, she always put down the phone when anyone answered. She
didn't steal food either. Though she did open the fridge sometimes
and just looked at it. Rows and rows of Diet Pepsi, lettuce, carrots,
celery, tomatoes, tins of spaghetti, Bovril, eggs.

She was winding the duck again, but she knew that the train was
running down and Gillmore was looking at it.

'How long will he want to do this?' she wondered.

Immediately this was followed with the usual answer. Did it
matter? Time was thick and heavy anyway, and events were never
consecutive. Sometimes she stopped wondering what they meant.
She was just winding mechanical toys. When Gillmore had got out his
toy box, he told her that he had many more at his home. His wife
Mary sometimes did the winding. Beth remembered Mary, who had
used to try and talk with her. Beth had thought her perhaps shy at the
time. Mary's bedroom was all in pink, and a lot of her clothes were
pink as well. She never heard Mary speak back to her husband or
argue with him in any way. He seemed to take care of her, though.
Bought her lots of things. Nice clothes, a car. Now she was jealous
of Mary and dreaded the day when Gillmore returned to her.

The Australian had stopped playing with his Bentley and came over
to watch from behind as she wound up toy after toy. The sound had
stopped making any sense to her. Instead it had become a single
structure, like time. Solid.

She could sense Gillmore kneeling down behind her and felt him
lift her dress. He pulled her knickers down and put his hand
underneath, on her sex. Reflexively, she caught her breath as she
reached for the Spitfire.

"Keep winding. Don't stop," Gillmore said as he pushed his
fingers into her.

His groping was crude, even rough. He ignored her clitoris and
just kept shoving his fingers in and out, his arm following her as she
moved around among the screaming toys. She was finding movement
a little awkward with her knickers at her knees and was relieved when
he removed his fingers and took them all the way off. Then she felt
him moving behind her, and she kept her hips still for a moment as he
shoved the tip of his penis into her. It was stretching her and hurting
a little, and she tried to adjust for him.

"The monkey has stopped, Beth."

She grabbed the monkey and wound crazily. He pushed harder into her.

"The soldiers, Beth. The train."

He was all the way in now and she felt stretched and flushed, frantically reaching for the dying toys.

"I don't want you to come, Beth," she heard him say.

She bit her lip when she heard it and didn't know what to think or do, but she was too busy with the toys. The toys helped. She snatched at them, one after the other. Her hands, fingers and wrists were aching. Gillmore increased his rhythm and she could hear him grunt over the screeching mechanical noise. He grunted three or four times, then pulled out suddenly after he came. She continued to wind the demented toys as he went to a table at the side of the room and unwrapped a parcel.

A large dildo landed in front of her, and for a moment or two she didn't know what it was. She very nearly picked it up to try and wind it up.

"I want you to come with this. I want to watch. With my toys around you." He was standing over her, staring down, his head between her and the desk lamp. "Turn over on your back and get that into you."

She took the dildo inexpertly in her hands. It was large and black and moulded like a penis, but it wasn't too hard to insert, with his sperm making her more slippery.

"Spread 'em, Beth. Good and wide." He was grinning at her.

She opened her legs as far as she could and fumbled to turn on the vibrating switch at the end of the thing. Immediately it began twisting inside her, going round and round. She used her other hand to stroke her clitoris and felt the heat inside her become more intense. The toys around her were winding down and stopping. She could just hear the little train still going on the desk, round and round, like the rubber penis inside her. Just before she began to come, she vaguely heard the monkey, the last toy, slowly banging his tambourine. Jangle, jangle . . . jangle . . . jangle. Jangle. Her hips rose off the floor with the spasms, and she arched her head back, moaning at first, then bellowing some words – she didn't know what they were because her consciousness was spiralling down and away from her. But somehow she knew that one of them was Thomas . . . How queer. Odd. Thomas? Thomas was dead. The spasms continued as her hips

266

bucked into the air and she stuffed the dildo deeper inside, feeling it rubbing against her cervix. Finally she began to subside and her bottom slumped to the floor. Her face was sweaty and hair stuck to her temples.

It was quiet for a few minutes. No sound at all. Except for distant traffic noise and the sound of her breathing. Then she heard him speak.

"Go fetch me a Diet Pepsi," he said as he walked away. "Then tidy up in here."

He turned again before he reached the door. "Be very careful with my toys when you put them in the box. I've had them a long time. Very, very dear to me." He held up a warning finger. "And don't forget to read your Bible tonight."

Julian van der Bijl was singing in the shower. He woke up on Thursday morning in a very good mood, relaxed and rested. This was only partly because he was expecting a call from Bernstein to say that one particular problem of this operation was solved. However, it was a problem on his patch, and Van der Bijl was proud of his reputation for efficiency within the organisation.

He was the head of Direct Action in European Operations, based in London, which everybody called DA. It was still growing slowly, but that was according to plan. Make sure that one stage is solid before you build the next one. It was, however, very difficult to get quality people. That was the biggest problem, partly solved a few years ago by bringing in Israeli mercenaries. Quality was determined by two things – recruitment and training. This was where the emphasis had now been shifted and he was beginning to see the results of his policy changes. Basically, they had begun with thugs and gradually a more sophisticated character had emerged. Piet, for instance, was from the old school. A criminal, a bully, a bouncer, wanted by the police in South Africa. Men like Piet had no morals, no ethics, no ideological motivation. Coetzee was another one from that school. He winced when he thought of Coetzee. They had been unable to sew his ear back on and he was having to use a colostomy bag because of damage to his back passage. But Fanie and Chaim were good. They shouldn't have failed in the first place, causing all this fuss, all this extra expense.

But that was not the only reason he was in a good mood. He had talked with Michael Regis, who had promised him a meal followed by an evening with one of his special prostitutes. He had heard of these hand-picked women and had always wanted to try one for himself – that is, if the operation last night went smoothly. Of course it had gone smoothly. Bernstein was in charge. Bernstein was the best he had, one of the best in the business. He was a little surprised that there was not a message on his answerphone when he woke up but immediately assumed that Bernstein would want to talk to him personally.

Van der Bijl got out of the shower and selected a large fresh towel. The mirror was steamed up, so he swiped at it with the towel and looked at what he considered a handsome figure of a man. He was going to do some lucky woman a favour that evening. He slapped his belly and frowned. Going a little too flabby because he was forgetting his jogging. Like this morning. He pointed a finger at himself in the mirror.

"Tomorrow then," he said to his image, "and every day afterwards, no cheating."

Wrapping the towel around his waist, he left the bathroom and went into his bedroom. As he dressed he looked at the bedside clock and frowned again. After ten o'clock already. He'd better check the answerphone again. Maybe the phone had rung while he was in the shower.

Van der Bijl entered his office and stopped dead in his tracks, his eyes growing wide. A chill froze his spine. Someone was sitting at the desk in his chair. He could not see who it was because the light from the window backlit the figure. But he was big. Could it be Piet?

"Piet?" he called softly as he crept forward towards the desk. "Piet—"

He was going to say something else but words would no longer form because they were crowded out by the rising drumbeat of horror. What he was seeing didn't make any sense. This man had no face, no throat. The throat was torn out and the head thrown back at an odd angle. Coagulated blood was everywhere. But it must be Piet. It couldn't be anyone else. Van der Bijl could no longer feel his body, which must have gone completely numb. To defend itself, his mind struggled for some astral plane where it would be emotion-free.

The door slammed. "I brought the monkey. Now I'm lookin' for the organ grinder."

Van der Bijl turned slowly, his eyes still wide and staring. A man stood on either side of the doorway. Two men. One black, one white. The white man stepped towards him, but he could not move at all. The white man was heavy-set with a bull neck and wore a leather jacket and jeans and boots. On his head was a baseball cap. It was not possible.

"Oooo . . ." Van der Bijl said, and started again. "Ooooo . . . oooooo . . ."

"You know *who*, asshole," Haug said to him, "but I'll introduce myself formally, if you want."

He took off his cap. "Joe Wayne Haug Esquire. And this feller is One Time Griffin. We have come to talk to you, asshole, and I just bought your friend here to show you exactly what we do to sons of bitches who fuck with us."

Haug replaced his cap, walked over to Van der Bijl and grabbed him by his lapels, slowly raising him on to his tiptoes. "Because obviously you folks do not know who you're fuckin' with."

He shoved the man backwards, propelling him against a leather armchair, where he came to a sudden stop and sat down ungracefully.

"Where is Bernstein?" Van der Bijl whispered faintly.

"Bernstein has got a carload of lame and physically impaired people, and if I get the right answers here he will be lookin' for somebody to put 'em all back together again. Bernstein himself is hoppin' on one leg and will be for some time to come. There were three dead, countin' this feller here. The other two are huggin' some heavy rocks at the bottom of the Atlantic Ocean. Now, that's all the questions I reckon I need to answer. It's your turn to talk now. Don't bother with your name. I already know that."

Van der Bijl was desperately trying to collect together his reeling thoughts. "I have no intention of saying anything to you or anyone else—"

With an angry movement Haug grabbed the man again by the lapels, pulled him up from the chair, spun him around, grabbed his arm and forced it halfway up his back. Then he pushed him towards the lolling corpse of Piet and, using the arm, wrenched his head forward inches from the demolished face.

Van der Bijl could feel his cornflakes on the way up and struggled to keep them down. His eyes were drawn to the torn and gouged face a few inches away. And he was also aware of the faintly sweet smell. Then he felt himself being pulled backwards. He finally fell again into the chair.

Haug put his face very close to the man in front of him.

"Contrary to a lot of malicious rumours, I do not like to hurt people. Even shitty assholes like you. But they make me do it, don't they? Under the circumstances I have made a reasonable request. You know what is going to happen if you don't tell me what the fuck is goin' on? I am gonna systematically break ever bone in your body, and I mean ever one of 'em. I'm gonna start with your little toe and end up with your skull, and you're gonna look worse than Frankenstein's monster over there when I finish with you. I'm gonna cut your dick off and stretch it to make a new five string on my banjo. But if you talk and tell me the truth, then I won't lay a finger on you and will just leave you with the relatively simple problem of disposin' of your late friend who's occupyin' your desk chair. Now, do you unnerstand what I'm tellin' you?"

Van der Bijl looked at Haug. "Who are you?"

Haug sighed. "You're tryin' my patience, Julian. Look at thangs real close. You are not in a position to ask me *any* questions."

Van der Bijl sagged back into the leather armchair. "What do you want to know?"

"Why the hell have you been tryin' to kill Miss Jennifer Montgomery?"

"Because she has a tape and presumably knows the contents of the tape," Van der Bijl answered reluctantly.

"In fact", said Haug, "she doesn't have the tape and never has. Who said that she did?"

"Michael Regis. He said that it belonged to Harvey Gillmore, who accidentally left it at her house."

"What was on the tape?"

Van der Bijl looked exasperated. "I don't know. I had no reason to know."

"What do you do?"

"I . . . am director of DA. Direct Action. Under European Operations. Which is run mainly by Michael Regis. Direct Action is the physical expression of policies decided by European Operations—"

"I think Direct Action is pretty clear to me," Haug said, "on account of the fact that I've been dealin' with 'em for the past week. But what is European Operations? What are their interests?"

Van der Bijl thought for a minute. He felt completely drained, but he tried to choose his words carefully. Give the hard man enough to satisfy him. But not too much.

"In South Africa I was one of the leaders of the RB, the Red and Black—"

"Explain."

"An organisation. The name comes from the Red Danger and . . ." he glanced at One Time, "and the Black Danger."

"One time," said One Time.

"Which was what you would call a secret paramilitary organisation," he went on. "Over a period of years we made contacts with other organisations with similar interests and gradually, naturally, we came under one umbrella. Which is now worldwide."

"And the Israeli angle?" Haug asked.

"Mercenaries mostly, used to train and provide a backbone to our Direct Action squads. Nothing to do with Israel itself, except that many of our recruits had excellent European, even worldwide, contacts through their own native organisation. In the Nazi hunt, for instance. And later, the Arab menace."

"Is this . . . European Operation . . . does it have anythang to do with the British Government?"

Van der Bijl sat stonily silent.

"Answer," Haug said menacingly.

"I don't know. Honestly. You see, amongst nearly all governments there are those who are sympathetic to our cause—"

"Which is?"

"The Red Danger."

"And the black one?"

"No," answered Van der Bijl unevenly. "Not so much. Only in southern Africa, perhaps Africa as a whole. But only because it has so much to do with the Red Danger there. For instance the ANC is Communist. We oppose this. So do many in European governments. Therefore we have the same, or closely overlapping, interests. Here in the UK there is no black danger but an Irish one, in France an Algerian one, in Holland an Indonesian one, and so forth. Everyone has local problems. Where we all agree, however, is the Red Danger."

Haug looked out of the window and studied the tops of the trees in Regent's Park.

"So, to put it in a nutshell, you guys are a bunch of right-wing loonies who run around Europe and the rest of the world puttin' pressure on anybody who doesn't agree with you. And if the pressure doesn't work, you send in your gang. What's it called? Direct Action. And they bring out the bag of money. If that doesn't work, you kneecap 'em. If they still won't play ball, they wind up in the foundations of a new bridge. Have I got the hang of thangs?"

"Roughly. There's actually very little violence, though. Most people come round in the end. And we're *not* right-wing loonies."

"I'll be the judge of that," Haug said, reaching into his jacket pocket and taking out a tape cassette. "Now I think this is what you have been lookin' for, Julian."

"I thought you said you didn't have it."

"At a great deal of trouble to myself, I have arranged to find it. To try and figger out what the hell's goin' on with my fuckin' life."

Haug walked over to the stereo system. "Now I'm gonna play the thang. It's a real short telephone conversation, and there's no information which sounds earth-shatterin'. One of the speakers I know. That scummy Australian who wipes his ass with paper and sells it to the public as news. The other guy I don't know. Maybe you do."

Haug studied the system, looking for the switch. He had picked up the tape from the post office on the way to the flat and listened to it in the pickup. Neither he nor One Time had a clue who the other speaker was. He inserted the cassette and pushed the play button.

" . . . *shouldn't take long, Mr Gillmore. Couple of things to tidy up. I'm going to OK WORLDWIDE, so long as—*"

"*Good, good, glad to hear it, mate.*"

"*So long as the arrangements and proxy are suitable for you—*"

"*Yeah, two and a half per cent, that's a quart of blood, all right.*"

"*But I want to make clear that my name doesn't come up anywhere. My proxy—*"

"Trust me, mate. We're all in it to make a buck, and that's nobody else's . . . nobody else's business."

"I'll also do what I can about the Star. *If we can swing it—"*

"You have to swing it," said Gillmore.

"Yeah, maybe. Got to be careful, though. I'll want some net on that too, through nominated proxy. I'm talking about preferential, not ordinary—"

"Yeah, yeah, we'll work something out."

"No, no, no! I want it agreed now before I OK this deal—"

"OK, OK, you got it. My fucking hands are tied. I need the cash. And I want The Johannesburg Star. *You're in. You're on the boat. In the cabin. First-class."*

"Right, right. Then Michael will sort things out on this, Mr Gillmore."

"Thank you very much for your help, mate . . ."

Haug ejected the cassette and put it back in his pocket. He had been watching Van der Bijl while the tape played.

"So. Who is this guy?"

"No idea," Van der Bijl lied.

He knew that voice very well indeed and it had been difficult to suppress his astonishment.

"Well," Haug said, "I think you do know who it is. But I'm tired, and I'm losin' my stomach for torture. On a good day I could get it out of you. I'm gonna do somethin' else, bo. So lissen like your life depends on it, which it does. I'm gonna put two or three copies of this tape in deep, safe places. If somethin' happens to me or Jennifer Montgomery or One Time or any of my friends, then these tapes are gonna float up somewhere and start smellin'. Do you get my drift?"

"You want to do a deal."

"I want to do a deal. That's right. I haven't got eyes in the back of my head, and I need to sleep some time. So if you keep sendin' 'em at me, one day one of your boy scouts is gonna get lucky and drill a hole in me. Me, I wanna die of old age. So does One Time. So does Miss Montgomery. From here on in I want a stand-off. You haven't got everthang you wanted, and I still don't know who's on the goddam' tape."

Van der Bijl chewed his upper lip. "I don't have the authority to do a deal with you."

"Don't hand me that crap, bo. Between you and that shitass Regis, I'm sure you can figger somethin' out."

"I'll try to convince Michael—"

"Tryin' is not good enough, asshole. I'm not gonna leave this place with you *trying* to do a deal for me."

Haug slapped the pocket with the tape. "If you don't agree, I'm gonna make this thang public today. Right now. Believe me, I'll find a way to make it hurt."

Van der Bijl held up his hands. "OK. OK. A deal. We'll back off. You'll never hear of us again. So long as we never hear of that tape. But if we do—"

"Any double cross and we'll resume battle stations."

Haug walked over to the telephone and picked it up, pushing the buttons. Keef answered and he told him to put Bernstein and the injured in his car and let them go. He asked after Jennifer and was told that she was asleep. He told Keef that all was well and that Jennifer should be safe now. Then he rang off.

Van der Bijl stood up. He had a faint smile on his lips. "Why don't you consider, Mr Haug, coming to work for us? The pay is very very good."

Haug stared at the South African. "Let's get outta here, One Time. Frankenstein's monster is startin' to stink. And I might just change my mind and kill this guy on account of my conscience."

They left Van der Bijl standing in the middle of his office, still smiling.

———————

When Haug got back to his own office, Lizzy wasn't there. But she had left two notes for him. The short one said that she had gone to pick up one of her kids from school to take her to the dentist. The longer note was a list of phone calls with bills to pay and cheques to sign. He checked through the post, most of it junk. Lizzy had put something on top. A fancy business card with a name on it. Sir Jonathan Mainwaring. On the back was a spidery handwritten note. *Meet me 1.00 p.m. in St James's Park, Palace end, nr Spur Rd. Thursday or Friday.*

He frowned and turned the card back over. Who the fuck was that? Today was Thursday, and it was already afternoon. Have to be tomorrow. Bound to have something to do with this business, though.

The garbage had been coming at him through the bottom trough. Now maybe it was going to start pouring down from the top. *Sir* Jonathan. A knight of the realm. He stuck the card in his wallet and sat down at the desk.

He finally found where Lizzy had moved the stationery and counted off three sheets. On each he scratched out a message with a pen. Then he pawed around in the bottom drawer until he found three Jiffy bags. One of these he addressed to his only close friend in the States. On the other two he used a marker pen and wrote in capitals: OPEN ON PRODUCTION OF DEATH CERTIFICATE JOE WAYNE HAUG AND POST TO ADDRESS INSIDE. He had addressed the letters inside to two different investigative journalists, one of them an acquaintance, a man known all over the country for his integrity.

He went upstairs and made three copies of the tape, then sealed them in the bags. The one to America he posted downstairs in the pillar box. Then he left a note for Lizzy. One parcel was to go to her solicitor and one to his, delivered by hand immediately. He thanked her, left twenty pounds for taxis and said that he was going to take a nap.

Haug stretched out on his bed, glad to be there. He didn't even take off his boots. He had driven directly to London with One Time, and they had stopped only once, for petrol. He was hungry and tired, but food could wait. He was also pretty sure that he had a cracked rib, and only felt comfortable on his back. That could wait too. Sleep couldn't.

Lizzy opened the door to his flat with her key and immediately heard the thunderous snoring. She carried the waste-paper basket over to his bed and left it standing on the side table. Inside the waste-paper basket she had discovered the most disgusting thing she had ever seen and realised that it was a wad of used chewing tobacco. There was no way that she was going to sit with that by her desk. Such things should go in the toilet.

She stopped in the doorway before closing the door and looked at the man spread-eagled on the bed, his head back, his mouth open. She felt her anger subside.

Whatever his faults, she thought, he was a good man. She closed the door quietly instead of slamming it as she had planned. When she returned to the office, she put the two parcels and the twenty-pound note in her handbag, turned the answerphone back on and left, locking the door behind her.

Chapter Nineteen

Haug pulled the Harley slowly into Spur Road. It was a full dress Electroglide and always attracted a lot of attention. This was the first time he had ridden it since last autumn. He only had just over 5,000 miles on the clock, and it gave him a lot of pleasure to get the hog out, even if it was only to burble around London in the traffic. The reaction of Londoners to his riding a full dress Harley was the same as though he were riding a pinball machine with all the lights flashing. Harleys could not be made anywhere on earth but the United States of America. The chrome, the lights, the sound, the size all announced that it was the fucking biggest and the fucking best and if you didn't like it, fuck you. Other motorcyclists could sneer, but you always detected a slight trace of envy in the twisted-down corners of their mouths. It was so over-the-top that it made pedestrians gasp. In fact it was a very old design, a V-twin long-stroke engine which still used pushrods in the days of the overhead camshaft. Nor was it fast by Jap standards. Even old British 650s and 750s would overhaul a Harley and beat it on top speed. But Haug loved his Harley partly because he loved the sense of the ridiculous. And partly because it was, despite its monstrous size, a very comfortable motorcycle to ride.

He pushed down the kickstand and revved the engine before switching off, a habit he had picked up from earlier days of motorcycling when you cleared the carburettors to save on fuel loss. Opening the top box, he dumped his helmet and gloves and took out his dozer cap. It was a bright day again and he wore his California Cop sunglasses. He locked the top box and the bike, unzipped his jacket and looked around. St James's Park. He had only been here maybe once or twice before and wondered why he didn't come more often. Probably because it tended to be infested with the wrong sorts. Either throngs of tourists or civil servants on their lunch breaks. It was a pretty place with a nice pond and a good feel. Now how, he wondered, am I gonna recognise Sir Jonathan Mainwaring?

He started walking slowly on the path by the pond, hands stuffed into his jeans pockets. He glanced along at the wooden benches and their occupants. Just as he had predicted. Tourists and civil servants eating lunch. He looked over at the other side. Same thing. Lots of ducks taking advantage of the English passion for all animals except foxes.

"Mr Haug?" It sounded a bit like Mr Hoog.

Haug turned to look at the man seated on the bench. He was a tall thin man, conservatively dressed, with a bowler hat on his head. He walked over to the gentleman.

"Mainwarin'?"

Mainwaring smiled. "I'm not sure about the pronunciation of your name actually."

"I'll answer to most anythang. It's How, with a g. How . . g."

He stuck out his hand and Mainwaring shook it briefly.

"Please, Mr Haug, sit down."

He moved his briefcase, raincoat and umbrella. "I saved you a place, despite the fact that it is always rather crowded here when the sun comes out. I wasn't sure that you would come."

"I only got your card yesterday afternoon, Mr Mainwarin'. For the last few days I been runnin' around like a dog with turpentine on his ass."

"I beg your pardon?"

Haug sat down. "I been busy, Mr Mainwarin'. And I got a strong feelin' that this is gonna be a continuation of that business. How did you recognise me? I never met you."

"I knew that you were American", said the Englishman, "and I'm afraid that you are a bit of a give-away. Though I had decided that you were going to be more of the Sam Spade type, with a fedora, a dangling cigarette and an ill-fitting suit with brown shoes. Now, what business do you think this might be a continuation of, Mr Haug?"

"Just call me Haug. Everbody else does. And what should I call you? I never know how to deal with titles and all that crap."

"Like you, I answer to almost anything, Mr Haug. Whatever makes you feel comfortable."

"Well, you sound like a decent sort of feller, Mr Mainwarin'. They've tried the rough and that didn't work, so now I guess you're tryin' the smooth."

"I'm afraid you've lost me. I admit that I have asked you to join me on no more than intuition. I work for the Department of Trade. The Permanent Secretary to the Minister. And your name crossed my desk in connection with a request from Mr Harvey Gillmore—"

"That jerkoff!" Haug spat out.

Mainwaring looked away. His ducks were still lurking, hoping for more, though he had finished lunch half an hour previously.

"I may take exception to your language but not your sentiments. Gillmore has made a somewhat irregular request for the Minister to revoke your licence. Or to put pressure on those who would. I thought I would like to hear your side of the matter. Informally."

Haug sighed and looked at his partner.

"OK, for your information, that jackass Gillmore is, in my opinion, implicated in the very recent attempt to murder my client and, incidentally, myself."

"Did you say murder?"

"That's exactly what I said, Mr Mainwarin'. Maybe wrongly I suspected that you were a part of the same shitty business. Then again, maybe you're gonna come out with some fancy sort of bribe. Like I can keep my licence and stay in this country and not get arrested by the police, if I am a nice boy and hand over the tape to you."

"Tape, you say?"

"Yeah, tape."

Mainwaring turned up the toe of one black shoe and examined it carefully. "I have no idea what you are talking about. I am making my own informal and discreet enquiries into some disturbing government irregularities. I know no more about you than your name, nationality and occupation. I know nothing of any tapes, though I admit the idea intrigues me. And I know nothing, God forbid, of any murder attempts upon you or anyone else. Mr Gillmore alleges that you assaulted him in his office."

"The son of a bitch refused to answer my questions, so I banged his head on the desk – simple as that."

Mainwaring put the tips of his long fingers together. "Mr Haug, I don't understand what you are talking about really. And I'm under the impression that the reverse may also be true. Would you tell me the story if I guaranteed that it remains confidential and goes no further than my own ears?"

Haug snorted. "What sorta guarantee do I get?"

"My word," Mainwaring said simply.

Haug looked at the two remaining ducks still hoping for a handout. He leaned forward on his elbows and took off his sunglasses.

"Mainwarin', you know I half believe you. Nobody has tried that one on me in a long time. My word. It's somethin' *I* unnerstand, but I didn't think there was anybody else who did. This world seems to have filled up with trash like Gillmore and Michael Regis—"

Mainwaring had raised his hand. "Excuse me, what was that last name?"

"Michael Regis. You probably don't know him. An arms dealer, a blackmailer and a pimp. And, I might add, an attempted murderer."

Mainwaring locked his fingers together and placed his hands in his lap. He turned to Haug.

"In fact I do know of Michael Regis, but it startles me that you mentioned his name."

"Are you a friend of his?"

"Hardly," Mainwaring said with chilly emphasis. "However, what you say, together with your obvious sentiments, encourages me to think that we may indeed share some common ground."

Haug thought carefully for a minute. "Well, it doesn't make sense you bein' out scavengin' for information if you are one of them. 'Cause they dam' well know the story. Inside out. The only real risk I can think of is that you may be some sorta fancy policeman who's gonna burn my ass 'cause I had to do a few illegal thangs to keep from bein' killed."

He held up his hands as Mainwaring started to protest. "It's OK. I don't think you're a cop, 'cause no cop I ever met would ever sit with a straight face and give me his word. Cops just don't think like that. Now, before I start talkin', I gotta warn you that what I tell you might be dangerous to you. I circled this park on the Harley before stoppin', lookin' for the give-away van. Or well-dressed men loiterin' in cars. But I gotta say that thangs are gettin' so sophisticated these days that it wouldn't surprise me if they could lissen by satellite. Or these tourists passin' by got somethin' fancy up their sleeves. So, there's a risk. Even out in the open."

"I'm aware of the risks, Mr Haug, and I think they are minimal here. Not non-existent, but minimal."

Haug leaned back and replaced his sunglasses. He started at the beginning and covered everything but the private matters between him and Jennifer. It took him over twenty minutes to tell the story. Through it all Mainwaring did not move, did not even swing his leg.

He sat as immobile as a statue. When Haug stopped to think or search for a word, he simply waited, staring stonily ahead across the pond. When clumps of tourists would linger in front to gaze or take snapshots, Haug would stop or lower his voice slightly, waiting for them to move on. Once a couple of Japanese pointed a camera in their direction, and Haug got up with a smile to ask them please not to bother. They politely bowed and moved away. He returned and took up the story again where he left off. All the time he talked, though, his eyes roved and paused briefly on a lounger, a young man leaning on a tree, two men sitting in shirtsleeves, anyone who looked at all suspicious. He was very aware that Mainwaring was a high-ranking civil servant and that, friend or foe, the meeting would be very interesting to certain groups of powerful people. But he had made a decision to tell the man the story without pulling punches. He was blunt and descriptive. At the end he mentioned the fact that Gillmore's chauffeur had died soon after Haug had obviously been spotted talking to him. Lizzy had saved the newspaper article for him. He waited for Mainwaring to speak.

The Permanent Secretary cleared his throat. "An extraordinary tale. And you seem to be an extraordinary man, Mr Haug."

"Naw, I don't think so. And that's not modesty. I was a little bit lucky, and the opposition made the mistake of underratin' me. A lotta folks do. Gives me a little advantage sometimes."

"Hmmm. I'll try not to make the same mistake myself. I admit that I am rather overawed at your courage and daring. Sounds like the stories I read as a child about frontiersmen in the colonies. How many men were involved in the assault on the house in Cornwall?"

"A total of nine. But there was only one of 'em worth a fuck. He damn near whipped my ass."

Mainwaring turned to Haug. "I don't mean to be rude, but the Americans seem to be obsessed with . . . their bottoms. An anal fixation of some sort."

Haug laughed. "Just the way we talk. Some of the Yanks who stick to this piece of flypaper take to your ways and change their accents, try to be more English than the English. Now, I'm ashamed of some of the thangs America does, but I'm not ashamed of the fact I'm American. On account of the fact I cain't help it. It's like bein' bald, isn't it?"

"Oh, I don't mind Americans so much, Mr Haug. I just sometimes wish they would pack up all their hamburgers and Coca Colas and take them back where they came from."

Haug laughed. "Hell, I agree with you. This is a different place, and I like it here. It's changed a lot since I arrived. The Limeys look silly drinkin' cocktails and wearin' hats like mine and tryin' to use West Coast slang. I mean, you make the best beer in the world and then you go into a pub and ask for Budweiser. American beer tastes like horse sweat. That's modern advertisin' for you, though. It works. Give 'em enough money and they'll sell bottled owl piss, and people in suits'll be talkin' about the bouquet and how it's astringent on the palate. Between the goddam' advertisers and pornographers like Gillmore, folks don't bother thinkin' anymore. They suck up the filth in newspapers along with candy-coated political horseshit that they wouldn't even be able to digest if they didn't sit in front of a television set until they fell asleep. I'm right with you, buddy. Get these highsteppin' slick bastards with their yuppie ad talk outta here and back to the States where everthing's lit up with neon anyway. If it gets much worse, I tell you, I'm gonna back my ass down to the Cornwall coast and be a hermit the rest of my life."

Mainwaring chuckled. "I sincerely hope you don't, Mr Haug. I can't reveal many details of my own investigations at the moment. We seem to share a few enemies, if not a few ideas. This tape which was the origin of all your problems – do you have any idea why they consider it so important?"

"I got an idea why, but not who. Funny thang is, I think I got the answer packed away somewhere in two different compartments, just cain't bring 'em together. It's somebody important talkin' to Gillmore, somebody who shouldn't be doin' what he's doin'. You say you're Department of Trade. Know anything about this arms deal?"

Mainwaring recrossed his legs. "As a matter of fact I do. I advised the Minister of my reservations regarding the shipment but I was overruled, I'm afraid."

"That's Ian Castleberry, right?"

"Very good, Mr Haug."

"Well . . . Ian Castleberry was a client of Miss Montgomery. Regis brought 'em together and introduced her as his cousin. Regis paid as well. Fifteen hundred quid. Where I come from that's as close as a gnat's ass to bein' a bribe."

"It is in this country as well."

"Two more clients were Tobias-Wyatt of the Bank of England and Lord Stourbridge."

"Ah," said Mainwaring. "The Lord Chief Justice."

"Now I assume", Haug went on, "that Miss Montgomery is not the only woman controlled by Regis, but I don't have any proof. He uses the girls as favours or treats to sweeten up folks he wants somethin' from or as rewards when they do it right. Must cost him a hell of a lot of dough, when you think about it. On the other hand, when you put it into a kind of perspective, you can see it as an investment, a business investment. Some people call it grease. Makes thangs slide along easier. If Regis is in the arms business, there's a shit pot of money in that, and along the way you need accommodatin' politicians, bankers who'll shrug at certain accounts and movements of money and a legal system that looks the other way. So Miss Montgomery sure had a good spread there. The executive, the judicial and the legislative. I assume they were gettin' some other kinds of backhanders as well. But I suppose you, bein' English and of the same class, probably won't want to look at that kind of picture and call it corruption—"

Mainwaring held up a long thin finger. "This particular Englishman – and a few more – do indeed object to such behaviour, Mr Haug. We too use the words 'bribe' and 'corruption', because they are accurate. As you suspect, Miss Montgomery was more a sweetener than an actual bribe. In Ian's case the bribe was an arrangement made by Michael Regis for the Castleberry estate to be extended by six hundred acres, an old and much valued piece of land."

"In that case, my hunch is that the current deal is only a little trickle to make sure they got a river bed. Then they can open the sluice gates. Is there anyone behind Regis?"

Mainwaring thought for a moment. Finally he folded one hand over the other.

"You must also wonder, Mr Haug, why I asked you to come today. Particularly now you know that I knew nothing of your recent adventures."

"I was about to come to that."

"How shall I put this?"

Mainwaring took off his bowler. Not a single hair on his head was disturbed. He placed his hat carefully on his knee, holding on to it with one hand.

"I have reason to believe that a dangerous conspiracy has been formed. It has a transnational character and, trying to be fair, many of the conspirators would never see themselves as traitors. I am chauvinist enough not to be overly worried about conspiracies elsewhere, even in Europe. My loyalty is to the Crown. Thus it is here in this country where my concern lies. Over the years I have observed what is going on, and your analogy of the river bed is apt. One can overlook individual avarice or poor judgement or ethical laxity and occasional depravity. When, however, they become an everyday event and, moreover, those everyday events seem to be orchestrated outside our parliamentary and answerable democratic system, then it is time that I examined my own loyalty. Do you follow me, Mr Haug? I refuse to be part of a conspiracy to subvert or undermine the specific interests of the Crown. These interests are being subverted and undermined. I have decided to do something about it."

Haug was interested. "Like what?"

Again Mainwaring held up a bony finger. "I have revealed too much already, Mr Haug, for my own peace of mind, for my own safety. I'm sure you can appreciate that."

"Yeah," Haug breathed out heavily, "I see what you mean. What I'm wonderin' is why you're tellin' me all this. I mean, I know what you're talkin' about. And I got a strong feelin' that you're right too. Somehow the right wing has made a clean sweep everwhere. It's like a plague—"

"It makes no difference to me which wing it is," Mainwaring interrupted. "I'm not interested in wings. If there were a Marxist conspiracy undermining the fabric of Parliament, I would fight them as relentlessly as I fight the ones on the right. *This* is the way *we* do it, Mr Haug. How you do it in America is only of academic interest to me. Perhaps I sympathise with one side or another, but ultimately it is up to the people over there to decide what kind of government they want. And it is not for Americans or anyone else to decide our form of government."

Haug chuckled. "It's an old-fashioned liberal argument—"

284

"Fashion is another item which does not interest me, old or new. Right and wrong have no fashion."

"No, no, I'm not tryin' to put you down, Mr Mainwarin'. I look at you and see the kind of Englishman I used to read about before I came. Straight as a ramrod, stiff upper lip, principles that won't bend under any weight and a kind of decency that goes all the way through, like Brighton in rock candy. There's somethin' kinda touchin' about it, kinda movin'. I didn't even think it existed any more. The so-called gents get more like Regis ever day, slippery as snot on a brass doorknob. I don't say I agree with you. On account of the fact that the old class of Englishmen were the best colonial administrators and kept the workin' class heads down at their benches, producin' sacks of profit so that you could afford to send your kids to private schools and Cambridge or Oxford, while the workin'-class kids went down the pits or into apprenticeship or provided cannon fodder for all your old conquests—"

Mainwaring raised his hat from his knee and brushed off a small piece of lint.

"Mr Haug, I have no wish to waste my time debating the minutiae of political philosophy. Hopefully we can put all this aside for the moment and consider instead our common ground. While it may intrigue me that you hold unusual views for an American, I am much more interested in your own 'old-fashioned' actions and sentiments. I sense an overlap with my own, Mr Haug, despite the fact that you were born outside our borders, now inevitably shrunk to this little island. I will therefore come to the point. Would you consider working with us?"

Haug did not conceal the fact that he was genuinely taken aback. "Who is 'us', and why me?"

"We are at the moment a very small core of people forming our own conspiracy. However, since this is a conspiracy to defend the Crown, it is not logically a conspiracy at all. I have taken the liberty of calling it the United Opposition. I cannot by honour and for security reasons divulge the names of any other members, but, if it will make you feel any better, their politics conform more to your ideas than my own. That's the answer to one of your questions. As for the other . . . to be quite brutally frank, we have no one at all at what you might call 'street level'. I have no idea how to go about recruiting such a person or persons for obvious reasons. The fact that you happen to be an American is annoying but something that I think I can learn to live with. We have a need for someone who knows how to acquire evidence, or 'tail' – is that the word? – a suspect, or let us know when a place is 'bugged'. I do loathe this kind of slang, but in the interests of transatlantic goodwill, I am making an effort."

Haug scratched the back of his neck. "What makes you think I won't just slide across to the other side of the street to see what they have to offer for my services."

Mainwaring smiled thinly. "From what you tell me, they have already made one offer which you turned down. And I also think that I am a good judge of character, Mr Haug. For instance, I don't believe that I underestimate you."

"I'm not a rich man, Mr Mainwarin'. However much I might sympathise with you and your project, I cain't live on sympathy. Yet I kinda hate to ask you for any money 'cause you seem to be such a nice man. But I got a part-time secretary to pay, rent, food, gas for the Harley and my old van and pickup. If you want tailin' done or buggin' cleared, I gotta pay somebody to do it. I know you English guys would rather talk about the warts on your dicks than discuss money, but if you want somebody at street level as you call it, well, that's how we have to operate. 'Cause we *are* at street level. We don't have your kind of credit."

Mainwaring sighed. "I had already anticipated your needs. Your reasonable expenses will be met – initially from my own pocket. However, I will need a budget so I know what to expect. No, Mr Haug, I did not expect to appeal to your charity."

It was now mid-afternoon, and Haug watched a group of kids from school walking towards an open space with cricket gear.

"The only charity *I* give to is Lord's Taverners."

Mainwaring uncrossed his legs and half turned to the American. "Are you serious? Do you like cricket?"

Haug pressed his lips together and nodded. "After a number of years of deep and thoughtful study, I have had to admit that it's the greatest game ever invented. At least it's the greatest one I know of. Now, I used to play football, what you call here gridiron football, and that is one hell of a game. So's baseball. I can still smell the mustard on the hotdogs, watchin' one of the games in the World Series. But cricket is really more than a game. It's sensitive, subtle, yet fulla interestin' surprises. The important point is," he said, turning to face

286

Mainwaring, "that passion in the spectator doesn't overwhelm the intellect. And *that* is genius."

"Well, you've quite taken my breath away, Mr Haug."

"A good test match", Haug went on, warming to his subject, "is like a magical theatrical event or the Ring Cycle at Bayreuth or a visit to The Hermitage or The Louvre. It's as much artistic as athletic. Now you cain't say that about American football or soccer. They're just straight out competitions, up-front entertainment. The only trouble with cricket is that you gotta be prepared to risk boredom to find the sublime. In a good game there are bursts of excitement, bursts of passion, but then you got time to swirl it around in your mouth, like a fine wine, before somethin' else happens. And I hope you don't mind my sayin' so, but one day cricket is a load of kangaroo shit. It's some other, crummier game played by the same folks."

"I'm afraid you've hit a soft spot in my centre. On the other hand, I'm happy to say it only confirms my intuition that you are the right man."

"It's the greatest thang you ever exported – that and motorsickles. Sorry it didn't grab my fellow Americans, but then we'd probably have fucked it up, even though there's plenty of time for commercials. I mean, the Australians are bad enough with shiny suits and white balls and names on the back of shirts."

He took off his cap. "And I wanna tell you somethin'. This is a *baseball* cap, not a cricket cap. What's the matter with people here? You lost your confidence or somethin'? Afraid of doin' thangs your way any more? The only thang you fight for any more is a place in the queue to kiss ass – Japanese ass, German ass, Yankee ass. I wanna shake people on the street and say, you got a lot to be proud of here – you don't have to kiss anybody's ass. You still got the greatest game in the world, the best television, the best national health service, and some of the best engineers. It's not the Garden of Eden, but neither is anywhere else."

Uncharacteristically Mainwaring stretched his legs out in front of him, placing his bowler beside him on the bench. "I don't know where it's gone, when it left, or even how it went. I am not a philosopher. I do know, however, that if something is not done soon, we'll only be a squalid little country of violent, selfish, ignorant, suspicious people with nothing *left* to fight for but a countryside

littered with jerry-built neo-Georgian terraces, soulless concrete
motorways, foul or irradiated beaches and parks like these, littered
with Kentucky fried chicken cartons. No one will care any longer.
Just as no one cares that egregiously corrupt cabinet ministers accept
bribes to line their pockets from gangsters who would be in prison,
but for the fact that no court in the land will convict them."

Like the Englishman, Haug stretched his legs and folded his arms
on his chest.

"Oh, I dunno, Mr Mainwarin'. I think you sellin' these folks
short. A lotta people just don't know what hit 'em in the '80s. That
goddam' woman prime minister had as much sense as you could slap
in a gnat's ass with a butter paddle. But she had a killer instinct all
right. She and that sorry bunch of varmints near cleaned house. And
all their good friends got in on the kill. Steel gone, coal goin', cars
and buses gone, electricity, gas and water makin' a fortune for a few
people, with the National Health Service and the BBC waitin' their
turns with their caps in their hands. The eatin' was good while the
hog lasted, but what now? A lotta people know that this is true, but
they got lies comin' at 'em from all directions, and most of 'em are
scared of losin' their jobs. I think they *know* that they gotta sweep
these heathens outta the temple but are just dreadin' doin' it on
account of all the garbage they gonna have to clean up and what it's
gonna cost 'em to put all that money back which has been dragged
away by the thieves."

"Perhaps it is hopeless, Mr Haug. I'm not sure that I share your
optimism about the people any more."

"Oh, I think you do. Why else would you put your career and
your title and your reputation on the line to try and do somethin' about
it?"

"Those things are of no importance if the basic human fabric is
filthy. In the value system in which I believe there is a right and a
wrong. It is simply my duty as a citizen and civil servant to serve one
and resist the other. I have no romantic illusions about the 'people'. I
have done my best within the system over these past dreadful years. I
have managed to slow down or seriously damage legislation and I
have leaked crucial pieces of information to the Press through a
tortuous series of channels. There are others as well who have
resisted. But in the end, too few. Too little and too few. There
always has been corruption in government and always will be, but

when the whole structure has been corrupted it is time, as you say, to clear out the rubbish. Not being a revolutionary – and despising the very word – I don't know how to go about it, Mr Haug. Except very carefully."

"Well," said Haug, "for a start you don't get into pissin' contests with skunks."

"I have to admit that I find your provincial homilies amusing sometimes, though the meaning occasionally escapes me."

"You don't meet 'em head on with their weapons until you're ready. Make 'em fight on your ground. Draw 'em into a place where you got the advantage."

"Easily said but practically difficult."

"Well, you're takin' on a pretty big project here, Mr Mainwarin'. Doesn't hurt to keep tactics in mind."

"The tactics of government I understand fully. Those of the street not at all."

"Then I think we got the grounds for a partnership, feller. Exactly the reverse is true with me. And as far as I'm concerned, you gotta deal."

Mainwaring winced. "I would be so grateful if you would indulge me by calling it an agreement."

"Okeydoke. An agreement. You got an agreement."

"I don't think we should be in touch by telephone."

"You're right there. No phones. No post, for that matter. We'll have to set up somethin', and there are several ways around that."

"For the moment it will have to be St James's Park, I'm afraid. I am usually here every lunchtime while Parliament is sitting, unless I am out of the country."

Haug pulled his legs under him and put on his cap.

"I gotta say that I kinda enjoyed this conversation, Mr Mainwarin'. I don't agree with everthang you say, and if I did it would be about as interestin' as talkin' to a mirror. At least what you do say is intelligent. Hard thang to find these days, intelligence."

"Indeed." Mainwaring carefully replaced his bowler on his head. "An agreeable afternoon, Mr Haug. I am very glad to have met you. I was wondering. It may be possible that I could just manage to get two seats at Lord's for the Ashes this summer. Would you be interested in joining me?"

"You're jokin'!"

"I'm afraid I don't joke. Cricket is my passion – as much passion as I allow myself, that is. And who knows? With a little luck perhaps we'll stuff those bastards this summer."

"I've been tryin' to get tickets to Lord's for years. Hell, if you can do that, I tell you what. I'll let you ride on my Harley."

Haug and Mainwaring got up together.

"Thank you very much for the generous offer, Mr Haug. I hope you won't be offended if I decline. I loathe motorcycles. However, if you wish to be sporting, perhaps we could go in my old Morgan."

Haug grinned. "You got a Morgan? Not a three-wheeler?"

"No, this is a later one and has a wheel at every corner."

"I'd be delighted. Meanwhile, I'll check in here at St James's once a week, and I got to say it won't be a chore."

Mainwaring picked up his coat, briefcase and umbrella. "Thank you very much."

He tipped his hat. "Until next time, then."

"Just one thang," Haug said, stopping him. "Just outta curiosity I'd like to know who the other feller is on the tape."

Mainwaring looked puzzled. "I'm afraid I can't help you there."

"Oh, I think you can," Haug replied. "I took the liberty of slippin' a copy in your jacket pocket while we were talkin'."

He winked and turned away, walking back to where he had parked the Harley.

There was no change in the expression on Mainwaring's face as he turned up the centre of the path, the umbrella performing its ritual as a walking stick. But there was a little extra spring in his step.

Chapter Twenty

Harvey Gillmore looked out at St Paul's wishing that he could bulldoze it. And Buckingham Palace. And the Tower of London. No, he'd save the Tower and bulldoze the rest of London. The fucking Poms have done it again, he thought. Every time I get near the top of the mountain, I find a big English boot on my fingers. A nation of lesbians and faggots, from the Royal Family right on down. Anyway, London ought to be done like Rome. Or was it Carthage? Fuck history. Everything should be smashed away and the whole place ploughed with salt. Then he'd start hanging them in the Tower.

"Pom," he said out loud, visualising the hangman's trap opening. "Pom, Pom, Pom, Pom . . ."

Every one of the swindling bastards, swinging on ropes.

Michael Regis had called him that morning and told him the news. The deal was off. Fucking Abdullah had pulled out, along with the rest of the two-faced cowardly Arabs. Regis had withdrawn. Orders had been cancelled. The Department of Trade had been informed. The whole thing was fucking dead and next week he had a very important meeting with his bankers.

An hour after Regis called, fucking Abdullah himself had called and in his slimy phoney public school accent had offered him cash for shares. He had told Abdullah to get on his camel and sell rugs, and put the phone down. They all wanted to dip into the honeypot.

His honeypot. But they were family shares. WORLDWIDE was not a public company. It was *his*. Like his newspapers. They were his too. The fucking workers thought *they* owned them, and he had shown them by applying his foot to their arses. Now they were selling pencils under the arches. Nobody really understood ownership in England, not even the fucking Tories. If you own something, it belongs to you personally. It's yours to do with as you wish. If someone works for you, he is *yours* while you are paying him. Or her. People are no different from property, and the sooner the Poms understood that the better. Every employee at *The News* would get down on their knees and suck his cock, from the editor on down. And they knew it. He had once lowered his trousers and made his editor,

Colin Greenaway, kiss his ass. Right in the hole. A man who would do that would do anything for you and that's the kind of employee he wanted.

Well, he thought, they've backed me into corners before. And he had always escaped, always made even more money. A lot of men had crossed him only to find themselves ruined. He laughed silently, thinking of a couple who had actually come to beg him to back off. He had caned them both over the desk and put them on the payroll. One of them was a big man, twice his size, who had actually cried with humiliation. Experiences like that made life worth living.

One day he would get Michael Regis. One day. Right now the man was useful. This deal may have fallen through, but there were others. He knew that Regis wanted to use WORLDWIDE to set up a new pipeline, so it was just going to cost the fucker. Then, one day, some day, he would have Regis in here on his fucking knees, begging. Something to look forward to.

Meanwhile, this afternoon, he had a meeting with Bilsten Vanguarde Holmes, his accountants. An old Pommie firm which now had one of his mates from Adelaide as a partner. One of the conditions of retaining them. Old Bill Fry. There wasn't any better financial wizard alive. An artist with figures. Turn red into black. Well, he was going to have to be a fucking Rembrandt to get out of this muck.

Gillmore went to the safe and span the dial. Swinging the door open, he bent down and collected the files he needed for the meeting. He put them on the desk and brushed the dust from them. Then he looked at his hand and swore. He rang the bell. When Beth came hurrying in, he sent her back for a damp cloth. When she returned, he held out his hand for her to clean. With his other hand he opened one of the files.

"While I'm going through these papers I want you to clean the inside of that safe for me. Dust is not supposed to get in safes, but it does."

Then suddenly he had a thought. Beth was drying his hand.

"Take off your clothes. Not your shoes. I don't want you to take those off."

Without a word Beth took the pins from her little hat and placed them carefully on the edge of the desk. Her hair was wet against the back of her neck because she had been cleaning the cooker. She took off her apron and pulled her dress over her head. It was a little damp at the back, but she folded it and placed it on the desk as well. She unhooked the bra Gillmore had asked her to wear because it pushed her breasts up and made them look larger than they were. Then she pushed down her knickers and stepped out of them, glancing anxiously at the gusset. She knew that she was due for her period in a few days and feared that Gillmore wasn't going to like it. It worried her. She didn't even have any tampons with her.

She stood waiting for him. He was leaning forward on his hands studying one of the files, his half glasses perched on the end of his nose.

Finally he turned to her. "How old are you?"

"Thirty-four," she said.

He shook his head. "That's too fucking old. But we might be able to do something anyway."

He put his glasses down and walked around her, looking speculatively, as he might examine a horse. He grabbed a fold of flesh on her stomach. "Still too fat."

He grabbed another fold at the top of her thigh. "Too much here as well – doesn't look good in stockings. And I like stockings. All the girls wore 'em when I was growing up. And your tits are hopeless. Open your mouth. I want to look at your teeth."

He peered inside. "Two crooked ones, and you've lost a couple as well. That's going to cost. Need a good clean."

He walked back over to the window and looked out at St Paul's again. "Pussy's nice and tight, though. What I'm going to do is get an estimate on you. Send you over to a good plastic surgeon, see what the price is to get some decent tits and rake out some of that fat."

He turned back to Beth, who still stood at the end of his desk. "You're only a five pound whore. I want to make you into something better. That fucker Regis must clean up with his little flock. No way I can make you worth fifteen hundred a night. Maybe two, five if the surgeon does a good job. Should get my investment back in ten to twenty tricks. Face isn't bad."

Beth was confused. "You want me to be a prostitute?"

"Shut up. I'm trying to think. Must be a way of getting cash. It's cash I need. Plenty of property but no cash. Might be cheaper to go and buy five or six women about twenty years old. A lot more value for money that way. I'd only get about two or three years' mileage out of you before you start wrinkling up."

"I . . . don't want anybody but you," Beth whispered.

"I told you to shut up."

He walked over to her, grabbed a handful of pubic hair and pulled her to him. "This is mine. I own it. Right?"

"Yes," she murmured. "Yes . . . but . . ."

"If I own it, I can sell it. And if I sell it, I want to make a profit. Are you too stupid to see that?"

His face was close to hers, looking at her impatiently.

"Yes, but, it's just that . . . I couldn't . . . I don't think I could do that."

Gillmore exploded and pushed her away. "What do you mean, you couldn't? Right now I could go down on the street and get six men, and you'd fuck 'em all if I said so."

Beth was trying to think.

"Yes, but that would be for you. Because you wanted it. It might excite you, something like that . . ."

Her voice trailed off and she looked down at her shoes.

Gillmore turned away and grabbed another file. "You'll do what you're told to do. I'll get the quack over tomorrow to give me an estimate. Put your clothes back on and get cracking on that safe."

He sat down and opened the file. He completely ignored her while she was dressing.

She went into the kitchen and fetched a damp sponge, two dry cloths and a can of furniture spray. When she returned, he appeared to be engrossed in his work. The safe was as tall as she was, a big one set into the wall. There was a series of doors and drawers, some with locks on them. The files had been lying on a bottom shelf and she could see the shadow made by the dust and cleaned it, first with the wet sponge, then with a dry cloth. She cleaned around the door underneath and realised that it was not locked. When she pushed it open, she saw a long narrow box full of audio tapes. She closed the door suddenly, then realised that she should start at the top and work down. What was wrong with her?

She felt a little ill as she straightened up and started wiping down the cold metal. It was going to come to an end. She could feel it. She didn't want to go into a hospital and be cut open like a melon. But if he wanted it, she had to. Something dark and indistinct moved at the edge of her mind, and it was frightening. He didn't understand, she knew that. He didn't understand that she loved him. She didn't want to be a prostitute, go to other men's houses. She didn't want other men. The darkness moved closer.

She heard Gillmore get up from his desk and leave the room. She looked around. The light was on, shining down at the spot where he worked, and beyond that was the closed office door. Before she knew what she was really doing, she had bent down and opened the bottom door, grabbing the long box of tapes. Clutching them to her bosom, she moved as quickly as she could across the room and pushed the box behind the black leather sofa.

Beth didn't know why she had done this. Her heart was pounding, and she listened for his footsteps in the hallway. With a sense of dread, she realised that she nearly wanted to be discovered clutching the box from the safe. The danger of what he would have said, what he would have done excited her. She leaned over and took the tapes from behind the sofa, kneeling on the carpet. She held them to her, looking at the door expectantly. Where was he? Where was Harvey Gillmore? Why didn't he come? She thought that she heard the toilet flush and realised that her heart was pounding even faster.

Beth looked down at the tapes, then up again at the door. The darkness was swelling up inside her again and she almost started to cry. A distant voice inside cried out, Who am I? She didn't know and couldn't answer. All she had were the tapes. What were they? They were his. Important. People wanted them. That's all she knew.

She looked up again at the door, expecting every second for it to open and the terrible eyes to see her kneeling with his Important Tapes – a thief. Didn't he realise that he was all she wanted? Couldn't he see that? The darkness was horrible, and she couldn't see properly, couldn't think. With a sudden impulse that shocked her, she forced herself to open her arms. The box rolled to the floor. She pushed it back behind the sofa, but left it this time so that the end of the box was showing, just the end. Then she got up and ran back to the safe.

She heard the office door open as she leaned over to pick up the sponge from the floor where she had dropped it and closed her eyes, waiting for him to stop in the middle of the room. And he stopped.

There was a long silence, and Beth knew that it was going to be very, very bad. He was bound to hurt her. The danger was there again and red panic shot through her consciousness like an electrical fire. Beth realised that she wasn't breathing. She was holding her breath, and her stomach churned in fear.

"What the fuck are you doing", Gillmore said finally, "bent over like that? You look frozen solid."

"Nothing," she managed to say.

"I can see that. Are you going insane? I don't like nutters, won't have 'em working for me."

"It's . . . just my back, I think," she lied. "From bending over."

Gillmore came around his desk and grabbed his glasses. "I don't like malingerers, either. Most people who complain got nothing wrong with them. Now get that safe done."

Beth stood up with the sponge and wiped the sides of a little inner safe. She didn't know whether to be relieved or not. She knew that he could still come across the box of tapes on the way out. It wasn't over yet. She could see that her hands were white, drained of blood, and they were trembling.

"*Are* you going insane?" she unexpectedly said out loud.

Gillmore spun round in his chair. "What did you say?"

"I'm sorry. I was talking to myself."

"No, you weren't. You just asked me if I was going insane. Didn't you?"

She turned around, not knowing what to do with the sponge. "I didn't mean you. I just . . . repeated something you said . . . asked. I was saying it to myself."

"You're a lying bitch!"

Gillmore sprang from his chair, throwing his glasses back on the desk. He walked over and grabbed her face with one hand, holding it. "Nobody calls me insane! Nobody!"

His eyes were rolling from side to side and bulging from their sockets.

"What gives you the right to call me insane? Huh? Huh?"

He spat on her face. "I'm talking to you. Why am I so rich, if I'm insane? People all over the would say I'm a genius. A genius!"

His voice, normally quiet to the point of a whisper, was now loud and rasping. "Fucking working-class scum don't know the difference between insanity and genius because none of you have any fucking brains at all. Your fucking husband wouldn't have died if he hadn't stolen one of my tapes. It's my soft heart that gives me away all the time. Because I'm a Christian, people take advantage of me. That's why, isn't it? You hate Christ. Out of the fucking goodness of my heart, I offer to rebuild you, give you a decent body. And I pay for it, right? With my money. But you don't understand class, do you? Well, you're going to learn! You're going to learn to speak properly and you're going to give me some sort of return on my investment in you, because that is the Christian way. Don't you understand the Bible you read every night? Those words are sacred! I'm going to make you into a high-class money-making machine, and all you can do is stand here and call me insane! It's *genius*! You need to be born again. Reborn in Jesus, my child."

He let go of her face, closed his eyes and placed both hands on the top of her head.

"O Holy Father, make this child understand that she is a part of a Great Plan which she is now too stupid to understand. Make her whole, O Holy Father, and take her unto Your service."

He opened his eyes and looked at Beth seriously. "I give a hell of a lot of money to the Church, you know. A hell of a lot. They get free advertising in my papers. And a ten per cent discount to all preachers of the True Faith on the cover price. Have you ever heard of anybody who's done more for Christ? Have you?"

Beth shook her head. She didn't know what he was talking about, and it was so confusing. Something he said kept reverberating in her mind. Thomas wouldn't have died if he hadn't stolen a tape? But Thomas had hanged himself, didn't he? Because of her? The darkness was overlaying everything now, making it difficult to see. Behind her eyes, day was changing to night. Harvey Gillmore didn't want her any more. She knew that. That certainty was spreading with the darkness.

Gillmore was staring at her, immobile.

"Get your arse back to work," he said finally, turning to his desk.

Beth turned back to the safe, wiping the tears and spit with one of the towels. As she started to work again, she realised something important. The fear had been there, the fear that she wanted, that she searched for. But the excitement wasn't. Some thread somewhere had broken, not just stretched. It had broken.

———

Jennifer Montgomery was sitting on a stool in her kitchen drinking a cup of tea and staring out of the window at her garden when she heard her front door open. With a surge of fury, she put down the cup, opened the cutlery drawer and selected a Sabatier boning knife. She gripped it tightly and held it in front of her, waiting.

Michael Regis came through the open kitchen door and smiled.

"Hello, Jennifer."

He glanced at the knife. "Going to disembowel someone?"

Jennifer spoke through her teeth. "Put your key to the front door on the counter and leave."

Regis smiled easily. He had on a grey lightweight suit and was holding a pair of expensive sunglasses in his hand.

"I brought back all the tapes taken from here. They're in a box just inside the door."

"Good," she said. "Now get out."

"We have much to discuss."

"We have nothing to discuss."

Again Regis smiled. "For a start I have a number of apologies to tender—"

"*Apologies!*"

"Apologies," he repeated. "Shall we go into the sitting room to talk about it?"

Regis turned and walked easily up the hallway towards the front. He opened the door to the sitting room, selected an armchair and sat down, crossing his legs.

She stood in the kitchen, rooted to the spot for a moment, then followed him into the front with the knife at her side. When she entered the room, he was holding her front door key up in the air. He placed this on the side table.

"I don't believe this, Michael," she said finally. "You invaded my privacy with these cameras and microphones."

She waved the knife at the walls of the room. "You had me kidnapped. I was raped and abused and nearly killed. Then you sent a bunch of gangsters to Cornwall to make sure that the job was done properly. Now, bold as brass, you come walking into my home, letting yourself in with a key and sit down in my front room as if you owned it."

"Well, legally speaking of course, I still do. Or partly own, to be more exact. My name is on the mortgage, as I provided the deposit."

He quickly held up his hand as she started to speak. "However, I am attending to that. My name will be withdrawn from the mortgage and title deeds and you will be sole owner. Now, if you will kindly put that knife aside, I think that I am entitled to explain my part in this series of disasters."

"I'll keep the knife," she said, "because I want to cut your heart out."

"You're not a killer, Jennifer. Not like your lover."

"Haug's not a killer. You forced him—"

"Oh, he is. Quite a prolific one in fact. It wasn't difficult finding out something about your simple private detective. He created quite a stir back in the 1970s in the United States. Since its inception by Congress, he was the only man to return the Congressional Medal of Honour. And a number of other medals. A Silver Star – whatever that means – and clusters, ditto. I can't remember all the names. He was a paratrooper with the Special Forces and his group fought behind enemy lines in Vietnam a great deal and, I believe, with a great deal of success. He received the Congressional Medal for action when he was attached to a division of marines who were fighting in the north of the country. His group was covering some flanking company action when attacked by the equivalent of at least battalion strength. Two of his group were killed and your man was wounded. However, he somehow held his position, and the company managed an escape. But your man was now cut off. In darkness he managed to slip away, carrying his wounded companion, and somehow fought his way to the coast over fifty miles away, where he was picked up eventually by a naval helicopter. His partner had been dead for several days, but he had carried him anyway, apparently to give him a decent burial."

Jennifer sat down on the sofa and looked at the floor. "He sounds like a hero to me."

"Very courageous. Indeed." Regis agreed. "As a former military man myself, I am unable to conceal my admiration for the gentleman. However, that was not all. Your man—"

"I wish you would stop calling him 'my man'. His name is Haug."

"As you wish. Mr Haug returned his medals about two years after he left the army, with a long diatribe against the army and American involvement in Vietnam. He also enclosed a detailed list, giving dates or approximate dates of atrocities that he and his group had committed during their tours. Atrocity was his word, not mine. Though, of course, I agree. These included murders where villagers were made to dig their own graves, lined up and shot so that they would fall into them. Men, women and children. Younger women were often raped—"

Her head shot up. "Not by him! I don't believe it."

Regis held up his hand. "No, not by him. Or so he claims. But two of his group raped and he did nothing to stop them. It could be called the same thing in law, couldn't it? He executed in cold blood two North Vietnamese majors and one colonel on behalf of the CIA. He called in air strikes innumerable times against villages which he only suspected of harbouring the enemy and which were later found to consist of only simple folk – old men, women and children. It was quite a long list and I can only recall a few of the choicest items. Your man – I'm sorry, Mr Haug – was in fact covered in blood and very little honour. Great courage, mind, I grant you that. Quite an elaborate serial killer in fact. Not a simple backstreet private investigator. So please put the knife away. You're nothing like him."

She leaned forward, her elbows on her jeans and stared at the carpet. "You don't understand anything, do you, Michael?"

"Oh, I understand perfectly. You will only see what you want to see."

"He did terrible things. I admit I didn't know what they were. But I sensed them anyway. But remember, he confessed. He changed."

"When you're a killer, you don't change. Remember, I too was in the army."

She shook the knife at him. "But don't you see? He was a young man, maybe not out of his teens. Believed everything you people told him. Yes, you people, Michael. People like you. Officers. Educated people who should know better. And you indoctrinate these kids from the countryside and fill their heads full of lies and give them the most dangerous weapons known to man and send them out to kill. A few are good at it. And you give them medals. Don't you understand that he could have said nothing and kept the medals and remained a hero. Instead he did something honourable—"

"Oh, Jennifer," Regis said, turning his head away. "It has nothing to do with honour. The man simply couldn't live with his conscience."

She straightened up in her chair. "It fits in, though. Who you are. Why you're here now. *You* don't understand what honour *is*, do you?"

He raised an eyebrow. "I didn't send someone else, did I? I came on my own. I didn't flinch when you threatened me with a knife. I knew that you deserve an explanation, and I came myself and am prepared to give one to you."

"Oh, I'm sure you have a wonderfully polished explanation, Michael. Normally I would listen to your 'explanation' and be eating out of your hand, if not out of your trousers, before you left. Did you hear what I told you a few minutes ago? *Much* has happened. Things have *changed*. I have been *raped*. Three times I have nearly been killed. I have endured the most horrific and nightmarish events set into motion by you. And yet you sit there as if everything were just as it was. Little Jennifer, sweet and wonderful in her expensive silk underwear and slinky stockings and high-heeled shoes, a little lollipop for your associates to slobber over. Someone for you to plunder while the going is good."

"Perhaps a little overdramatic, but that's to be expected, eh?" He smiled charmingly. "You always received your fee. As generous as London provides."

"Oh, you're nothing if not generous, Michael."

"I do, however, wish to clarify some justifiable misconceptions you may have gained about me during the past week or so—"

"Misconceptions!"

"Your misfortunes had nothing at all to do with me, Jennifer. It is true that I knew some of these people, and I trusted them when I shouldn't have. The benefit of hindsight. . ."

"You're going to deny it all, aren't you?"

"Jennifer. I'm going to tell you the truth. What have I to gain by lying?"

"The cameras and microphones? I suppose you are going to swear blind that it was all done by someone else. Nothing to do with you. And those tapes out in the hallway. . ."

Regis looked away, out of the window.

"I had them installed. I freely admit that. For the simple reason that I had to ensure this house could not be a source for the leaking of confidences. It was a matter of national security, after all. The men you entertained were of high social and political rank. A very tricky area, I do admit. It is something I now sincerely regret. Contrary to your Mr Haug's lowly opinion, I had no mind at all to use them for blackmail. The thought had not even occurred to me. And if I were ever to use such a thing for such a purpose, just imagine what it would do to *my* career. I would be finished – socially, financially, politically, in all respects. No, the unfortunate installation of surveillance was purely for security. That of the nation – and, of course, of yourself."

She leaned back on the sofa and couldn't stop herself from laughing. "It was put in for *my* security?"

She stuck the end of the sleeve of her sweatshirt in her mouth to stop the giggles.

"Of course," he replied smoothly. "You were very vulnerable here. Alone in a house with a man whom you might not even know, engaging in what legal circles would call prostitution, which anyone would agree is a dangerous profession. Harvey Gillmore always worried me—"

"I find this extraordinary, Michael, I really do. You sit there so relaxed and confident that I will believe this desperate lie, simply because it is so bold. It takes my breath away. So let me get this straight. I must remember it. One of the reasons you *secretly* installed cameras and microphones in my house, my bedroom, over my bed, in my bathroom, was so they could be used in evidence in case I was attacked? Or did you have some direct line with little men waiting outside to bound through the door should I be struck or abused by a cowardly client?"

He laughed gently. "Of course it now sounds somewhat incredible. But that is simply because of subsequent events. It must appear to you to be a gigantic conspiracy with the puppet master Michael Regis at the centre of the web, raising his eyebrow for this to happen, snapping his fingers for that to occur. I am simply not that powerful—"

"Michael, let me stop you there. To return to the surveillance: it never occurred to you that it was a gross and criminal intrusion into my privacy? To have all this done without even telling the owner-occupier? You simply made the decision from your lofty eyrie with your superior judgement, knowing that I am only a woman? A young woman at that? A whore, additionally? Despite the smoothness of your words, I can't tell you how insulting that is. You are a confection of lies which sound so convincing until you expose them to one whiff of fresh air."

"Which I gather is your Mr Haug."

"For the last time, he is not *my* Mr Haug. People only belong to each other in your world. But that's not the real world. In that world, I still belong to you, don't I? I am still 'indebted' to you, no doubt, for the lifestyle I lead. Average of a couple of clients a week, say five hours altogether – you must be doing me a very real favour."

"It amounts to well over £150,000 per annum, Jennifer. A tidy sum for someone your age."

"Whatever it is, your gain is at least as much! In fact, much, much more! How would you feel, Michael Regis, about a profit share? Eh? How about fifty-fifty? Surely that would be more than a hundred and fifty grand a year."

He put the tips of his fingers together and smiled indulgently. "You see, my dear, you are talking of things about which you know nothing. These favours given to various friends and acquaintances are impossible to quantify. It would be ridiculous to try and distil it all into an accounts ledger. A few pounds for a meal, this amount for a taxi, tickets to the opera or Ascot or Wimbledon—"

"Or a blow job by Jennifer Montgomery."

"Men will be men, won't they?"

"And, come to that, Michael, what about all your freebies?"

"I beg your pardon?"

"The skirt-lifting I've done for you, at the snap of a finger or the lift of a eyebrow. Or, as today, whenever you feel like letting yourself into my house. Jennifer, get rid of your guest, get off the phone, turn off the TV, put the script away, get off the jeans and into the expensive glad rags, preferably without knickers. Get some slap on your face, comb your hair so it looks nice and fluffy because Mr Michael Regis is so very particular, so very concerned about his image. Smile, laugh at his jokes, listen attentively to his little anecdotes, say the things he wants to hear. Then, when *he* is ready, flip on your back so that he can play with your tits and stick his dick in you. So, it comes down to the same thing in the end, doesn't it? Except that you don't pay. You get yours any time you want it."

"I expect that you have acquired this coarseness from your association with this man, Haug. I admit that I was immodest enough to believe you were physically attracted to me, that the motive for making love came from your own desire. But then, perhaps you are a better actress than I thought. After all, you did tell me once that you loved me. And I believed you, Jennifer. I loved you myself. Still do, if the truth be known."

"Bullshit."

"The coarseness doesn't become you. And that is an American word."

She laughed. "You couldn't love anyone but yourself if your life depended on it."

"Perhaps, perhaps not. I have never pretended to be an expert in love. If not love, I am certainly fond of you."

"Fond enough to have me killed no doubt."

Again Regis smiled, this time with charm.

"It doesn't surprise me that you see my hand in these matters. I suppose that I was a kind of father figure for you. Now you are the rebellious daughter who has found her own life and her own man. The attempts on your life were made by agents answering to someone else, not me. I had no idea that they contemplated such extreme measures. In fact I was assured that no harm would come to you. I insisted on that."

She pointed the knife at him angrily. "Don't take me for a complete fool, Michael. These other friends of yours were not even necessary in the first place. All you had to do was to ask me. Use your key. Come in the door. Get up my skirt first, if you wanted, then simply ask a simple question: 'Jennifer, do you have a tape that might have dropped from a client's pocket?' 'No, Michael, I'm afraid I haven't seen one, but if I do, I will let you know immediately.' It was *that* simple. Instead you chose the more complicated way.

"Someone tried to run me down in the street. Then there was an elaborate ruse to kidnap me in the West End under the pretence of an audition. Do you know what I went through then? You haven't even asked. I was tied up so tightly that I couldn't move and tape was put over my mouth. I was fondled by every man with a pair of hands, dumped in the back of a van and taken somewhere north to a hellish place where I was thrown on the bed and raped. Then I was taken before an awful and frightening man who terrified me beyond the limits of reason. He was holding some kind of dreadful whip and threatened to flay me with it. Do you have any understanding at all of what I went through? Or what I will probably go through in the future, waking up in the middle of the night screaming? Eh, Michael? It's more likely that what you are thinking is that I am just a hysterical female exaggerating as usual about what was really a minor 'misconception', I think you called it."

She paused, but he said nothing.

"So answer me. *Why didn't you just ask me for the fucking tape?*"

Regis shook his head. He looked very serious. "The tape is extremely sensitive. The implications, should the identity of the speaker be known, are beyond computation. You'll have to trust me on this."

"I don't trust you on this or anything else. And that, by the way, is not an answer to my question."

Michael Regis was supplicating with his hands.

"My interests were not the only ones involved, and others made decisions which went beyond reason. If I had known what they were going to do or how they were going to go about it, I would have thrown myself in front of them. I would have killed them with my bare hands."

"Yes," she snapped, "but in reality someone else had to do that, eh? It wasn't Michael Regis killing men with his bare hands. It was someone I knew a lot less well. Someone who has given me a little something to hold on to when the world around me was falling apart."

"Your new hero-lover. The serial killer."

"Yes, my *friend*. Joe Wayne Haug. I never knew what a friend was before. Nor a lover, come to that. I thought that they were supposed to be like you."

"So the earth moved for you?" he asked ironically.

"Well, since you ask, I enjoyed sex for the first time in my life. I never thought that I was supposed to enjoy it. Oh, yes, it occasionally tickled in the right places at the right times, but I never felt that oneness . . . that . . . oh, fuck it. It's useless talking to you about this. I may as well be talking about the flora and fauna of Mars to a deaf Chinaman."

Regis got up from the chair and shot his cuffs. He carefully brushed an imaginary fleck of lint from his sleeve.

"I know you very well, Jennifer. Better than you know yourself. Much better, I think you'll realise as you grow a little older. I know, for instance, that you'll be back."

He glanced over to the table where he had left the key. "In no time at all you'll give that back to me and you'll be your smiling, perky self again. I'm willing to wait until this infatuation is over. After all, I care a great deal for you."

Jennifer Montgomery got up and swiftly lunged at Regis with the knife. She held it in front of her, like a spear. But Michael Regis was a fit man. He moved quickly to one side, grabbed her wrist and easily twisted the knife away from her. He held on to the wrist and threw the knife to a corner of the room. She stood glaring at him with hatred.

Regis put his other arm around her shoulders and drew her to him. "I know you, Jennifer. I know you very well."

His face was close to hers, and he had a slight smile on his lips.

Jennifer Montgomery looked into Michael Regis's eyes and felt a dense collision inside between a glowing boulder of hatred and a completely unexpected electrical charge.

Regis moved his lips closer to her, holding her with a steady gaze.

She put her arms around his neck, knowing that she wanted to strangle him. And, as his lips moved closer, she closed her eyes and they kissed. She felt his tongue explore confidently. She was going to bite. She really was. She was going to bite off the man's tongue. But she didn't. He withdrew and held her a moment, and she dropped her arms to her side. The hatred she felt for him swam before her eyes. Now, however, it was self-hatred.

He turned at the door and looked back. "I'll give you a month."

Again, that confident half-smile. He put on his sunglasses and closed the door silently.

Jennifer Montgomery stood in the middle of her sitting room motionless. She heard the front door close. Then she spat on the floor, again and again, wiping her mouth with the back of her hands. She threw herself on the sofa, curling up in a foetal position around the cushion and cried.

Chapter Twenty-One

Beth fumbled in her purse for the taxi fare. The driver was looking at her a little strangely. Perhaps it was because it was Friday, a warm day, and she was wearing her long coat buttoned up to her chin. Or maybe it was because of the make-up. Gillmore always liked bright red lipstick and heavy mascara. And her hands were trembling as she gave the man two five-pound notes and took the change.

"Thank you," she mumbled and turned to the doorway next to the Asian shop.

She looked at the nameplates carefully, clutching the box in her left arm, and went in.

Lizzy was at the desk typing and at first did not hear the knocking on the office door. It was really a tap rather than a knock, followed by another two tentative taps.

"Come in! It's open!" she shouted.

There was no response, so Lizzy exhaled a great sigh, slipped her shoes back on and heaved her bulk from the chair. She had just got comfortable and was muttering irascibly under her breath when she opened the door. She looked out and at first thought no one was there after all. Then she spotted a figure at the top of the stairs, leaning against the railings, clutching something.

"Are you all right, love?" Lizzy asked, walking towards the figure.

"I'm sorry," said Beth. "I was looking for Mr, er . . . H-A-U-G." She spelt it out. "And I don't suppose he's in."

"No," said Lizzy. "But I am. And I've got more brains than he has anyway. And I'm nicer. And I don't chew tobacco. So you're lucky really that you got me and not him. Come on in. Get the weight off."

She glanced down at the shoes the woman was wearing. The heels must have been at least four inches and looked generally spattered and water-soaked. She let the woman walk in front of her into the office.

"Take your coat off and have a seat," she said. "No, wait a minute."

She fetched a bath towel from a side cupboard and spread it on the sofa. "Sit here, love. It's more comfortable than the chair. I tell you, Haug is an animal. He comes in after working on that motorcycle and sits here reading magazines without washing his hands . . . Come on, over here, it's clean enough now that I've put the towel down. Let me take your coat."

She held out her hands.

Beth shook her head. "No. No, that's all right. I think I'll keep it on."

"Look!" Lizzy said. "I've got the windows open. I was thinking about getting the fan out. Like a sauna up here today."

"No, if it's all the same, I think I'll keep it on. Thank you."

She sat on the edge of the sofa.

"Suit yourself," said Lizzy as she went to the kettle and plugged it in. "Cup of tea or coffee?"

"Oh, yes, thank you. Please."

Lizzy sensed something in her voice. "Maybe a biscuit? Or two or three?"

Beth smiled. "If it wouldn't be any trouble."

Lizzy went to the fridge. "Listen. I bought two sandwiches for my lunch today, but I'm desperately trying to lose weight. So I just ate one."

She got the sandwich out and put in on a paper plate. Then she found a clean mug, threw in a teabag and looked around. "Sugar?"

She added a spoonful when the woman nodded and poured the hot water, followed by a splash of milk. Adding four chocolate biscuits to the little paper plate, she carried them over to the woman on the sofa. Lizzy watched carefully as the woman placed the box close beside her and took the plate and mug gratefully. She did not so much eat the sandwich as wolf it, swallowing bites after chewing only once or twice. Halfway through she looked at Lizzy self-consciously and tried to slow down, picking up the mug and drinking slowly. But then she forgot herself and grabbed the rest of the sandwich, which quickly disappeared. The biscuits followed rapidly.

"You haven't eaten for a while, have you?" Lizzy asked.

Beth shook her head, looking down at her mug. "No. No, I haven't. I'm sorry if I ate too fast."

"Well now, I want to tell you a secret," said Lizzy. "I'm one of the best cooks in North London. And today I've just bought a big fresh chicken. I've got potatoes, spring greens and last night I just baked an apple pie. I live just over the road and this evening you're going to come to my house for tea. Do you understand me?"

Beth smiled at her, eyes bright. "Thank you very, very much. That's so kind. But I can't. I can't stay long. I have to go soon. There's not much time."

"Well, I think you should stay for tea, and I want you to."

"No. Listen." Beth picked up the box of tapes. "This is for Mr Haug. Tell him they are from Mr Harvey Gillmore—"

Lizzy's ears pricked up. "You work for Harvey Gillmore?"

"I do. I did, I was. Well, it wasn't working so much. It's hard to explain. I don't know how to."

She started speaking quickly. "Yes, I suppose I work for him, yes, I do. And I'm in love with him, I think. No, I shouldn't have said that. I don't know what I should say or how to explain why I bought this box of tapes to you. I saw your name . . . no, Mr Haug's name when Mr Gillmore wrote it down, and somehow I remembered it. These tapes are important somehow and while I was cleaning the safe he told me two things that made me feel sick, a little sick. No, please let me finish. He said that my husband, Thomas – no, my ex-husband, Thomas – had been killed, and I thought it was a suicide . . . killed because he had one of these tapes. Anyway I used to love Thomas a long time ago . . . and I wanted him, desperately wanted him to stand up for me, but he didn't . . . no, you won't understand that. And then, somehow, I started falling in love with Mr Gillmore and I was living there in his flat in Fleet Street and doing what he wanted me to do . . . Oh, I'm glad it's you and not Mr Haug I'm having to tell this to. I can see that you . . . But I want to tell you the other thing and this is just as important. I don't mind cleaning for Mr Gillmore and feeding him and dressing whichever way he likes . . . This is getting so complicated. Please forgive me. You probably don't understand a word I'm saying. I don't know if I do. But the main thing – or at least as important as Thomas . . . it's tied in, really – is that he wants to make me into a prostitute, you know, with a plastic surgeon, because I'm not pretty enough. Even that I might do, if it was for him, you see? For him. But he wants me to go with other men and earn money for him. You know, go to their houses and be with other men, and I don't want other men, you know? I mean you . . . you probably think I'm horrible, and maybe I am. Of course I am, because of Thomas. I didn't mean him harm, Thomas. I just stopped thinking about him because of Mr Gillmore. I wanted to feel needed and wanted, you see, and I thought that Thomas didn't want me but Mr Gillmore did. Do you see? Well, it makes sense to me, anyway. And it was so exciting, the fear. Oh, my God. It made me feel alive. And now Thomas is dead. Killed, probably my fault. Mr Gillmore doesn't want me and I don't know what to do . . ."

Lizzy watched as the woman put down her mug and covered her face with her hands. Her shoulders were shaking.

"Holy Mary, Mother of God," she murmured. "What has that devil done to you?"

She grabbed a handful of tissues from her handbag, went over to the sofa, sat down and put her arms around the woman.

"You go ahead and cry, baby, it's all right. It'll be all right now you got it all out."

She rocked gently back and forth. "It would be better if some men had never been born, for all the damage they do . . . Now listen to me. It's nothing to do with you. It's not your fault. You did the right thing, coming here, bringing those tapes. We'll see that they're put to the best use. We'll do it for you. I promise. You and . . . Thomas."

She patted her head gently. "Now let me guess something. You won't take off your coat because you're wearing something skimpy, something Gillmore wants you to wear, right? Well, that's fine. But I'm going to go out now, just three doors down from here to a little shop where I'm going to buy you something nice to wear and some comfortable shoes."

"No," said Beth, turning to Lizzy. "I can't take these off. He likes them. He wants me to wear them all the time."

"Oh, he does, does he? Well, we will send them to him, and he can wear them himself. Now, I'm going to get you some nice comfortable clothes, and you are going to come home with me. I'll close up the office as soon as I get back, and we'll walk over to my house. While I'm getting the tea, you can lie down on my bed, have a little rest. Now, how is that? OK?"

Beth didn't answer. She was sitting with her elbows on her knees, dabbing at her face with a tissue. Lizzy got up and went to the desk. She turned on the answerphone and grabbed her handbag.

"I won't be long. Just a few minutes. Will you be all right here?"

Again Beth was silent. So Lizzy walked quietly to the door, turning back once more before she opened it. Her own eyes were a little moist and she reached for another tissue after she closed the door.

When Lizzy returned fifteen minutes later, after hurrying up the stairs, Beth was gone. The box of tapes was sitting in the middle of the desk, but there was no note.

"Damn!" she said, slamming the parcel down in the middle of the floor. "Damn! Bloody hell!"

Beth Howell walked along Blackfriars Bridge slowly, her hands in her pockets, her head down. It was late in the afternoon and office workers were moving swiftly, most of them coming towards her from the south. Some glanced in her direction, and a few made certain that they didn't come too close. One or two men turned and looked back at her when she passed. The traffic was heavy too and Beth didn't notice when one car slowed down and the electric passenger window was lowered. The driver said something to her, but she heard nothing because she was looking at the toes of her shoes and counting.

Forty-five, forty-six, forty-seven . . . for some reason she had started counting steps as she approached the bridge. It seemed to keep the dark dragon at bay, but the claws still showed at the rims of consciousness, so she knew that it was there, lurking in the shadows. She didn't know why she was on Blackfriars Bridge. She had alighted from the taxi on Fleet Street but, instead of walking back to Harvey Gillmore, her feet had led her down to Ludgate Circus, where she turned towards the bridge. Maybe she wanted to know how many steps it took to cross the bridge, maybe that's why she counted. But what happened when she got to the other side, what then? Would the darkness come back again?

She stopped midway on Blackfriars and looked up at the rushing people, the incomprehensible traffic. Are you insane? Some of them looked at her as though she were. A fat, bald man grinned at her and smacked his lips together. What did that mean? There were little seats at the side made of concrete. They were for people to sit on and look at the river, she knew that. Because, across the road, some people were sitting. One of them had a camera, taking pictures.

Beth walked slowly over to the seat, intending to sit for a while until she decided what to do. She remembered her count. Fifty-four, fifty-five, fifty-six, fifty-seven . . .

She stepped up on to the seat. Fifty-eight. Without stopping she stepped on to the rail. Fifty-nine.

Someone behind her shouted, but she didn't hear what he said.

Sixty. And the world was turning slowly upside down. Very, very slowly.

Beth looked back and saw the underside of the bridge and people looking over the edge. She very nearly laughed at them, but then the darkness spread all over and she couldn't see anything at all any more.

It was Sunday morning, and Haug sat in the chair that Michael Regis had used on his last visit. His feet were bare, he needed a shave and a few hairs had worked loose from his ponytail. His red checked shirt was outside his jeans and was open to his waist. He had just got up, gone into the kitchen and made two mugs of tea. One he carried back to the bedroom and placed on the bedside table. Jennifer was lying on her side, staring at the wall. She thanked him and he left her there. The bedroom was dark and he wanted some light.

When he opened the curtains in the sitting room, he was disappointed to see that it was raining. A pity, he thought. He had been looking forward to a nice long walk on the Heath. He had been lying in bed thinking about that, taking a picnic to the Heath, having a nice quiet day, not much talking, letting things drift.

They had not made love the night before. Jennifer had gone to sleep in his arms, as she had done before Cornwall. They hadn't talked much either. Just had a few drinks from the bottle he had bought and listened to a bit of jazz. She liked cool jazz, and he didn't mind it at all. Just the thing for the mood he was in. Nothing was said about the events of the past two weeks. It had been a little awkward, and under other circumstances Haug would have thought that the best thing to do was leave, not stay the night. But these were unusual times. He had expected a severe reaction to set in eventually with all that had happened to her, and the best thing to do was to try and support her when she needed it.

He turned and looked out of the window. It was a proper rain, not just mist. Friday afternoon and early evening he had spent looking for

Beth Howell. When he had returned from St James's Park, Lizzy was in a state and he had had to calm her down before he could make any sense of what had happened. He glanced at the tapes, which were all labelled and dated, then told Lizzy that he would come round to her house whether he found Beth or not. He grabbed an extra helmet, threw it in the topbox of the Harley and set off towards Fleet Street.

The big Rolls-Royce was not in the underground car park, so Haug tried the lift and flat doorbell. Nothing. He couldn't even find a security man on duty. The place was locked up tight as a jail. He looked for a fire escape but couldn't find one. He even tried to pick the locks on the door, but they were too good for him.

So he got back on the Harley and cruised the streets of the City, stopping occasionally to check on figures huddled in doorways. London was becoming an awful place. As the workers deserted it at 5 p.m. every day, the other tenants moved in. The night tenants. Sleeping bags and blankets and cardboard were laid in every deep recess. Hands were held out.

"Any spare change?" echoed over and over again through the canyons of concrete and glass. Was it like that when Dickens was alive, a Parliamentary reporter and, later, a novelist? Probably. And every year it got worse. When he had first arrived in England, there was only the occasional drunk sleeping rough. Now there were young people. The homeless and the hopeless huddled together against a society which now thought that it could afford to ignore them all. The mad had been turned out of asylums to save money. So had the aged and the ill. A country which had surprised Haug with its warmth and concern had slowly turned its back and divested itself of humanity and progress. The clock was turned back to earlier, meaner days. Sharks and barracudas now cruised openly on the streets in their Mercedes and Porsches and Rollers, snapping up all the spare change for which the poor were now calling in desperation.

Haug was already in a bad mood when he turned towards Blackfriars Bridge. There were a couple of emergency vehicles in the middle of the bridge with their blue lights flashing. Somehow, as the Harley pulled up alongside the police van, he *knew* it was her. Of course, it could be anybody. People who had had enough – too much – threw themselves off bridges all the time. But there was a catch in the back of his throat, something that wouldn't go down.

He parked the Harley and wandered over to a policeman. The policeman wasn't minded to talk at first until Haug told him that he might possibly know her, if it was a woman. Noting his accent, the policeman loosened up a little and told him that the body had been pulled out of the water further down the river. The identity of the party was not known, but, yes, it had been a woman. Haug tried to get a description, but the cop knew nothing.

While Haug was staring into the water below, cursing mankind in general and newspaper proprietors in particular, the policeman came back over to him. He had had a word with the sergeant. They had found a shoe on the bench where the party had jumped and he could have a look at it if he wished. As soon as Haug saw the shoe he recognised it. He said that he didn't know her name but told the policemen she worked for Harvey Gillmore.

When he returned to Lizzy's house, she was inconsolable and Haug had to provide a shoulder for her to cry on, telling her over and over again that she mustn't blame herself. She had done her best and you couldn't demand more than that. He made her drink a glass of whisky, followed by a mild sleeping pill, and he read the kids a story and put them to bed.

He slept on the sofa in her sitting room.

Jennifer came through the door with two fresh mugs of tea, passed one to Haug and sat down on the sofa. She was wearing a dressing-gown and crossed one bare leg over the other one. She stared out of the window, looking at the rain. Her face told him that she hadn't slept very well. As a matter of fact he hadn't either, waking up several times, thinking of the woman and the bridge, thinking of Jennifer and the likely emotional backfire through which she was about to go, wondering about the strength of his own feelings for her.

"I have to tell you something," she said finally, ominously.

"Well, if you have to tell me, you better tell me," he replied genially.

"Michael was here yesterday."

"Regis? That asshole? How the fuck did he get in?"

"He had a key."

She told him the story, hesitating before the kiss, then took a sip of tea and a deep breath before plunging on.

"You know," Haug said after listening carefully to her words, "I figger folks like Regis are really kinda stupid. I mean, when you come down to it, he doesn't have enough brains to hit the ground with his hat if he had two tries. What they are is evil artists. Confidence men. Part of the confidence act is to make themselves look smart. Which they're not. They're *cunning*. Yeah. Rats are cunning like you wouldn't believe."

She was looking at him. "You're not surprised that I kissed him? That the trick worked yet again, even after what I know?"

"No, it doesn't surprise me, Jenny. He's a good con man and you're not some kinda machine. Don't feel bad about it."

"I expected you to be angry. I thought you would turn around and leave."

Haug laughed. "What the hell for? Unless I read you wrong, you don't love him. You hate him. You hate all he stands for. Human beings are complex, not simple. You gotta lot of emotion sloppin' around inside right now. Hate, both the outward and inward variety, maybe love, fear, resentment, pain, anger, and probably some too complex to have names. Now along comes somebody with an act. And it is an act. They seem confident. Now, in my experience, nobody is really confident. But if you put enough coats of varnish on the top surface, you might convince other people that you are. And that's a cute trick. It's like watchin' a magician. If you know the trick, it's not magic any more, right? But they use that varnished surface like a shield. They hold on for dear life. Until the other person lets go. And that is how people like Regis float to the top. Not by brains. Intelligence is a handicap for a con man, and that's the truth. Intelligence questions thangs, asks why they're there, what their purpose is, how everthang fits together, what it's made of. Yeah, I'd get up and leave if you sat there and told me you believed his lies and wanted to trail around after him, kissin' his ass. But that's not what you're sayin', is it?"

"Oh, Haug, I was so disgusted with myself. I actually put my arms around his neck and let him put his tongue in my mouth."

She looked at him steadily. "I enjoyed it."

"Does that *upset* you?"

"Doesn't it upset *you*?"

"Nope. A little tingle of jealousy, of course. Yeah. I find it a little unpleasant thinkin' of you tonguin' a horse's ass—"

"Haug—"

"But the fact that you enjoyed it . . . well, he's a good-lookin' man. Now, if the situation was reversed, and I got a woman in front of me that looks as good as a hot fudge sundae, and she sticks her tongue in my mouth, I'm probably gonna shiver all the way down to my toes and all the way back again. Even if you're upstairs in bed waitin' for me. I wouldn't fuck her, particularly if I hated her guts and on account of the fact that I like you too much right now to fuck anybody else. But she'd get a response from me. What's wrong with admittin' that?"

"Haug, I understand what you are saying, but what I'm talking about is . . . well, last night I couldn't sleep very well, thinking about all this. You know, down at the bottom of the barrel?"

"Yep."

"And I have tried all my life, right from the time I became aware of sex and the fact that I was going to be a woman. Right from the start, when my father was fucking me, I decided that I was not going to be a victim. I didn't use those words then. Then I just wanted to win, to turn the tables, to get out, to try and push back the loneliness and shame I felt. I don't know anyone who has tried any harder. Yet I don't seem to be getting anywhere or, if I do, I fall back to where I started. I suppose Michael was about as close as I ever came to love, but there were others like him. Smooth, sleek, confident. Like you say. And in the end I'm the loser. Just like the situation with Michael now. He wins, I lose. OK, I get the house. But, like you say, I'm a human being. I have other needs. And those needs *always* lead me to situations where I'm the loser. Why can't I be like him? Snap my fingers, pick a man up, put him down, walk away. I want to do the confidence trick too. They have all the fun. They win all the games, don't they?"

Haug put his mug on the table where Regis had left the key. He noticed that it was still there.

"They come up with the games. They make the rules. They hold the cards. Is it any wonder that they win 'em? There's nothin' that I can do to the man either. He's a criminal, he's a murderer, a blackmailer and a pimp. In the eyes of the law, not just me. But I cain't touch him. Oh, yeah, I could go bust him up, but he'd probably win that in the end by turnin' the law on me. If I go along to the police station and tell them all this, they'd just laugh at me. I could go to the Prime Minister, I could go to the Queen, I could write letters to MPs and ever judge in the system. And it would amount to less'n a hill of beans. You got a man who'd steal flies from a blind spider, and everbody knows it. But he's built himself into the system."

She made a sound of disgust. "So he's just going to get away with it – everything."

"Oh, yeah. He's got away with it. Clean away. But I tell you somethin', Jenny. I'm still on his trail."

"I hope you get him."

She stopped and looked out of the window again. It was still raining.

"He also told me about you."

"What did he tell about me?"

"Vietnam. The Congressional Medal. Your sending it back. Your confessions."

"Only a matter of time before somebody dug that up, I reckon."

"He called you a serial killer. I defended you."

"I don't need defendin'. But thank you."

"I'm glad to know it, though. I wish you had told me yourself."

Haug got up and walked over to the window. He sat on the arm of the sofa, looking out at the driving rain.

"Not an easy thang to talk about. Not easy to think about, either. But he's right. I'm a serial killer. One of the few thangs I was really good at. I gotta tell you I never minded shootin' those people, not then. I believed that they were the enemies of the United States of America, the enemies of democracy. So I pointed a gun at 'em and pulled the trigger. That was the right thang to do. I see now that it was the wrong thang. But I did right as I saw it then. I don't make any excuses. I cain't bring 'em back to life."

"I can't believe that it doesn't affect you," she said softly.

"I'm not gonna lie to you. It affects me. That's why I sent the fuckin' medals back. After that I just wanted to forget it all. I know that might not make sense, but it's because I want to put that in the past. I decided to change. To try and find out how thangs work – 'cause if I know how they work maybe I can help change it so that the next young killer won't be sent out to slaughter innocent folks when he doesn't know any better. Now I even think that's too big a master plan for me. We're both victims in a lotta ways."

"It's reassuring to hear you admit it. You seem so solid to me, like the Rock of Gibraltar. Isn't that like a confidence man?"

Haug chuckled. "No, I got my doubts like anybody else. But I see a few thangs clearly. Not many, just a few. I don't think there's any eternal good or bad, right and wrong written on tablets somewhere. The problem is, human beings gettin' along and makin' some sorta progress. You could probably have an ultimate Right and an ultimate Wrong if it wasn't for change. You gotta have rights and wrongs that take account of movement in time."

He turned to her, looking in her eyes. "You know Zeno's Paradox? When you shoot an arrow at a target, it goes halfway first, then half of the remainin' distance, then half of what's left and so on. Therefore, the arrow never gets to the target. Well, the solution to that paradox is that that isn't the right way to look at movement. Though it looks logical as hell. And it's hard to see what movement is when you're a part of it."

"Well," she said, "you obviously think some things are really wrong. Like racism."

"Now that's a good example. 'Cause a long, long time ago, racism might have been a 'good' thang. Good in the sense of people dispersin' all over the earth, tryin' different thangs in different ways. So if somebody comes to your tribe covered in purple spots, the best thang to do is get him outta there. But we've moved on since then. Thangs have changed. The earth is covered with people now, people who need to get along and who need to work together. We need enrichment from all the tribes now. Racism isn't only bad, it's fuckin' useless and harmful. Same as fascism, monarchies and, to my mind, capitalism. There's still a lotta life in it yet, but now it's throwin' up more evil than good. The human race is a lot like the individuals in it. We get a little ways, then we slide back, sometimes further than where we started from, like you were talkin' about before."

They sat in silence for a while. Haug got up from the arm of the sofa and sat down beside her. She moved her legs and he put his head in her lap, looking up at her.

She looked down at him and put her hand on his head.

"So. What do *we* do now?"

"Fuck?"

"Not in the mood."

"Then why not do just what we're doin'? I'm comfortable."

"No," she said. "I meant what about us in the future?"

"Well, you're safe now. So the job's done. I c'n walk off into the sunset. Or maybe we can walk off into the sunset together – who knows. As usual a lot depends on chance."

"I wonder what it would be like living with you."

"Absolute hell," he admitted. "Stubborn as a blue-nosed mule. Contrary. If you throw me in the river, I'll float upstream."

She laughed. "Just what I thought."

"How come we have to live together?"

"We don't. I was only wondering. For your edification you're the first man I've even considered living with."

"I don't think we'll get that far."

"So, how long have we got?"

"I think the more complications you got, the more kinks in the vine, the less chance you got of a nice, long, smooth relationship. I suppose if you grow up expectin' to get married, have a brood of kids, farm or have the same job from one day to the next, if you don't have to know what's at the end of the rainbow or what's on top of the next hill, and you got a partner who feels the same way, then you got some kind of chance. Or maybe you got one that's wild marryin' one that will take any kind of hell – that might work, too. I tried marriage and found that it wasn't for me. I go from flower to flower havin' a sniff. I won't say I'm not lookin' for a partner, but I won't say I am either. Lookin' for somethin', cain't put a handle on it."

"That just about sums it up for me as well," she said. "But my plans are shot to hell now. I've still got a big mortgage to pay and there's not enough acting work to cover it yet."

"Think you'll go back to whorin'?"

"Whoring," she repeated ironically. "That's the word for it, isn't it? But it's no worse than people I know who marry men for what they can provide. Like mortgages, cars, position. And they get to stay at home and open their legs when required. As a matter of fact I think my way is better. More honest."

"Sure is expensive pussy."

"Not really. It's all wrapped in the best designer cocoons. A Hampstead address overlooking the Heath. And a girl who's willing to do anything within reason in the best possible taste."

Haug grunted. "Why don't I get a feel of those fancy threads? How come I gotta make do with pullin' a pair of tight jeans off you? I'm not gonna complain if you sit around in high-class underwear and see-through dresses."

She thumped his nose with her finger. "*You* get it free. So *I* get to choose what to wear. Those are the rules."

He opened the top of her dressing-gown. "I gotta admit those are the best-lookin' tits I think I've ever seen. If I was a tit-makin' god, I'd make 'em all just like those."

She leaned over and put one of them in his mouth. "Boys are just babies. One way to shut you up. Though I admit you do it well, you bald-headed randy old bastard. Hmm."

She caressed his chest and stomach with her hand as his shirt fell open. His lips and tongue felt good on her nipple, and he was cradling her other breast with his hand. She opened his belt and unbuttoned the top of his trousers, sliding her hand underneath, where she found his penis already getting hard. He wasn't wearing underpants and she pushed his trousers further down. Her hand went under his balls, feeling the weight, and his penis stood up like a truncheon. She started moving and his mouth came away from her breast.

"Hey," he said. "What's the big idea?"

"Time for breakfast," she said, shrugging out of her dressing-gown and moving her head towards his penis.

With her legs, she straddled his head.

"How did you know?" she heard him say. "It's my favourite. Raw fish."

She delicately wrapped her fingers around his organ. "Sorry, I prefer sausage and eggs myself."

She felt his hands on her bottom, moving round to the top of her thighs.

"You got peculiar tastes. Except your recent one in men—"

She settled her hips down over his head. "Only way to shut you up is to put something in your mouth."

With her tongue she went round the glans like a lollipop before slowly opening her mouth wide to take the head inside. Slowly she pushed on to him to the point until she began to gag, then slowly she withdrew, ending again with her tongue. She could feel his tongue exploring her clitoris and it felt so good. She closed her eyes and took him slowly inside her mouth again.

Chapter Twenty-Two

Harvey Gillmore was rocking inside the private ambulance and the rocking made him feel worse. An attendant was hovering over him with phoney concern in his eyes, gurgling comforting words and watching a monitor. Gillmore could hear the sound from the monitor. Beep . . . beep . . . beep . . . beep.

But the fucking driver was hitting every bump in the road, every pothole, and each shock reverberated in pain. The pain was in his chest and he knew that he must be close to death. Death. It was something he had never thought would happen to him. The siren went on again. They must be approaching a junction. How long to the hospital? Would he make it? It couldn't happen. It was impossible. If he had the energy, he would wring the driver's neck. He made a mental note to get the clumsy bastard fired when he got better.

The heart attack had happened at his home on Sunday late in the afternoon. Gillmore thought back to the phone calls and started grinding his teeth again. The stupid attendant was patting his fucking arm and whimpering something.

He didn't bother to listen because his mind recalled the perfidy of Regis and the slimy unctuousness of Abdullah. Then there was the police. And Bilsten Vanguarde Holmes, his accountants. And his bankers. Like Furies, they were all aswarm around his honeypot. When he was on top, they all bowed and scraped, couldn't wait to join the queue to kiss his arse. Then they sensed a weakness and changed into jackals, trying to tear the flesh from his bones before his heart even stopped beating.

His heart. Beep . . .beep . . . beep. Well, it was still beating, wasn't it? The pain in his chest and upper left arm was excruciating and made him want to vomit. His lips formed into a snarl as the attendant leaned over once more, concerned.

And it was all because of a sheila. A woman. A queer and strange woman, if ever he'd known one. And women were all strange. Only good for one thing and even that cost more than it was worth. Beth. The stupid blackmailing bitch. She had run off with his precious box of tapes and fuck knows what had happened to them.

Personally he was pretty sure that they were at the bottom of the
Thames, but Regis and Abdullah thought otherwise. They were
convinced that she had given them to somebody. But *who*? he had
screamed at them on the telephone. *Who*? Who does she know?
Who *did* she know? Nobody. Nobody at all. That's why logic said
that they were in the Thames. Because she was a nobody. Nobodies
knew nobody. Simple deduction.

But the fat Arab and the Pom were pointing fingers and accusing
and threatening. They threatened *him*. Harvey Gillmore. Half an
hour after talking to them, his bankers were on the phone telling him
that they were going to force him either to sell part of WORLDWIDE or
float the company with share sales, and that was unthinkable in this
financial climate. Either way Gillmore would lose, and Gillmore was
not used to losing. Minutes after the bankers had rung off frostily, his
accountants called to say that they could do nothing in the
circumstances. It was clear to Gillmore that they were all closing
ranks against him. But he would win yet. There were still some
arrows in his quiver.

The ambulance lurched into another pothole, and Harvey Gillmore
groaned. His skin was cold, but he was sweating. The attendant
looked very concerned and was filling a giant hypodermic needle.

Was this it? Was he going now? Maybe the sweat was caused by
the fear. So long as he thought of the traitors he was angry and not at
all afraid. But he could smell the danger in the air, transmitted by the
worthless attendant. The driver had the siren on again and he realised
that the ambulance was going faster. He was much too young to die.
There had never been heart trouble in his family. And he was deeply
religious. So *why*? The bleached lights seemed dimmer, and the pain
was increasing in his chest.

Gillmore realised that he was crying for the first time since he was
a child after one of his father's beatings. His hands were cold and
trembling.

"Please don't let me die," he murmured to the attendant or to God.
He wasn't sure which.

"You'll be all right, Mr Gillmore," said the attendant. "I may
have to give you an injection directly into the chest. But we are
almost there. Another couple of minutes."

Tears were streaming down the Australian publisher's cheeks now
and he didn't have the energy to wipe them away. When he opened

his eyes, the attendant was Beth, looking down at him. She was dressed smartly in a suit and was laughing at him.

"Well, Harvey," she said. "Look what we all come to."

"Don't call me Harvey," he snarled weakly.

"Yes! Harvey! Harvey! Harvey! You can't do anything about it now, Harvey. I'm going to take over WORLDWIDE, you know. It was all a plan and it worked perfectly."

"Liar!" Gillmore moaned. "I have signed nothing. Only Mary will get anything—"

"Oh, but you're wrong, Harvey. You signed some papers and I have them here in my briefcase. It used to be *your* briefcase, Harvey."

"Don't call me Harvey."

She leaned over, her face close to his. "Die, Harvey. Die painfully. Die slowly. And after you're dead I'm going to cut your dick off and have it stuffed and mounted as a table lamp. Are you dead yet? Shall I cut it off now?"

Gillmore squeezed his legs together instinctively and closed his eyes again. Where had she come from? How did she get into the ambulance? Where was the attendant? He felt his shirt being unbuttoned and his trousers being loosened and he began to panic. He opened his eyes and saw with relief the attendant standing over him with the big needle. No, it wasn't the attendant. It was Beth with a carving knife. She was pushing his legs apart, pulling his trousers down. The pale light flashed on the blade.

Gillmore screamed as he imagined his penis being sawn off. He screamed and screamed.

The ambulance stopped at the doors of the hospital's emergency entrance. The rear doors were thrown open and Harvey Gillmore was rushed into cardiac surgery. He survived the operation, which took over five hours. But it was two weeks after the operation before he realised that he was impotent and could not achieve an erection.

———

Haug parked the Harley in the same place, opened the topbox, took out a Dillons Books shopping bag and put his helmet and gloves inside. He looked around. The rain of the day before had cleared, but the clouds hadn't. Rain was possible. Rain was always possible in England.

There weren't as many people in St James's Park as on Friday and he could see Mainwaring sitting on his bench feeding the fucking ducks. He walked over carrying the Dillons bag and put it between them when he sat down.

"I bought you a book on the way over," Haug said, dipping into the bag. "It's a big one on Morgans. Hope you don't have it already."

Mainwaring brushed the remaining crumbs from his hands and carefully took the book.

"It's marvellous," he said. "No, I don't have this one. I didn't even know it existed. What a splendid gesture, Mr Haug."

He leafed through the book, clearly very pleased.

"In the bottom of the bag is somethin' even more splendid. It's a pile of tapes from Harvey Gillmore's office. Mainly telephone calls between him and a lotta important people. I don't recognise any of the voices, though some sound familiar, but I expect you'll know or know somebody who knows."

Mainwaring nodded his head carefully. He had the book open at a colour photograph of a 1934 Morgan three-wheeler in British racing green.

"How very interesting. May I ask how you acquired the tapes?"

"It's a long story, Mr Mainwarin'. And a little painful at the moment. I can tell you that these came right outta his safe, and he has no idea I got 'em. Nobody knows. So I suggest that you use the information very, very carefully 'cause a lotta people gonna have their ears to the railroad line lissenin' for the train."

"Sound advice, Mr Haug," Mainwaring replied, turning a page of the book.

There was a detailed picture of a JAP engine, its distinctive V shape mounted in the front of another Morgan three-wheeler.

"You move rather quickly, I must say."

"Well, these just happened to drop into my lap, so to speak. Unsolicited. I personally hope that you can use them one by one as bullets to drill into his carcass. The tapes came from a dear lady he treated like shit on his boot. A lady who killed herself on account of him. Took a lotta self-discipline to keep myself from goin' over there, grabbin' him by the ankles and knockin' his head against the wall."

"I look forward to going through them with great anticipation. The first tape you gave me was certainly a powerful revelation."

"Yeah? So who's the big cheese?"

Mainwaring raised a thin forefinger. "The big cheese. That's more like it. That sounds like American detective language."

He withdrew the finger to join the others and laid his hand on the book. "I don't want to tell you his name, Mr Haug, for similar reasons to those you gave me, warning me about the use of information."

"Well, hell," he muttered. "I'm dyin' to know."

"But I can tell you this much. He is South African. He is black. He is a high-ranking official of the African National Congress."

"Not Mandela?"

"No. But quite close to him. A man with a long history in the movement. A trusted lieutenant."

Haug smacked his lips together. "It must have been the Nigerian."

"I beg your pardon?"

"That's why they were tryin' to kill Jennifer Montgomery. They thought she had the tape. If she listened to it, she might well have recognised the man who had visited her as a client. A man who told her that he was from Nigeria, not South Africa. Yep. That was it. They couldn't risk her puttin' two and two together and exposin' their man at the ANC."

"He wouldn't have been talking on the telephone at all but for the fact that Gillmore's was one of the very few non-government secure telephones."

"How does he rate that?" asked Haug. "Naw, I can answer that question myself. Gillmore's rags are the string section of the Tory orchestra. Without him, you could hear the tune, 'Never give a sucker an even break.'"

"I had heard the faintest of rumours that such tapes existed, but I never thought that they would fall into my hands like pennies from heaven."

"The pennies came from hell, Mainwarin'. Goddammit, you mind if I call you Jonathan or John?"

Mainwaring winced visibly. "Please. Anything but John. I would be delighted if you called me Jonathan."

"And I want you to call me Haug. Only people call me mister are people who want money from me."

"Done, Haug."

"Thank you, Jonathan. I feel better now."

He looked out over the pond. The ducks had wandered off. Maybe they knew now that, when he showed up, the feeding was over.

"The ANC. Yeah, that's how they do it all right. Keep testin' the links till you find a loose one. Even if you got a band of angels, eventually you gonna find one of 'em wants somethin' the others haven't got. One bad apple will spoil the whole barrel eventually. It's an old story and part of the politics of power. The rest of it's simple as far as South Africa's concerned. The serious money works at corruptin' the top and Gillmore and his reptiles slime the rest of 'em with filth. Get a decent government, they find that they can't get any credit with the main industrial countries. The IMF won't loan 'em anythang till they promise to throw all the poor out on the streets and then tax 'em for livin' there. The banks conspire against you because most of the big ones are owned outside the country. Therefore your currency is undermined, and before long it's worthless and you can't trade at all, except by barter. Wealth goes outta the country but isn't allowed in. Meanwhile the trashy Press whips up old fears, old emotions, sets man against man and even man against woman. Splits form in the old solidarity, factions are fanned and encouraged. Then, outta the chaos comes a man drippin' with gold braid and a hat like a ski jump who says he's takin' over and restorin' order. Order meanin' the old three shell game, with the usual people movin' the shells around. Final score: Establishment Five, People Nothin'. Look, folks! Socialism doesn't work!"

Mainwaring was still engrossed in his book on Morgans and didn't look up when he spoke.

"Yes, it works something like that. Of course it does. The only surprise is that people are surprised. I have had a strong sympathy with the ANC but have always assumed that such forces were at work. I'm not sure how you stop them. Except with time and determination."

"You mean, with enough patience and enough Vaseline you can fuck a cat?"

Mainwaring turned from the book to look at Haug. "Do you mind if I enquire about the origins of these little aphorisms of yours? I don't know whether I find them amusing or disturbing."

"Come from the South, same as me. Yankees – which to us are folks born north of the Mason-Dixon line – tend to look down their noses at us just 'cause they can talk fast. Don't realise that we're poets."

He turned back to his book. "It's poetry, is it?"

Haug shrugged. "Doesn't have to rhyme."

"Indeed."

"What are you gonna do with this information about the ANC?"

Mainwaring looked up and stared across the pond. "You have made your claim on artistic heritage, Haug, and perhaps I may be allowed to place a small claim of my own. There are elements of the British civil service which are second to none in the world. Perhaps it came from the colonial tradition. Or three hundred years of relative political stability. There are some in the service who can place a dagger with the grace of a bullfighter. There is little pain, and at times the victim even dies believing that his is a natural death."

Haug chuckled. "So this guy is likely to drown while eatin' his soup."

"Figuratively speaking, of course. His exposure will take place at the point where it will make the most difference. Then again, it may be best to use it as a threat. The fine tuning will give me the greatest pleasure. Democracy may not triumph, but they won't find us toothless."

"I wish you'd stop usin' that word democracy. Worries me. I've never seen democracy yet, so I get a little unhappy when folks use it with every breath, like any fool knows what they're talkin' 'bout. Freedom is another one of those words. The ordinary citizen's got free choice all right. Just like the man dropped into the middle of the Pacific Ocean and told he's got free choice. He can swim north. south, east or west. And democracy? In this country and mine, it's another three shell game. Simple as the hand in front of your face. It takes money to run for office, more money than any one man's got. Only the big parties got money. The one with the most usually wins. You wanna run, you gotta do thangs their way. So whichever shell you pick up, you never gonna find the pea. Democracy is supposed to work the other way. The people pick who they want and push him or her forward. But you never get that, except maybe in a union. Here it's the other way around. *They* do the pickin'. They pick somebody radical, like Stuart Easton, then they wheel out all their newspapers, and the bankers start squealin', landlords and heads of companies howl, and the United States ambassador sidles over to have a quiet word in your ear, to tell you some facts of life. Naw, they won't pick Easton. And he's not even a fuckin' revolutionary."

Mainwaring had raised an eyebrow at the mention of Easton's name. "It will do no harm to tell you that Stuart is one of us."

Haug grinned. "If he's in, I'm damn proud you asked me. Matter of fact, you're not so bad yourself, even if you are a little dumb about democracy. I just hope you don't have to roll up your trouser leg or have a secret handshake or somethin'. Cain't stand all that shit."

Mainwaring closed the book carefully and placed it in the bag. He put the bag on top of his briefcase and glanced at his wristwatch.

"I'm afraid I must go now, though I find your company not unpleasant. I look forward to this evening, reading your book and listening to all this lovely music. Looks like there's enough here to keep me occupied for a week or so."

"Must be a slow lissener."

Mainwaring nodded as he got up. "Sometimes I enjoy savouring each individual word."

He hooked his umbrella over his arm, picked up the bag and briefcase.

"Good day, Haug. And, again, thank you very much."

"See you later, Jonathan."

Haug sat on the bench watching the retreating figure of Mainwaring as he strode down the pathway, looking neither to the right nor the left. He knew that the whole aura of the man was the result of a system of privilege. But he had a soft spot for that kind of old-fashioned honour.

Michael Regis was leaning back in the leather chair behind his desk. His feet were crossed, resting on top of the desk, and he was aiming a paper dart he had just made. After two or three judging movements with the wrist, he released the dart. At first it went high, nearly to the ceiling. Then it stalled and nose-dived briskly into the floor. Regis shrugged. In earlier days he had been very good at making paper darts. He must have lost the knack. He put his arms behind his head and locked his fingers together.

Sometimes the macrocosm repeated itself in the microcosm. Like the paper dart, things were not going so well. Plans needed adjustment. Decisions should be made. Courses must be altered.

Money and time were being lost. And now, added to all the other troubles, there was a distinct danger. A danger which could not be extinguished easily. The unfortunate Gillmore was truly a loose cannon on a pitching ship, rolling this way and that, threatening everyone. The lost tapes were going to be a nightmare for him – for everyone. Yes, they had probably gone into the Thames. *Probably*. Probably was not good enough, given what was on those tapes. He didn't know exactly. Neither did Gillmore. But what the Australian had remembered was truly frightening.

Regis was quite aware that tapes were practically worthless in courts of law, but that was not the point. It was the knowledge which was priceless. Men who thought that they were safe, speaking candidly, references to others, linkages. The poor woman had known no one, that is true. In desperation she could have only sent them to, say, the Prime Minister. Or the Queen. That thought made Regis laugh out loud. If so, the tapes would be recovered intact, and no one would be the wiser. But Michael Regis didn't like not knowing for certain. If the tapes did not surface, then there was another way. Wait. Wait until someone had information they shouldn't have. Wait and listen.

Regis shrugged. Well, that was all he could really do in the circumstances. It wasn't the best choice, but it was the only one. He turned his attention to Gillmore's future. The move on WORLDWIDE was quite simply a strategy to control the man. They couldn't really do without him at the moment. Gillmore was a phenomenon, a rogue. He had played a vital part in the advance of their fortunes and in providing the glue for the international linkups. In this country alone he shared the responsibility for splitting the left vote, undermining trade union strength and supporting every effort in much needed reform, including the sustained dismantling of the welfare state. Yet the man was an utter fool. And difficult to manipulate. A cross, unfortunately, they had to continue to bear.

Or maybe not. The news of Gillmore's massive heart attack had come last night and it wasn't yet certain that he would survive. Regis had immediately sent flowers and a card. If he was allowed visitors tomorrow, he would have to see him. Perhaps they had put too much pressure on the man too soon, another possible misjudgement. The truth was that they still needed Gillmore.

Regis unclasped his hands and stretched, swinging his legs down and swivelling around to survey his lovely garden. He must learn to look on the bright side. There are always going to be setbacks. But the events of the past fourteen years had been earth-shattering. The Labour Party had been crushed and was still in total disarray, headless and without spirit. Finished. The Soviet Union had collapsed in upon itself as if by magic. A true paper tiger. The left was in retreat everywhere, all over the world. The ideas of freedom and democracy were in the ascendant, and they would remain there. Regis was convinced of that. But constant vigilance was necessary. And pressure. And dissemination of their ideas. Michael Regis smiled comfortably.

Then he frowned as he thought of Jennifer Montgomery and her big American lover. He felt the need for something soft and smooth and soothing for the evening. Something wearing only gold earrings moaning underneath him. Jennifer had been perfect and always made him look good when he had guests. Again he shrugged and picked up the telephone. Oh, well. There was always Glenda Howard. Or Deirdre. Or Helen. Or Samantha. His fingers paused over the buttons of the telephone. It was like selecting from a menu at a fine restaurant. Glenda. A nice Sloane with rounded vowel sounds and large breasts. Just the ticket. His forefinger pressed the buttons and the telephone rang.

"Hello, Glenda. Michael here . . ."

It was a humid day and hot in the gym. There was no air conditioning. If you wanted air, you opened the windows. Too bad if there was no breeze. Haug was training with Keef and One Time.

They had all missed some days recently, and it was hard getting back into it again. Muscles and joints complained while half your mind called you a fool and urged you to go back home. That's why it was always good to train with partners. Because you have to maintain face at all costs. If one does a certain weight, the next one must do it. If someone forces the pace, you have to keep up.

Slowly the three friends were working themselves into a jolly mood. They had started with bench presses today. You lie on your back, take the weight at arm's length, lower it to your chest and push it back up. Quite a bit of weight can be handled like this, and people start taking you seriously when you approach 300 lbs. Keef, Haug and One Time were fairly close with regard to strength, and they were all three doing quite a bit more than that. Working together, one would lift, one would help – or spot – while the third man rested. Keef was just sliding out from under the bar.

"Where you buy your shoes, man?" One Time asked him derisively.

"Gets 'em out of a skip," said Haug. "Same place he gets the rest of his clothes."

"And those socks," One Time added, pointing.

Haug laughed, looking at the mismatched old Argyles that Keef was wearing. "He got off the boat from Jamaica in the 60s and somebody sold him two dozen for three and six."

He slid underneath the bar.

"What's wrong with my socks, man? My woman was hasslin' me this morning."

Haug took the weight from One Time. It felt heavy as fuck, but he lowered it and pushed. Then again. And again. Was it anger deep inside which drove him to lift weights instead of, say, jogging? Or tennis? It just seemed so satisfying. And it wasn't competitive, not really. It was just you and an inert weight, cold and impersonal – a weight that threatened to crush the life out of you. You let it get close, bought it to your chest, then pushed with a rush of anger or deep emotion to move it to arm's length once more. You pushed with all your strength and, moreover, you *willed* it to rise. To be able to do that, to be able to fight the dead iron dragon and win brought with it a sense of peace. A little satisfaction. Haug liked it a lot better than beating someone at a game, because that involved another person. To win a game you grapple with other things, including the crushing of confidence. Or dominance. Well, you can be dominant with a barbell without anyone else suffering loss. Just you and the impossible mists of your own consciousness. There were good days and bad days – sometimes you could, and sometimes you couldn't. His friends knew this though because it was the same for them. He squeezed out the sixth rep.

"Hey," said One Time. "Spring fever?"

Haug usually did eight to ten reps on that weight but didn't have it in him this morning. "Fuck it."

"Some other kind of fever," Keef said with a smile, stroking his little goatee.

One Time was under the bar and took it from Keef. "Right now. One time."

He had a smooth motion and managed seven without help. He got up with a catlike grace and held up one finger. "One time. The man at the top, climbing high."

"The higher you climb, the more you show your ass," Haug muttered in good humour.

One Time laughed, snapping his fingers. "Comin' round the track, up on the inside, don't see nothing but a shadow pass. That's me."

Keef was under the bar pushing while Haug spotted. He did eight reps with a struggle. Haug went to the weight rack and brought back two ten-kilo plates. He slapped them on to the bar, making the total nearly 450 lbs.

He slipped under the bar again and looked up at One Time. "Look after me, Tonto."

"Right now," said One Time, helping him lift the weight from the cradle.

He had done this weight before, but today it felt oppressive. Like the weight of the whole world. The bones in his arms seemed to be bending. As he bought the weight to his chest he thought suddenly of Harvey Gillmore. And exploded. Rage itself seemed to lift the bar. One Time didn't even need to help. Again he lowered it. Regis! Slowly the weight went up again as loathing seeped from every pore along with the sweat. And again he lowered it. A sudden image of all the cold slimy night creatures flapping about, falling wetly on to innocent necks to suck blood and infect the hosts with the unspeakable contents of their reptilian stomachs. Then slithering back to their foul damp nests to suckle their young with sticky poisonous milk, each little disgusting mouth another clammy parasite . . .

The third rep went slowly, slowly, slowly up. It seemed as though seconds had turned to hours. The bar stopped dead, and Haug screamed at One Time not to touch it, not to help at all. He remembered what had happened to Beth and Thomas. And Jennifer. The bar began to move again and Haug could hear blood pounding in his ears, deafening. Gillmore. Regis. Van der Bijl. Bernstein.

They have to be fought. They can't be allowed to win. The bar was up.

He rolled off the bench with as much flourish as he could manage. "Suck on that, meatballs."

Later he sat in the cab of the pickup staring through the windscreen. Wind*shield*, goddammit. There's no more reason for me to be English than for the English to be American, he thought. Different ways of doing things, different ways of thinking always helped in the end.

He turned and looked at the entrance of the gym, its big red painted doors. He realised that his friends there, the gym itself, was about the only sense of community he had any more. He could relax and joke, feel the warmth and maybe return it. He and Keef and One Time poked fun at each other. Took the piss, as they say here. Project images. Everybody there loved his pickup truck, thought it was great. But it was only an image, he knew that. The Harley, the Triumph, the pickup, the dozer cap, the ponytail. Images weren't dangerous so long as they were fun. It was a way to keep playing like a child as an adult, exercise the mind, relax. Men like Regis, though, sculpted images for alliances or for use against enemies. For those men images were used like tools to feed their greed.

'What a way to live,' he thought.

What a way to live. He put the key in the ignition and started the pickup. The powerful V8 roared to life. He put it into gear and pulled carefully out into the traffic.